*R*eal *V*ampires

and the Viking

GERRY BARTLETT

REAL VAMPIRES AND THE VIKING
Copyright © 2016 Gerry Bartlett
Dragon Lady Publishing. League City, Texas, USA
Cover artist: Donna Maloy
All rights reserved.
ISBN: 0991486072
ISBN-13: 978-0-9914860-7-6

Dear Reader,

Thank you for picking up **_Real Vampires and the Viking_**. This is lucky number thirteen in the Real Vampires series, the twelfth full-length novel. Full-figured vampire Gloriana St. Clair finally married her sire and long-time lover Jeremiah Campbell, Jeremy Blade this century. Now they're off to celebrate their honeymoon. As is typical for this couple, there's adventure waiting for them in Sweden, including an ancient Viking. I hope you enjoy the ride.

I had fun with my imaginary visit and sprinkled in some of the language of the country. At the back of the book you'll find a dictionary with the Swedish words I used in case you can't figure them out from the context. Native speakers, if you see mistakes, blame the Internet. I also put in a short Italian section for when Glory's best friend Florence Da Vinci arrives. Oh, you knew I'd have to bring along some of your favorite characters, didn't you?

So sit back and enjoy this ride either on your favorite e-reader or in paperback form. I'm one of those dinosaurs who still loves to hold a book in my hands so I'll always try to provide my work in paper for you.

I want to thank Donna Maloy of Frontrunner Publications for my fabulous cover art. She and pal Nina Bangs are also my critique partners and go along with me every step of the way as I write these books. They know this series as well as my long-time supportive fans. You know who you are. As always, it's the fans of the series who keep me going. I wouldn't keep writing these books if I didn't hear from you on Facebook and by email about how much you enjoy Glory's adventures. Let me know what you think about this one!

Gerry Bartlett
http://gerrybartlett.com

Praise for the Real Vampires Series

"This has got to be the best series I have ever read."—
Night Owl Reviews

"...fast-paced and funny entertainment expected from
the series. Glory is hysterical..." —*Fresh Fiction*

"Glory gives girl power a whole new meaning,
especially in the undead way." —*All About Romance*

" I am completely enamored of Glory St. Clair and
enjoy seeing what she gets herself into through each
new book." —*Once Upon a Romance*

"Real vampires, real fun, real sexy!" —**Kerrelyn
Sparks,** *New York Times* bestselling author of the
Love At Stake series

Titles by *Gerry Bartlett*

REAL VAMPIRES HAVE CURVES

REAL VAMPIRES LIVE LARGE

REAL VAMPIRES GET LUCKY

REAL VAMPIRES DON'T DIET

REAL VAMPIRES HATE THEIR THIGHS

REAL VAMPIRES HAVE MORE TO LOVE

REAL VAMPIRES DON'T WEAR SIZE SIX

REAL VAMPIRES HATE SKINNY JEANS

REAL VAMPIRES KNOW HIPS HAPPEN

REAL VAMPIRES KNOW SIZE MATTERS

Novella: REAL VAMPIRES TAKE A BITE OUT
OF CHRISTMAS

REAL VAMPIRES SAY READ MY HIPS

REAL VAMPIRES AND THE VIKING

Also RAFE AND THE REDHEAD

ONE

"Are you ever going to tell me where we're going?" I snuggled closer to my new husband. Glory St. Clair married. Would I ever get used to that? Didn't matter. We were hitched and I had to accept it. Was I sorry to be tied to the love of my life forever? I slid a hand down his scarred and very masculine chest. Are you kidding me? I couldn't quit smiling.

"You'll see when we get there." He grinned and grabbed my hand when it dove under the sheet. "You're going to have me too weak to get off the plane, you insatiable wench."

"Wench? You'll pay for that." Laughing, I threw him to his back and climbed on top. I couldn't imagine ever tiring of our love play. Amazing after over four hundred years. "Jeremiah Campbell, I've never known you to be too weak for anything. Now," I wiggled over his erection, "you've just shown me proof you're up for another round before we land." I leaned down to drag a fang over his jugular. "I promise not to take your blood this time if that will help you save your strength, poor baby. What do you say?"

He grinned and was running his hands down my back to draw me even closer when the intercom came alive.

"We'll be landing in about thirty minutes, Jerry. You might want to get ready to leave the plane." The pilot cleared his throat. "I know you two are on your honeymoon and all, cuz, but the locals will expect you to be wearing clothes. And the weather is a brisk twenty-seven degrees."

"All right, Sean. We'll be ready. Now shut off the intercom and mind your manners." Jerry flipped us so that I was under him and kissed me thoroughly. "That's what I get for asking my cousin to fly us here. Cheeky bastard. But he's right. Time to face the public. Now stay where you are. I have a surprise for you."

I lay there watching him untangle the covers and stride to the closet. Oh, but I loved the way the muscles twitched in his perfect butt. Hmm. If I followed him and kissed the dimple there . . . But he flung open the door, surprising me that it was full of clothes *I* certainly hadn't packed. We'd both brought suitcases aboard the private plane, packed for cool weather per Jerry's cryptic instructions. Now he plucked a white velvet cape out of the small closet and tossed it on the bed.

"Jerry!" I stroked the white fur lining the hood. It was an exquisite vintage piece and exactly the kind of thing I loved. "Where did you get this?"

"Lacy at your shop helped me order it on-line. Like it?" He tossed a few more things on the bed--tan wool pants, cashmere sweaters in bright red and emerald green, and a pair of brown suede boots that made my mouth water.

"Love it all!" I jumped out of bed and hugged him tight. "You are so amazingly thoughtful. How did I get so lucky?"

"You stuck with me through a hell of a lot, my wife. You deserve everything I can give you and more." He smiled down at me.

"You put up with even more. We've fought demons and my parents who have to be the worst in-laws any man could imagine." I stood on tiptoe to kiss his chin. I loved that he was bigger, stronger than I could ever be. And the way we fit together so perfectly. Even though I could hear the jet engine's sound change as we obviously must be approaching an airport, I knew I wanted him again. And I could feel Jerry's cock, eager against my stomach. I needed him inside me. Now.

"My parents have been horrible to you, lass. It's a wonder you didn't leave me long ago. My mother…" He shut up when I grasped him and backed us toward the bed, knocking those beautiful clothes to the floor with a sweep of my other hand.

"You seriously don't want to talk about your mother now, do you, Jer?" I whispered in his ear as I sat on the edge of the bed and guided him into me. I was wet and welcoming, sighing as he filled me. God, but I loved him. I wrapped my legs around his waist, my hands on his back.

"Hell, no." He kissed me then, moving as he held me with one hand and braced us on the bed with the other. The aircraft angled toward the earth, the shift sending me tighter against my man. I moaned with pleasure as we surged against each other, gaining momentum as the plane raced toward the ground. By the time the wheels hit the tarmac, we were jolted into climax, each shaking with pleasure. Our mouths and tongues tangled, words impossible.

As the plane rolled to a stop, we peeled ourselves off of each other, agreeing that it hadn't been our most elegant bedding but right for a honeymoon—hot, eager and with a little of the unusual. Now I had only minutes to pull myself together and slip on a new outfit. I could feel cold seeping into the plane already. Jerry didn't seem to care. He had a relaxed, well-loved stride to his step. I was trying to add some makeup to cover whisker burn and to brush out tangles that seemed permanent.

The outer door opened and the cold air became frigid.

"Welcome to Stockholm." Sean, our pilot and one of the Campbell cousins who had attended our wedding, now wore a parka, his breath making white clouds. "It's a clear night and should be perfect for your journey north."

"You brought me to Sweden for our honeymoon?" I stared at Jerry. "Why?"

"Twenty hours of darkest night out of every twenty-four, darling. Why do you think?" He frowned.

"Oh. I guess I didn't sound exactly thrilled, did I?" I rushed to wrap an arm around his waist. "Twenty hours to stay awake? What a brilliant idea!"

"It really is, lass." Sean grinned. "And the Ice Palace north of here is famous for its spa and other excellent accommodations. It's a great place for a honeymoon." He looked around to make sure the ground crew wasn't close by. "Especially for vampires."

"I called ahead and another of our cousins has stocked our honeymoon suite with everything we need to drink, including that synthetic blood with champagne you like, Gloriana. I know it'll be cold, but I've been assured that the rooms are climate controlled and very comfortable." Jerry looked like he was worried that he'd made a mistake.

"I'm sure it'll be wonderful. It just took me by surprise, that's all." I kissed his frown. "Now let's go. I packed my new clothes and left some of my old ones on the bed. Is that a problem, Sean?"

"No, I'm going to spend the day here sleeping then I'll refuel and head back to Austin to pick up the family for the trip home to Scotland. I'll leave your clothes with one of your friends at your shop." He held out his hand to Jerry to shake. "I'm going to be here in three weeks to pick you up. That's on the family. Have fun, you two. The limo will take you north until you catch the dogsled to the hotel." He laughed. "Enjoy the adventure!" He hugged me then grabbed our suitcases and bounded down the steps.

"Dogsled?" I started to follow Sean.

"Like my cousin said. It's an adventure." Jerry put his hands on my shoulders to stop me before I stepped outside and settled my new cape around me. "There will be lots of surprises when we get there. Is that okay?"

"I'm not big on surprises, Jer. You should know that by

now. But so far, this is a good one. As long as it stays that way? We're fine." I turned in his arms. "It's our honeymoon. We laugh, make love and enjoy being together. No worries. Right?"

"Exactly. And no nasty surprises." Jerry held out his hand. "What could possibly go wrong?"

I took his hand and let him help me down steps that had become icy in the short time since workers had rolled them out to the plane. What could go wrong? I hated when people said things like that. It was like tempting fate to come at us with both barrels. No, everything would be fine, starting with the black stretch limo waiting at the curb a short distance away. I was warm in my fabulous new cape and Jerry was close by my side, eager to be with me for the longest nights I could imagine. It was a dream come true for a vampire. Three weeks of bliss. I walked carefully across the icy pavement and slid into the warm cocoon of the limo. No more negative thoughts. This was going to be the best honeymoon in the history of the world.

When the limo stopped we were at a cluster of what looked like igloos to me. Not that I'd ever seen an actual igloo. But I'd accidentally stumbled upon a special on the History Channel. Know what I mean? Anyway, these were neat looking places and there were people milling around, not to mention barking dogs and dog sleds. I was trying not to shiver. I know, vampires aren't supposed to feel the cold. That's a myth. Trust me, when it's below freezing? You feel it. My new boots were cute but I could have enjoyed some warm fur lined Uggs about then.

"Glory, we're going to each have our own dog sled. Is that okay? The double ones were already taken and we do have a lot of luggage." Jerry had to drag me out of the warm and toasty igloo where I was sticking close to the fire. The igloo had a pot-bellied stove. Who knew?

"Whatever gets us to the hotel the quickest, Jer." I eyed the sled, not sure it wasn't going to topple over as soon as the driver "mushed" us into action. "Those things don't look too stable."

"Relax. The guys swear they've made these runs hundreds of times. It'll take just about thirty minutes to get there." Jerry pulled up my hood. "You look beautiful in your new cape. Did I remember to tell you that?"

"No. Thanks." I smiled and patted his chest. I had on leather gloves and wasn't about to take them off. "Your parka makes you look like a giant. I hope the dog sled can hold you, big guy."

"You're stalling. Get on board, Gloriana."

"Wait! Look at those dogs. Can I pet them?" I could see them frisking in the snow like they were actually eager to get running. Their breaths were making clouds in the air and they were barking like they were saying "Let's go!"

"I know you love dogs, but you're still stalling. These are working dogs." Jerry lifted a heavy fur robe in the back of the sled and gestured for me to get in under it. "I've checked that there are no shape-shifters here. Valdez didn't make the trip." He whispered this last in my ear as he tucked the robe around me.

"Aw, too bad. You know how close we are and he was my favorite dog for a long time." I laughed when Jerry frowned. "I have it on good authority that he's proposing to Lacy soon, so relax, husband. Now get in your own sled and let's mush or whatever they say in Sweden."

The driver turned around and grinned. "Mush? No, we say 'Hike'." He pulled up the hood on his parka. "Ready to go, Madame?"

"Sure. I think the adventure is about to begin." I glanced at Jerry, cramming his legs into his own sled. "First one to the hotel gets her back washed." I squealed when our sled suddenly lurched into action. Apparently my driver was competitive, even if he wasn't the one in on the prize. I laughed, enjoying the feeling of being close to the snow. My body was warm and the hood drooped over my face enough to keep me from freezing. I realized there was some kind of heater in the bottom of the sled too. No wonder I wasn't feeling the cold. Well, except for my nose. I was sure it was bright pink.

Jerry's sled was drawing close, I turned and waved as my sled hit a bump and we flew across the snow. The dogs barked excitedly and kept running. The drivers yelled at their dogs and each other in Swedish, clearly enjoying the competition. Jerry had pulled out some money and waved it around. Oh, no fair. But I knew how he liked to win.

I have goddess powers but had promised Jer that I wouldn't use them on this trip, not on him anyway. But then again, I hadn't promised I wouldn't use them at all. I could tell his sled was about to pass us. Was there anything I could do that wouldn't hurt the dogs? Oh, really, was anyone the loser when there was back washing involved? I knew where that would lead. I held onto the sides of the sled and just enjoyed the ride. What a surprise this trip was. Twenty hours of nighttime. For a vampire that was just an unimaginable treat. I was in the middle of a fantasy when I went airborne and landed in a snowdrift.

"Madame! Madame! I am so sorry."

I heard the driver but couldn't see a damn thing. I was face down in cold wet snow. I struggled to dig myself out, cursing the fact that my lovely velvet cape was getting ruined.

"What did you do?" Jerry's voice was close as I was jerked out of the snow by strong hands on my waist. "Gloriana, sweetheart? Are you hurt?"

"Just my pride." I spit out snow and brushed it off of my face. "And my beautiful cape! What happened?"

"We hit a rock. I swear I've travelled this path dozens of times. But there is warming. A melt and the rock just appeared. I am so sorry, Madame." The driver shook his head. "Please excuse me. I must see to the dogs."

"Of course. I hope none of them are hurt." I shook out the cape. "Wet velvet. I think it can be restored. At least the snow was clean." I was getting Jerry wet because he was still holding me in his arms. "You can put me down now."

"God, Gloriana, when I saw you fly through the air like that I swear my heart stopped." He held me tighter. "Maybe coming here was a bad idea."

"No, I love it. Long nights with you? What could be better?" But I was shivering. "It looks like the dogs are all right." I saw the driver had righted the sled and was waiting for me. "Put me down, love. Let's get to the hotel. I want a hot bath. And you're washing my back, no matter who gets there first."

"You've got it." He slid me down his body then kissed me, brushing more snow off my cheeks. "You're freezing. Okay, get in and we'll slow down. No more racing."

I patted his cheek, getting snow all over his face. I was tempted to rub it in. A freezing honeymoon? What had he been thinking? I couldn't feel my toes. "Sorry. I admit the race was fun. That'll be the agenda for this honeymoon. We're going to have fun for the next three weeks. Even if I am freezing my butt off, I'm going to love this trip. There's nothing wrong with taking me out of my comfort zone. It's a good thing. So quit frowning. Okay?"

"Okay. You're being a good sport about it but I know how you feel about your vintage clothes. If that cape can't be fixed, I'll haunt the Internet until I find you another one." He walked me back to my sled and tucked me in again. Then he ordered my driver to proceed carefully. Trust me, Jerry issuing stern orders could scare even a hard man into following through. Our driver was shaking as he "Hiked" again.

I warmed up as we ran smoothly through the snow this time. It was a well-worn path and we could sometimes see small towns in the distance. I had a feeling there were roads and civilization not far away but the Ice Palace had deliberately made this access for guests part of the package Jerry had arranged for us. I'd have to get on the Internet myself and find out more about the place and what else it had to offer.

It wasn't long before I saw a glittering complex of

buildings rising out of the snowy landscape. It did look like a palace. Could it really be made out of ice like a man inside the igloo had claimed? Impossible. But then I'd been living in Austin, Texas for the past few years where winters were mild. Even a few snow flurries got school cancelled and everyone afraid to drive on the icy roads.

The dog sleds carried us to an entrance on one side of the hotel obviously designed for their arrivals. The drivers helped us out then assured us they'd see to our luggage while each man pocketed Jerry's generous tips. I was busy studying the huge wooden double doors set into the ice. They must have come from a castle or something equally imposing and were obviously antique.

A doorman bowed us in, holding one side open for us. Inside, towering ceilings were decorated with gorgeous crystal chandeliers. There were glowing Oriental runners on the floors leading to a front desk made of... ice. Yep, the entire building was constructed of the stuff. I gave my new husband a hard look but he just grinned.

"Jerry, seriously? Are we sleeping on ice too? Cause I don't think that's going to be good for your love life, sweetheart." I shivered in my wet cape and tried to wiggle my frozen toes. "Not at all."

"Wait and see, my love." He held my hand as we approached the desk.

I could tell he was trying not to laugh. Ha. The joke might be on him if I refused to sleep with him.

Luckily for the desk clerks, there was a cloth runner over the desk then computers just as you would expect in any high-end hotel. Every hotel worker wore a uniform in blue and gold. The men and women working behind the counter were obviously the top of the chain, their uniforms consisting of blazers and pants with a fancy logo on the breast pockets. To my relief, English seemed to come naturally to all of them. Of course Jerry knew a dozen or more languages and showed off his Swedish when he checked in.

"Of course, Mr. Blade. Your special suite is ready for you and Mrs. Blade." The clerk answered in English anyway as he took our American passports.

I gave Jerry a narrow look. He knew I was keeping my last name. This century my Highlander was going by Jeremy Blade, which was fine with me. But I was not going to be "Mrs. Blade."

"Thank you." Jer didn't correct the mistake. Of course he wanted everyone to know he'd finally tied me down. "Did my cousin leave something in the suite for us?"

"Yes, indeed. And nothing has been disturbed since she left, per your orders. No one will be coming in to clean or bother you." The clerk actually winked at me. "We deal with honeymooners on a regular basis, you understand. If you decide to have the sheets changed, need fresh towels, or require anything, merely press 9 on your telephone and it will be done while you are out of the room on an excursion. There will be no need for you to ever be disturbed."

"Excursion?" I took a brochure from a stack beside the computer. "What do you offer?"

"Madame, there are many wonderful amenities that you might enjoy. A cable car ride over the mountains while you both enjoy your own private steam bath." The clerk's eyes twinkled. "My wife and I have taken that one many times. It lasts approximately an hour and a half. Most, um, relaxing."

"Oh, Jerry, we will definitely do that one." I slid my arm around his waist.

"Can you book it for us for tomorrow night?" Jerry was already imagining it, I could tell.

"Very wise to get it set up now. It is very popular." The clerk typed in something. "I'm afraid you'll have to wait until next week for that one. But the reindeer sleigh ride is also very romantic and I can set you up for that one right away. The drivers are very discreet and we can arrange a picnic supper for you in an ice cave. Add champagne and you will find it most rewarding."

"We won't need a driver. I can handle a sleigh myself."

Jerry kept his arm around me. "I like the sound of a sleigh ride, Gloriana. Just the two of us to see the Northern Lights."

"Have you ever driven a horse drawn carriage, sir? It's not anything like steering a car, you know." The man shook his head like he already knew the answer. "The reindeer are well trained but need a firm hand. Our drivers also know where to take you so that you can enjoy privacy safely. Not all the ice caves are right for a getaway. Global warming. It is something we deal with here in the North on a daily basis."

"Trust me, I have driven all kinds of horse-drawn carriages. Who do I need to talk to about this?" Jerry leaned closer and slid a large bill across the counter. "As long as we have a map …"

"Certainly, sir. Sven is the man in charge of the stables. Convince him you can handle the reindeer and I'm sure there will be no problems." The clerk smiled and tucked the bill in his pocket. "Now I see Madame is shivering. Can't have that. Was it snowing outside?"

"No, her sled had a spill." Jerry glanced around. "I assume the chalet I requested is heated."

"Certainly, sir. It is not one of our ice chalets. It is made of wood and fully heated with all the luxury appointments that I'm sure you and Mrs. Blade are accustomed to in the finest hotels. There is also a fire going in the fireplace." The clerk typed some more. "If you will set her wet things outside your door, I will have our very experienced dry cleaner get to work right away restoring her things." He looked up, his face serious. "We are so very sorry, Madame. May I send a bottle of our finest Vodka to your room as an apology for the mishap? It is sure to warm you, Mrs. Blade." He smiled tentatively, probably worried about a lawsuit. Americans had a certain reputation for being difficult. It was easy to read that in his mind.

"I don't think so." I leaned against Jerry. "My husband will take care of warming me. But I appreciate the offer. I know accidents happen. The driver was most apologetic. No harm done."

The clerk laughed with relief. "Of course. It is your honeymoon." He sighed, looking wistful. "I myself have been married for ten years. But we still enjoy a cuddle on a cold night. Eh?" He went back to his computer. "Now be sure to let us attempt to clean your clothes at our expense. And if anything was damaged, we will replace it, of course."

Jerry grinned, obviously as eager for me to get warm as I was. "Excellent. Now we are more than ready to get to our room." Jerry looked around. "I assume our chalet is outside."

"Yes, sir. Your bags are already there." The clerk signaled and a bellman hurried over. "Viktor, take Mr. and Mrs. Blade to the *Sluten* Suite. Here are your keys."

I frowned. "Did he just call us sluts?"

Jerry laughed. "*Sluten* means club or exclusive. It's their best chalet. Relax, wife." He leaned closer. "Are you mad because he's calling you Mrs. Blade?"

"I'm dealing with it. But back home I'm still Glory St. Clair, remember?"

He kissed the frown line between my brows. "Not liking it but I know. Your independence is just one thing I love about you. Now let's get you out of those wet things. It's surprisingly warm in here but he's right, you're shivering."

We followed the bellman, Viktor, as he pointed out a beautiful restaurant, explaining the menu of continental cuisine. Bet he'd be surprised when we never ate there. Then he told us where the workout facilities were. Fat chance I'd ever get on a treadmill. I was stuck with my extra pounds and no amount of walks or runs to nowhere would ever get rid of them. Finally we came to another wooden doorway.

"There's a great venue for dancing down the hall to the right." He pointed to another wooden doorway. "Tonight is a seventies discotheque event. This part of Sweden has wonderful vodka and we feature drink specials nightly. Plus there is a good disc jockey. If you like to dance, you might enjoy it." Viktor made a dance move that almost knocked Jerry into me.

"Oh, Jerry!" I held onto his arm. "You know I love to dance."

"Yes, Gloriana." He sighed. "And you know I'm not Patrick Swayze. But I'll do my best." He turned to Viktor. "What time is the dancing?"

"There are brochures in your room with all the details." The man grinned. "I understand, sir. My wife drags me to dances too. I just stand there and she treats me like a May pole. You have those in America?"

Jerry laughed and clapped Viktor on the shoulder. "No, but I know exactly what you mean. The ladies do all the work and we're there to make them look good."

"Exactly, gentlemen." I couldn't help it. I could hear my teeth chattering. "Where is this room where we are staying?"

"Sorry, Madame." Viktor stopped in front of yet another fancily carved wooden door. "We'll be stepping outside now. To a covered walkway out to the individual chalets. Yours is at the very end because it is the largest. While I'm sure you've noticed that the main building of the hotel is carved out of solid blocks of ice, the rest of the Ice Palace is a combination of ice and wood. There are cold suites and warm suites. You have chosen a warm one and it's built of locally grown wood." He laughed. "Well, imported from Denmark anyway. You will find it very comfortable. The ice portions of the hotel change from time to time as thaws take place but we are nearly at our deepest winter now so you need have no worries about the main structures. In the summer, we don't rent the smaller cold places."

"Good to know in case we come back. I understand there is almost no night in the summer here. Midnight sun, they call it." Jerry grinned at me. "That must be interesting."

I wasn't talking. We were hurrying down a path that was obviously packed snow topped by a carpet runner. There were chalets of varying sizes that we passed set back from the main walkway, some farther than others. I couldn't concentrate on any of it because I was so damned frozen in my wet clothes. And these two men were chatting like old friends!

"People who like outdoor sports really enjoy it." Viktor stopped in front of yet another fancy wooden door and used a modern key card to open it. "Here we are. I can show you where everything is if you wish."

"No, that's fine. We'll figure things out. Thanks, Viktor." Jerry handed him a wad of bills. "My wife is cold and wet. We need to get her into a hot bath."

"The bathroom is--" The bellman was trying to point to it but Jerry slammed the door in his face.

"I thought we'd never be rid of him. God, Gloriana, your hands are like ice, even through your gloves."

"I know. Hot bath, sounds good." I threw off my cape and sat on a bench. I was very afraid my new suede boots were ruined. I unzipped them and tugged them down to drop them on the floor beside me. I was glad to see our luggage had been deposited next to the king-sized bed.

"I'll bet the hotel can fix the cape and boots, don't worry." Jerry didn't have to read my mind to know what had me frowning. "I'll start the water in the tub." He headed for what I could see was a luxurious bathroom. The entire building was well appointed.

Thank God Jerry had opted for the warm room. A brochure on a table had pictures of the cold rooms. We could pick a night to try one if there was one available. Insane. The platform bed in those was a block of ice covered with furs that would supposedly make it comfortable. Yeah, right. I'd always been partial to pillow-top mattresses.

A fire roared in the large stone fireplace and I moved closer. I was chilled to the bone and quickly shucked my damp clothes. By the time I'd dropped my bra and panties onto the pile, I had at least stopped shivering in the warm room. Central heat. Thank goodness. Because my nightwear consisted of sexy and very skimpy nighties.

"Your bath is ready." Jerry's voice was low and almost a growl.

I loved the way he looked at me. As if he couldn't ever get enough. Considering I wasn't exactly a skinny Minnie, it was enough to make a woman throw back her shoulders and do a sexy strut. I sauntered over to him and trailed a finger down his open parka.

"You're overdressed. You promised to wash my back." I glanced into the bathroom. Enormous tub with jets. Ah, yes. We were in the slut suite for sure and I was more than ready to bring it. "Get naked and join me."

He didn't have to be told twice. I pinned up my hair and had just settled into the blissfully warm water with a sigh when I felt him at my back. His legs bracketed mine and I knew that once more my man was ready to make me very happy.

"This soap smells funny." He held it in front of my face. "I recognize it but can't think... What is this scent?"

I sniffed. "Hmm. Oranges." I laughed. "I read once that it's an ancient aphrodisiac. As if we need that." I sighed as he rubbed the bar between my shoulder blades.

"I'm not complaining. I like it. And no, we don't need it but anything that puts us in a loving mood is all right by me." He soaped his hands then brought them around my back to work the soap onto my breasts. "How's that?"

"Wonderful. You always know how to please me, Jerry." I sighed and leaned against him. We were in no hurry. Three weeks to relax and play. I'd left my cell phone in airplane mode and hadn't even considered turning it back on yet. He hadn't checked his messages either. We both had competent people handling our businesses back home and we deserved this uninterrupted time together.

"You're not falling asleep, are you?" Jerry kissed behind my ear. "I know we won't have much daylight here, but our body clocks may not realize it."

"Mmm. I'm not about to fall asleep. I was counting our blessings." I turned in his arms, an awkward business that sloshed water onto the marble floor. I saw that we had a half dozen or more fluffy towels with bright blue embroidered letters on them. Good. So I didn't worry when I sloshed some more as I got comfortable, my legs around Jerry's waist.

"Blessings. Yes, we certainly have those." He set the bar of soap on the tiled ledge next to him and pulled me against him. "Thank you for marrying me, Gloriana. I know it wasn't what you planned."

"I don't plan, Jer. Haven't you realized that by now? Because things keep happening that would have messed up anything I 'planned'." I kissed his chin then his jugular. As usual his blood called to me but there was plenty of time for that later.

"It's true. We have had some mishaps through the years." He brought his hands around and used his thumbs to rub my nipples. I felt the touch all the way to my inner thighs.

"Mishaps. Yes, I guess that's one way to put them. Everything from demons to my parents showing up from Olympus." I licked his ear and felt that wonderfully male part of him jerk between my legs. Oh, I did know what pleased my man.

"Yes, you do come with some baggage." He kissed me deeply then, drinking in my taste as if he could never get enough.

I was feeling the same way. Jerry, my lover. My soul mate. By the time we pulled back and smiled at each other, I knew there were things I wanted to say. From my heart.

"I think I've always been afraid to make long-range plans, Jeremiah." I raised my hands out of the water where they'd drifted down his body to set them on his shoulders. "But that stops now. I want us to think about the future. Make plans together. Set goals, work toward them. What do you think?"

"I'd like that." His smile reached his eyes, warm dark brown eyes that could be hard as stone when he was acting the warrior. "Any idea what you want to aim for? A string of shops? A new home? Tell me, Gloriana. What do you want in the future?"

I ran my fingers through his thick dark hair then closed my eyes and leaned my forehead against his. I tried to concentrate but the warm water and the smell of his body and his blood overwhelmed my senses. What did I want in the future? I couldn't imagine wanting more than what I had right at this moment. I had a man who loved me completely, every bit of me. I had enough money to live comfortably and friends who would always have my back. I shivered, suddenly wondering if there was another shoe ready to drop somewhere. Glory St. Clair had never had things easy. Never.

"What is it, lass? Surely there's not something you're afraid to tell me. Not after all we've been through together." Jerry pushed my head down to his shoulder and just held me there, his arms strong and comforting. "If I can't give you what you want now, I'll find a way to make it happen."

"I'm scared, Jerry." I said this against his skin, the words barely a whisper. He heard me, of course. Vampire hearing.

"Why? Surely you know by now that I'll protect you with my life." He ran his hand over my head, careful not to dislodge the pins that were keeping it from getting wet. "Has someone threatened you?"

"No, that's just it. For the first time in a long while, I'm completely happy. No threats, no problems." I sighed and kissed the skin over his heart. "No reason to be worried at all."

"Then stop your nonsense and remember what you said a while ago." He pushed me away from him so he could look me in the eyes. "This is our time, Gloriana. To be happy, to have fun, to play and forget the rest of the world. Soon enough we can go home and let reality try to bite us again. As it always does."

I smiled and kissed his mouth, lingering over it until he

grasped my head again, not so carefully this time. I was the one to push back when he was ready to take me then and there.

"Wait. I want to go back to the original question."

"What question?" He had managed to slide his cock into me, making me gasp. "I think I have the answer right here." He slid his hands onto my hips and held me so he could begin to move. "What do you think?"

"I think you're distracting me." I let him do it until I was beating on his shoulders with my fists and screeching his name. We both came with a shout and the bathroom floor was awash. More water there than was left in the tub.

"Well, that was interesting." I climbed out and grabbed one of the thick terry robes the hotel had provided, waiting until I was out of the flooded bathroom before I slipped it on.

"Interesting and very satisfying." Jerry wore the matching robe and pulled me close to the fireplace. He added a couple of logs and poked the fire until it blazed again.

"Now about that answer."

"To a question I have forgotten." He grinned at me and pulled me into his lap when he sat on a bench conveniently placed in front of the fire.

"It was what did I want in the future, you silly man." I snuggled closer. "I know you never forget anything, so don't start trying to claim that now."

"I was letting you off the hook. That seems awfully serious for a honeymoon. If you don't want to think ahead, I understand." He pulled my robe closed, obviously still worried that I was chilled.

Chilled? Our romp in the tub had warmed me through and through. "That's just it, Jer. I agree. I don't think ahead. Never have. So asking me what goals I have or plans for the future is getting me all stirred up." I wiggled in his lap. "And not in the way you want me to be on a honeymoon."

"Then let's forget it. Table the discussion." He pulled

the pins from my hair and let it cascade to my shoulders. "You want to go dancing. I'm game."

"Good. Because that's about as serious as I want to be during this trip. You may not be Patrick Swayze or John Travolta, but you're mine. So I'll get you on the dance floor and make you look good. Are you sure you're up for that?"

"Gloriana, I am up for anything you throw my way. Try me." He grinned and stood, tossing me on the bed. "Now let's make sure the *Sluten* Suite bed is named correctly. How does the bed feel?" He grinned down at me when I threw open my robe.

"Lonely. Come here, husband, and show me your horizontal moves. I'm convinced you've got the makings of a dance star in you. Because you definitely have rhythm." I laughed when he landed on top of me.

Rhythm. Oh yes, he did. It was very late by the time we were dressed and ready to find the discotheque. But there was no hurry. Twenty hours of night. A luxury. I dragged him down the hall, still glowing after the latest romp with my man. Too bad that niggling worry wouldn't let me relax and enjoy. My long life had convinced me of one thing. Highs were always followed by lows. Damned if that wasn't the truth.

TWO

"Not sure this was a good idea, Jer." I huddled under the fur lap robe. Jerry didn't seem to feel the cold, in his element as he steered the reindeer away from the safety of a massive barn where dogs and more reindeer were kept.

"We can't just stay inside the entire three weeks, Gloriana. Don't you want to see a bit of the countryside?" He had the shaggy creature with its massive horns actually trotting as it followed a well-worn path across the snow.

"Snow, ice." I waved a hand toward the monotonous landscape. "Oh, look. More snow and ice. Honestly, Jer, no one would be surprised if honeymooners never left their room at all." I had to quit whining. Not attractive. But the biting cold and the unsteady sleigh made me remember doing a facer in a snowbank. No word yet on my beautiful cape and boots. If they were ruined...

"Gloriana, you and I will have plenty of time for lovemaking. Pretend you are human. Breathe in the fresh air." Jerry moved both reins to one hand and squeezed my thigh, even though I wasn't sure how he found it under the mounds of furs and my insulated parka that was long enough to cover my knees. I'd had a lot of fun shopping in the hotel boutique. "Work up an appetite." His hand moved upward.

"You know what appetite I mean. And look up at the sky. It's a beautiful night and the Northern Lights are putting on a fine show for us."

I leaned against him. "Okay, you're right. They're beautiful." I covered his hand with my own. I had a new pair of gloves too. Jerry wouldn't wear any. Macho man. "Where are we going?"

"One of the drivers told me about an ice cave not too far from here. It will be a perfect place for our picnic." Jerry laughed, his teeth gleaming in the starlight. "I guess we'll dump the food the hotel packed for us and let wild animals enjoy it. It's the hotel's standard package. But don't worry. I have plenty of blood, some with the champagne kick, for us in a pack in the back of the sleigh."

"That sounds lovely if we don't freeze our buns off." Oops, more whining.

"I have a heater that runs on batteries too. We'll set it up next to our furs." Jerry glanced at me, his eyes twinkling. "I think I showed my moves last night to be up to your standards, vertical as well as horizontal."

I cupped his cheek in one hand. "You did! I can't believe you managed to surprise me like that. I swear you put all the other men on the dance floor to shame."

"Florence gets all the credit. She drilled me until I mastered those dance steps. I'm surprised your best friend actually managed to keep it a secret." He bit my glove and almost pulled it off. "The look on your face when I spun you out the first time made every minute spent with Flo the dance Nazi worth it."

I laughed, wishing I could have seen their sessions together. I knew he should be watching the path the reindeer had decided to gallop down but I couldn't resist pulling Jerry's face to mine for a long deep kiss. "It was a wonderful surprise. The best." I sighed then snuggled against his hard body. "That you can still rock my world unexpectedly after all these years is just one reason I married you."

Jerry smiled then looked ahead at the path we were

taking. "Now look what you've done. Distracted me so much I think we've taken a wrong turn. Not that I'm complaining."

I gazed around us. It was all snowy landscape and hills. Then I checked behind us. "How lost can we be? I can still see the Ice Palace in the distance. I'm sure Rudolph will trot home when he gets hungry."

"Rudolph? You're giving this beast too lofty a name. This reindeer is contrary. One minute he's running like his hooves are on fire, now he acts like he's done for the night. Look at him, he's barely moving." Jerry had his hands full. The trail had disappeared altogether and, yes, Rudolph seemed to have run out of gas.

"You're doing a good job with him." I held on when we hit a bump. We were definitely off the regular path. Jerry slapped the reins and I grabbed the railing when Rudolph took off again. He *was* contrary.

"All right, there are the hills the drivers mentioned. We should be seeing some caves soon. The men said this area was riddled with them. But I was warned that the ice isn't always stable and that we should be careful where we set up our picnic." Jerry steered toward a nearby hill.

"Look!" I pointed a well-insulated finger. "Do you think that's a cave?"

Jerry headed toward the dark opening in the hillside. Sure enough, as we got closer we could see the broad mouth of a cave, icicles hanging from it.

"Icicles? That could mean there's been some recent weather warm enough to cause melting here." Jerry pulled the sleigh to a halt. "Doesn't look too safe to me. Perhaps we should keep going."

"The icicles are frozen solid now. Not dripping. I like this cave. It's big enough for you to stand up in and we'll be out of the wind. You could toss down some of that hay the driver gave you for Rudolph and we could set up our furs for the picnic right inside." I threw back the cover and leaped out of the sleigh. I'd had enough riding for a while.

The sleigh wasn't well-sprung, the seat little more than a board, and my butt felt it.

"Let me check it out first, Gloriana." Jerry jumped down, pitched some hay in front of the reindeer, and pulled out one of his knives. My man never went anywhere without at least three knives on his body. Why do you think he'd chosen the last name Blade this century?

"Be careful. Are you seriously thinking there could be animals in there? Wolves?" I shivered, imagining a pack of starving wild beasts coming at us. I grabbed the picnic basket and checked inside to see if we had wolf bait that I could lure them away with. Not really, unless they'd stop for chocolate cake. Too bad I couldn't try it. The smell made my mouth water.

"You never know." Jerry's voice stopped my memories of a chocolate feast in Olympus. Not that I was eager to go up there again. Long story. "Gloriana, maybe you should get back in the sleigh while you wait to see what I find." Jerry put on his fierce warrior face and stepped into the cave.

"You're enjoying this! Man against beast." I wasn't about to cower in the sleigh. "Really, Jerry, I don't think Rudolph would be calmly chowing down on hay if he sensed wolves in the area. Would he?"

"No, you're right." Jerry stopped in mid-march and looked over his shoulder. "I thank you for the reassurance and your vast knowledge of wildlife, Gloriana. You must have been watching the National Geographic channel again."

I muttered my opinion of that putdown and he grinned before he came back to kiss me. "Can't I just know things? Huh?" I slapped his chest.

"I love you, darling, but I know where you get your information. Nothing wrong with using the TV for it. Or the Internet. My twenty-first century woman." He laughed, patted my bottom, and then headed into the cave again. He still had his knife at the ready before he disappeared from sight.

"I'm unpacking! You're wasting your time when you

could be getting me naked." I grabbed a pile of furs and arranged them just inside the cave. We could see Rudolph and the sleigh but were downwind of him. He was pretty in a Christmassy kind of way but smelled like any barnyard animal. I pulled out the pack with the bottles of synthetic blood and two crystal goblets. Then I found the heater Jerry had mentioned. It was easy to use and I anchored it nearby, pushing the button to get it going on high. Soon the area around us was warm enough for me to shed my coat and gloves. Too bad it was also making the walls melt a little.

"Well, this is a cozy scene." Jerry strode back, sliding his knife into his ankle holster.

"No wolf pelts with you? What a disappointment." I poured blood into a goblet and handed it to him. "Drink a toast with me."

He settled on the furs beside me. "What are we toasting, my love?"

"To us, may we always be as happy as we are right now." I clinked my glass against his.

"Perfect." He stared into my eyes before we drained our glasses. He was leaning in for a kiss when a boom shook the ground beneath us so hard we knocked our heads together. The empty glasses tipped over, bottles rattled and icicles fell to the snow from the edge of the cave opening.

"What in the hell was that?" I held onto Jerry and looked around frantically. Had one of our ancient enemies decided this was the time to settle an old score and ruin our honeymoon?

"Ice-quake. The stable master told me we might hear one." Jerry rubbed my back. "It happens out here sometimes. Like an earthquake, but caused by shifts in the ice." He glanced around the cave. "Seriously. Relax." He stood and surveyed the new piles of icicles near the entrance. "This doesn't look too bad but we can't see beneath the ice. Maybe we should move on. Go back to the hotel."

"So soon? I know I was reluctant, but now that we're here, I'm into it. And we haven't gotten to the main event yet, have we?" My heart was beating like a drum. That sudden sound had brought back all kinds of bad memories. We'd faced danger before and not always come out of it unharmed. I sat back. No sign of danger here though except from Mother Nature. I sure wasn't letting a little noise ruin a chance for romance.

"It was just a sound, Jer. The ground we're on seems safe." I looked up at solid ice. "Roof too. I see no reason to run." I unzipped my leather vest. "Not when it's play time."

"I'm all for that. Let's play." Jerry reached for a bottle of the champagne blood but stopped, his eyes on the cave entrance. "Where the hell is Rudolph? Damned contrary beast. The noise must have spooked him. He's not where we left him."

"Oh, great. I don't fancy walking back to the hotel." I lay back on the furs. "Talk about a mood killer."

"Maybe he's close enough for me to catch him. Let me see before you lose your mood." Jerry kissed me then headed for the cave opening. "He was dragging a sleigh so I doubt he could go too far. Don't worry, if I can't find him, we can always call the hotel for a pick-up."

I knew Jerry really didn't want to do that. He'd laid it on thick at the barn, bragging to the stable master about his experience handling the reins. Even so it had taken a big bribe to get us out of there without a driver. Admitting he'd lost his sleigh and reindeer would kill Jerry's reputation with the locals who'd watched us closely as we'd headed out this evening.

"You'll find him. Calling the hotel is a last resort. Definitely." I hid a smile, refilling my glass. "I'm going to wait here, working on my mood while you round up Rudolph. Don't keep me waiting too long, lover boy." I ran a fingertip down my scenic route, stopping Jerry in his tracks.

"Gloriana, I'd say to hell with the reindeer except it's a long walk back to the hotel and I don't think we want to fly in, taking a chance we might be seen, do we?" He came back to give me a deep kiss, along with a fondle that had me sighing. "I'll find that animal and be back before you can finish that glass." He winked and loped out of the cave, a man on a mission.

I sipped slowly, enjoying the light buzz from champagne. But then I had to see what Jerry was up against. Luckily he wasn't that far away, talking to Rudolph as he grabbed for the reins. Rudolph treated it like a game, trotting along and shaking his horns when Jerry got close. I bit back a laugh when Jer used some strong language as the reindeer zig-zagged through the snow. A chill wind chased me back inside just as Jerry finally caught the edge of the sleigh and vaulted inside. Nicely done.

I felt compelled to explore a little, to see what was further along the narrow path that led inside the cave. It was bigger than I'd first thought. I walked along what was barely a trail between fallen rocks and ice. The ice-quake had shaken loose more of the ceiling back here. I should really turn around, maybe even encourage Jerry to pack up and head back. But I couldn't. I didn't understand it, but I needed to keep going. Something called to my paranormal instincts. I laughed at myself. Yeah right. I had seen ghosts before, even in my own shop back home, but I didn't sense them in this frigid place where my breath made clouds. I was letting my imagination run wild.

I turned to head back when another ice-quake knocked me off my feet. Ice, rocks and debris fell all around me and I screamed, trying to protect my head.

"Gloriana!" Jerry called my name. "Are you all right?"

"Yes. Stay there. I'm coming. I stayed against the wall, crawling toward the entrance when another loud boom and a crack made me stop. There was a huge crash and something landed next to me while more ice fell all around. I waited, wondering if I was going to be buried here, stuck forever in this cold and dark place.

I could hear Jerry calling my name over and over again as I tried to move my arms. Rocks, ice. It was on top of me, around me, weighing me down. But Jerry was close. I could hear him digging, desperate to get to me. I sobbed, spitting out dirt as I wiggled my arms to dislodge the rocks holding them down.

"I see you. Stay still. I'm getting you out!" Jerry sounded frantic but he was tossing rocks like a mad man, heaving them away until I felt a blast of cold air hit my face. "Gloriana. Are you hurt?" He reached for my hair and gently pushed it back. "Say something."

"I'm, I'm okay. Just get me out of here. I can't move my arms." I wasn't going to cry. But I felt so damned helpless. God, I hated that.

"Working on it, my love. I've almost got it." He brushed dirt from my face then kept digging, pulling aside chunks of ice from my right side. "See if you can pull your arm up now."

I realized he had made enough space around it for me to push it free myself. After that it was easy. I could heave rocks away myself and soon he was lifting me away from the piles of debris to hold me in his arms.

"Jerry." I rested against his chest and just held on. "I was scared I was going to be buried alive."

"I would never have left you here." He breathed against my hair. "Are you hurt?"

"No, no. Just shaky." I saw that he had scraped his hands and they were bleeding. "Look at you."

"Never mind that. We have to get out of here. This place isn't safe now." He started to carry me out of the cave toward where we had laid our furs.

"Wait!" I knew there was something I had seen and felt as I'd been trapped in the ice. "Put me down. I need . . ." I wobbled but I could stand. I gazed around the mess that had been a large cave and there it was. Something dark against the unrelenting white of the snow and ice. Not a rock. Those were almost as white as the snow and ice that covered them.

"Jerry, look!" I pointed with a shaking finger.

Jerry squatted down and peered at what I was showing

him. "What the hell?"

"It's, it's a man. Holy shit, Jer. This guy was frozen in here." I shivered, thinking how it could happen. How it had almost happened to me. Despite being encased in ice, he looked in pretty decent shape. "We have to dig this person out, Jerry. We have to take him to the heater and furs." I tugged at his coat. "There's a chance that we can thaw him and he might be able to come back. Alive!"

"Now that's nonsense. No one could survive being frozen like that." Jerry stood and pulled out his phone. "I can't believe I've got a signal. We should tell the authorities. The poor soul is obviously dead. The police should handle this. You've found a victim of the elements, Gloriana."

"The authorities? Really?" We exchanged a look. We both had spent long lives avoiding entanglements and usually impossible explanations with government types.

"All right. Maybe we'll see what we've got here first." Jerry shoved his phone back into his hip pocket.

"I'm telling you, Jer. I saw this thing on TV. People almost frozen were brought back to life."

Jerry actually rolled his eyes. "There's no 'almost' for this person, Gloriana. Look at the situation. We're in the middle of nowhere. And there's no telling how long this poor fool has been on ice."

"Okay, okay. So there's a slim chance. But check out the condition of his body. It's not a skeleton. Or decayed like a corpse would be." I swallowed, thinking about that. Yeah, I'm a vampire but that doesn't mean I can't be grossed out. "He's flesh and blood. Buried in ice and left for dead." I ran back to get my gloves. "Come on. Humor me." I shoved on my gloves then began digging around the body. "What are you waiting for? Please? Help me."

"Here we go." Jerry gave me his "She's crazy but I love her anyway" look and muttered under his breath about this not being his idea of a "honeymoon activity."

"That's my guy. Or not." I flinched when Jer began hacking at the snow next to me with one of his knives. "You want to finish him off? Kill him if he's not already dead?"

"I can't watch. I'm going to get the heater." I hurried to do just that.

"There's excess ice around him, Gloriana. No need to drag more than necessary." He continued to cut away snow and ice. "Look at him." Jerry was working around the man's head. Yes, we could see it was a man, a big one. "Bring that heater closer. Poor bastard. This must be some poor soul who either got lost out here and froze or was put on ice, I guess you could say, while still living. I've heard of the practice. It's a cruel punishment. Something the Vikings might have done centuries ago."

"God, Jerry, so this might be someone forced out here? Left for dead?" I realized the ice *was* melting as I pulled the heater closer. I could see bare feet now, bigger than Jerry's own which were a size eleven. This was no lost traveler. A man, dragged out here without shoes, no clothes either that I could see. Probably doused with water to make sure he was encased with ice as the temperature dropped. God. The cruelty made me shudder.

"An enemy, I would say, with a vendetta. But it would take a small army to bring down a man of this size." Jerry frowned. "The ice is melting. If your theory that he could come alive when he's thawed holds true, then you'd better step back. Take one of my knives."

"What? You want me to stab the ice man?" I couldn't just step away of course.

"Son of a bitch!" Jerry exclaimed when the hand he was working on reached up and grabbed his wrist.

The legs near me moved, no, writhed. It was as if the man was desperately trying to work his way loose from the ice. Jerry looked conflicted, trying to decide whether to pry off the fingers that gripped him or stick them with his knife.

"Don't stab him!" I did back up when one of the feet almost hit me in the face.

"He's strong. I can't believe how strong." Jerry broke free then started digging around the man's frozen head. "If I had been buried alive like that, I'd be going mad, trying to get air."

I got on the opposite other side and began digging too. "Come on, whoever you are, you can do it. Hold on. We're not here to hurt you. We want to help."

"You think he can understand English? Someone buried here?" Jerry shouted some words in what I was coming to recognize as Swedish. I assumed he was telling the man we were here to help. The ice heaved, then the man was free. He looked like some kind of abominable snowman, his harsh features caked in frost. He shook himself like a dog and roared, throwing himself on Jerry like he was going to kill him with his bare hands.

Jerry yelled something in Swedish before knocking the man on his ass. Then Jer held his knife defensively, ready to cut the stranger if he had to, just to keep us safe. I scuttled through the snow to get away from the fight. The man staggered to his feet again then swore. Sounded like swearing to me anyway. Some things are universal. He looked down at his body before he collapsed like a felled tree, shaking and shivering. His hands and feet were blue and apparently useless.

"I'll get the furs!" I ran for them as Jerry approached the man and kept talking. I was so glad my husband knew languages. I tossed the furs at Jerry and watched as he wrapped the man in them. The poor guy we'd uncovered wore little more than a loin cloth. He lay there shuddering and making feeble attempts to take swipes at Jerry but I could tell he didn't have the strength to do any damage. Apparently his first efforts had cost him whatever energy he'd had.

I ran to the sleigh. Jerry had secured the reins with a stack of rocks next to the cave entrance and I pulled out the picnic basket. I could only imagine how hungry and thirsty the man must be. I found a container of chicken and bottles of water and carried them back to where Jerry was standing guard. Jer had pulled the heater close to him and the man was starting to look a little more human as the blue tinge left his lips and ears. Cave Man had long tangled hair and a beard.

"Here. Can you tell him I brought him food and drink? There's wine if he'd rather have that." I opened the container with the chicken. Roasted meat. The smell had to appeal to a starving man so I expected him to grab it. Instead he ignored it, looking at me and licking his lips. Oh, no. Surely not.

Jerry noticed and his Swedish was short and obviously to the point. "I just assured him that my wife is not on the menu. Can you believe this guy is thinking about sex before food? Maybe that's what got him put in his ice prison."

"Ridiculous." I stayed well out of reach and on my feet. Yes, he looked harmless at the moment but that first burst of energy had been scary. "Has he told you anything? Like his name, what happened to him? Anything?"

"Not yet. He seems to understand Swedish but he isn't speaking. I'm going to try something else. He looks Viking to me. I've seen pictures of the assholes and he has that look." Jerry spoke a few words in Celtic. I recognized that language because Jer spoke it occasionally with his family in Scotland. The man's eyebrows rose and he finally spoke.

"What did he say?" I was tired of standing and threw down one of the furs so I could sit. This night had been way longer than I was used to.

"His name. He's called Gunnar." Jerry shook his head and sat beside me though he kept his knife in his hand. "I can't believe this. The man has actually raided Scotland enough to know the old language."

"That means he's been frozen here for a long, long time." I rested my hand on Jerry's taut back. I knew how he felt about the Viking raiders. They'd done a number on the Highlands, centuries ago. "Ask him when he was brought out here."

Jerry did ask the question. More than one if the length of his speech was anything to go by. Gunnar stared at him, his eyes narrowing as he obviously got his second wind. Finally Jerry said something I understood. "Speak English?"

"Little." Gunnar picked up the container of chicken, smelled it then tossed it aside. "Must feed."

"Feed?" I couldn't believe he knew English. He had to have raided all the way past the Scottish border and along the English coast. There was only one species that used th term "feed" that I knew of. I inhaled, finally realizing that there was more than just the familiar in the air. "Are you--" I couldn't say it. Didn't want it out there if it wasn't true.

Gunnar inhaled too then snarled, showing us an impressive set of fangs. "Like you, I am vampire."

"Well, hell." Jerry got up and fetched a bottle of synthetic blood. "What are the odds we would dig up a fucking vampire?"

"Jerry!" I glanced at Gunnar. "Is that why they froze you? Because of what you are?"

"Mayhap. And how they caught me. In my death sleep. I was betrayed by a human lover." Gunnar stared at the bottle Jer had tossed in his lap. "What this? Did I not say I need to feed?"

"Blood."

"Nay. I don't believe you." He looked at me. His eyes, so blue they might have been painted to match a fjord, raked over me. "I will take the woman."

"You want me to cut off your cock?" Jerry moved his knife, making it clear he could take care of that business if provoked. "I told you, the woman is my wife. You will not touch a bloody fang to her." Jerry snarled, showing his own fangs. "Drink from the bottle or die for all I care."

"I need real blood." Gunnar stared at the bottle.

"Jerry." I squeezed my husband's hard bicep. "I don't think he even knows how to open the bottle."

"Give me a break." Jerry took the bottle and twisted off the cap. "Now drink." He practically threw it back to Gunnar, spilling some on the fur. It was a premium brand and one of my favorite flavors, AB-Negative.

"Try it. It's delicious." I dragged a finger through the puddle on the fur and licked it off.

Gunnar growled and I realized I'd made a mistake.

"Gloriana, I'm going to have to kill him if you keep doing things like that." Jerry pushed me behind him. "Gunnar, drink from the fucking bottle."

Gunnar put the bottle to his lips and tasted. Then he drank, gulp after gulp until the bottle was empty. He tossed it aside and belched, then wiped his mouth with the back of his hand.

"Not bad. But not the woman."

"I agree. But that's all you're getting." Jerry stayed between me and the Viking. "Now what the hell are we going to do with you?"

Gunnar stood, almost hitting his head on the cave ceiling. He was huge, bigger than Jerry, and that was saying something. I was really afraid that if he got his strength back and still wanted me, we'd have a bad situation on our hands. Luckily I had some powers that could freeze him in his tracks. Not that I wanted to use them. But I would.

"I must needs wash off my filth." He ripped off the little he wore, ignoring my gasp as I saw that all of him was giant-sized. Then he staggered past me to the cave entrance, fell into a snowbank and rolled around with a grunt of either pleasure or pain.

"Is he crazy? What's he doing?" I had to admit he was a solid hunk of a man, ripped, from his broad shoulders to his narrow hips and down his long legs to his big feet. His hair and beard were wild, but I guess that was to be expected after what were apparently centuries of being on ice. Amazing that he hadn't lost any muscle tone.

"Bathing. And he's not shy about it. It's his culture." Jerry grabbed a fur throw and stalked out to hand it to Gunnar. "Cover yourself."

"This is a problem, isn't it? He needs everything and what *are* we going to do with him?" I ran out to the sleigh when I realized Gunnar was eyeing Rudolph like he was his next meal. "You are not drinking the reindeer's blood!"

"Not a good choice but fresh." Gunnar smiled at me, showing decent teeth for his time period, "At least 'tis not out of a bottle."

"You speak pretty good English. How?" I still kept my distance.

"My father had an English mistress. She taught all of his children her language." Gunnar finally wrapped the fur around himself. "Two vampires here. Are there many vampires now? What year is this? How long was I," He swept his arm toward the cave, "here?"

I told him. He swayed then just sat, right in the snow.

"You lie! It cannot be." He looked up when Jerry came to stand beside me. "She say it is the year two thousand and sixteen. Is she making a foul joke?"

"No. What year did they put you in the ice?"

"A thousand years ago. No, more than that. It is too much! I cannot think!" Gunnar moaned and leaned his head onto his knees. "My family, my children. All gone." He sat there for a long time, his shoulders heaving.

"Weren't they vampire too?" I barely resisted the urge to touch him. His grief was real and hard to watch.

He raised his head, his eyes bleak and red-rimmed. "No. I could not do it. At first, when I was made while raiding, I tried to keep it a secret." He drew his hands through his wild hair. "But such a thing has a way of coming out. Vampires are monsters, are they not? Even my wife feared me. My villagers were scared of me." He pulled at his beard. "I could not blame them."

"I would. Since you ended up here." Jerry stared down at him. "What they did to you…"

"Not my village. I had enemies, whispering about me until even my friends and my liege turned against me." Gunnar looked away to stare at the hills in the distance. "They must pay. Of a certainty they are all dead now but their descendants will feel the edge of my sword." His face seemed carved from stone. "You will give me one. I saw your knife. You handled it like a warrior."

Jerry shook his head. "I was one. Once. Still can be if I need to fight. But no, I'll not arm you now."

"Why not? What are your names?" Gunnar's eyes narrowed on us, but he was glaring at Jerry. "I demand you say them!"

"Why?" Jerry held up a hand when I would have answered. "Are you thinking *we* are your enemies? Saving you only so we can torture you some more?"

"It is possible." Gunnar stood, staggered then sat again. He muttered something in a foreign language that even Jerry didn't seem to know then reached for another bottle of blood and stared at it. "They wanted me in hell. But that seemed too easy. Buried me here instead. Snow and ice would not kill me but I cannot get out without help." He flinched when Jerry took the bottle and opened it for him then handed it back. He took a deep swallow then gave Jerry a narrow look. "You found me. An accident? Or a plan? Explain yourself."

"First, you are in no position to demand anything here, Viking." Jerry was getting wound up and I grabbed his hand.

"It was an accident. I was exploring." I had to calm things down here. "We don't want to hurt you. We will help you." I ignored the warning squeeze I got from Jerry. "If we can."

"Why should I trust you?" Gunnar drank some more. "Why won't you tell me your names? Is it Brodin? Did one of the Brodins send you?"

"Brodin?" I looked at Jerry. "No. I am Gloriana St. Clair. This is my husband Jeremy Blade or Jeremiah Campbell. He goes by both names. But neither of us is a Brodin."

"Don't bother, Gloriana. The man isn't going to believe you unless you let him read your mind." Jerry faced Gunnar. "We are not from the Brodin family. I swear it." He dropped my hand and held his out to Gunnar. The Viking gave him a hard look before he finally took it. Mind reading. Of course.

"Get inside next to the heater and drink some more blood." Jer tossed him another bottle of synthetic. "You need your strength before you can think about revenge."

"Heater. The box that makes heat." Gunnar nodded. "Yes. I need more strength."

I stared at him as he walked barefoot across the snow and into the cave. "What now, Jerry?" Of course we were going to help Gunnar. Vampires helped each other if they could. But how?

"First, we've got to go back to the hotel." Jerry suddenly seemed to snap to the fact that our coats were inside the cave. He stalked inside and brought them out, wrapping me in mine. At least it was relatively free of rock dust from the cave-in. I shook out my hair, dismayed by what fell out of it. I put up the hood on the coat. What would the people at the hotel think when they saw us like this?

"Then where do we put him?" I stuffed my gloves in my pocket, needing to touch Jerry and feel his skin against mine more than I needed to get warm. "I'm not sharing my honeymoon suite with him."

"No, of course not." Jerry kissed my palm.

"You cannot just leave me here." Gunnar was outside again, watching us. He must have decided that we were his ticket to civilization. Or we were tricky so he was keeping an eye on us.

"We could but we're not. I don't know what we're doing with you yet." I went back into the cave to collect our stuff. We'd put a deposit on the furs and the heater. I wasn't used to being married to a rich man and I wasn't about to let Jerry lose any money because of this new development.

"Where are you going?" Gunnar's fur kept flapping open.

I wasn't about to look. It would drive Jerry insane, he'd do something crazy and then where would we be? First thing on our list would be clothes for Gunnar, size big and tallest.

"Our hotel." Jerry picked up our picnic basket and

stowed it in the sleigh. "Rudolph can't pull three of us back there."

"What is a hotel?" Gunnar slammed a bottle against a rock, his solution to opening it, and drank until it was empty.

"An inn. A palace actually. Made of ice." I sighed. "Be careful, Gunnar. You'll cut yourself." I could smell his blood which meant he already had.

Gunnar grinned. "Aye. You would like my blood I think." He winked, backing up when Jerry growled. "But I heal fast." He tossed away the empty and picked up another bottle from a stack on the ice beside him. "I need more. This is good." He staggered back to the cave and smacked open a fresh one.

I realized he was into the champagne blood now. Great. A tipsy Viking. And obviously a horny one. I kept my eyes on Jerry who wasn't letting Gunnar within ten feet of me.

"One of us should shift and fly back." I could tell this suggestion wasn't going over with Jerry. "But then we've got to get Gunnar into the hotel, explain him, put him somewhere that doesn't cramp our style. After we find him some clothes." At Jerry's stormy look I quit listing.

"Yes." Jerry loaded the last of the things into the sleigh. "I have to drive the sleigh, remember? You can't and I'm sure not having Gunnar handle the reins. I don't know a damn thing about the man."

"I can drive a sleigh." Gunnar stomped toward us, his eyes not quite focusing.

"Not this one." Jerry helped me into the sleigh then got in beside me. "Here's what we'll do. I'm driving Gloriana back to the hotel and turning in the sleigh at the barn. You shift and follow along but stay out of sight until we get to our room at the Ice Palace. Then we'll work on what happens next. You *can* shift, can't you? Into a bird or bat or something?"

"Of course I can shift. But I am tired of being cold. Why do you stay in a palace made of ice?" Gunnar shivered.

"Our room is warm. You'll see." I patted Jerry's hand when he stiffened. "Temporarily."

"So I will shift to follow you. I will become something with fur. A wolf. I can be a magnificent wolf." Gunnar had no more than said it than he tossed the fur he wore at me and shape-shifted.

Rudolph went crazy. His eyes rolled back into his head, he squealed then peeled out like he was being chased by a whole pack of wolves. In this case it was only the one wolf, loping along and laughing like a freaking hyena, a drunk one. Which made Jerry's arrival in the stable yard something of a spectacle. He was barely controlling his animal, disgraced in the eyes of the stable master and the gathered sleigh drivers who witnessed the scene. At least the wolf vanished before anyone else saw him. But that didn't help. Jer was definitely hot under the collar by the time we arrived in front of our door. Luckily the hallway was empty. Because a very naked Viking arrived right behind us, grinning as he clapped us on the backs.

"That was a good time. Now what do you have for me in here?" Gunnar pushed us aside and walked into the room as soon as Jerry threw open the door.

"Mr. and Mrs. Blade?"

Jerry and I turned to see a pale Viktor carrying my cape and boots. "Um, your clothes are clean and ready for you, Mrs. Blade." The bellman thrust the cape at me and the boots at Jerry then ran away down the hall before Jerry could dig a tip out of his pocket.

"Oh, great." I turned to Jerry then burst out laughing. "Now we're swingers."

"As if I'd share my wife with that Viking throwback." Jerry stomped into the room after me, slamming the door behind him.

THREE

Jerry wasn't a happy camper when he finally came out of the bathroom and threw himself on the bed.

"He's in the bathtub. I showed him how to use the shampoo and now he's knee deep in bubbles. Idiot." My husband beckoned and I crawled onto the bed to cuddle next to him.

"How'd you get wet?" I plucked at the front of Jerry's damp shirt.

"The hot running water freaked him out. I didn't dare show him the shower with all the jets. He needs scissors and a razor too but those will have to wait." Jerry pulled me close. "Clothes first. I won't have the bastard showing himself to you every chance he gets."

"Now, Jerry. You know I could care less about that." I had looked my fill though. Not comparing the men. Jerry was all I wanted or needed. And size doesn't matter to me. Really.

"None of my things will fit, of course. The man is a damned giant and still asking for a weapon."

"Oh, I'm sure you aren't about to give him one." It

was scary how little we really knew about the man we'd pulled out of the ice. Giant versus Jerry? Much as I loved and respected my man, I was afraid Gunnar could take him in hand to hand combat. "Maybe you could call your cousin. The one who arranged for the blood to be in our room?" I knew it was a woman and I was dying to meet her. The fact that Jerry had cousins in this area had certainly been news to me. "She must have connections around here and might know some local history."

"Gretchen. Yes, I'll have to make the call. The Viking is making serious inroads on our blood supply. She'll have to bring us more and then go to the hotel boutique to see if she can find anything to fit Gunnar. Will she know anything about a man buried in ice centuries ago? I can't imagine it." Jerry stared at the ceiling. "This pisses me off, Gloriana."

"Now, Jerry." I crawled on top of him. "We won't let this ruin our honeymoon." Somehow I was feeling guilty, like this was all my fault. If I hadn't gone exploring in the cave… "You know we couldn't have just left him in the ice. And it was lucky that vampires found him. If a mortal had run across Gunnar and he'd broken through the ice, well, blood lust would have made it a slaughter."

Jerry absently ran his hands over my back as I snuggled closer. "I don't believe in luck or coincidence, Gloriana. You must have sensed vampire in the cave and that drew you to him." Jerry frowned. "Bad timing for us but good for the Viking. He might have stayed there for another century unless global warming freed him."

"God, Jerry." I laid my head on his chest. "Can you imagine waking up and finding out a thousand years have passed? Everyone you loved dead for centuries."

"It would be maddening. Which is why we need to be careful around him." Jerry kissed my hair.

"I will be." I sat up and smoothed the worry line between his dark brows. "Why don't I run down to the boutique now? You know shopping is my thing. I'll pick out something for Gunnar to wear while you call Gretchen and get her to bring in some more blood. Ask her about the Brodin family. What they are up to today or if any of them survived." I ran my hands through Jerry's soft hair, trying to coax him into a better mood. "You can probably figure out a way to foist Gunnar onto her, if you put your mind to it. Is she pretty? In a relationship?"

"You aren't seriously suggesting I fix up my cousin with that Neanderthal Viking, Gloriana." Jerry sat up, gently moving me off of him. "We have no idea what he did to deserve being put on ice for centuries. He could have been a rogue vampire, on a killing spree for all we know."

"I am not a rogue." Gunnar spoke from the bathroom doorway. He wore a towel around his narrow hips, his wet hair and beard stringing around his face and head. He looked marginally more civilized but still loomed large. He gave off a menacing vibe and not just because of his size.

"Are we supposed to take your word for that?" Jerry jumped to his feet, effectively putting himself between me and Gunnar. He did that a lot, protected me. I didn't mind it this time because he'd brought up a valid point.

"Look in my eyes. Read my mind. 'Tis no lie I tell you. The bastards who put me in the ice wanted my village, my wife, my fortune. They got me out of the way so they could have it all." Gunnar looked away from us and ran his hand through his wet hair, droplets scattering everywhere. "What happened after I was gone..? I can only imagine it." He said some words in another language. They were bitter and he shuddered before he met Jerry's gaze straight on. "By Thor's hammer, I swear that any who carry the Brodin name will suffer as I did. Nay, tenfold." His fist pounded his massive chest.

Jerry stared at him, reading the truth. He finally stepped forward and offered his hand. "Bastards. I'm sorry. Yes. Some men can never have enough. The ones who did this are long gone though. Their family…"

"Will pay." Gunnar wasn't about to hear an argument against a rampage to wipe Brodin kin from the face of the earth. Not yet anyway.

I had jumped off the bed as soon as Gunnar strode into the room. Now I grabbed my purse.

"I'm going after some clothes. Jerry, call Gretchen then see if Gunnar will let you use some scissors on that mane and beard. There are some in my makeup kit." I looked Gunnar up and down. I was good at judging sizes, did it all the time in my vintage clothing shop, Vintage Vamp's Emporium. "I'll charge everything to our room."

"I have no money. Yet. But I will repay you somehow, I swear it." Gunnar took the bottle of synthetic Jerry handed him. He was about to break it open against the door jamb when Jer snatched it back and twisted off the cap.

"We'll figure it out." Jerry gestured toward the fireplace. "Sit. I have to make a call."

I left just as Gunnar settled on a bench in front of

the fire. The look on his face when Jerry started talking into his phone was priceless. I couldn't imagine the culture shock the Viking was going through and had ahead of him. As for me? I ran into Victor in the hall. I smiled, pretending that the last time I'd seen him hadn't been when I'd been escorting a naked Viking into our room. The bellman rushed past, eyes downcast, cheeks pink. Swell.

Lucky for me the boutique catered to all sizes. There must be Viking descendants in the area. I picked out some jeans for a big and tall man, a comfy sweater in a blue that would match Gunnar's eyes then boots that should fit. I added socks, an insulated coat and a sweatshirt, enough to get Gunnar ready to hit the road if we could persuade Gretchen to take him on. Ah, I was ever the optimist. With gloves and a knitted cap, I was done. Just the thought of centuries stuck frozen made me shiver.

I ran into Viktor again on my way back to the room but didn't let him get away this time. I had to explain our visitor.

"Viktor!" I gestured and juggled my packages and of course he hurried to take them. "I guess you're wondering about the man you saw with my husband and me earlier."

"Oh, no. It's not my place, Madame." Viktor followed me down the hall, ears pink.

"You can imagine our surprise when we ran into one of Jerry's cousins in the area. Jerry has relatives everywhere. He's from Scotland and the Vikings raided there centuries ago."

"Yes, Madame. Many Scots find they have Scandinavian relations here. I guess your husband's cousin is a naturalist. There is a commune close by."

Viktor held up one of the bulging bags. "You have persuaded him to put on clothes? For his visit? Thank you. We don't allow the naturalists in the dining room or disco without them."

"Yes, yes! Exactly. So glad you understand." I dug a big tip out of my purse as we got to our door. "Of course I don't think he'll be staying here. Another cousin is coming by and I hope she'll picking him up. But we did want to take him around the hotel before he left. It is so beautiful. And, frankly," I put my hand on Viktor's arm. "I'm a little uncomfortable with all that nudity."

"It is a lifestyle, so they say." Viktor looked sympathetic. "I have relatives who do things that embarrass me. I try to understand. And avoid them."

"And when you marry into a family, you never know what you're getting into. Right?" I laughed and nodded. "Just put the bags down here. Thank you for carrying them."

"Of course. Enjoy your visit." Viktor pocketed the tip, smiling broadly as if he either accepted my explanation or decided he didn't care as long as I was generous. Then he rushed back down the hallway.

I picked up the bags then kicked at the door. Jerry was being cautious and asked who was there before he opened it to let me in.

"Seems like you had some luck." He took my packages. "Gretchen will be here soon. She had to pick up some more supplies for us." Jerry stepped back. "Look at Gunnar."

I did look and then did a double take. Jerry had trimmed Gunnar's hair and beard. The tangles had probably got the best of him because he'd cut off a lot of both. It wasn't exactly a style, since Jerry had just hacked inches off the bottom but Gunnar's natural curl had made it work. His hair had dried a dark blond and just grazed his shoulders. The real transformation was his beard, now short enough to show off a strong chin. The man looked less wild cave man and more like a modern movie star set to play a pirate. He even had that wicked gleam in his eyes, like he'd ravish you then make you want to say "Again, please." I took a breath before I said something silly. Like, um, wow. Just wow.

"Shut your mouth, Gloriana." Jerry took my arm and led me to a chair. "He turned out well, I think."

"Yes. You did a good job. He looks very, um, civilized." I stared down at my lap when Gunnar dropped his towel and stepped into the jeans. I guess he hadn't noticed the underwear I'd purchased.

"Fit good but how you close these?" He walked up to me. The zipper was open and of course he hadn't snapped them either. He tucked himself in, so there was just a nice path of hair roughened skin showing below his navel.

"I'll show you." Jerry shoved Gunnar back and proceeded to give the man a lesson in dressing in the new century. By the time the Viking had on his new sweater and boots, you'd think he belonged in this era. I had to remember to keep closing my mouth. Damn, but he looked hot.

"I will pay for these things. I don't take charity. Now owe you for clothes as well as this fake blood." Gunnar was learning and actually twisted off the cap of yet another bottle. "I may have way to get gold."

"Really?" I couldn't imagine how he thought he could find gold after all this time. Of course he hadn't seen much of the modern world yet. Nothing beyond this hotel and this room. For now, we'd humor him.

Jerry and I smiled at each other.

"Tell us, Gunnar. Where do you think you will get gold now?" Jerry sat in a chair, ready to listen.

"You don't believe me. Listen to me." Gunnar took a swallow, his cheeks showing good color now. "I was a cautious man and always hid my treasure. The ones who froze me wanted it of course." Gunnar stared into the fire for a moment then shook his head. "'Tis possible they didn't find it. We can go look. You will take a portion for saving me."

"I don't need your gold." Jerry wasn't having it. He obviously just wanted to get rid of Gunnar, the sooner the better. "But it's true you will need money to survive in today's world."

"Wait a minute." I couldn't so easily dismiss a chance to pick up an extra fortune. After all, I was the one who'd actually found the Viking. Right? "You have a hidden stash somewhere?"

"Stash? What do you mean?" Gunnar sat on the bench in front of the fire.

"Stash is like a big pile of gold. Your fortune." I moved closer, intrigued.

"Yes, stash. I always kept my gold away from my village. In a special place. No one knew where and I did not let them read my mind. They tried of course. The Brodins." He stared down at the bottle in his hand. "They tortured me. But a warrior will not break if he is determined. Is it not so, Blade?" He turned to Jerry who nodded. The men shared an experience that I was glad I didn't.

"You must have been important in your time." Jerry looked at Gunnar with new respect.

"I served my king. It *was* an important position. I led many men." Gunnar's shoulders were back, chin up.

"So it is a big stash. I saved for a long time. Not even my wife knew where I kept it." He glared at me. "Move back, woman. Your man warned me not to touch you." His fangs were down. "I can smell you this close and have been a thousand years without a woman. You hear me?"

"Uh, yeah." I scooted away, next to Jerry who nodded and looped his arm around me, pulling me into his lap. Obviously more than hair cutting had gone on while I'd been shopping.

"Did this gold come from your raids? In England and Scotland?" Jerry's hand tightened on my waist.

"What does it matter?" Gunnar obviously knew Jerry had issues with that. "It is hidden. The people I took it from are long dead. You help me get it and you can have half. What say you?"

I could tell Jerry wanted to blow him off. Of course. Jerry had his own fortune. He had been a rich man for so long that money meant nothing to him. Hell, he'd even been born rich, son of the Laird of Clan Campbell. Me? I'd been found wandering in London in 1600 with amnesia, digging in the trash for food and coming up empty.

You ever hear the phrase more money than God? Well, that was my family. I'd finally discovered who they were recently. Yeah, Mom and Pop are Gods in Olympus and rolling in it. But they had so many strings attached to their gifts I would never consider taking a dime from either of them. Seems they weren't happy that I'd turned vampire. And when I married Jerry, the vampire who'd sired me? Well, enough said.

So here I was, on Earth, where I'd scrounged for every dollar for so long I could never relax about the subject of money. My business was in the black now, but barely, and I didn't cut myself a decent paycheck very often because of that. I refused to let Jerry just take care of me, much as he claimed he wanted to. Call it pride but I valued my independence. I guess the truth was I thought if I relaxed and did rely totally on someone else, the rug might get pulled out from under me.

Hey, I've had an exciting life. Shit happens around me. A lot. Jerry loves me now but could I really count on him being around forever? Yes, I'm insecure. My history made me that way. So a pile of gold of my own would certainly go a long way toward making my dream of permanent independence and security become a reality.

"Gloriana, I know what you're thinking." Jerry turned me around so I faced him, his hands on my shoulders. "But I don't want to spend our honeymoon on a damned treasure hunt."

"It could be fun, Jer." I couldn't believe I'd just said that. Fun? I'd hated the sleigh ride. How were we going to find Gunnar's treasure? It had surely been lost or stolen centuries before. At least I doubted it could be far from where he'd been stuck in the ice with the way transportation had been in ancient times.

Of course a Viking didn't tuck his gold into a vault in a nice warm bank either. I had hit the Internet while I'd waited for the clerk in the boutique to hunt up some of the extra-long pants in Gunnar's size. Vikings had been active around here in the eight hundreds.

Not only had that made me realize what a fluke it was that we'd found Gunnar and that he'd survived, but now it made the likelihood that his treasure was where he'd left it highly unlikely. I didn't tell the Viking that. Soon enough he'd realize just how much the world had changed since he'd left it.

"We'll have plenty of time to play honeymoon games." I ran a finger across Jerry's firm lips. "I promise."

"What is a honeymoon?" Gunnar picked up a poker from beside the fireplace, obviously deciding it would do for lack of a better weapon.

"We were married just a few days ago. We are on our wedding trip." Jerry glared at Gunnar and stepped in front of me, a knife suddenly in his hand. "Use that rod at your own risk. I know you were a warrior in your time, but you need to understand how things are now before you start carrying a weapon."

"How are things? You have a knife." Gunnar slapped his palm with the black iron poker. "Tell me. Do people in the hotel know what you are? Does a vampire feed in the open? Show his fangs to mortals. Or do we hide in this room? Pretend to be like others."

"We are still a secret. We work hard to keep it that way." I'd heard disdain in Gunnar's voice and saw it in his hard gaze. "We stay," I started to say below the radar and realized that would confuse him, "invisible to mortals so that we can survive. You know they are afraid of us, so they would try to destroy us."

"'Tis so." Gunnar nodded. "I slept in dirt, burying myself in a different place each day. I saw fear in the eyes of even my own children who once loved me." At least the disdain was gone. "Nothing has changed?"

"No. Jerry only pulls a knife when he feels threatened. Or when he's protecting me. He won't hesitate to kill if he thinks you mean to harm me. I hope you get that." I held onto Jerry's knife throwing arm, waiting for another nod. I finally got it. What a shame if Gunnar woke up after centuries on ice only to be killed his first day back. "We drink the fake blood because taking blood from mortals is complicated and a risk we don't have to take anymore."

"Fake blood." Gunnar spit on the hardwood floor.

I cringed. At least he'd missed the white Flokati rug. Gunnar was too busy working up steam to notice.

"Ha! Vampires now seem weak. Who make these rules? Why do you follow them?" He addressed this to Jerry. "Are you a man?"

Jerry shook off my grip and jumped up, moving toward the Viking. "You don't have a fucking clue how things are today. A man can't take a piss outside without a picture of it showing up somewhere." Jer shook his head as if realizing that explaining cameras and computers would take more time and energy than he wanted to give at the moment.

"What do you mean?" Gunnar glared at Jerry but didn't back down.

"Modern communication has made the secrecy you'd need to act like you did back in your time impossible." Jerry looked pointedly at the poker in Gunnar's hand. "You might want to think before you start hurling insults, Gunnar. We did take the trouble to dig you out of what could have been your grave."

"Aye, it is so." Gunnar finally noticed me staring at the mess on the floor. "Sorry. I have no manners. My wife," He swallowed, "would be shamed by me." He picked up his discarded towel and wiped up the spit. Then he stared at the towel and took a breath.

I could see him struggling. With his pride? Obviously he'd been a powerful man in his time. Now he was like a newborn baby, having to trust two strangers to steer him through the maze ahead of him. I knew better than to reach out to him, Jerry would hate that, but I really wanted to offer Gunnar some comfort.

He finally looked up and let the poker fall to his side, though he didn't let it go. "New world. New time. So I must learn. Please. Will you show me how to act here? I need," His fingers flexed on the poker. "help."

"More than you know." Jerry stalked to the door before we even heard the knock. "Gretchen is here. This woman is my kinswoman. Do not disrespect her, Viking." He threw open the door and took a box from the tall blond who stood in the hall. "Come in."

"I was glad to get your call, Jeremiah. This must be Gloriana." She breezed in, her tall slim body bringing the chill of the outdoors with her. She had the Scandinavian look that I would have expected--blue eyes, a tumble of light blond hair and a creamy complexion that made me want to add a layer to my makeup. She could have been a model with her perfect figure and height of almost six feet in heels.

I loved her dark green velvet dress when she threw off her heavy wool cape and tossed it on the bed. Yes, she made me feel short and wide but her bright smile was so friendly that I found myself returning her hug and inhaling her delicious perfume. I never wore any. Jerry thought it was unsafe for vampires to confuse their sense of smell. We do have enemies and he's all about defense.

"Gretchen. Thanks so much for the supplies. We have been enjoying every bit of it." I looped my arm through hers. "Jerry had never told me he had family here in Sweden. This entire trip was a big surprise."

"It is the perfect time to come. Long nights for a honeymoon, eh?" She gazed around the room. "Ah. This must be your find in the hills." She began speaking to Gunnar in Swedish.

Gunnar was speechless, staring at her as if he'd just found his treasure trove.

"He speaks English, Gretchen. Apparently his father had an English mistress who taught him English as a child." Jerry set the box on the table, walked over and kissed her cheek. "Be careful. He can be dangerous."

"I am not. Especially to a beautiful woman." Gunnar finally spoke. "Gunnar Ellstrom." He made an elegant bow.

"Gretchen Marken." She smiled at him. "It seems a miracle that you are alive."

"He's a vampire. We aren't alive, Gretchen." Jerry seemed determined to be surly.

"I know what you mean, cousin." Gretchen moved closer to Gunnar. "I would like to hear the story of how you came to be put into the ice. I'm sure it is very interesting." She flipped her hair back over her shoulder and I saw Gunnar's eyes fix on her neck as she exposed it.

Of course Gretchen was vampire too. It was a thing in the Campbell family, passed down from generation to generation. Parents stayed mortal until they had children then, when those children became adults, they gave them a choice to be turned vampire or to stay mortal. Of course the parents waited until the next generation was born. I wonder if Gretchen had children. Probably. She looked late twenties. But she could have been turned vampire hundreds of years ago. Just like Jerry had been. Don't worry if this is confusing. It took me a long time to wrap my head around the Campbell traditions.

"So, Gretchen, Gunnar wants to go looking for treasure which must be not far from his old village. You think you could help us get transportation?" I knew this wasn't what Jerry wanted to hear but I was on board with the treasure hunt.

"Of course. Gunnar, what was your village?" She leaned closer to him and Gunnar actually dropped the poker on the rug. He told her and she shook her head.

"Oh, dear. That's going to be a problem. Stockholm has grown so much it has swallowed up many of those tiny villages. We will have to see if there are any remnants of it left." She laid her hand on Gunnar's sleeve. "Have you fed, Gunnar?"

"Only that *skitprat* in the bottles." Gunnar gestured at his pile of empties on the hearth.

"Oh, I'm sure that wasn't very satisfying." She glanced at Jerry and me. "You know I wouldn't mind letting him feed from me. Just enough to help him get his strength back."

"That's not necessary, Gretchen. Look at him." Jerry wasn't in favor of it. "He's perfectly fine. Gloriana and I do quite well on the synthetic blood." Of course he didn't add that he usually liked fresh blood from mortals himself when he could manage it.

Gretchen laughed. "Really? Are you telling me you don't share from each other during sex?" She shook her head while I cursed the fact that I had flushed. "Don't be embarrassed, Gloriana. It's only natural. Healthy. Isn't that right, Gunnar?"

"You are torturing me, *gullig*." Gunnar rubbed his face with his hands. "It was my greatest pleasure."

"Then come with me. I will take care of you." Gretchen took his hand. "Jeremiah, put your knife away. I'm a woman with a mind of my own. We will be back in an hour or so."

"Where the hell are you going?" Jerry stood

between Gretchen and the door. She had Gunnar in thrall. He was going wherever she led if he didn't trip over his tongue.

It was obvious that he couldn't believe his luck. Women of this new century were too good to be true. I wanted to laugh and exchange a high five with him but poor Gunnar would have no idea what that was. I gave Jerry's arm a squeeze, trying to get him to back off.

"I have a friend on staff here. He will give me a room for a few hours. This man is in pain. Can't you see that?" Gretchen patted Gunnar's cheek. "I am happy to help."

"Yes, she will help me." Gunnar's look said it all. He was on his way to Nirvana and no one was getting in the way. "Move."

"You are mad." Jerry did step aside when I tugged on his arm. "I've of a mind to tell your husband about this, Gretchen."

"Fredrick won't care. We have an open marriage. It's wise when you live forever." Gretchen winked at me. "Gloriana, you would do well to get this straight with Jeremiah early in your marriage. Fidelity is boring after the first five decades, I can attest to that. Fredrick and I find we appreciate each other much more when we are free to indulge our appetites elsewhere. Then, when we do get together, it's like coming home. Know what I mean?" She jumped when Gunnar pressed against her from behind. "Well, I guess someone is in a hurry."

"You promised. If you want me to kill this husband, say the word." Gunnar slid a hand under her hair to her jugular. "We must go now. Find this room."

"I see we are going to have to work on patience." Gretchen sighed. "I'm sure the first time will be fast. So many centuries of pent up frustration." She reached back and touched his zipper. "Impressive. Yes, let's go."

Jerry and I stood at the door and watched them walk down the hall and out of sight.

"Damn, I'm suddenly desperate to be inside you, Gloriana." Jerry slammed the door and picked me up, throwing me on the bed.

"Now who's crazy?" I laughed, sat up and ripped off my sweater. "But you're right. I'm not about to let Gunnar get his rocks off and leave you frustrated. The room fairly sizzled with sexual energy. Get over here."

"My cousin had an interesting attitude toward marriage. What did you think?" Jerry had made quick work of my wool pants, pulling them down my legs and throwing them across the room.

"I think it was sad." I slid my hand inside his jeans. Of course he was ready for me. How could I ever get tired of him? I certainly hadn't in four hundred plus years. Yes, his macho attitudes chaffed sometimes but sexually we were compatible in every way. Practice made perfect as far as I was concerned. Oh, yes! His clever fingers were revving me up just as I shoved down his jeans.

"Gloriana." Jerry raised his head from where he'd been giving my breasts some expert attention. "You know I hate it when you lie with other men, don't you?"

"Yes. Believe me when I say that I wouldn't have taken those marriage vows if I weren't ready to forsake all others, Jerry." I brushed his hair back from his dark eyes. My lover. My love. "I am yours. Forever. Only yours." I guided him into me, desperate for that deep connection. I meant every word of that. I'd had my flings, more than a few since we'd met. But I always came back to this man. Call it the bond of a vampire to her sire. Whatever. Jerry completed me like no other man ever had.

"I meant those vows as well." He held himself over me, pressing deeper as he gazed into my eyes. "You have my mind, my soul, my fidelity. Put a stake through my heart if I ever give you cause to doubt that."

I drew his face down for a kiss of affirmation. That kind of talk made my nerves skitter. Of course I was superstitious. A long, hard life had proven to me that tempting fate was a sure way to bring on challenges. Jerry should have known better. But he was ever the optimist. Me? Not so much.

I let his face go then ran my hands over his hard body, urging him on as he proved once again that he knew how to bring me to a screaming climax. Good thing these were detached bungalows off the hallway or I'm sure the people next door would be pounding on the walls asking for quiet. And we weren't done yet. It had been a long, long night and there were still half a dozen hours left of it. I caught Jer unawares and flipped us, laughing down at him when I tweaked his nipples then bit into his neck to take his life force.

Of course Gretchen had been right on target. Sharing blood during sex was the best and Jerry and I had made it a habit. I savored his taste, felt the surge of power from his ancient blood and swallowed the salty zest of a vintage that no one else could top, at least not in my experience.

I finally licked the punctures closed and slid down his body, running my lips over his still firm erection. Got to love a vampire's stamina. It wasn't long before I was pulled into position so that he could sink his own fangs into that sweet spot on my inner thigh. Jerry pressed his lips into the crevice and drank deeply. But he was careful not to take too much, just as I had been. I heard his sigh of satisfaction as he eased away from me then drove his tongue into the place where I still quivered from the last orgasm he'd given me.

"God! Jerry!" I bucked against his mouth, caught off guard by the sheer intensity of the pleasure. "You're killing me."

He leaned back and grinned, full of himself and his power to please me. "Never. But I don't mind if you want to beg me a little. To finish you off?"

"Ass!" I took him into my mouth then, tracing veins with my fangs and then drawing hard until his hips left the mattress and he groaned. Pain, pleasure? We both knew they could be too close to call. I kept at it until he cried out and dug his hands into my hips, his pleasure complete.

After several moments to recover and a love pat, I finally slid off of him and nestled by his side.

"How are you feeling?" I rubbed his chest, startled to realize his heart was pounding. Unusual in a vampire.

"You surpassed yourself, wench." He gripped my bottom and pulled me on top of him. "I love you so much it sometimes scares me."

I gazed down at him. His eyes were glittering. No, impossible. My man did not shed tears.

"Stop it. Now *I'm* scared. It was just a really good roll in the hay." I laughed and rubbed my cheek against his. His whiskers were rough, his evening beard growing in because of the long night.

"No, it was much more than that and you know it." Jerry rested his palm on my head. "We made love like we couldn't get enough of each other. And it was unselfish. You know how rare that is?"

"I have an inkling." I smiled against his skin. He was right. We had a rare thing and I was going to treasure it. It was good to know that he was on the same page.

"I'm glad we're married. You are mine and I am yours. Forever." His arm tightened around me.

"Amen to that." We were as close as we could be, skin to skin. I ran my toes up and down his leg, loving the contrasts of masculine and feminine. Happiness. This forever? I couldn't imagine being so lucky.

I finally sighed. "Guess we should get dressed in case Gretchen drags Gunnar back here soon. She was right about one thing. He'll go off like a rocket after a thousand years of celibacy."

Jerry laughed loudly and long. "I can just imagine it." He sat up, taking me with him. "Seems a shame to interrupt our honeymoon but I understand why the treasure is important to you. If you want to help him find it, we'll do it."

"Thanks, Jer. I know it seems silly, but--" He stopped me with a finger on my lips.

"Not silly at all. You want your own fortune. I understand completely. You never wanted to be a kept woman. Just one of the many things I love about you. That and your very fine ass." He swatted that as he climbed out of bed. "I'm for a shower." He held out his hand. "Join me?"

"After such a compliment? Just try to keep me away." I let him pull me into the bathroom. Just to be safe, I closed and locked the bathroom door. If Gretchen and Gunnar did come back while we were in there, they could just wait for us. And see for themselves that we'd made very good use of the king-sized bed. Newlyweds. We were definitely taking our roles seriously.

FOUR

Gunnar strutted into the room like a conquering hero. He'd obviously had a very fine time with Gretchen and his cheeks were flushed. Sex and blood. What more could a vampire want?

"Are you all right, Gretchen?" Jerry met her at the door and helped her to a seat in front of the fire. She did look pale.

"I'm fine. The Viking is insatiable of course. Who wouldn't be after more than a thousand years without a woman? He said he remembers nothing from the time in the ice so I explained to him that it was like he went to sleep one day and woke up in the cave with you two the next night. He was not denied for all those years. So he needed to," Gretchen swayed, "slow the hell down."

"Here." I handed her a bottle of synthetic. She'd obviously let the man feed too long. "Drink it all."

"Yes, thank you, Gloriana. He did get a little carried away and he's strong as an ox." Gretchen drank deeply.

"She is a fine wench. Too bad she is already

spoken for." Gunnar stood in front of the fire, staring at Gretchen. He was clearly enamored.

"But she is. She may help us while we are here, but that's all. She is not for you." Jerry sat next to his cousin, a second bottle in his hand. When she finished the first, he took the empty and pushed the new one on her. "Drink another. The Viking was obviously greedy." That got Gunnar a dirty look.

"I'm sorry. I couldn't stop. She was so," Gunnar's slow smile said it all, "good."

"I will be all right. Now what about today? Sleeping arrangements." Gretchen looked at the rug in front of the fire. "Why not let him sleep here? I'm sure it will be as good if not better than what he's used to and you will all be dead anyway."

"This isn't going to work." Jerry jumped to his feet. "I'll be damned if I'm stuck on my honeymoon sharing a room with Gloriana and another man. There are privacy issues."

"'Tis not my idea of a good arrangement." Gunnar still stared at Gretchen. "You think me a mere thrall, used to sleeping at the foot of my master's bed?"

"I never said that." She looked down at her lap. "Clearly you were well educated. The very fact that you speak other languages…"

"Yes! I commanded many long ships, served King Olaf himself. It was on a mission for him that I was captured and turned vampire. It was not of my own choosing." He showed his fangs, more of a snarl, and aimed it at Jerry. "That was the beginning of my troubles."

"A touching story but that doesn't change the fact that Gloriana and I want our privacy." Jerry picked up the house phone and called the front desk. "Do you have a room available? One night." He listened. "Tonight. Now." His face made it clear there was nothing available. "How about tomorrow?" He glared at Gunnar. "Book it and put it on my credit card. Yes, Jeremy Blade." He listened for a moment. "No, I don't know how long. Can you make it open ended? I don't care what it costs." He slammed the phone down. "Guess we're stuck with you. For one night at least."

"Do you see me glad of it?" Gunnar sat beside Gretchen and picked up her hand. "I do not want to stay here. May I come with you, dearling? Where do you abide?"

"I have to go home to my husband. He's waiting for me. I got a text a few minutes ago." Gretchen was looking better after finishing the second bottle. "Never mind. You have no idea what a text is but that means I can't bring you with me." She patted his hand then put some space between them. "You're safer here, Gunnar. The staff at the hotel knows not to disturb the honeymooners and you will be safe here during your death sleep. It is only a few hours this time of year, during the cold months you would have called them."

"Aye. I saw the *Bifröst* in the sky. The rainbow of lights." Gunnar nodded. "Long nights. Short days. 'Tis not to my liking to stay here but I will make my bed on the floor in front of the fire for this one night. At least it will be warm." He grabbed her hand again and pulled it to his lips. "But not as warm as it would be if you were to lie with me, *min kärlek*."

Gretchen rolled her eyes while Jerry looked like he was about to stomp his foot like a petulant boy.

"You are not going to have my cousin for your mistress, Viking. Or ruin my honeymoon." Jerry gave me a hot look. "Damn you for falling into our path."

"I did not fall into your path apurpose, sir. And I am mightily sorry if you mislike my wooing of Lady Gretchen. But she is not minding it, are you, sweet lady?" Gunnar had the nerve to grin. Now I had two little boys in the room. "I promise to look away if the Lady Gloriana wishes to dance naked around the room for you. That would be a honeymoon pleasure, eh?" He laughed, clearly recovering the fine mood he'd been in after his visit with Gretchen.

"There will be no dancing, naked or otherwise, while you are here with us." I held onto Jerry before he threw a punch. "You heard Jerry. This is for one day only. Which is almost upon us." I smiled at Gretchen. "I'm sure Gretchen is anxious to get home before sunrise."

"Yes, I must go." She stood, patting Gunnar on the chest when he hurried to help her stand in case she was still weak. "I am fine. Really. And it's not a problem getting home. I live but a short drive from here."

"I'm sure we will find Gunnar's gold soon, very soon, and then we can help him set up his own place. Right?" I walked her to the door, staying between Jerry and Gunnar. "Until then we can pay for his room and give them the same instructions we did for us."

"It is to be hoped he can pay me back some day." Jerry jerked open the door, putting his hand on Gretchen's shoulder. "Are you sure you're all right to drive home?"

"Surely you have a driver for your sleigh. Outriders." Gunnar looked worried. "You are clearly highborn and shouldn't ride about unprotected."

Gretchen laughed. "I have something better than a sleigh. I can't wait to show you tomorrow night. And don't worry about me, Gunnar. I am used to taking care of myself. I have for hundreds of years. My husband is usually too busy to hover over me." She sighed but then let her eyes linger on Gunnar. "Which I'm beginning to appreciate."

I hugged her goodbye. "Thanks for coming. Take care."

"I will. If I feel weak when I get outside, I'll take a taxi." She blew a kiss to Gunnar who seemed to realize he'd been boxed out by us but was letting it go. "I'll see you all tomorrow night. As soon as I can get away. Since Fredrick is actually in town I must make a small effort to be with him. Spend a little time proving I am still his wife. It won't take long, never does these days." She laughed. "Of course no one is as quick as my Viking."

"Gunnar, you have just been insulted." Jerry was in a better mood as he shut the door.

"She did not complain to me." Gunnar still stared at the door. "But I know there is much to learn in this time. The women, they are different, I think."

"You'd better believe it." Jerry winked at me. "There's a spare pillow and blanket in the closet in the bathroom. I'll get them."

"What do you say, Gloriana? She said I was quick." Gunnar pulled off his new sweater and tossed it on the bench at the foot of the bed. "Is quick a bad thing? My wife was always eager to be done with our bedsport." He sat down to pull off his boots.

"Women these days prefer that men take their time, get them ready before a man . . ." I knew Jerry wouldn't like this line of conversation. "Ask Gretchen to tell you what she likes. If she allows you to lie with her again." I saw he was thinking of taking off his jeans. "Leave your pants on, Gunnar. Jerry doesn't want you to get naked in front of me."

"He is acting like one of the priests who used to come to our village. Don't do this, don't do that. The man needs to--"

"He gets jealous, Gunnar. Didn't you protect your wife from other men and their lustful looks?" I hoped Jerry wasn't listening to this conversation. Gunnar had basically said Jer had a stick up his butt.

"But you have already seen me." Gunnar stretched, watching me to see if I was watching him. Of course I was. "No matter. I am sure Gretchen will let me have her again. She screamed her delight." He grinned and wiggled his toes in the soft rug. "Some things never change, no matter the century. Now, I want a hot bath again. I liked that bathing tub with the endless water."

"Jerry will fix you up." I sat in a chair and picked up the remote for the TV. Time for a little culture shock. "See this? I am going to turn on a television set. It is a box with pictures and sound. For entertainment. Watch." I hit the on button and the flat screen above the fireplace came to life.

"*Fostra av Gud*!" Gunnar jumped a foot and ran for the fireplace poker. And no wonder. There was a movie on with a really good battle going. World War II was being won or lost on the beaches of Normandy.

"Don't you dare!" I threw myself between him and the really expensive HD TV. Jerry arrived just in time to wrestle the poker away from Gunnar.

"Hey, relax. It's not real." Jerry was trying not to laugh. Of course it seemed very realistic with the surround sound--bombs dropping, screams of pain and heavy artillery taking aim at the men on the beach.

I ran for the remote and hit mute.

"What is it?" Gunnar sat on the bench, mesmerized. "Blood. I can't smell… Not real?"

Jerry reached up and touched the bright red on the screen then held his finger out for Gunnar to examine. "No. See? It's just a picture. A show. For amusement."

"People enjoy watching death? War?" Gunnar was not exactly turning away in disgust himself.

"Some do." I took off the mute, pushed a button and the screen changed to the Weather Channel in Swedish.

"They say we are having snow tonight and tomorrow. Why? I could look out a window and see that." Gunnar glanced at me. "You do that? Change the picture?"

"Yes, this button changes what you can watch." I hit it again and we were at a soccer game.

"Leave it there. I'd like to see how England did yesterday." Jerry sat on the bed.

"Men playing with a ball. We used to have challenges of strength. These men look like they are testing their skills with the ball against each other." Gunnar leaned closer to the screen. "You like this, Jeremiah? Do you play this game?"

I realized this was the first time Gunnar had called Jerry by his first name and he'd used the one Gretchen and Jerry's family preferred. This was progress. Some male bonding. Jerry started explaining some of the rules of the game and where the teams were from as I went into the bathroom. I brushed my teeth and got ready for bed. But I had a problem. What to wear. I'd only brought the skimpiest, sexiest nighties I owned. I wasn't about to put on one of those. So I settled for wearing one of the toweling robes the hotel had provided. I could slip out of it after we got under the down comforter in bed. At least Jerry and I could snuggle right before we died at sunrise.

I was beginning to understand Jerry's frustration. A third wheel on my honeymoon. Was any fortune worth that? And what were the odds the fortune would be there after over a thousand years anyway?

Gunnar had been traumatized. That was the only word for it. He clutched the seat so hard that the leather would probably have permanent finger marks on it. Gretchen patted him when she took her hand off the wheel. She'd picked us up in a luxury SUV. The hotel had a driveway on the side opposite from where we'd arrived by dogsled. Taxis and cars used the paved road and it led to a modern highway that was kept cleared of snow.

Our Viking couldn't seem to take it all in. Motorized vehicles were new, terrifying and fascinating to him. Jerry could relate. He'd suffered from amnesia not too long ago, stuck in a time before any of this had been invented. I remembered all too well how scared he'd been riding in his favorite sports car. Fortunately he'd recovered his memories. At least this shared experience made him sympathetic. He patiently explained everything we saw to Gunnar and even talked him into the car, offering to sit in the back with him. Not happening of course. Gunnar wanted to stay near Gretchen. She strapped him in, ignoring his complaints. Sweden had a law about seatbelts, just like Texas did.

"We should be getting close to the area that Google Maps says used to be Gunnar's village." Gretchen had driven us into Stockholm. The city was a bustling metropolis. The area Gunnar had named was in what Gretchen called "Old Town."

"No, this cannot be. Where is the forest? The sea?" Gunnar jumped when Gretchen lowered his window from her side.

"This is it all right. And you look sick. Is the car's motion making you ill?" She touched his fist where it rested on his knee. "If you have to vomit, say something and I'll pull over."

"A man does not do that. I stood on the deck of my longship and never once did my stomach heave." But he swallowed, like maybe he wouldn't have a choice.

"Was your village on the sea, Gunnar?" Jerry leaned forward. "I'm not surprised the forest is gone. We call it progress. They cut down trees to build houses and shops." He glanced at me. "There are even some shops here Gloriana would probably enjoy visiting."

Jerry knew me so well. We'd already passed a couple of resale shops with displays that made me hang onto the door handle. Not that I'd leap out of the car, but, oh, did I want to explore a little. No, we were on a mission for Gunnar.

"Stop this thing!" Gunnar leaned out of the open window. "I can't--"

Gretchen pulled over to the curb and parked. Jerry jumped out, jerked open the door and dragged Gunnar out after a brief struggle with that seat belt. Jer helped the Viking to a spot next to a bush and we heard retching.

"Well, I guess he did get car sick. How mortifying for him." Gretchen tapped her fingers on the steering wheel. "We'll pretend we didn't see a thing. For his pride."

"Why are things so different here? I understand about the trees being gone, but what about the sea?" I eyed those shops just a few yards away. Maybe Jerry and I could come back another time without the Viking.

"This area used to be on the Baltic Sea but dirt, silt, I guess you call it, has built up. Now we are on a lake, Mälaren. And it is farther away. Poor Gunnar will not recognize any of this." Gretchen turned around and made a wry face at me. "We figured out that it has been more than a thousand years since his time! I feel sorry for him, I do. But this talk of treasure is foolish. He won't find it."

"I will. By Thor, I vow it." Gunnar pushed his head in the open window. "You think me a fool. I am not." He stomped away, looking around like he just knew there would be a sign of his ancient civilization somewhere.

"Let me talk to him." I got out of the car.

"Give him this water to rinse out his mouth." Gretchen handed me a bottle.

"Gloriana." Jerry leaned against the car. "What good will talking to him do?"

"I don't know. Humor me." I didn't remind Jerry that I had some experience in dealing with a man who was stuck in a time he didn't know. I followed Gunnar, saw him lean down and pick up a handful of snow, then the soil beneath it, sifting it through his fingers before tossing it away. He muttered something when he noticed me behind him.

"Is this a joke to you? Watching me when there is no hope?" He stood, his shoulders back but his eyes bleak.

"Not at all. I want you to hope. Here." I gave him the water and he rinsed out his mouth then spit on the ground.

"I thank you. That machine…"

"Didn't move like a ship. I understand." I took his arm. "Let's keep walking." I inhaled and caught a whiff of what must be the lake nearby. "Come with me." I pulled him down the sidewalk. I knew Jerry was following us, not trusting Gunnar alone with me. I heard Gretchen's car start. She was following too.

"What are you doing?" Gunnar let me lead him though. I think he was too discouraged to resist.

"Looking for clues." I knew we were getting closer and even the Viking sensed it, his nose flaring as he suddenly walked faster. "You had a long ship, you said. Were you a captain?"

"More than that. I had a *flotta*, many long ships. I sailed for King Olaf to many lands." His shoulders were back again, as if he remembered his glory days.

"You must have been very important."

"I was a warrior, well respected. Olaf knew he could trust me to know who was *fiende* and who was a friend." He inhaled again. "I smell the sea. How did you know?" He was the one pulling me now as we hurried down the street. Sure enough a quay was just ahead, boats tied up to docks. "These *batars* look strange. Where are their masts, their rigging?"

"You know how Gretchen's car runs on a motor? So do these boats." I pulled my hand from his tight grip. "Was your treasure near here?"

"Nay, it was on an island." Gunnar peered into the darkness, the lights on the pier did little to help us see if there was an island across the dark water. "It was *en timmes* hard rowing to get there." He pointed into the mist which had formed near the piers. "Across the sea. That direction."

"He means an hour. There is an island out there."

Gretchen had parked and walked up on his other side.

"Shouldn't take much time at all in a motor boat." Jerry stepped to my side and he took my hand. "What do you know about the island he's talking about, Gretchen?"

"Was it Bjärkö, Gunnar?" Gretchen touched his shoulder. "It's still there but was abandoned right after King Olaf died. We call it Birka now."

"Dead. Yes, of course he died." Gunnar looked down at the ground. "All dead. All the fine men that I knew and fought beside." He stared across the water. "Bjärkö. Yes, that is where I hid my treasure. I can take you right to it."

"What's out there now?" Jerry was eager to get on with this treasure hunt.

"It's an archaeological dig. And," Gretchen laughed, "a museum that is supposed to show how the Vikings once lived. Gunnar will have to tell us if it's accurate."

"We should go now." Gunnar eyed the boats.

"No, we'll have to hire a boat to get over there. And we'll need to do some advanced planning, won't we, Gretchen? Research. I can't see us just jumping into a boat tonight and showing up over there with a shovel." I wondered about this archaeological dig. Of course they wouldn't be working it at night. Probably not in the winter at all. The museum wouldn't be open either. Though many shops were open after dark because of the short daylight hours.

"Why not? We should go now. What do we wait for?" Gunnar turned to Jerry, clearly ready to go. "Jeremiah, do you know how to captain one of these *bätar* with motors?"

"I think so. But we need a chart, or a guide who

knows these waters. What do you think, Gretchen?" Jerry was just eager enough to get rid of Gunnar that I could see he was thinking about hijacking someone's boat.

"Now, Jerry…" I could only shake my head.

"Fredrick has a boat and I've driven it many times. He keeps it at a marina not far from here." Gretchen sighed. "I don't know if we should take it without discussing it with him first."

"You want to tell your husband about me?" Gunnar gripped her arms. "What will happen if he senses we are lovers?"

"We are not lovers." Gretchen stepped back from him. "We had a moment, that's all. But you are right, I don't want to throw you in his face. Our open marriage isn't working at the moment. Fredrick has decided to be possessive this time. He smelled you on me last night when I came home and it upset him. I don't usually take vampire lovers." She flushed. "Not that we are lovers."

"How upset was he? Did he beat you?" Gunnar showed his fangs while the rest of us quickly looked around to make sure no mortals were nearby. Fortunately most of the boats had been put up for the winter and this wasn't exactly a good night for a stroll along the harbor. It was freezing cold and we all wore heavy coats.

"It's none of your business what happens between me and my husband." Gretchen turned as if to go back to her car.

"That is not an answer, woman." Gunnar laid a gentle hand on her shoulder and she winced. "Why are you making a face? Is this where he hurt you? Show us!" He tried to make her open her coat and she slapped at his hand.

"Leave me alone! I said it is my business, none of yours." She looked near tears.

"Wait a damned minute." Jerry jumped in front of her. "Gunnar is right. You didn't answer. And now it's obvious the man did hurt you." Jerry touched her cheek when a tear slid down it. "You don't have to put up with that shit, Gretchen. Are you unhappy? Do we need to have a talk with Fredrick? Gunnar and I would be glad to intervene for you. Right, Gunnar?"

"If you mean we would go see the bastard, stuff his cock in his mouth then make him swallow it before we drive a stake through his black heart. Yes." Gunnar dropped to his knees beside Gretchen and took her hand. "Dearling, you must not allow this man to hurt you. Jeremiah and I will take much pleasure in killing him for you and setting you free."

"That wasn't exactly what I had in mind, but it would work." Jerry gave Gunnar a nod of approval.

"No! Fredrick will come around. You can't kill him. We have been together for hundreds of years. Something is making him change lately. He has never been this short of temper with me before." Gretchen was wringing her hands and her shoulders were hunched. The strong confident woman was gone and a shaking, scared woman had taken her place.

"So he did beat you." Gunnar was on his feet again. He looked around and saw a wooden fence nearby. With a quick jerk he pulled up a picket and waved it around above his head like he had a sword and was ready for war. "I will put this through his heart and he will never touch you again."

"I said no." Gretchen had tears running down her cheeks now. "Let me find out what is wrong with him.

We must go ask about the boat first. You do need money if you are to survive in this time. That is our first priority."

"Priority. If you mean that is the first thing we must do, I think you mistake things." Gunnar slapped the makeshift stake against his palm. "Jeremiah and I think the first thing we do is to make sure you are safe. Are we agreed?" He looked at Jerry.

"Aye." Jerry wore his fighting face and I could see he was itching to pull out a knife. "Why is it I have never met your husband before this? Have you kept him away from your family in Scotland deliberately? Will I see his cruelty to you when I finally meet him face to face?"

"Jeremiah, stop it. Fredrick is a busy man. A successful man. I didn't keep him away on purpose. He had his reasons for not coming with me when I visited." Gretchen wiped away her tears. "You are making too much of this."

"I don't think so. I begin to think you need your family to help you get away from this abusive bastard." Jerry did have a knife out. I should have known. "Say the word and you will never have to see him again."

"Great. Now we have two ancient warriors on our hands. Jerry, stop this. You two aren't killing anyone. Can't you see how you're distressing Gretchen? Get in the car, all of you." I herded them toward the SUV. To my surprise Gunnar let me have the stake without an argument. I think Jerry must have sent him a mental message warning him off a struggle with me. "I'll put this in the back where it will be handy if you need it, Gunnar."

"You will let me have it if I ask?" He wasn't happy.

"I promise that if the situation calls for it, I will

place it in your hands myself." I made sure that was worded carefully and he seemed to accept that.

"We are going to your house, Gretchen." Jerry made that an order. "Will Fredrick be there?"

"I think so. He said he had work to do today and he does it from home on his computer." Gretchen started the car. "Seatbelts, everyone." She reached over and gestured until Gunnar handed her the end of his and she inserted it into the lock. "It's for your safety, Gunnar."

"Ha! You seem to have no care for your own, *älskling*."

"I am not your sweetheart." She sniffled and pulled a tissue out of the side pocket of her door. "All of you need to calm down. Fredrick is not a bad man. I swear it."

"We shall see." Jerry stretched forward and touched her hair which she'd pulled back into a ponytail tonight. "I am a good judge of character. If this man doesn't convince me that he means you well, he won't live to see another night."

"Stop it!" Gretchen blew her nose. "Gloriana, help me."

"I'm with the guys on this, Gretchen. You don't deserve to be mistreated. If he's an abusive bastard, at the very least I'll help you pack a bag." I rubbed Jerry's knee. "Now let's go. Gentlemen, remember that Gretchen can leave him. He doesn't have to die tonight."

"We'll see." Jerry and Gunnar exchanged a look.

"Yes, we will." I sighed. This was going to be a long night.

Gretchen lived in a castle. That was my first

impression. My second was that she and Fredrick had excellent security. She punched in a code at the fancy iron gate with spikes at the top and even talked to a guard on an intercom. Pretty extreme considering she was the mistress of the household. Even more extreme, the guard quizzed her about her "guests." He could see she wasn't alone because of the cameras beside the driveway scanning the car.

"Rolf, let me in. I am bringing my cousin, his wife and their friend to meet Fredrick. Is your master at home?"

"Certainly, Madame. I'll open the entrance at once. Would you mind giving me your guests' names?" The man behind the voice still hadn't swung open the massive iron gates.

"I would mind very much. Now, Rolf. Or I shall tell your master that you have overstepped your authority." She rattled off some angry Swedish and the groaning sound announced movement in front of us. Gretchen gripped the steering wheel. "Sorry about that. Fredrick has become paranoid lately. He has obviously tightened security."

"It's a good idea for vampires to be well protected." Jerry was studying our surroundings and nodded approvingly. "I'm impressed."

"I don't like the way he made you tell him twice, *min älskling*. Where is his respect?" Gunnar laid his hand over hers.

"Let go of me. Cameras are recording your every move." Gretchen jerked her hand away. "And Fredrick is certainly seeing this."

"What do you mean? Cameras?" Gunnar looked around as we sped down a brick driveway that wound through snow-covered trees. "Is that a new kind of weapon? Is this an ambush?"

"No, no." Gretchen shook her head. "I wish we'd never come. I don't suppose you will just wait in the car, Gunnar."

"Wait? Like some scared *liten pojek*?" Gunnar glanced back at Jerry. "You ask too much."

"He's coming in with us, Gretchen." Jerry nodded to Gunnar. "The Viking is right. He's no little boy to be told to wait in the car."

"Oh, so that's what he said." I was sorry to see we'd arrived in front of a massive front door. Yes, the stone castle guess had been right on the money. It was surrounded by forest and had a kind of creepy vibe with turrets on the corners and stained glass windows. I had a feeling though that it was beautiful inside. Gretchen wouldn't live in anything less than the best if her high-end wardrobe was anything to go by.

She turned off the car engine and unbuckled her seatbelt. "All right. We're here. Now please promise me you'll let me do the talking. I don't want anyone hurt."

"Nay, I cannot promise that. You were already hurt." Gunnar stroked a finger down her cheek. "The *pultron* will pay."

"*Pultron?*" I was ready to get this over with. Or not. I don't suppose *I* could wait in the car.

"He called Fredrick a coward. Any man who beats his wife is one in my book too." Jerry opened his car door. "Gunnar's right. Come on, Gretchen, introduce us to your husband. I want to see this man for myself and decide how this should play out." He reached my side of the car and helped me out. "Gunnar, we're not rushing in with stakes in our hands. Did you notice the security force here? We will be outnumbered."

"As if I care about that." Gunnar hadn't figured

out how to open the car door yet. When it finally yielded to him he shouted in relief. "I have defeated five times my number in battle. But I had my sword then. Are you sure you won't give me at least one of your knives, Jeremiah?" He strode around the car just as Gretchen slammed her own car door.

"No, he will not." She spun, her face pale, when the front door to the house opened and a man stepped out. "Fredrick, I have brought my family to meet you."

"So I see." The tall slim man had an elegant look to him as he walked down the freshly swept stone steps. His black wool suit was tailored to perfection so that it showed off broad shoulders and a narrow waist. He had a blue silk tie knotted at the neck of his crisp white shirt. Of course the blue matched eyes that were studying us with a keen intelligence that I found unsettling. His blond hair was worn long but tied at the back of his neck with a leather thong. He was strikingly handsome in the cold, formal way of an ancient vampire. He would have looked at home in a Renaissance doublet, tights and thigh high boots. I wouldn't be surprised if he'd been turned vampire back then.

I shivered as he bowed over my hand. Of course he had impeccable manners, approaching the lady in the group first.

"You must be Gloriana, Jeremiah's new bride. How lovely you are." His cold lips brushed my knuckles.

"Why thank you, Fredrick." I smiled, determined to show off my own manners. "Of course this is Jeremiah, though he's going by Jeremy Blade at the hotel. It is his name this century." I held up Jerry's right hand since he had grabbed my left as soon as Fredrick had come out of the house.

"Fredrick." Jerry finally released me to shake the other vampire's hand. Good manners demanded it and it would help him look into Fredrick's mind too. "I'm sorry for the surprise visit but Gretchen gave me cause for concern tonight and I wanted to meet you in person."

"Concern?" Fredrick's gaze turned to Gunnar who had stayed surprisingly silent while he hovered near Gretchen. "It is I who am concerned. You arrive in my country and suddenly my wife comes home smelling of sex with an ancient vampire." His nostrils flared. "It was not you so it must be this creature."

"Creature?" Gunnar roared the word. "And what is it *I* smell? Is it a sniveling coward who tries to make himself feel more like a man by taking out his anger on a woman?"

"Watch your tongue!" Fredrick stepped up to Gunnar, his fangs down, his eyes blazing. "You fucked my wife. Are you surprised that I would not like it? Can't you find a woman of your own?" He wheeled on Jerry. "But, no, I suppose not. You had her cousin pimp for you. Do you blame me for treating a whore like a whore?"

"You will die for that." Gunnar snarled and threw himself at Fredrick. The last sounds we heard before everything went dark were the clicks of a dozen rifles being cocked.

FIVE

It was dark and I realized I had a wool blanket over my head. Why? I was lying on a cold stone floor. I shook off the cover and sat up to look around. Iron bars. Like in a cell. Fredrick's castle. Holy hell, I was in a dungeon.

"Jerry?" I had to find him. "Jerry!" What had happened to us? I rubbed my eyes, feeling like maybe I would throw up if I moved too fast. I finally heard a moan from across the way. I crawled to the door and used the bars to pull myself to my feet. Swaying there for a moment, I peered into the gloom. My cell wasn't the only one. Dim lights hung from the ceiling in a hallway between my cell and another row of them. I could see a lump of clothing stirring in the cell across from me.

"Jerry!" I inhaled. Was it him? I couldn't tell and didn't that freak me out? All I could smell was mold and my own fear. It was as if my vampire senses had deserted me. Impossible. Surely I could shift into something small enough to squeeze through these bars and get out of here. I concentrated. I hate mice but it was the logical choice. Nothing happened. My grip tightened on the steel and I shook the bars. They didn't give an inch.

"Jerry!"

"He won't wake up for a while." Fredrick strolled into view in front of me. He was flanked by two men who were obviously bodyguards. "Gloriana, what are you?"

"Huh?" *Brilliant comeback, Glory.* I held onto the bars to keep from sliding to the floor. Whatever he'd done to me had left me weak. He'd taken my coat, probably Jerry and Gunnar's too. No wonder I couldn't stop shivering.

"I'm a weapons manufacturer. Quite a good one." Fredrick smiled. "My latest invention worked just as I expected on your husband and that Viking you brought along with you. But you didn't even blink when I used it on you. So I had to resort to old school techniques."

"Old school?" I rubbed my sore arm. "Drugs, you mean. You freaking drugged me. Is that any way to treat family?"

He laughed, his teeth gleaming in the light. "Family? The Campbells claim that faithless whore Gretchen but they are not related to me, thank God." He glanced behind him when Jerry made a sound that must have been a curse. When Fredrick turned back he examined me with narrowed eyes. "I will ask you again, Gloriana, and I expect an answer this time. What the hell are you? I have tested my new weapon on dozens of ordinary vampires and shape-shifters. It always works flawlessly." He leaned closer. "Why didn't it work on you?"

"How the hell would I know? You ever try it on a woman before? Everyone knows that the human race would have died out millennia ago if left up to men. You'd never suffer through pushing out a baby." I pulled back before he could touch me. The effort made me wobble and I fell onto a narrow cot pushed against one wall. "We are far superior to men."

He laughed and the men with him laughed too. Big joke. "Get serious. Of course I've tried it on other women. Hit my own wife with it just last night when she came home smelling like sex with another man." He snarled, his fangs down, and the guards gave him plenty of space. "The faithless bitch fell down unconscious just like your husband and her lover did as soon as I turned the Eliminator on her." He gathered himself, obviously determined not to lose control in front of a mere woman. Then he patted what looked like a space age weapon. He wore it strapped across his chest. "The Eliminator. That's what I call my special weapon. Like I said, you are the only vampire that's been immune to its power."

"Lucky me. Now what are you going to do to us?" I was glad to see that he was the only one wearing an "Eliminator." Poor Gretchen. Her own husband had knocked her out with that thing? We had to get her away from him.

"Well, that depends on you." He gestured and one of his men pulled out a sharp and lethal looking knife. "Cooperate or it would be my pleasure to spoil your honeymoon by slicing off your husband's cock."

"God! No!" I leaped off the bed, suddenly finding my strength. "Tell me what you want."

"I already did. What are you, Gloriana? How is it that my perfectly good weapon won't work on you?" Fredrick took the knife. "Open the Scot's cell."

"All right." I was back to holding onto the bars

again. "So maybe I am a little different from what you call your 'ordinary' vampire. Just leave Jerry alone. Swear it."

"Tell me first. Then we'll see what I do or don't do." Fredrick gestured. "Bring him out."

"Stop! It's a weird story." I could feel my senses start to sharpen. His drug really was wearing off and that made me hope I could save Jerry. "You may not believe me."

"Try me." Fredrick was nobody's fool. Not only wouldn't he look me in the eyes but he wore tinted glasses.

I knew about special lenses and just bet these were the kind that kept him from being mesmerized by "ordinary" vampires. Unfortunately, they would also protect him from *my* mesmerizing power. I grabbed the blanket and threw it around my shoulders to hide my shivers. It was freezing in this damned dungeon.

"Go ahead, Gloriana. Tell me your story." Fredrick nodded and his goons dragged Jerry out of his cell. He came alive, struggling to get away, but he lost the battle as they knocked him to the floor and held him down with boots on his back.

"My parents are gods from Olympus. I'm a demigoddess. I suppose that's what made it harder to control me. Your weapon obviously wasn't strong enough to do the job." I couldn't breathe, terrified that Fredrick would laugh off the truth and start fileting my husband for fun. He toyed with the knife as if he was thinking about it.

"Olympus. Really? Does that mean you have special powers?" Fredrick smirked, as if this was a big joke.

"Uh, not here on Earth. Only on Olympus." As if

I'd admit to this yahoo what I was capable of when I hadn't been drugged. I'd already tried to shift, teleport, do something, but whatever Fredrick had injected me with had short circuited my abilities. Thank God I could at least make up a story. "Here I thought I was just like you. Don't know why I didn't respond to whatever it was you shot at us." I rubbed my sore arm. "What *was* that Eliminator thing? What does it do?"

"My very special weapon is powerful." Fredrick cut Jerry's shirt down the front until the point of his blade stopped against Jerry's zipper. My husband's eyes were wild and I could see he was afraid to move. "You are trying my patience with your silly story. Tell me the truth, Gloriana."

"I told you. On Olympus I can freeze people. Like statues. So they can't move. Really. And I can dematerialize. You know. Disappear so that I'm here one second and over there the next. Trust me, if my powers were working I'd be gone already and you wouldn't have seen me leave."

"Really? You can do that?" Fredrick flicked the knife and the button at Jerry's waistband flew across stone floor. "Have you seen your wife do those things, Campbell?"

Jerry stood still as one of the statues I'd made many times. His eyes were full of hatred as he glared at Fredrick. "Yes, in Olympus. I was there with her. She's really a goddess. Her mother is Hebe, daughter of Zeus, and her father is the god of war, Mars. You don't want her to call on them or you'll be in a world of hurt. I suffered at their hands and it was hell."

"Zeus? The god of war?" Fredrick laughed like he was going to bust a gut, the knife quivering in his hand until I was sure he'd castrate Jerry, maybe by accident.

Finally Fredrick cursed and stepped away when Jerry went for a head butt. "Put him back in his cell." He paced the corridor while the two men wrestled Jerry back inside and locked the door. "What do you take me for? A gullible fool?" Fredrick kicked the cell door when Jerry made a grab for his ankle. "I should have already killed you."

"No!" I leaned against the bars, desperately trying to send Jerry mental messages. Could he even hear them? I wanted him to calm down. To bide his time. I felt stronger and was sure I could shift once we were left alone.

"You're disposable, Campbell. It's your wife who interests me." Fredrick turned his back on Jerry.

"Touch her and die, asshole." Jerry was livid.

"Empty threats." Fredrick looked me over. "Now, Gloriana, suppose I believe this nonsense. Why haven't you already called these illustrious parents for help? Olympus must be reached by something more interesting than a mere cell phone. I took yours, of course. Do you communicate mind to mind perhaps?" His grin was pure mockery. "I know if I were locked in a dungeon and had powerful people like that on my side, I'd be screaming for their aid."

"Oh, I'm sure you *would* be crying for your mommy." Jerry gripped the iron bars. His payment for that remark was a hard hit on his knuckles by one of the guards with what looked like a nightstick.

I gasped but tried to keep my cool. I stared at Fredrick, caught his gaze, and tried to mesmerize him anyway. No luck. Those damned glasses worked. "First, I haven't given up trying to get myself out of this mess." I sat on the cot. "Second, my parents love me but they're a lot of trouble. I don't want to owe them a favor. Payback's a bitch on Olympus."

"Olympus. Home of the Gods. Bet they just love having a vampire daughter." He laughed again and punched one of his guards on the arm. They all were in stitches, laughing at me. "Really, Gloriana, you spin a fine tale." Fredrick got serious, gesturing to his men. "But enough of this. I do believe you have something different in you so I drew blood while you were out. I'm analyzing it now. Perhaps I can use it to create something useful. A new and more effective drug."

"Knock yourself out. Just don't hurt my husband." I continued to play the pitifully weak victim. Too bad I could see that there were cameras at each end of the dungeon scanning the cells. Oh, well, when I finally managed to make a move, it would have to be fast and timed perfectly.

"For now he's useful as leverage. Since he's obviously important to you, my dear." Fredrick looked down his nose at Jerry like he couldn't understand my loyalty to an "ordinary" vampire.

"And my friends—the Viking and Gretchen? Where are they?"

"I am here. In a cell near you." Gunnar's voice echoed down the hall. "I haven't seen Gretchen. That bastard had better not have killed her."

"Gretchen!" I called for her. Was she in yet another cell?

"Don't bother calling for my wife. Surely you don't think I'd put her down here." Fredrick laughed. "Though I admit I was tempted. Gretchen's mercy fuck made her develop a soft spot for the Viking." Fredrick stalked down the corridor. "Oh, yes, I had the whole story out of her, Gunnar."

I heard Gunnar roar his hatred. Fredrick just

laughed, but it sounded bitter. He strode back to stand in front of my cell, apparently considering me the only vampire worth his time.

"My wife cries and begs for mercy for all of you." Fredrick spit on the floor. "Disgusting. If I threaten to hurt the Viking oaf, Gretchen becomes most loving to me. Pathetic."

"Leave her alone." I couldn't help it. It made me sick to think of kind, sweet Gretchen married to this monster.

He came closer and looked at me with hard eyes. "You know, Gloriana, it would be a kind of justice if I were to take *you* to bed now." He turned to Jerry. "How would you like that, Cousin Campbell?"

"You must have a death wish." Jerry lunged at the bars again.

Fredrick ignored him then nodded to one of his men. "Open her cell."

I wasn't about to let him drag me out of there without a fight. I clawed and kicked and screamed every curse word I knew. It didn't save me. Before I could stop them, the guards had me wrapped in their arms and held in front of Fredrick like a gift.

"Well, Gloriana, that fight was impressive but very ordinary. Any mortal female could resist as much." Fredrick reached out and dragged a finger down my cheek while the men held my arms behind my back. I kicked again, landing a good one on Fredrick's shin.

"I see we should have taken your boots." He shook his head. "You really don't want to make me angry, *min fina*. You would not like what happens then. I could have them hold you down on the cot." He hooked a finger into the neck of my red top. "I like the color and you do fill out a sweater." He glanced at Jerry before he grabbed a handful of my left breast. Then he danced out of the way of my kicks with a laugh. Jerry was beside himself, launching his body at the bars as if he could knock them down by sheer force.

"God damn you, leave her alone." Jerry reached through the bars, desperately trying to get a hand on Fredrick. "Coward. Do that again when you don't have me locked up and see what happens."

"Ha! Don't you realize you are as powerless as a mere mortal now? I could toss you around like a child, rip open your throat and watch you bleed out on the floor." Fredrick did stay out of reach. "But your wife is safe from me. I find her too *köttiga* for my taste."

"Bastard!" Jerry hit the bars with his fists. "I will see you in hell for this."

"Where is Gretchen? What have you done to her?" Gunnar's voice roared down the hallway.

"Ah, the lovesick swain speaks again." Fredrick nodded and his men threw me back in my cell and locked the door. "Gretchen is fine. She is my wife after all. It took some punishment to convince her, but she now knows that our open marriage is closed." He walked down the hall and I heard him bang something against the iron. "Mind your fingers, Viking. You will not heal now as fast as you usually do."

"What did you do to us? Why can we not shift?" Gunnar asked the question again.

"I have created the perfect weapon to use against vampires." Fredrick paced up and down the hall. He smiled as if deciding this was his chance to show off his genius. "My family has been in the weaponry business for centuries, since we made swords for Vikings such as you in ancient times." He banged on a cell again. "Then we turned to guns, making fortunes during the many wars that followed." He laughed. "When one of our number became vampire, it presented a unique opportunity. And who doesn't want to live forever?"

"You are clearly mad. Why would you want to destroy your own kind?" Gunnar was voicing all our thoughts.

"I like a challenge. And power." Fredrick walked over to study me again. "Gretchen is from another ancient family. I married her to make an alliance. But our families have not always been cordial. We have been enemies too. I like to be able to kill my enemies. To show them who has the most power." He glanced at Jerry. "You have the look of a warrior. I'm sure you understand my thinking."

"I don't understand you at all." Jerry stared at me. "But I do understand the urge to kill."

"Jerry, let's listen to him. Tell me, Fredrick, about this weapon you created. How does it work? When will its effects wear off?" I was desperate for that answer. I was getting my own powers back but I couldn't get Jerry and Gunnar out of here if they didn't have theirs restored soon.

"I'm sure you'd like to know. It's a secret, my pet." Fredrick laughed. "I will be back later. I am finding your blood very interesting. It has possibilities. And keeping you is proving to be entertaining." He nodded. "I'll be back later. A man will bring you fresh blood to drink. Use it to gain your strength because I want to know why my weapon didn't work on you even if I have to cut you apart to study your physiology."

"What?" I shrank back into a corner of my cell. What did he mean? Was he thinking of dissecting me like a lab rat?

"Oh yes." Fredrick put a hand on his own chest.

"There's a mystery here and I will get to the bottom of it, even if it kills you." He laughed suddenly. "Olympus." He wiped tears of mirth from his eyes. "By God, where do you come up with these things?" He strode down the corridor. "Oh, and don't even think of attempting an escape. Your husband will suffer for it. We will see if you try anyway." He gestured at the cameras then left through an iron door that clanged when it slammed shut behind the last guard.

We were alone. No guards stayed with us because of those security cameras at both ends of the dungeon. The door clanged again and a man in black brought in a bottle of blood and set it just inside my cell. He didn't say a word just left it and strode away again. I saw him toss the cell keys in an iron box by the door before he left. I sniffed the bottle suspiciously but it was obviously fresh and safe. It was a relief that I could tell that. I drank it down and felt better immediately. I got as close to Jerry as I could and saw he had collapsed on the floor of the cell a few feet away. No cot for him.

"Jerry! How do you feel?"

"Like hell. Save yourself, Gloriana, if you can. The bastard's obviously insane." Jerry sat up slowly and leaned against the bars.

"You're right. Fredrick *is* insane." I leaned my cheek against the cold bars. It was so damned freezing in here I could see my breath. A castle dungeon. At least Fredrick had upgraded it with electric lights but a quick sweep showed me that the ancient area still boasted iron rings in the walls where prisoners had once been chained. He hadn't bothered chaining us but that only worried me more. He counted on keeping us weak and helpless with his drugs and weapon.

"You're shivering." Jerry was shaking his cell door

or trying to. "I've lost my strength and I can't shift. Whatever he did to us sapped all my powers. That's never happened to me before. And I'd like to know how long we've been down here. I pray this effect will wear off soon."

"Can you get a mental message if I send one?" I tried but Jerry looked blank. "Guess not."

"This is impossible. I would think you should recover first."

I leaned low and whispered. "I'm feeling better. Stronger. We need to be careful, the cameras may have audio." I held onto my blanket. Of course Jerry didn't have one. Chivalry, Fredrick style. We'd had high-tech weaponry aimed at us but not central heat. I guess we knew Fredrick's priorities.

"Really?" Jerry sat up straighter but did keep his voice low. "Do you think you'll be able to shift soon?"

"I hope so." I glanced up at the cameras then just put my finger to my lips.

"I'm worried about Gretchen." Gunnar's voice came from what was probably the cell next to me.

"I am too, Gunnar. But I think he's probably afraid to kill her. He did say she was from a powerful family." I settled back against the stone wall and started to plan. As soon as I could shift, I was going to have to get the keys to let out the men. We wouldn't have long to make a break for it, not with those cameras aimed at us.

There was a small opening at the top of each wall between cells. If I could climb up and squeeze through that opening, I could work my way down to the end of the hall and disable the cameras somehow.

"Get ready. I think I can shift now. But we'll have to move fast." I stared across at Jerry.

His head shot up from where he'd been staring at the floor. "What are you thinking, love?"

"I'm going after the keys as soon as I disable the cameras." I took a chance and hissed Gunnar's name.

"I heard you whispering, Gloriana. What's happening?" Gunnar didn't know how to whisper. "I am ready to fight, though my chest hurts. Whatever that weapon does, it hurt my heart." Gunnar slammed something against his cell.

Jerry was on his feet. "Mine too. I can't shift yet either. Fredrick was right about one thing. I'm as weak as a mortal and I have none of my vampire senses." Jerry was playing it up for the cameras.

"Calm down, Gunnar. Save your strength." I concentrated and managed to shift, finally, into a bird, flying over the bars as fast as I could. I landed next to the first camera and pecked out the lens then quickly hit the other one. Then I shifted into my human form and found the cell keys in the metal box, running down to let Jerry out of his cell then Gunnar.

"By Thor's holy rod! You are special, Gloriana. Olympus? I would like to see you there, I think." Gunnar waited while I stopped long enough to hug Jerry then we were running down the hall. Thank God no one had thought to lock the big iron door. We opened the door carefully. A room with a TV monitor was just outside but no one was on duty. Fredrick must have been too sure of himself to post a guard. He'd pay for that.

Just then we heard someone coming. Jerry and Gunnar kept trying to shift but weren't having any luck. They did claim in whispers that they were feeling stronger though. We ducked into an alcove and that strength was tested when they jumped on top of two guards who were coming to check on us. The element of surprise worked in our favor and I got a good look in the guards' eyes, leaving them both statues that we shoved into a closet. I wasn't sure how long they'd stay frozen since I was still a little unsure of my powers.

"Good trick, Glory." Gunnar was impressed. "If Fredrick had seen that, he'd have to believe your story."

"Yes, and he'd never let me go." I grabbed Jerry's arm as we made our way very quietly up the stone stairs. Each man had a gun now, though Gunnar wasn't happy with using one. We were on our way to finding Gretchen. We weren't about to leave her behind. The upper floors of the castle were completely modernized. Except for one thing. Apparently a man who ran a multi-billion dollar munitions and weapons company took pride in his craft. He had displays of many kinds of weapons on the walls. They were in fancy locked cases behind glass but an angry Viking doesn't let that stop him.

Gunnar was delighted to spot an old Viking sword and ran a fist through the safety glass. He grabbed it and a scabbard to sling over his shoulder. Jerry added a broadsword to his arsenal then handed me a short dagger. I knew there were probably silent alarms going off in a secure room somewhere but we had to keep moving. We crept down halls covered in lavish and colorful Oriental rugs. At one point a pair of soldiers hurried past on the way to the dungeon. I guess they'd expected a report from the two guards who'd gone down earlier. More shape-shifters. Jerry and Gunnar jumped them, eager to use their weapons. When it became obvious that my guys were no match for the shifters, I jumped in with my Olympus freeze technique again.

"If I were fully recovered, you wouldn't have had to do that, Gloriana." Jerry was not a happy man. "I wonder how long it's going to take me to get my strength back? This is maddening." He had landed on the floor after a shifter had wrestled his sword away from him.

"Obviously whatever the 'Eliminator' does, it's serious. We need to take it and figure it out when we get Gretchen. If we can." I helped Gunnar to his feet. He didn't take the help well either.

"The man must die." Gunnar helped Jerry grapple with the shifters' bodies, shoving them behind a couch in a library that looked seldom used. "Can you smell her, Glory?"

I concentrated. Actually, I could. I pointed upward and we dashed up a broad staircase. I was terrified we'd be caught in mid-stair but no one was on patrol there. We heard shouting below us, a sign that the alarms had sent guards down to the weapons displays and the dungeon but not up the stairs yet. Naturally they'd assume we'd head outside and for freedom anyway.

At the top of the stairs I inhaled again and pointed to the right. It was a broad beautiful hallway with a half-dozen doors leading off of it. Then there was a set of double doors at the end. The master suite? We stopped and listened. Voices on the other side. Arguing. Surprisingly it was in English. Maybe they didn't want any of Fredrick's guards to overhear them.

"Fredrick, you cannot hold my cousin and his wife like this. The Campbells will come after you and there will be an endless feud. Do you really want to start that kind of war?" Gretchen sounded hoarse, as if this argument had gone on for a while.

"What do I care? I have the means to make it all

come to a swift end." He laughed. "You never should have taken up with that Viking. What made you flaunt the affair in my face like that?" He was not laughing now. He actually sounded hurt. "We agreed to be discreet."

"Like you are with Birgett? That *slyna* is everywhere on your arm. All my friends laugh at me." Gretchen's voice quavered.

"She is a vice president of my company. Of course she goes with me to business meetings."

"In hotel rooms?" Gretchen must have thrown something because there was a crash. "I am not a fool, Fredrick. I've had enough of your humiliating me. Gunnar was kind, different. I don't know him well enough to say that I love him, but he was certainly better to me than a man who thinks he is God."

"Shut your mouth, woman. The only *slyna* I know is standing in front of me."

Gunnar roared and threw open the double doors. He was on Fredrick before we could stop him. And I certainly wasn't trying to anyway. His sword sliced through Fredrick's arm before the men grappled and rolled on the floor. Gunnar had the advantage in height and weight but the Viking still had only a mortal's strength and powers. Fredrick's wound didn't slow him. He used his fangs to go for Gunnar's throat. The smell of blood was heady in the room and my own fangs slid down.

"Jerry, help him." I pushed Jerry toward the men. I knew he was staying out of it to give the Viking a chance to defend his woman. But when we saw that Gunnar was on the losing side, it was time to jump in. Gretchen had run to try to help, picking up a lamp and hitting Fredrick on the back. It didn't faze him. Now

Jerry grabbed Fredrick's bleeding arm, pulling him off of Gunnar and holding his own sword at Fredrick's neck.

"Stop, all of you!" I was trying to restore order but then I realized there was an army coming when I heard feet pounding up the stairs. Forget order. "Gretchen, come with us." I held out my hand. "Can you help us get out of here?"

"Yes!" She ran to where Gunnar and Jerry held Fredrick and reached into her husband's pocket to pull out what looked like a small flash drive.

"Gretchen, no! Where's your loyalty?" Fredrick tried to fight her. "You do this and I'll kill you."

"I'm as loyal as you are, Fredrick. And we'll see who survives this." She picked up the "Eliminator" which was on the dresser and plugged the drive into the end of it, then aimed it at her husband's chest. As soon as her finger flexed on the trigger, Fredrick slumped to the floor, unconscious. Then she grabbed a large leather purse and slung it over her shoulder.

"Now this way." She pointed to an ordinary looking door next to a bathroom. "We can go down the back stairs." She pushed us inside then through another door. This one was made of iron and she closed and bolted it. "This should hold them for a while."

We ran down the narrow staircase, ignoring the shouting and banging on the door above us. At the foot of the stairs was another iron door. This one creaked from disuse as Gretchen, with Gunnar's help, opened it. We were next to a driveway that led away from the castle and into the snow-covered woods that surrounded it. Of course it was cold, freezing, but at least it had stopped snowing. I was glad for my blanket but the other three had nothing to keep them warm.

Gretchen pointed to a shed and we found an old four-wheel-drive vehicle inside. Gretchen jumped in the driver's seat and the engine came to life, the car obviously well-maintained in case of emergency. We were soon bumping across the field. Luckily it started snowing heavily and I looked back and saw that it would probably soon hide our tracks. I breathed a grateful sigh when the heater started blowing hot air. The men were trying to hide it, but I could see them shivering and Gretchen hadn't bothered to hide the fact that she was clearly miserable with cold.

When we were about fifteen minutes from the castle, we came to a paved road and Gretchen stopped the car. She picked up the gun she'd brought with her and pulled out the flash drive.

"I'd hate for this to go off accidentally and hurt one of us." She looked at Gunnar. "How are you feeling?"

"Fine now that you are with us, *älskling*." He grabbed her hand and kissed it. "You were very brave back there."

"I should have done something like that a long time ago." She sighed. "It will take Fredrick a while to find his backup 'Eliminator' and the controller, if he ever does. I hid it long ago, as soon as I realized what he'd made. He won't come after us until he does find it. It took him years to make this one."

"But he will come after us." I snuggled into Jerry's arms. "Quite a husband you have there."

"He's changed since I married him. After he discovered this new weapon, he has been crazy for power. The other vampires in Sweden hate him for it. Once word got out what it could do, there has been a movement to have it destroyed. Since he refuses to give it up, that means Fredrick must be destroyed with it." She shrugged. "That is why he surrounds himself with an army now and has turned our home into a fortress."

"I'm sorry, Gretchen. But we've just seen how dangerous that thing is in the wrong hands." Jerry rested my hand on his thigh. "But when there are evil vampires in the world, it could be a useful weapon. It's a shame there couldn't be a way for it and Fredrick to be used correctly."

"He's a dead man." Gunnar wasn't going to listen to reason. "Then Gretchen will be free." He pulled Gretchen's hand to his lips. "I will make you love me. You will see what it is like to be worshiped as you deserve, *min vackra lady*."

"What does *vackra* mean?" I whispered to Jerry.

"Beautiful, pretty. Take your pick." He smiled at me. "Gunnar's laying it on thick."

"And while we're translating, tell me what Fredrick said about me. He called me *köttiga*." I saw by the look on Jerry's face that it wasn't good. I raised my voice. "Gretchen? What does *köttiga* mean?"

"Fleshy. Why? Who said that?" She handed the "Eliminator" to Gunnar. "Be careful with that thing. Even without the booster, it's dangerous. So whatever you do, don't hit that switch when you aim it at someone." She pointed at the silver one in the middle. "If you do, the person will fall unconscious, just like you all did before and Fredrick did at the castle." She started driving again, fast, down that paved road.

"Never mind." Fleshy. Otherwise known as fat. Bastard. Fredrick was going down.

"Not all of us. Gloriana didn't fall asleep." Gunnar looked back at me. "She is a goddess." He winked at me, clearly thinking I had made the whole thing up.

Not even the fact that I'd shown I could make statues had totally convinced him apparently. "No matter. This machine is magic." Gunnar set the box in his lap.

"Do you know how it works, Gretchen?" I really wanted to know that.

"Not a clue. Fredrick wouldn't ever share such a secret with a mere woman."

"He's a fool. You are wonderful. The best thing that ever happened to him." Gunnar kept up the sweet talk while we drove for several hours past fields of trees and snow. Jerry dozed next to me, still not fully recovered. I tried to test my senses, relieved that I could pick out each of my fellow vampire's scents in the car. My eyesight was sharper too. Finally Gretchen steered the car into a side road that was definitely not a main highway. It was bumpy and got me worried about that stupid gun going off accidentally.

"Where are we going?"

"My family has a hunting lodge not too far from here. I'm pretty sure Fredrick has forgotten about it." She glanced at Gunnar. "It's on the water and there may even be a boat there so we can still hunt for Gunnar's treasure. Obviously we're not getting near Fredrick again so using his boat is out of the question now."

"Obviously? No, you are wrong. We must get near him and make him pay for what he did to us." Gunnar looked fiercely Viking. "Jeremiah, are you with me?"

"Aye. He needs to be brought low for what he did to Gloriana and to us. We must do something about this weapon of his too, of course." Jerry reached out his hand. "Will you let me look at it, Gretchen?"

"Yes, of course. When we get to the cabin." She was concentrating on the road which was little more than a narrow track, dark between rows of trees.

I was just relieved Gunnar didn't try to pass that machine back to Jerry while she was driving. We had to be careful with that thing. What did those other switches do? There were two others next to the middle one. We couldn't afford to experiment with it or even try to disable it. I loved Jerry but a technological genius, he wasn't. Who did I know who was really good with that kind of stuff and could figure this out? Oh, no, I wasn't thinking of inviting friends along on my honeymoon, was I?

I glanced at Jerry. He stared at me and rolled his eyes. Great. So he'd read my mind. At least that special sense had returned to him and he could see his honeymoon plans going down the tubes at warp speed. I just wished for my cell phone. I had techno nerds on my speed dial. This was an emergency, honeymoon or not.

SIX

Gretchen's designer bag proved to be its own treasure trove. She'd managed to find my cell phone and Jerry's and hide them in there while Fredrick had been interrogating us.

"My husband always underestimates women," she explained grimly as she handed us our phones.

"Lucky for us that he does." I hugged her before heading for the shower. I was desperate to wash off the stink of that dungeon while Jerry got on the phone. Fredrick had certainly underestimated his resourceful wife. Gretchen had driven us to a roomy hunting lodge with three bedrooms and a living room. It had a stone fireplace large enough to keep the entire place cozy. Lucky for us it had been stocked with the family's synthetic blood and firewood. It was a perfect hiding place as long as Fredrick didn't remember it existed.

"Our friends will be here tomorrow night." Jerry told me after I joined him in the bedroom where Gretchen had brought us some extra clothes her family had left there.

"It must have been fun explaining all this to our best friends." I was lucky my borrowed sweater was roomy and a flattering blue. I gave up on changing pants and stuck with my jeans.

"It took a while even though I left out some details to save time." He stared down at his hands.

"Everything okay?" I sat on the bed next to him and picked up one of them. His knuckles were bruised and they should have already healed. "Did you drink some synthetic?"

"Of course." He shook his head when I kissed his fist. "Damn it. What did Fredrick's weapon do to us?"

"We'll figure it out." I leaned against him. He still felt solid and I knew he was getting his powers back, just not right away or all at once.

"At least we'll have help now. Guess who's coming with them." Jerry's frown gave me a clue. "Who do we know with a comprehensive knowledge of all things scientific and technical, not to mention medical?"

"Ian?" Jerry wasn't happy but I was glad that Ian MacDonald was coming. The doctor was brilliant and did have a mind that was at least as diabolical as Fredrick's.

"He had a private plane available and Richard made a case for getting him in on this. Of course Florence wouldn't be left behind either." Jerry pulled me down beside him on the double bed.

"Other than the fact that I hate for any of my friends to be in danger, and we certainly have proof Fredrick is dangerous, I'll be glad to see all three of them." Especially my best bud Flo. She'd been my matron of honor at our wedding and I missed her. I could tell Flo just about anything and couldn't wait to see what she said when she saw Gunnar. As for our honeymoon? Hey, Jerry and I had been "together" off and on for hundreds of years. Did we really need privacy for a traditional honeymoon? Of course the way Jerry's hands were sliding under my sweater I had to think privacy wasn't a bad thing.

"Mmm. Don't you think we should go out and tell Gretchen and Gunnar about our friends coming here?" I closed my eyes when Jerry's thumb ran across my nipple.

"What's the hurry?" He lifted my sweater and unclipped the front fastening of my bra. "Damn it all to hell. I knew it. That bastard bruised you when he grabbed your breast." He kissed the places where there were clearly fingerprints. "I should have killed him when I had the chance."

"Jerry." I was breathless by the time he sat back. "Why didn't you? I admit I was waiting for it. Dreading it."

"Gunnar and I were sending each other mental messages. Thank God we could by then. It wasn't the right time. Or the right way for it to happen. Gunnar wanted a fair fight. Probably to impress Gretchen." Jerry carefully closed the bra and pulled down my sweater. "Murdering a man in cold blood is a coward's way. I would have liked to have a fair fight too, but not with you and Gretchen in harm's way. We both knew Fredrick's men would be on us any minute."

"Fredrick's not worth risking your immortal soul for either." I put all my love into the kiss I gave him.

Jerry was smiling ruefully by the time I sat up. "You're worrying about my immortal soul? That ship sailed a long time ago, Gloriana." He shook his head. "I know you pray, go to church, all those things in case there's a heaven and a hell, but it is much too late for me to worry about the afterlife. I'm fairly sure it's the fiery furnace for me. I've killed many men in my time. Too many to count. But I've told myself it was done for a good cause. In war or self-defense. At least that's always been my excuse." He brushed my hair back from my face, his fingers lingering at my ears then at the veins at my neck.

"Hush. You're a good man, Jeremiah Campbell. It's Fredrick who's bound for hell. Look at how he treated Gretchen. And us! He needs to be punished. And his weapon should either be destroyed or turned into something helpful, not harmful to good vampires." I wiggled against Jerry's hard body and felt his rising interest.

"At least Fredrick's Eliminator didn't damage this." I stroked the bulge in his jeans. "I thought I'd die when he threatened you with that knife."

Jerry pulled me on top of him and kissed me thoroughly. "Would you stay with me, lass if I could not--"

I put a hand over his mouth. "I will be with you always, Jeremiah Campbell, even if you are cockless, fangless, hairless--"

He laughed and rolled me under him. "Enough. If any of that comes to pass, I will fall on a stake myself." His eyes gleamed as he touched me until I sighed.

"I could stay like this forever, my lover." Oh, how I meant that! "Unfortunately Gretchen might think we're safe here but clearly Fredrick is too damned clever not to figure out where she could take us, don't you think? He's probably checking out all her family's holdings already."

"That's why we're bringing in our clever friends as backup." Jerry grunted when I shoved him off of me and rolled off the bed. "Now where are you going?"

"Gretchen and Gunnar are waiting. I say we search for the Viking's treasure tonight, before our friends get here. At least get a boat and make a trip across to the island."

"That treasure. You think there's a chance in hell we'll find it?" Jerry sat up and slipped on wool socks.

"Probably not, but it'll keep Gunnar occupied. You know he's itching to run back to Fredrick's castle and challenge him to a sword fight." I sat down to zip on my boots.

"As if an asshole like Fredrick would ever agree to a fair fight." Jerry got up and slid his arms around me. "Whether he agrees or not, I'm not forgetting what he did to you. Never. He will pay. You have my word on that."

"Okay, okay, make him pay. But not necessarily with his life. That will complicate things here. His family is apparently prominent, respected, even if Fredrick isn't. Gretchen can divorce him if she wants to but the weapon is a breakthrough. He knows how to make more. If he can be persuaded to work with reasonable men, like Ian and Richard, it could be a game changer. For all decent vampires. Just promise to think about that, Jer." I took his hand. "Okay?"

"I will. Remember though that weapons never only get into the hands of the good guys." Jerry ran his hands through his hair. "History has shown us that. And then there's the problem of our Viking. What are we to do about him? If he doesn't find this treasure, he's going to be destitute and lost in our time." Jerry stepped into his own boots and tied the laces. "I don't fancy supporting him forever and I'm sure his pride wouldn't allow it anyway."

"You're right. We need to start thinking of a way for him to earn a living." I glanced at our closed door. Gretchen would be a wealthy woman once she shed herself of Fredrick but a man with Gunnar's background would never agree to be a kept man. I could relate.

"We'd better not think about it now. He'll read your mind and start worrying too." Jerry slung his arm around my shoulders. "Gretchen says there's a speed boat hanging in the boathouse down at the dock. If the lake isn't too icy here, we can lower it into the water and go across to the island from here."

"Good. Maybe we'll get lucky." I threw open the door and saw Gretchen and Gunnar sitting close to each other on the sofa in front of the fireplace. Both of them were smiling dreamily, as if there might have been more going on than just a change of clothes in one of the other bedrooms in the hour since we'd been shut in ours. Obviously Gunnar had fed if his ruddy cheeks were to be believed. By contrast, Gretchen looked a little pale.

"Lucky?" Gunnar held Gretchen's hand and didn't let it go. "By Thor, I hope so. We were just talking about going to the island tonight. To see about the treasure. There is a boat here."

"Good. That's what we hope to do too." I sat on Gretchen's other side. I noticed she'd taken off her wedding rings, a very large diamond ring and platinum band, and had set it on the wooden coffee table in front of her.

Jerry told them about our friends coming to help us.

"What can they do that we cannot?" Gunnar stood and strapped his sword on his back. He'd picked up the entire rig from the wall at the castle. "Are they fighting men?"

"Yes, of course. Both of them have been warriors in their time. But that is not the reason we asked them to come. " Jerry nodded at Gretchen. "I'm sure my cousin can appreciate the fact that we need men who can understand this new weapon of Fredrick's. How it works. How to make our own if we need to."

"We must persuade Fredrick that it would be wise to ally himself *with* us instead of against us, Gunnar." I stepped back when the Viking took out his sword and checked the blade.

"Or we could kill him and the problem would be solved." Gunnar ran the blade over his thumb and blood welled. "For us and for Gretchen." He stuck his thumb in his mouth and licked off the blood. "I want justice." He put away his sword and laid his hand on Gretchen's shoulder. "For this woman."

"I understand. But we should wait for reinforcements first. You saw Fredrick's army. We are outnumbered." Jerry grabbed his borrowed coat and shrugged into it.

"A Viking is worth ten men." Gunnar puffed out his chest. "Where are you going?"

"You want and need your treasure. Let's go down to the dock and take a look at the boat there." Jerry kissed my cheek. "Gloriana, I hope you will drink some synthetic while we're gone so your bruises will heal." He turned to Gretchen. "You look like you could use some too, cousin."

"Yes, I do need something." Gretchen had been too quiet while Gunnar had done all the talking. "Gunnar, please calm down and listen to Jeremiah. He knows this time. It is just good sense to take his advice."

"If it will make you happy, *älskling*." Gunnar kissed Gretchen's cheek then took a coat off a hook by the door, zipping it up over his sword as if he'd done it forever before he followed Jerry outside.

I waved them off. I had no desire to go out in the freezing cold until I absolutely had to.

"Gunnar looks good in the pale blue cashmere sweater." I got up and found two bottles of synthetic blood in the kitchen. Since it was so cold outside, I gave them a few seconds in the microwave before carrying them back to the couch.

"I agree. My brother's clothes look well on him, I think." Gretchen took the bottle and sipped. She rubbed her empty ring finger as if missing that wedding set.

"Gunnar is handsome, but he's going to have some problems, coming from another time." I settled into a corner of the couch. "Are you thinking about a future with him?"

"It's too soon. I told him that." She stared down at her drink. "For him to make plans too. He has no idea what other women of our time are like. He thinks I'm so wonderful." She glanced at me, her eyes shining. "He is a fool. Doesn't he know that many modern women would have been happy to sleep with such a handsome man who needed her?"

"Seriously? You thought of his needs before your own." I sighed. "I certainly wasn't going to offer myself to him."

"Of course not!" Gretchen smiled. "You are newly married. Jeremiah wouldn't have allowed it."

"Well, I won't debate you on whether Jerry allows me to do things or not." I played with my own beautiful wedding ring. "But it can't have been easy, being with a man frozen for a thousand years."

"He wasn't an animal." Gretchen sighed. "Just very... hungry."

"What you did was a purely selfless act. And now I think you have feelings for him. Not just because he is handsome, but because he is kind and cares for you."

"So he says." She stared into the fire. "What is to become of him? He will never find his treasure. After all this time?"

"We must at least help him look for it. Who knows? Maybe we *will* get lucky." I got up and took our empties to the kitchen sink to rinse them out, tossing them into her recycle bin. "I hear them coming back. I don't know what you want to do with him, but I feel some responsibility for Gunnar. We did find him in the ice."

"Yes. Thank God for that. You're right. It is refreshing to have a kind man care for me. Fredrick hasn't for a long, long time." Gretchen got up and slipped on her coat then picked up her cell phone off the coffee table. She slipped it into her pocket. "Shall we go out to meet them?"

The guys assured us that they were fully recovered from their encounter with the Eliminator and had even done a quick test outside to see if they could shift. To everyone's relief, they were all systems go. Even Jerry's knuckles looked better after a second bottle of synthetic.

Jerry and Gunnar had lowered the small speedboat into the water and we all managed to fit into it. The water was choppy and there was an icy wind that took my breath but at least the lake hadn't frozen. There were navigation lights on the shore of the island and a clear night made it a simple thing to find our way to Birka. Good vampire vision and an almost full moon helped too. Gunnar pushed Jerry aside as soon as we left the dock and took the wheel.

"You can take care of that engine thing, Jeremiah. I will steer." Gunnar was practically jumping out of the boat with excitement. The fact that this boat used a motor fascinated him. But we could all tell that he was a seaman through and through. He stood behind the wheel as if he'd done it all his life, steering us around buoys and through a channel until we came to a rocky harbor.

"Let me slow it down now, Gunnar. You have no idea how to handle a throttle." It was Jerry's turn to take over and he wasn't taking no for an answer. Gunnar didn't argue. He was looking up at the rocky cliffs in dismay.

"Odin save me but this is different from what I remember," Gunnar muttered under his breath as he helped Jerry avoid the rocks and abandoned boats to find a place where we could dock. "There was once a town at the top of the cliff, many houses made of wood."

"Birka was abandoned centuries ago, Gunnar." Gretchen rested her hand on his arm. "It won't be anything like you remember. There's a museum, but we're late enough that it will be closed."

We landed at a pier and the men tied up the boat next to a wooden walkway. There were stone stairs cut into the side of the cliff with a sign pointing the way. A sign in several languages, including English, let us know that we could walk up to the top and visit that museum and the remnants of a Viking village.

"Let's go see what they've done." I needed Jerry's help climbing out of the rocking boat and waited for Gretchen to join me. We were very afraid that Gunnar was going to be disappointed but he strode off in front of us, a man with a mission.

"He should lead the way. Yes, the island has changed but maybe what he's looking for is still here." Jerry stayed at our backs, I guess in case one of us stumbled.

"I don't suppose we could use a flashlight." I could see but it was pretty dark and I had to watch my step as we got higher up the cliff. One wrong move and I could go plunging off the side. Would it have killed them to install handrails? The water would break my fall but I didn't look forward to an ice bath.

"There's bound to be some security here." Jerry put his hand on my elbow. "Stay quiet. It's best not to draw attention."

Gretchen hurried to catch up to Gunnar and hissed at him. "Would you slow down and be careful? I told you, things are different here now."

He stopped at the top of the cliff and looked around. "Yes, I can see that." His shoulders slumped. "I expected..." He shook his head. "*Det gör mig galen.*"

"What did he say, Jerry?" I whispered.

"He said it makes him crazy." Jerry stepped up to Gunnar and squeezed his shoulder. "I understand. But take a moment. Get your bearings. Look for landmarks. Where did you hide your coin?"

"In a grave. A special one. Far from the center of the village." Gunnar nodded and took off again. "Yes, I think I can find it. If grave robbers have not beat me to it. *Tack*, Jeremiah."

"Grave robbers. Yes, that's been a problem here.

For centuries." Gretchen looked stricken.

"It's the same everywhere." I hurried to keep up with Gunnar whose long legs made that difficult. "Gunnar, wait up."

"*Stopp! Vi är stangda!*" The voice came out of the darkness.

I didn't move and neither did Gretchen or Jerry. Gunnar disappeared and I hoped the man in the uniform hadn't seen him. Gretchen answered the man in rapid Swedish. I guess she was weaving a story.

"I told him you were my American friends. That you thought you'd left your purse here when we came to tour the museum today, Gloriana." Gretchen took my arm. "He's agreed to let us look inside, to see if it's there. I let him know you have a plane to catch and can't leave without your passport."

"Clever girl." I whispered.

Jerry walked up to the man, pressing a large bill into his hand and obviously thanking him profusely. Jer always had money in his pockets and, surprisingly, Fredrick hadn't taken it from him. I'd crammed my cell into my pocket, along with my lipstick of course. Gretchen had loaned me a flattering color.

We stopped at the large wooden building and waited while the security guard unlocked the door. He flipped on lights and allowed us a few minutes to pretend to search. It was a fascinating place and I was sure Gunnar would have loved it. Viking figures stood in vignettes in front of small wooden houses or holding swords. They looked much like Gunnar had when he'd fallen out of the ice except that they were wearing complete outfits, including furs. Some had swords strapped on their backs.

Jerry had left his sword in Gretchen's cabin but

had found some knives there to his liking and had them on him of course. Gretchen had the Eliminator under her coat but it was unplugged, the activator in her pocket.

My phone rang. I dug it out and saw Jerry's number before I answered.

"Pretend you're getting a call saying that your passport was found at a restaurant where we ate lunch. Got it?" He was whispering, out of sight of the guard who had chosen to trail Gretchen and me as we looked around the ladies restroom and snack bar area.

"Oh, thank you! What a relief!" I ended the call, turned to the guard and explained the call. "Thank you so much for allowing us to look for it here." I shook his hand. "You have such a wonderful job, guarding these Viking treasures."

He answered me in halting English with a smile. "So many old things we find. Look at the bowl there. Very old. A real treasure as you say."

"Treasure?" The voice boomed from the darkness. "Is this man saying he has my treasure?" Gunnar strode into view, his sword in his hand. "Tell me where it is and I might spare your life, *tjuv.*"

"Oh, shit." I jumped in front of the guard who was thumbing his two-way radio. "Give me that." I snatched the radio before the guard could send a message and looked into his eyes. He was frozen in place before he could say a word.

"Gloriana! How did you do that?" Gretchen stared at me open-mouthed when it was clear the guard couldn't move a muscle.

"Long story." I heard the radio squawk in my hand.

"Rolf, *vad händer?*

Jerry snatched the radio out of my hand. *"Inga problem. Tappede min radio."*

There was laughter and a comment before the radio went silent again.

"What did you say?" I had to admire the way Jerry had sounded like the guard.

"Just that there was no problem. I'd dropped my radio." Jerry shook his head. "Gunnar, the guard does not have your treasure, put the sword away."

"I heard him." Gunnar looked ready for action.

"He thinks anything old from Viking times is a treasure." I stayed in front of the guard protectively.

"Obviously you didn't find what you were looking for." Gretchen approached Gunnar. "Put away the sword."

"The graves have been disturbed but I am not finished searching. There is so much change. The black dirt is thicker now. I need tools." Gunnar's eyes lit up when he saw the displays of Viking life. "Ah, just what I need." He grabbed a sharp pointed staff and what looked like a primitive shovel. "Jeremiah, get another one and we dig. Are you with me?"

"Yes, of course. But how deep can we go with these things?" He gestured at photographs the archaeological society had posted. "The people who have worked this site used backhoes, machinery."

"I know not what those may be, but I can put my back into this and dig a fine hole. If you are too weak, mayhap one of the ladies will take over for you." Gunnar grinned, showing that he was merely goading Jerry into helping.

"I can dig." I grabbed a tool. "I'm sure Gretchen can too. Let's just get on with it."

"What about him?" Gretchen pointed at the guard

who was still standing exactly as I'd left him.

"He will be fine until we're ready to leave. Then I'll thaw him out and order him to forget that he ever saw us. Okay?" I smiled and stalked toward the door with my primitive shovel over my shoulder.

"I suppose. But I want to hear this long story as soon as we're back at the cabin." Gretchen picked out what looked like a hoe and followed me.

"All right. With all four of us digging, maybe we can find Gunnar's treasure." Jerry grabbed a tool. "I just hope like hell that grave robbers didn't beat you to it, Viking."

"It cannot be. I have prayed to Freya and know it cannot be." He glanced at Gretchen. "If I am to live in this time and place, I must have gold." He turned and straightened his shoulders. "So we will find it." He marched off like he was going into battle.

We all exchanged looks then went after him. What he'd said was merely the truth. Freya? Okay, so maybe Gunnar wasn't Christian. I smiled at Gretchen. She would certainly have her hands full if she decided to have him long term.

SEVEN

We dug for hours. It was a good thing the Northern Lights were so beautiful and bright. The black earth as Gunnar called it was deep but not hard or frozen solid thanks to what Gretchen assured us was a mild winter. Could have fooled me. If she wanted to see a mild winter, she should come to Texas. I invited her to visit while we were taking turns digging until our muscles quivered.

Gunnar had carefully selected a sunken area after looking at various landmarks. He swore this was where one of the ancient kings of Sweden had buried his favorite mistress. We worked quietly, aware of other security guards on the island. Jerry checked a few times on our frozen guard but it seemed the men on patrol didn't report to each other on a regular basis. No alarm went off and no flashlights were seen scanning our section of the island.

It was cold, so cold. And of course there was the ice and snow to contend with. Even with heavy coats and gloves and my vampire senses that usually protected me from feeling too much from the weather,

I was absolutely miserable.

"I see the stone! The door to the tomb!" Gunnar grabbed Gretchen and kissed her. "Look, there is her name, carved on the door."

"Astrid? That's who you've been talking about?" Gretchen wiped the dirt away from the carving. "I have heard her story. The king adored her but his wife hated her. Some say his wife poisoned the king because he loved his mistress more than his wife." She turned to Gunnar. "You were very clever to hide your fortune here. Everyone knows Helga cleaned out the tomb even before her husband's body was cold. It is a famous story. There are even songs about it."

"We shall soon see if I am so clever." Gunnar looked serious as he nodded to Jerry. "Will you help me move this? It will be hard work."

"I can't wait." Jerry put his shoulder to it and between the two of them the stone slowly rolled aside. . . but not enough.

"I cannot look or begin to fit. Can you squeeze inside and see…" Gunnar touched Gretchen's face. "If I have wasted our time?"

"Here." I turned on my phone's flashlight and handed it to her. "Watch your step. I don't know how these tombs are laid out. Try not to trip on bones."

"I'll be careful." Gretchen smiled. "And, Gunnar, pray to my Christian god that your gold will be there. Where exactly did you hide it?"

"She had a bed of stone and was laid upon it. I piled rocks at the head of the bed. My fortune is under the pile in two hide sacks. There are many gold and silver coins so they should be heavy." Gunnar pulled Gretchen into his arms and kissed her with his heart in it. "Yes, I'll pray to your god. Now find my treasure, beautiful woman."

Gretchen was flushed as she wiped her eyes, smearing dirt across her cheek. Then she turned and squeezed through the entrance. We could see the faint glow of the flashlight moving around as she walked inside.

"How big is this tomb?" I sat right where I was, in the dirt and snow. We'd been digging in a hillside. It had been a surprise to find a cave with a rock in front of it after pushing aside so much dirt. I turned and saw the dark water behind us. Lights bobbed on the surface. Some were buoys marking a channel but one was moving fast, a boat headed toward the island. At this time of night? Surely we hadn't been followed. None of us had mentioned Birka to Fredrick but that didn't mean he hadn't read it in Gretchen's mind.

"Not so big. I'm hoping it's taking a while because she is moving rocks." Gunnar paced in front of the opening, trying to peer inside. "I cannot see her."

"Jerry, look out there, at the water. Is that a speedboat coming into the harbor? I think it's going to dock where we left our boat." I whispered, not wanting to distract Gunnar.

"You're right." Jerry walked closer to the edge of the cliff. "Shit. There are four men in the boat and they're tying up next to our boat." He glanced at Gunnar. "You know who it must be."

"Gretchen!" Gunnar had waited long enough. "Are you all right?"

"Yes. Give me a minute. The ground is uneven and rocky. I finally found the bed. The cave is unstable. I think there's been a rockslide." Her voice was strained, like she might have hurt herself in there.

"She has to come out now, Gunnar. I'm afraid

Fredrick and his men just docked down below. They've followed us here." Jerry grabbed Gunnar's arm.

"How is that possible?" Gunnar shrugged off Jerry's hand. "We can't stop now. If we leave this cave open someone else will come and finish what we started." He pressed his face into the cave opening. "You must hurry, *min söta*."

"He's right about the treasure, Jerry." I kept my eyes on the men down below. I recognized Fredrick in the lead. They headed straight for the stairs and started up the ones marked with the directions to the museum. They would find the helpless guard. "I have to go get the guard. I don't want him left to Fredrick's mercy. You know he has none."

Jerry pulled out a knife. "You're right, no one can find the guard like that. I'll go."

"You can't release the freeze. I have to do it." I touched Gunnar's back. "We're going back to the museum. We have to free the guard. Meet us at the boat with Gretchen as soon as she's done. Hurry!"

"You're sure it's Fredrick?" He pulled out his sword. "How did he know where we would go?"

"I don't know. He could have used the GPS in Gretchen's cell phone." I gave up at Gunnar's blank look. Of course the Viking had no idea what I was talking about. "Anyway, we can't leave the guard exposed. When Gretchen comes out, take her phone out of her pocket and kill it with a rock. Understand?"

"Kill a phone?" He shook his head. "No matter. Gretchen will know what to do. Go. We'll meet you at the boat." Gunnar leaned against the rock. "Gretchen, your bastard of a husband is here. We must go now. Forget the treasure." He sounded resigned and my heart went out to him. "You are more valuable to me than all the gold in Sweden, *älskling*."

Jerry muttered something about the Viking having it bad then grabbed my hand. We ran toward the museum. I was determined that the guard wouldn't be turned into collateral damage. When we got there, we could hear Fredrick and his men talking as they worked their way up the cliff stairs.

"Why they hell would they come here? The Viking with her is crazy if he thinks anything he left here a thousand years ago would still be here." Fredrick laughed and so did his men. He said something in Swedish and that got them really going. "I should give her a divorce and let her have him. She has no idea that I have been listening to them and their stupid love talk. The man is a throwback!"

"But what if he does have a fortune, chief? Some say there is still gold to be found here. You know what one old gold Viking coin is worth these days?" This bodyguard was clearly an American hired gun.

Jerry and I couldn't stand around listening. It was horrifying to think that Fredrick must have planted some kind of bug in Gretchen's cell phone or purse as well as tracking her movements. Whatever he'd done, he knew everything. No wonder it had been easy for him to follow us.

I found the guard exactly where we'd left him and stared into his eyes. I gave him a quick case of amnesia, just for the past few hours, then thawed him out. After relieving him of his gun Jerry shoved him into a closet and locked him inside. We'd just taken care of this when we realized we weren't alone.

"Well, well, well. If it isn't the two honeymooners. Where are your friends?" Fredrick strolled into the museum, looking very pleased with himself. His three guards aimed rifles at us.

"I thought there were gun laws in Sweden." I held onto Jerry, who was aiming the gun he'd taken from the guard at Fredrick.

"There are. Your husband is breaking them. My friends and I are going hunting. Perfectly legal to carry our guns with us if we're members of a gun club. See our matching patches?" Fredrick pointed to the coat of arms sewn on his jacket. And, yes, his men had identical patches sewn on theirs. I couldn't read what the symbol said, but the crossed rifles made it clear what it meant.

"Hunting? On an abandoned island with a museum? Don't think the authorities would buy it." Jerry kept his gun pointed at Fredrick's heart. "And a regular bullet will barely slow us down anyway."

"Ah, but there I have once again proven my ability to produce a weapon just for vampires." Fredrick nodded and one of his men dug in his pocket and handed him a bullet. "These bullets are special. We have loaded our rifles with this ammunition made of a hard wood guaranteed to kill if it hits a vampire's heart. Be assured, my men are excellent marksmen." His smile gave me chills. "Would you like for me to have Finn demonstrate on your wife?"

"Bastard. What the hell? Do you sell to vampire hunters?" Jerry's fangs were down and I was afraid he was going to jump Fredrick and take his chances.

"It's a lucrative market. Why not? I do it on-line so there is no danger to me." Fredrick's smile was self-satisfied.

"You are a disgrace to your kind."

"Quit whining, Campbell. I find it boring."

"Then we will get out of your way." Jerry kept his arm around me and moved toward the door. "You know we are not who you want to kill tonight so we're leaving now. Don't try to stop us."

"You're right. I'm not interested in you two. The authorities are funny about things like missing American tourists. I don't need them looking into my affairs." He waved his hand and the rifles aimed at the floor. "I'm looking for my wife of course. Have you seen her?" Fredrick pulled out his cell phone. "Oh, there she is. A few hundred yards away. What could she be doing there?" He gestured and his men moved closer. "Hand over that gun, Campbell. Or is it Blade this century? Vampires. We lead such complicated lives, don't we?"

"Why should I give you the gun?" Jerry kept it aimed at Fredrick's heart. "You could be seriously wounded before your men got off a shot."

"Not likely. I'm wearing a bulletproof vest. Are you? Better yet, is your wife?" Fredrick laughed. "Drop the gun and stop wasting my time."

"Do it, Jer. I just want to get away from this creep." I tugged on his arm. Not his shooting arm. For all I knew that gun had a hair trigger.

"Fine. We're leaving. If you're smart, you'll let your wife have a dignified divorce. Our family will make sure you'll regret it if she comes to any more harm. Understand? As you say, you don't need the authorities looking into your business dealings." Jerry tossed the gun to Fredrick who caught it deftly.

"You're careless. I could have been hurt just then. But you're also a Campbell and they are all a bit reckless. I have good reason to know that. Get out of my sight." He looked down at his phone. "*Jaklar!* Her phone has gone dead." He gestured to his men. "Come. We must go to her last known location and hurry."

"Do you think..?" I ran to keep up with Jerry as he headed for the cliff and the way down to the boat.

"I don't know but we have to be ready to cast off as soon as they get to us. Watch your step on these stairs but hurry." He was nimble as he jogged down the stone steps, taking them two at a time.

"Gretchen has the Eliminator. Maybe . . ."

"The odds are against them, Gloriana." Jerry jumped the last few feet to the dock then held out his hand to help me onto the boat.

"At least he didn't have his favorite anti-vampire device with him. Gretchen must have found a great hiding place for his spare." I worked with a grim Jerry to cast off the lines, holding one loosely while he started the engine. We scanned the cliff eagerly but didn't expect to see two large white birds fly overhead, land on the deck and then shift in front of us.

"We made it. Shove off." Gunnar was out of breath as he pulled Gretchen down to a seat in the back of the boat. It was a good thing because Jerry gunned the motor as soon as I tossed away the last rope. The boat went shooting across the water. "Slow down. Remember the rocks."

"Watch above us. They can all shift too, you know." Gretchen leaned against Gunnar for a moment then looked across at me. "I can't believe Fredrick followed me using my cell phone. I should have thought of that."

"Obviously he's into all the high tech stuff." I was glad when Gunnar stepped up behind the wheel and took over from a frowning Jerry to steer us safely out of the harbor. "But forget that. What I want to know is if you found Gunnar's treasure." She and Gunnar both wore bulky coats, his the biggest because of that ever-present sword sticking out of the back. Could there be bags of gold in her pockets? His?

Gretchen didn't answer, just stared at Gunnar whose face was a serious mask of concentration as he held onto the wheel. No clue there.

"Gretchen, a simple yes or no would work." I wanted to shake her.

"Later." Gretchen looked skyward where a trio of large black and white birds had dived off the cliff and landed on the speedboat. It was a matter of moments before it roared to life and came racing after us. "Storm Petrels. Naturally Fredrick would have them shift into a bird like that. Very common. It is a good idea." She glanced at Gunnar. "But one of them has stayed behind. I wonder why."

I wanted to shake the information out of her. *What about the treasure?* Was that extra shifter at Gunnar's cave now, looting it? But she was right. We had more important things to worry about at the moment. Like the fact that our boat wasn't as fast as the red cigarette boat chasing us, maybe because we had one more person aboard weighing us down. The solution might be for two of us to take off. We could meet somewhere.

I thought longingly of my honeymoon suite at the Ice Palace. Would we be safe there? Why not? Fredrick had already shown a lack of interest in Jerry and me. It was Gretchen and Gunnar he really wanted.

"You sure there's nothing else on you that could send a signal to Fredrick?" I looked her over. "Ditch your watch." It was pretty but digital. Clever Fredrick might have planted a bug in that thing too. She'd left her purse in the boat and now she dug through it.

"I don't see anything obvious that he could have

used to track me." But Gretchen tossed a pack of gum and a ball point pen overboard. "Oh, the hell with it." She pulled cash out of her wallet then threw her entire purse into the water.

I gasped as I saw a designer bag worth thousands of dollars sink beneath the waves.

"That bastard." Gretchen stuffed the cash into her coat pocket. "I wonder how long he's been spying on me."

I had no answer for that and no time to mourn her purse. But I did have an idea. "What if we all shift into birds and fly in four different directions? There seem to be a lot of those Storm Petrels. We can blend with them. Jerry and I can safely go back to the hotel, I think. You have somewhere you can go with Gunnar that Fredrick won't know about?" I glanced back. Damn, but that other boat was almost within shooting distance. In fact, I could see one of the men picking up a rifle and taking aim. The other one got the idea and grabbed one too. It might be Fredrick at the wheel. He seemed like the type who would want to be at the controls.

"Yes." She grabbed Gunnar's hand. "We're going to shift now. After we get away from them, Gunnar, head for that tall building you see on the point. I'll meet you there soon. On the roof. Do you see it?"

Gunnar let go of the wheel, turning it over to Jerry. "Yes, I see it. But the boat..."

"Is expendable. We don't care what happens to it." I made sure Gunnar knew I was serious when I could see he had a hard time with that idea. "Just leave it. We have to hurry and shift or one of us will get a wooden bullet through the heart. Fredrick told us that's the ammunition in his guns. By using wooden bullets, he's made them lethal to vampires." I grabbed Jerry and kissed him, not caring that the boat veered when I did it. "Jer, meet me at the Ice Palace. We all should go in different directions now."

"I heard you. We're shifting. But I don't like leaving you on your own, Gloriana." Jerry frowned at me before kissing me again.

"You should know by now that I can take care of myself." I glanced back. "Hurry, they're getting ready to shoot at us. All of us shift at the same time, birds like the ones Fredrick and his guys turned into a few minutes ago. On the count of three, we all go." I could see the shifters aiming at us. "One, two, three!"

"Gloriana!" Jerry had no choice and shifted before he took off and flew away from me.

Gretchen didn't waste time. She was gone too, just another Storm Petrel. Gunnar and I did the same, streaking through the sky with gunshots echoing as we flew as fast as our wings could take us.

Our boat still zoomed across the water so Gunnar and Jerry must have left it on full throttle. Fredrick gestured and his two men threw down their guns and shifted, hitting the sky to follow us. To my relief it soon became apparent that they didn't know which one of the birds was a priority.

We were careful to avoid each other and, as luck would have it, a flock of real petrels fished nearby, diving into the water. Gunnar headed that way so I made a sharp right, leading one of the shifters away from him and toward yet another group of birds soaring toward the shore. It didn't take long before I realized I'd left all signs of pursuit behind. I hoped the others also had that kind of luck.

I finally relaxed enough to look down and try to

get my bearings. I was still over the water but very near the coast. Hopelessly lost? Possibly. At least I could see the lights of Stockholm and headed toward them. The sky was blazing with a beautiful display of the Northern Lights. Too bad I couldn't really enjoy it. I was desperate to hit the ground and get warm. The icy wind was much worse when I flew into it as fast as my wings could take me. I watched for a major highway or the spires of the Ice Palace. No such luck. Snow and ice. This country was ridiculously beautiful but not giving me landmarks I could use.

Obviously I should head for the city. Surely it would be easier if I just landed where I could catch a taxi and take it back to the hotel. The other petrels stayed near the water so I was the only bird in sight now. That reassured me that I'd lost Fredrick's shifter anyway. I hoped the others had lost their pursuers as easily.

As for taking a taxi? I had a credit card in my pocket. Hey, I'm an addicted shopper. You don't think I'd ever leave home without at least one of those or some cash, do you? Not even the idea that maybe there'd be a nice shop in town helped me on my journey. The last few miles nearly killed me. I was almost numb from cold. I was cursing my new husband for his clever honeymoon surprise. Yes, we had those long, endless nights for fun and games, but it was freezing. And, to cap off my misery, it started snowing just as I finally hit the city center.

Flying was way harder than it looked. Flapping your wings aka arms wasn't fun in the best of conditions. When ice crystals started forming on my poor wings, I decided to land and shift no matter where I was. Fortunately I found the perfect spot to change back into my human form behind a tree. Bingo. The park with snow-laden evergreens was handily surrounded by luxury hotels all dressed for the holiday season with twinkling lights. It was almost Christmas and I had somehow let that important fact get lost in the rush of getting married, this trip, and now a crazy and dangerous adventure.

I hurried across the street and into the warmth of a hotel lobby that was centered by a beautiful tree that blazed with colored lights. I hadn't seen a taxi out front but that wasn't surprising this late. There was a doorman though so I knew he could call one for me when I was ready to leave. First, I had to thaw out. After I brushed my hair back from my face and freshened my lipstick of course.

A glance at the clock above the check-in desk assured me I still had a few hours before what passed for sunrise in these parts. I wandered into the bar and stood in front of its roaring fireplace. Too bad the bartender didn't serve synthetic blood but he stood in front of a big screen TV. The reporter looked excited and had planted herself in front of what I recognized as the museum on Birka. I asked the bartender to translate her Swedish. There had been a break-in of some sort and there was our guard who looked a little dazed as she questioned him. The reporter quickly got frustrated when it became obvious that he didn't have any juicy details for her and the scene changed.

To a boat crash. Gretchen's boat had apparently finally come to rest in a marina where it had slammed into the end of a floating dock. Luckily no one had been hurt and that reporter was having a tough time finding witnesses or an explanation for why an unmanned boat had been left running until it crashed.

The poor boat looked totaled while the dock seemed to have sustained minimal damage. No sign of Fredrick or his men as the camera panned the scene but I did notice a familiar red cigarette boat tied up nearby. Hmm.

I took advantage of the open gift shop to pick up a gift for Jerry. The clerk even wrapped it in holiday paper for me. I tucked it into my pocket then headed to the front of the hotel to ask the doorman for a cab. Hopefully Jerry would be waiting for me at the Ice Palace. We'd get one more night of privacy if we were lucky and then meet our friends at the airport tomorrow night. I wished we would hear from Gretchen before then so we'd know she and Gunnar were safe but there was really nothing we could do for now.

I sighed as I settled into the taxi and asked for the Ice Palace. I could use a little honeymoon action with my husband. Adventure was fine in small doses but the timing for this one sucked.

EIGHT

"Mrs. Blade!" Viktor came running up to me as soon as I finished signing the credit card slip and stepped out of the cab. "I'm so glad you're back. I tried to keep them out. I did. But they pushed right past me." He looked a little wild-eyed. "And your room! I had no idea it needed so much attention. May I send in a housekeeper now?"

"Who, Viktor? What are you talking about?" I pulled him out of the hotel doorway and into an alcove where we couldn't be seen by anyone coming into the hotel. I glanced around the lobby first. Had Fredrick sent men here after all? Was he going to snatch Jerry and me and try to get Gretchen's location out of us?

"What's this about attention? Mr. Blade and I left the room in perfect order." Well, except for a few towels on the floor in the bathroom. That was Jerry. He would never hang up a damp towel.

"I am sorry if I seem to be criticizing, Madame. Perhaps it is an American custom to pull out all the drawers and dump them on the floor." Viktor nodded.

"I was surprised, though, that the mattress was tossed aside and off the bed. I would think you'd be more comfortable--"

"We didn't do that, Viktor. Obviously someone made mischief in our room. You say it was like that when you let these people into our room? And they're still here? Who are they?" I wasn't about to go to our room if Fredrick's men were waiting to ambush me.

"Two men and a woman, Mrs. Blade. They insisted that they were your friends, from America. They were as shocked as I was when they saw the state of your room." Viktor was wringing his hands. "Oh, if you have been robbed we must notify the police. Take inventory, if you please. Make a list of what is missing."

"Viktor, I don't want to call the police. Tell me about these people who claim to be my friends." I grabbed his hands. "Calm down."

"I can't. This never happens here. We are a safe place to stay. Our guests must feel that they can trust our security." Viktor looked behind me. "Where is your husband, Mrs. Blade? I expected you to be together."

"He's coming." At least I hoped he was. This new development had me freaked out. Had Jerry arrived first and then been taken by force back to Fredrick's dungeon? God. I tried to put on a calm face, even forced a smile. "Mrs. Blade". Jerry had registered us that way and it pleased him. Of course he was all right. I would tease him about the Mrs. Blade thing again. Give him the little gift I'd bought him and we'd... I swallowed, my smile slipping.

"Please describe these 'friends.' We are expecting some people to join us. But much later tonight. You say they're waiting in our room now?"

"Yes, yes they are!" Viktor dug in his pocket. "I

will give you back the huge tip the blond one gave me if I did the wrong thing. Well, both men are blond, now that I think about it. One man is very blond, his hair almost white. Blue eyes. Which is common in our country. So I think that is not unusual but they were hard eyes. The men were not the kind I would want to meet in a dark alley, if you know what I mean." Viktor shuddered. "They were very angry at the state of your room. I can send a housekeeper--"

"Fuck the housekeeper!" Oh, I'd shocked him. Too bad. "Sorry. But I need you to go on. Please." I took a breath. So far he could have described any of the men who worked for Fredrick. Jerry! "You said there was a woman with them?" Fredrick would never hire a woman to do his heavy lifting. Okay, I took another breath and let go of Viktor's arm when he moaned. Poor man. I'd probably bruised him.

Viktor rubbed his arm and nodded. "Yes. She was Italian, I think. Short, very curvy. Dark hair." Viktor studied his shiny black shoes. "Oh, I knew I shouldn't have let them in. Aren't your friends Americans? I speak a little Italian. It is good to know languages in this job." He looked up again, eyes wide. "She let me know in that language that I should stop trying to keep them out of your room. Called me a few names I would rather not repeat to a lady." He took a shaky breath, clearly reassessing the lady thing. "If they are not your friends, Mrs. Blade, I will lose my job."

I laughed and hugged him, suddenly sure things were going to be okay. "No, you have just described my three friends from America perfectly. As I said, we were expecting them. I would have warned you but I didn't think they'd get here until tonight. They're early." I stepped back. "If I had any cash on me I would add to that enormous tip." I waved my credit card. "I'll make it up to you when we check out."

Viktor sagged against a pole then leaped away from it. "Ice, very cold. Be careful not to touch it with your bare hands, Madame. And thank you. I cannot tell you how relieved I am." He straightened his tie then smiled. "They asked if we had rooms available. I didn't admit anything, afraid it would not please you. Shall I go check now?"

"I believe Mr. Blade has reserved two suites for them. Hopefully they are already available." I patted his shoulder. "They should have checked at the front desk instead of scaring you to death. I will have a sharp word with them about that. Will you go see about getting their keys? One room is under the name MacDonald, Dr. Ian MacDonald, and the other is for Richard Mainwaring, a suite for two people—the Italian lady and her husband."

"Excellent, Madame. I will bring the keys to your room in a matter of moments if the rooms are ready and see about their luggage. They walked in here without it. You can see why that concerned me." Viktor bowed and moved off toward the check-in desk.

I hurried down the hall toward our room. How had they arrived so quickly? They must have gone straight to the airport after Jerry's call. Amazing since Flo usually took forever to pack. I was touched by their speed and really glad to have reinforcements.

When I used my key card to let myself into the room, I braced myself. Good thing. Flo rushed me, hugging me to her petite frame and almost squeezing the life out of me. My little buddy is stronger than she looks.

"*Amica*! What's going on here? Your room seems

as if *teppisti* came and tore it apart. Have you been robbed? You must check your jewelry first." Flo held me back and looked me over. "Your hair looks as if you've been in a wind storm. Sit. Tell us everything."

I needed to sit but took a moment to hug both of the men before I collapsed. I didn't know what *teppisti* meant, probably bad guys. But the room didn't look so bad now. Obviously Ian and Richard had lifted the mattress back onto its platform and thrown the bedspread back on top of it. All of them had been busy since the drawers were back in their places.

"I didn't bring any good jewelry, Flo, so you can relax on that score. Just my ring which I never take off." I waved my wonderful wedding set in front of her. "Viktor, the bellman someone gave a big tip to, told me the room was torn apart. I guess Fredrick sent men here to look for his device." I took the brush Flo handed me and ran it through my hair. "Thanks, pal."

"It is what we do for each other, am I right?" She frowned at me. "Is that a feather in your hair?" She plucked it out. "Yes, it is. Obviously you have much to tell us. We tried to call you but got voice mail. Your phone must be turned off."

"Yes. We had to shift and you know you can't risk a ringing phone when you're doing that." I pulled my phone out of my pocket and turned it on. No message from Jerry or Gretchen. Well, of course not Gretchen. She'd have to buy a burner phone first. No unknown calls either. Or texts. I shook my head then inhaled. No recent sign of Jerry. Okay, that was good. So he hadn't beaten me back here only to be kidnapped by Fredrick's thugs. I blinked back sudden tears. I couldn't melt down now.

"Take a moment, Gloriana, and then tell us what

happened." Richard could always calm me down. The former priest had a way of getting to the heart of matters. He gave Flo a look and she quit fluttering around me and sat beside me to hold my hand.

I took a breath, squeezed Flo's hand, and then gave them the details about our adventures on Birka. The television was on, the volume low. I had no idea if any of them spoke Swedish but I could see a news recap of the night's excitement on Birka being shown.

"They're talking about a break-in at the museum on TV. So that was you." Ian pulled up a chair across from the bench where I sat in front of the fire. He looked into my eyes, obviously in doctor mode. "Richard and I speak Swedish."

"Of course you do. I'm surprised you don't, Flo." I seemed to be the only vampire on the planet who didn't have an ear for languages.

"Pah. Of course I don't. I love the romantic languages. Italian, Spanish, Portuguese. They are music to my ears. I struggled to master English but it is used so widely, I had to do it." She waved her hand. "Tell us more about what happened on this island."

"Yes. Well," I was finally warm but still appreciated it when Richard laid a blanket over my shoulders. "Thanks. I think Jerry told you we went there to try to find the Viking's treasure." I shook my head, still not believing that Gretchen hadn't told me their outcome. "I don't know if Gunnar got out with it or not, but we did find the cave where he hid it centuries ago."

"Amazing." Richard glanced at the television. "I guess that wrecked boat was yours too."

"Yes. We had to abandon it and shift into birds to escape Fredrick's sharpshooters. We flew off in four

different directions. Jerry's supposed to meet me here."
I checked the clock. We had about an hour before
dawn. "I expect him any minute."

"They shot at you? Did any of you get hit?" Ian
picked up my wrist as if to take my pulse. Stupid since
vampires barely have one. "You aren't hurt, are you?"

"Ever the doctor." I snatched my hand away. "No,
we all moved pretty fast. Then mingled with real birds.
I don't think the shooters managed to hit anyone." I
stood, suddenly alert. "Jerry's here." I ran to throw
open the door to the hall. "Oh, my God!" The smell of
my husband's blood hit me hard and I grabbed him
when he almost fell into the room.

"Guess the assholes were better shots than we
gave them credit for." Jerry staggered against me,
clutching his stomach. Blood covered his hand and had
soaked through his sweater and coat.

"Let me, Gloriana." Richard gently shoved me out
of the way, helping Jerry into the room. "What the hell,
Jeremiah? Didn't you stop to drink from a mortal?"

"Yes." Jerry groaned when Richard and I eased his
coat off of his shoulders. "Didn't help. Wooden bullets.
Asshole sells to vampire hunters."

"Son of a bitch!" Ian grabbed Jerry's other arm
and helped Richard get Jerry to the bed. "The man uses
those against his own kind?"

"Yes. He bragged about it." I tugged off Jerry's
boots. God, he looked so pale when he collapsed
against the pillows, his eyes closed. "Jerry?"

"Hurts like a son of a bitch." Jerry slapped at Ian's
hand when he started to lift his sweater. "Get away
from me, MacDonald."

"Don't be stupid." Ian gently eased me out of the
way and moved to the side of the bed. "Let me take a

look."

Jerry opened one eye. "I'll be all right. Glory, toss me a bottle of synthetic."

"No. Ignore him, Glory. You need fresh blood, not that synthetic shit." Ian lifted Jerry's sweater and sucked in a breath. "This is serious. The way this is bleeding it's clear there's a bullet still in there. It has to come out."

"He should drink from me." I offered my wrist.

"You're exhausted. I don't think that's wise." Ian held up his hand when I moved closer to Jerry.

"I can give him blood." Richard spoke up.

"So can I, *amica*. We would be happy to help you, Jeremiah." Flo dabbed at her eyes with a handkerchief.

"Very generous. But vampire blood may not be the best remedy here." Ian grabbed a black case that he'd obviously brought with him from beside the door. "I've been doing research on this lately—the effects of drinking human blood versus drinking vampire blood on the healing process. We need to bring in a mortal. There's something in the blood chemistry from a living human being that can be more effective."

"He's healed just fine before after drinking from me." I didn't want to think about Ian's "research". I had visions of the doctor slashing some poor vampire with a knife, and then calmly timing the healing process while he watched.

"I'm sure he did. But this is a serious wound, deep and festering already from the wood. He needs to heal as quickly as possible. Fresh blood from a mortal will speed up things. First, of course, I've got to get that bullet out. You don't want the wound to close with the bullet inside. Clearly it's a special wood and it's poisoning his system." Ian began pulling instruments out of his case. He handed me a pair of scissors. "Cut off his sweater. Mainwaring, help her strip him."

Richard did more than that, ripping away the bedspread and efficiently taking the scissors out of my shaking hands. "Gloriana, you and Florence get some towels from the bathroom and find something that will hold water. We need to clean Jerry. He's covered with blood." Richard nodded to Flo. "Hurry, darling. Take Gloriana with you."

I cried out when Richard ruthlessly stripped Jerry's jeans down his legs. My man writhed in pain though he didn't make a sound.

"*Amica*, come with me. They will take care of him." Flo dragged me to the bathroom. She'd stopped crying and now looked full of fight.

"How? He's got a hole in his stomach as big as my fist, Flo." I swiped at the tears that ran down my cheeks. "Damn it. If I lose control it will make it harder for Jerry to handle this."

"You're right. Now blow your nose and take these towels in there. Be strong. For Jeremiah. *Capiscimi?*" Flo had her steely look in place but I saw the glitter of tears in her eyes too.

"Yes, yes, pulling myself together now." I took the wad of toilet paper she handed me and wiped my eyes then blew my nose. Straightening my shoulders I headed back to the bedroom.

"This is going to hurt like hell, Campbell." Ian didn't look sorry about that.

"Don't you have anything to dull the pain? Or a way to put him out completely?" I dumped the towels on the bed then climbed onto the other side so I could reach Jerry's hand.

"Gloriana, I'm not a weak, sniveling coward who

can't handle a simple extraction. This isn't the first bullet I've taken or even the tenth." Jerry did grip my hand though. "Do your worst, MacDonald." He nodded at Richard. "If it looks like the doctor is taking this opportunity to end an old enemy, Richard, end *him*. Are you hearing me?"

"Of course. You know I have your back. That's why I'm here." Richard stayed close, his look grim.

"What can I do?" Flo came out with the large basin that had held the designer shampoos and shower gels the hotel had provided. "Should I fill this with hot water?"

"Yes, do it." Ian nodded. "The hotter, the better."

"First, I help you protect the sheets." Careful not to hurt Jerry, Flo and Richard tucked towels around him. "We put these around him so he won't stain the bed linens. You do have to sleep here when the sun rises."

"Thanks." I smiled at her. She looked worried sick. "Viktor is supposed to bring your room keys soon. Jerry has reserved rooms for all of you. When he gets here, we can drag him inside and make him Jerry's blood donor."

"Viktor?" Flo looked confused.

"The bellman who tried to keep you out of here earlier. Someone gave him a big tip." I heard Jerry hiss when Ian dumped a clear liquid over the wound. "Hey, could you ease up?"

"Just cleaning the wound, Glory. I have to be able to see what I'm doing." Ian didn't spare me a glance. He was too busy mopping away blood with gauze and examining that horrendous hole in Jerry's stomach near his navel.

I blinked. Could not cry. Vampires are supposed to

heal easily. The fact that blood still bubbled up from that hole scared the hell out of me. Jerry had already been slow to heal after Fredrick's weapon had zapped him. Now the wooden bullet... I told Ian about the earlier problem with Jerry's knuckles. He grunted and looked at Jerry's hand which had finally healed. Then he kept working on the new wound with a grim determination. I couldn't watch, afraid I was going to be sick.

Flo picked up the basin. "The little man. Yes, I will drag him in here. He was *molto irritante*, keeping us out of your room when we told him we were expected. But his blood did smell fresh and healthy." Flo glanced at Jerry's wound then looked away. "I cannot stand to watch. *Medico*, you kill him and Ricardo and I will see you ripped to shreds. Count on it." She ran back to the bathroom and we could hear running water. Then she carefully brought back the basin full of steaming water and set it on the night stand without spilling a drop. "Call me if you need more." She staggered over to a chair next to the window and sank into it. She'd done all of this in five inch heels. My best friend is amazing.

"I'm not going to kill him, Florence, but this bullet might. Fucking vampire hunters. And this Fredrick sells to them you say. Shit." Ian held a scalpel in his hand. "I'm going to have to cut you now, Campbell, to get a better look at what we've got." He glanced at me. "You might want to make sure he can't get to any of his knives."

"Why? So he won't stab you when you hurt him?" I did reach for the one I could see. It was one Jerry usually had tucked into his belt. Richard had laid it on the bed next to me. "Put this between your teeth, love. And grip my hand. I think Ian would enjoy it way too much if you screamed."

"You're right. Help me." Jerry's face was pale. Blood loss. He opened his mouth and I carefully put in the handle so he could bite down on it.

I was just in time because Ian sliced into Jerry's skin, digging his scalpel into my lover's flesh. I was the one who wanted to scream but didn't dare. I was pretty sure I was going to have some crushed fingers but let Jerry hold my hand as hard as he wanted to. His face was strained and I used my other hand to brush his hair back from his damp face. He was sweating, clammy. I couldn't look at what Ian was doing but he seemed to take forever.

Jerry grunted and I saw Richard move to the side of the bed and put his hand on Jerry's shoulder to steady him. I was very afraid Jerry would move and cause himself more injury.

"Got it." Ian had switched to forceps at some point and now waved a very bloody bullet around at us before he dropped it into the basin. Then he grabbed gauze and pushed it into the large wound he'd created. It absorbed blood instantly, turning bright red. The damage looked much worse now than when he'd started.

We all jumped when there was a knock on the door.

"I've got it, *amica*." Flo pushed herself out of the chair and ran to answer. She opened the door just a little then we heard her speak. "Ah, you are Viktor, *sì*?"

"Yes, Madame. Mrs. Mainwaring? I have your key and can show you and your husband to your room. It's right down this hall. Dr. MacDonald will be next door to you. Do you have luggage that we can arrange to have brought there?"

"Ah, yes. Please step inside and my husband will give you directions." Flo held Viktor's arm when they walked inside the room. She locked the door and leaned against it. Good thing because as soon as the bellman saw Jerry lying on the bed with bloody towels around him and Ian, his hands bloody up to his wrists, standing over him, he made a lunge for that door.

"Viktor! Please stay. We need your help." I looked down at Jerry and he let go of my hand. I think he was close to passing out though he'd probably deny it.

"Mrs. Blade. This is most irregular. Is your husband hurt? What happened? Should I summon a doctor?" Viktor was inches from Flo and tried to go around her. "Yes, I will do that. At once. We have an excellent physician on call here twenty-four hours a day."

"No, that won't be necessary." I crawled off the bed and walked up to Viktor. "You see, our friend Dr. MacDonald has taken care of him. All we need from you is," I smiled. "Something you won't even remember." I stared into his eyes and he was mesmerized. "Come here, Viktor. Hold out your wrist." I led him to the bedside. He was like a windup doll now and I soon had him sitting on the edge of the mattress within Jerry's reach.

"You sure this is necessary?" Jerry was mumbling, clearly on the verge of losing consciousness.

"Yes, and don't delay." Ian was getting impatient. He took his scalpel and ran it across Viktor's wrist. Fresh blood welled from the cut and fangs went down around the room. Then Ian thrust the mortal's wrist into Jerry's mouth. Instinct took over after that and Jerry drank. It didn't take long for some color to come into his cheeks.

I watched his wound. I expected it to close immediately. When it didn't, I turned to Ian. "What's wrong?"

"It's that wood. It's going to take a while for its poison to get out of his system. I'm going to stitch him up as a precaution. Give him some time to heal. He can drink another minute or two then we'll have to pull him off." Ian got busy with his equipment and soon had a row of black stitches closing the wound. "It's almost dawn. We need to get to our rooms and settle before then."

I leaned over Jerry, kissed his forehead then wrenched Viktor's wrist out of his mouth when he didn't let go when Ian asked him to. I licked Viktor's punctures and incision closed myself and walked him to the door. I gave him a quick suggestion that he'd just arrived at my door and was ready to escort my guests to their rooms. Then I shoved him into the hall to wait.

"I'll be back to check on Jerry as soon as the sun sets." Ian gathered up the bloody towels and tossed them into the bathtub. "You both will benefit from a day's rest. As for how that machine the weapons manufacturer hit him with will affect the healing?" Ian shrugged. "I can't speak to that. You say it's been a while since that happened. I'd hope that he's recovered from whatever the weapon did to him by now."

"He seemed recovered. He could shift anyway. And his bruises from the fight healed, though it took longer than usual." I felt the sunrise pulling at me, though we still had a little time before then. Worry also dragged me down. Jerry had just closed his eyes and hadn't said a word since the operation. Was he unconscious? Maybe that was a good thing since he had to be in a great deal of pain.

"We will go, Glory. Don't worry. I'm sure he will be fine when he wakes at sunset." Flo kissed my cheek.

"Obviously your room was ransacked earlier. Fredrick's men looking for something. Do you know what?" Richard wasn't quite ready to leave me.

"Gretchen has Fredrick's device. He calls it his Eliminator. I guess they hoped she'd left it here. She didn't, of course." I'd already looked around. As far as I could tell nothing was missing, the men had just made a thorough search.

"Is there any reason they'd come back?" Richard stared at Jerry. "You said the man hires shifters. I don't like the idea of how vulnerable you are during death sleep."

"How vulnerable we *all* are. But Fredrick's really after Gunnar and Gretchen, his wife. Since he's satisfied we don't have his weapon, I think we're safe. He already had a chance to hurt us earlier and didn't take it. He let us go." I touched Richard's strong sturdy chest. "Thank you, for coming and caring."

"Always at your service." Richard smiled when Flo tugged at his sleeve. "Yes, darling, I know it's late and we need our luggage. I'll give the bellman our keys and directions so he can fetch it." He shrugged. "We left the luggage in a rental car outside here. You know my wife will not face the sunset without her makeup and wardrobe close at hand."

"And I have the most wonderful fur coats and boots, Glory." Flo dragged him to the door. "I never get to wear them in Austin. This trip is serious business, I know. But also a chance to wear some of my better cold weather things for a change." She ran back to give me a hug. "I pray for Jeremiah. I know he will be fine. And thank you for calling us. It is an adventure, eh?"

"An adventure with almost deadly consequences for Campbell." Ian ignored Flo's very Italian gesture before she flounced out the door. "Lock yourself in, Glory. Use the deadbolt." He'd put a dressing over Jerry's wound while I'd been talking to Flo and Richard. "When you wake up, drink some synthetic then let him feed from you. It will help. If we need to, we'll find another mortal tomorrow. That little guy probably can't take another feeding."

He threw the bedspread over Jerry then picked up his case. "I'm the big tipper. I'm going to give Viktor another one when he brings my luggage. Then I'll insist with a little mind control that he treat himself to a rare steak dinner as soon as he leaves us at our doors."

"Thanks, Ian. You were brilliant tonight as usual." I kissed his cheek. "And thanks for providing the plane."

"As Florence says, it's an adventure. I'm just sorry it's taken such a nasty turn." He glanced back at Jerry and frowned. "But we all need an adventure now and then. When you live forever, things can get dull without a little excitement occasionally." Ian stalked to the door. "Damned wooden bullets. They should be outlawed. And a vampire who turns against his own kind needs to be put down. I'd be happy to take care of that."

"Um, let's discuss that before we start murdering people, okay?" I don't know why I was reluctant to see Fredrick 'put down'. Gretchen's husband certainly had no qualms about taking people out. "See you after sunset."

"You have a soft heart." Ian stopped with his hand on the doorknob. "Get over it, Glory. Some people are more trouble than they're worth. We'd be doing the vampire world a favor if we rid it of this man. Think about that."

I thought of little else as I stripped off my clothes and took a quick shower. Then I dipped a washcloth in the warm water and gently cleaned any remaining blood from Jerry's way too still body. He was sleeping. So, so rare in a vampire. Or was he unconscious? I still couldn't tell and didn't want to know as I slipped into bed beside him. Sunrise was definitely trying to suck me under. I touched his skin, alarmed when I realized it was hot, not vampire cool as it should be. Fever. Damned wooden bullets. Maybe Ian was right. Fredrick had to go and every weapon he'd ever made had to go with him.

NINE

I woke at sunset but I knew we'd only had a few hours of rest, the downside of these long winter nights. I didn't mind but knew it hadn't helped Jerry. He hadn't moved yet. I reached over to feel his forehead then jumped when his hand clamped on my wrist, his knife at my throat. Uh oh. I'd forgotten about the knife. Last time I'd seen it, he'd had it between his teeth. Trust Jerry, even in pain and almost unconscious, to tuck a knife under his pillow.

"What the hell do you want?" His eyes were unfocused. He didn't know me or see me.

"Jerry, Jeremiah. It's me, Glory." I couldn't move or he'd cut me. He'd hate himself later if he did that. "Lover, you've been hurt." I carefully wiggled my fingers, managing to brush them against his skin. Hot. Still feverish.

"Glory. Hurt." He let me go, the knife relaxing in his hand.

I gently took it from him and set it on the bedside table within easy reach. If Fredrick's men came back, it could come in handy. "Let me call Ian. He'll have something to help you."

"MacDonald?" Jerry rolled toward me. "No. Drink from you. Heal me."

"In a minute." I eased out of bed. Ian had said I should take care of myself first. I grabbed a bottle of synthetic out of the mini-fridge and popped it open. I gulped it down, not even tasting it. Jerry's hand fell on me as soon as I slid in beside him again.

"Want you." He obviously meant that in the sexiest way possible but I doubted he could follow through with a raging fever and a wound in his stomach.

"Blood first." I slid down the sheet. Holy shit! He was still bleeding. This wasn't right. He'd soaked through the bandage Ian had placed over his wound. I had to clear my throat before I could even speak. "Uh, Jer, be careful now and use my wrist. I don't want to hurt you." I settled next to him and laid my wrist against his lips.

"Fuck the wrist. Need your vein." His fingers tangled in my hair and he pulled me closer with surprising strength. "Come. Here."

My jugular. Of course he wanted it. We never used the wrist. Not when the intimate connection of the jugular was so much better. I was willing. But I'd have to practically crawl on top for him to reach it. It was worth a try but if he gasped in pain I was going to have to figure out some other way to give him my blood. He was almost out of it with his eyes closed. If I had to just slash my wrist, surely he'd go ahead and take it.

"Gloriana," he groaned, pulling firmly yet gently. I moved closer so, so carefully, stopping when he kissed me. I broke the kiss to look into his eyes. Oh, God. He was struggling to stay with me, his eyes fever glazed.

"Jerry. I love you. Don't you dare leave me." I kissed him deeply then, with all my fear and love.

His fingers fell out of my hair to caress my breast. His mouth moved over mine again while he still fought to stay conscious. Damn, but I could tell he was losing that battle. I pulled away to offer my neck so he could take what he needed, bracing my hands on the bed as best I could.

When he plunged his fangs into my vein, I dug my

fingers into the sheets to keep from gasping. Of course it hurt. He hadn't made any effort to sooth my skin like he usually did. But I sighed when he began drinking. I felt the pull deep inside me and closed my eyes, praying that this would be the magic that would heal him. I loved this primal connection between us and let it go on longer than I should have.

The sinking feeling that I was in danger of losing myself warned me that he was on the verge of taking too much. I murmured his name and thank God he got the message. He slipped his fangs free and used his tongue to seal the wounds before he kissed my vein tenderly.

"Thank you, love. That helped more than you know." He settled back against the pillows. "But you'd better call MacDonald. The bleeding hasn't stopped."

"What? Still?" I rolled off of him. Yes, he was right. His bandage was even brighter red and now my gown was stained as well.

"The wood . . ." He grimaced and moved restlessly, obviously in pain. "It's toxic. There must still be a piece in there. Maybe I was hit by more than one bullet. That's the only reason I can think of to explain why I haven't already healed."

"God, Jerry!" I grabbed my phone from the nightstand and hit the speed dial for Ian. A few words and Ian assured me that he was on his way. I had to hurry to strip off my soiled gown and rinse the blood off my own body before the doctor arrived.

"Where are you going?" Jerry sounded weak when he tried to snag my hand as I headed to the bathroom.

"I can't greet Ian naked, now can I?" I managed a smile as I tore off my gown and tossed it aside. "You would probably rise from your sick bed to put a knife in his gut if Ian so much as gave me a wink." I did grip his hand then. "We need Ian now so I'm not taking any chances."

"Need a MacDonald. I've sunk low, haven't I? But you're right." He pulled me closer. "Come here before you get dressed."

How could I resist? I leaned in. "He's only a few doors away, Jer. I have to hurry."

"I know. But this is my honeymoon, damn it." He traced my nipples with a fingertip. "And you're so damned beautiful." He groaned and closed his eyes. "Shit. This is not how I planned it."

I sighed and kissed him. "We'll have the rest of our lives together. So relax and let me throw on a robe." I heard a knock at the door. "There's Ian now." I smoothed Jerry's hair. He was still too warm for a vampire even after taking my blood. This was freaking me out.

"Just a minute!" I called as I rushed into the bathroom and grabbed that toweling robe that covered every inch of my body. Adding jealousy to Jerry's feelings about Ian was the last thing I wanted to do. I hurried over to the door, taking a deep breath.

"Who is it?" Smelled like vampire but I'd be stupid not to be cautious.

"Ian. Let me in, Glory."

I threw open the door. "He's bleeding again. Jerry thinks there may be another bullet in him."

"That's bad news. You did let him feed from you this morning, didn't you?" Ian had brought his case and strode straight to the bed.

"Yes, of course. He almost took more than he should have."

Ian frowned and touched Jerry's forehead with his palm. "How do you feel, Campbell?"

"Like there's a fire in my belly." Jerry stared at me. "Gloriana, go take a shower. Get dressed. Let MacDonald and me take care of this."

"I want to help." I looked from Ian's grim face to Jerry's.

"Drink some synthetic then do what he says." Ian pulled open his case.

"I'll drink but there's bound to be something I can do."

I hated the sight of the scalpel again. The doctor had cleaned all the instruments and they were shiny and ready for action. That made me shiver as I pulled out a bottle of the fake blood and opened it.

"You've done all you can for now, Glory. Campbell is right. Take care of yourself and leave him to me." Ian took my elbow and steered me to the bathroom then lowered his voice. "A man would rather not have his woman around when he's in pain. I'm getting ready to put him through hell while I probe for another bullet. You really want him to have to put on a brave front during that while you're watching?"

"Oh. If I'm not here he could cry out. Not be so stoic." I glanced at Jerry. His eyes were closed, his jaw tight. Like he was waiting for Ian to do his worst. "I get it. Tell him I won't be able to hear a thing while I'm in the shower, washing my hair."

"Good girl." Ian smiled. "I promise I'll get every bit of wood out of him this time and he'll heal faster. I'm sorry I didn't do more of an exploratory last night but he really couldn't have taken a prolonged surgery then."

"No, he was very weak." I touched Ian's hand. "Don't blame yourself. Who would think those shifters would be such crack shots that they could have hit him twice while he was flying?"

"Exactly. Now take your time. This won't be quick." He wasn't smiling now as he patted my shoulder then pushed me into the bathroom and shut the door.

I slumped against it. He was going to dig into Jerry again with that scalpel. No anesthetic. God. I couldn't bear the thought. But I also couldn't stand the idea that Jerry would hold all his pain inside for fear I'd think less of him. So I turned on the shower and threw off my robe. I spent a long time doing everything I could think of--washing and conditioning my hair, shaving my legs, even blowing my hair dry with the loudest dryer I'd heard this side of the Atlantic. I applied makeup and put on clothes I selected from the closet that luckily was part of the luxurious bathroom.

At one point I thought I heard Jerry cry out. I wanted desperately to go to him but didn't. Instead I blinked back tears and waited until I couldn't stall a moment longer. I eased open the door and peeked into the bedroom. Ian was sitting in a chair next to the window, his bag at his feet. He was finishing a bottle of synthetic blood. If I didn't know better, I'd think he was upset by the surgery he'd had to perform.

Forget Ian. I rushed to Jerry's side, his middle swathed in a bandage. He was very, very pale and there were lines around his eyes and mouth from the unspeakable pain he must have endured. I fell to my knees and laid my head on his hand. Prayers. That was all I could manage for the moment. Finally I raised my head and turned to Ian.

"He's sleeping." Ian sounded tired.

"How is he? Did you get it all?"

"I hope to God I did." Ian didn't look so great himself. He set his empty bottle on the table next to him. "He was almost right, Glory. It wasn't another bullet but a splinter from the one I took out of him last night." Ian shook his head. "My fault, damn it. Careless. I should have studied the thing more closely. Noticed that it wasn't intact." He ran a hand through his hair but it fell back into place as if by magic. He was a handsome man though a little on the scary side with his very blond hair and brilliant blue eyes. Intense only began to describe him.

"But you got it all this time? You're sure?" I forced myself to stand on wobbly legs.

"As sure as I can be in these circumstances. I probed his gut so much it became a form of torture. Campbell and I simply couldn't take any more. Time will tell if I got it all. I think I did. If I had proper equipment here, I could know for a certainty. A CT scan would help, even an X-ray machine." Ian stood. "I need a shower. Then you'd better find him another mortal to drink from."

"Who? Some hapless housekeeper? I don't like that." I stepped back to Jerry's side and wished he'd open his eyes.

"But it's necessary. Call for fresh towels. God knows you need them." Ian gestured at a pile of blood soaked towels he'd dumped into that basin Flo had left in the bedroom. "Do what you call the whammy on the person and get this done. You're clever enough to handle it. Explain away the blood soaked towels with an accident. I'm sure you'll think of something. Anyway, you can handle the mortal and the blood exchange. I know you've done it before."

"Yes, of course. But I don't like to do it now that we have synthetic available." I brushed my hand over Jerry's brow. Warm. "Do you think he has a fever?"

"Yes. But that mortal blood should take care of it. Forget your scruples, Glory, and take care of it. Or do I have to call the housekeeper myself?" Ian walked over to the house phone.

"No, I'll do it. Jerry's in my hands now and I'll do whatever is best for him whether I like it or not." I sighed. "Just go. Take your shower. Let's all meet here in an hour. That should give me enough time to take care of 'housekeeping.'"

"Excellent. I'll stop by Mainwaring's room and let them know the plan." Ian leaned down to kiss my cheek. "You've been very brave about this, Glory. Campbell's a lucky man."

"Thanks. I'm grateful for what you've done. I know I didn't sound like it just now." I squeezed his hand.

"You're worried, I get it." And with that he was gone.

I stared at the closed door for a moment. Brave, hah! And worried, of course. Almost out of my mind. So I called housekeeping and asked for fresh towels, assured they'd be here in minutes. I tidied the room as best I could, covering Jerry with a sheet and the bedspread. He didn't move, obviously exhausted from the recent "exploratory" as Ian had called it.

Less than ten minutes passed before there was a knock on the door and a soft female voice claimed to be from "Housekeeping." I inhaled. Mortal. Then I cautiously opened the door. I still wasn't sure Fredrick's men wouldn't show up looking for Gretchen. But it was a tall sturdy woman in a hotel uniform who looked like she'd be able to flip a mattress one-handed. She stood next to a cart and held a pile of fresh towels in her hands.

"Thank you for being so prompt. We had a little accident in here and used up all our towels." I gestured to the pile of blood soaked ones.

"*Herregud*! Some accident. Where's the dead body?" She laughed nervously but looked from the towels to Jerry, laid out like a corpse on the bed. "Oh, I didn't mean . . . Is it serious?"

"He'll be fine. Our doctor just left. But my husband takes blood thinners and it's almost impossible to get the bleeding to stop. He cut himself accidentally you see." I took her by the elbow. "He's merely sleeping. It takes a lot out of you when you lose blood."

"I'm sure, Madame. Don't you think he should be in hospital? He looks very pale. How did you say he cut himself?" She pulled free of me with another nervous giggle and backed toward the door.

Oops, she'd spotted Jerry's knife on the bedside table. I'd just left it there, too used to the damned things lying around to think to put it out of sight.

"A silly accident. Men. He was showing off his knife skills to one of our friends." I grabbed her elbow. "What's your name?"

"Klara, Madame. Perhaps he would like his sheets changed. I always say a fresh bed makes me feel better. Can he get up and move to a chair?" She wouldn't look at me, which was what I was waiting for. I needed to catch her gaze to mesmerize her. "The sheets are on the cart outside." She jerked free and made a dash for the door.

I jumped between her and the door then grabbed her shoulders so I could force her to look into my eyes. "Klara, you will not leave." Just like Viktor, she was in my power then and unable to move. Now I could put her where I wanted her. By the time we were back next to the bed, Jerry had opened his eyes.

"What's this?" He licked his lips. "You bring me another mortal? Breakfast in bed?"

"Ian says it's for the best. Can you take her wrist?" I pushed it next to his mouth.

"Yes. I'm not too weak to drink, Gloriana." He took her wrist and sank his fangs into her vein. I saw him begin to drink while Klara just stood there, not even able to wince if he'd hurt her. Which he probably had. I counted, making sure Jerry didn't take too much. Luckily this mortal was bulky enough to give even more blood than Viktor had and I let Jerry enjoy a good long feed.

"That's enough." I tapped Jerry's shoulder. "Let her go." I was grateful when he did that without a struggle. I didn't relish forcing the matter again. It wasn't something vampire males took lightly or forgot. I watched while Jerry licked the punctures closed. Then I led Klara over to the door. She unloaded fresh towels and sheets then took the soiled ones with her. I persuaded her that Jerry and I would change the sheets ourselves and leave the dirty ones in the hall for her later. Then I wiped her memory of everything except the essentials about delivering linens for a sick man.

"Thank you, Madame. I hope your husband feels better soon." Klara pocketed the generous tip I gave her.

"I'm sure he will. We are on our honeymoon, you know. He has to feel well." I winked at her. I'd had to let her remember my story about the bleeding to explain all those soiled towels to whoever did the laundry. Boy, did staying in a hotel complicate matters. At least in most places where we travelled, we tried to stay in hotels owned and run by paranormals. I guess there hadn't been one available in Sweden when Jerry had booked this trip.

My phone rang as I closed the hall door and I ran to answer it.

"Gloriana?"

I checked the caller ID. Unknown caller. "Who is this?"

I glanced at Jerry. He did look better and he was staring at me.

"Gretchen. I bought a burner phone. Did you and Jeremiah make it back to your hotel all right?"

"Not exactly all right. Jerry was shot." I blinked back tears. "But he's getting better. How about you and Gunnar?"

"We are fine. Hiding out. I'm sorry about Jeremiah. We need to meet. Plan. I have a place but now I'm thinking it might be better if Gunnar and I just disappear from your lives. We have put you in terrible danger."

"Wait a minute. You pulled us into this. You can't just vanish. We need to help you figure out what to do about Fredrick and his weapon." I signaled to Jerry. "Gretchen, I mean it. Our friends from America are here. We all want to help. To make sure Fredrick can't hurt you and to stop his weapon from being used against vampires everywhere." I jumped when I realized Jerry now stood behind me. He took my phone.

"Gretchen." Then he started speaking to her in Swedish.

I hated that I couldn't understand what he was saying. His frown meant she was arguing with him but then he finally gave me a thumb's up. Okay, so he'd convinced her to accept our help.

"Fine, we'll meet you there later tonight. Midnight. You sure that's a safe place?" He sat on the side of the bed. Obviously he wasn't back to full strength yet. "Okay, see you then." He punched off the phone.

"You got her to agree?" I sat beside him.

"It wasn't easy. She's feeling guilty. Because I got hit." Jerry rubbed the bandage over his stomach. "I think that last dose of human blood did the trick. And MacDonald's surgery. He must have finally gotten rid all of that wood."

"God, Jerry. I know it must have been excruciating." I leaned against him.

"You could say that." He kissed the top of my head. "I'm glad you weren't in the room. I shed a few tears between curses. Not manly at all."

"I abandoned you." I slid my arm around his waist. He was still naked. Which was the way I liked him. Not that we were going to do anything about it now.

"There are times, Gloriana, when a man needs his privacy. I have MacDonald to thank for steering you out of here for that." He stood on wobbly legs. "Damn but I hate to be indebted to that man." He headed for the bathroom. "Now I need a shower. I reek of fear, pain and blood. Not a pleasant smell."

"It doesn't bother me. But let me help you." I rushed to his side and had him lean on me for the few steps it took to get him into the large shower.

"Wait out here. You're looking beautiful, clean and ready for our meeting. I'll just be a few minutes. But if you see me fall, come and scrape me off the floor." He grinned and slammed the shower door then turned on the water.

I watched him every minute while he scrubbed his hair and his body. I gasped when he tore away his bandage to clean his wound but I guess it was all right because I didn't see any blood dripping. I breathed a sigh of relief when he finally turned off the water and hurried to wrap him into a warm towel from the electric towel racks, a Swedish luxury. The floors were heated too.

"How are you feeling?" I rubbed his back dry, almost afraid to see his front and that wound.

"Like I'll live." He turned so we could both check out his stomach. The incision was fading, a pale red instead of the angry red it had been the night before. Ian must have put in new stitches but they had popped loose and I plucked them out with my fingers.

"So Ian was right. Mortal blood *is* more effective. Good to know. I'll have to get over my aversion to using mortals when we have a crisis like we did tonight." I kissed Jerry's chin.

"I prefer to drink from you, my love, but I want to be at full strength so we can get this honeymoon back on track." Jerry's arms went around me. "Do we have time to see if I'm completely healed?" His grin made me laugh.

"If only." I leaned against him, thrilled that he was at normal vampire temperature—cool and just right for me to snuggle with. Too bad we didn't have time to test his strength. I stepped back. "The gang will be here any minute and you can tell them what Gretchen told you. Me too." I walked to the closet and picked out some pants that had a simple waistband that wouldn't rub against that wound. No snug jeans tonight.

"It wasn't much." Jerry stepped into the black trousers. "I forgot to ask if Gunnar found his treasure."

"You're kidding." I tossed Jerry a dark blue cashmere sweater. "Where are they hiding?"

"She didn't say, just told me where to meet them. It's an abandoned warehouse. Not anywhere Fredrick would think to look she hopes. She said she used to visit an artist there but he has since moved to a bigger building."

"Abandoned. No heat then. I hope you're right and that's not where they're staying. Sounds horrible." I sensed company and left him to walk to the bedroom. One whiff and I threw open the hall door. I would know my best friend's favorite perfume anywhere.

"Ready for another adventure?" I grinned at Flo and Richard. Ian was right behind them. They all had eyes only for Jerry who strode to the door and let them look him over.

"It is a miracle!" Flo hugged everyone.

"No, just the skill of a brilliant doctor." Ian jerked up Jerry's sweater and examined his healing wound.

"I give full credit to the loving care of my nurse." Jerry pulled me next to him and kissed my cheek.

"All of the above. Now let's get to the business of the night." I was anxious to get this Gunnar and Fredrick thing settled so I could get back to my honeymoon. Almost losing Jerry had my priorities in order. My new husband was number one on my agenda from now on. Everything else? A distant second.

TEN

It took some skillful maneuvering to even get into the car Ian had rented. We might be considered paranoid but we didn't want to take a chance that Fredrick was having us watched. So Ian drove the car away from the hotel by himself and we all took turns shifting to meet him at a prearranged spot. Of course it was cold and snowing. Beautiful. But I wasn't sure I'd ever get used to the weather here. I was longing for my mild Texas winters. Flo was in her element wearing a chic black fur coat and matching hat. Her suede boots were the latest style in a black and white pony print. I was in serious boot envy though I had new things from the boutique that she exclaimed over.

"I must go there when this adventure is over, Glory. Your gloves and scarf are so cute." Flo settled in the back seat between Richard and me. Jerry was riding shotgun in the front while Ian drove.

"Put the address into the GPS, Campbell, and let's get this going." Ian was clearly excited. "I didn't come all the way to Stockholm just to do my doctor thing on you. I want to see this Viking. Examine him and see what a thousand years on ice did to him."

"You may have some trouble getting him to cooperate with that, Ian." I leaned forward to talk between the seats. "He was a high-placed Viking, powerful before he was turned vampire. I hope he found his treasure. It would be a shame if he had to start over in this time without money to support him."

"Glory's right. Gunnar was a leader. Was in tight with the King of that time. He won't just let you poke and prod him, MacDonald, like a science experiment. You'll have to convince him that there's something in it for him." Jerry smiled as if he liked the idea of Ian getting some brushback from Gunnar. "But if we save him from Fredrick, he'll be grateful."

"There you go. I know quite a bit about physics. If I can do something with that infernal weapon, we can turn it on this rogue vampire and save the day." Ian chuckled. "What do you think, Mainwaring?"

"I want to see it, examine this weapon. You said your chest hurt after you woke up so I think it must do something to the heart. Could be sound waves, electric shock. Any number of things. But Gloriana wasn't affected. I wonder why." Richard turned to look at me like I was under a microscope.

"Beats me. He had to use a drug to put me to sleep." I grimaced. "Those work on me like they would on any vampire. Puzzle that out."

"I'll leave you scientists to analyze this whole thing. The rest of us were incapacitated for hours with our powers shot even after we woke. It was a nightmare." Jerry smiled at me over his shoulder. "You know why Gloriana is different. Guess that made her immune to Fredrick's Eliminator somehow. For once, I'm grateful to Olympus."

"Ah, yes. My friend is special." Flo patted my hand. "She is a demi-goddess. I am glad we are friends, *amica*. Otherwise you would scare me with your powers. *Capiscimi?*"

"Sure. This Olympus connection is no joke." I squeezed her hand. "And my parents definitely scare me. My grandfather?" He was Zeus. "Well, no one messes with him." I sighed. "I can't believe I'm saying this but if we can't handle this ourselves, I can always call them for a favor."

"No!" Flo crossed herself. So did Richard.

I had to hide a smile. Gods and goddesses versus their Catholic upbringing? I wasn't taking sides in that contest. I prayed and just hoped someone was listening who was more benevolent than the folks I'd met in Olympus.

"Gloriana, don't even think of asking your parents for help. You know asking for a favor from them always ends with payback. If you get your folks down here, then you'll probably have to go back up there with them afterwards. The way time moves up there, it could be a century before I see you again." Jerry was serious as hell. "No Olympus. We'll figure this out ourselves."

"Of course. We've got the dream team on it. Right, gang?" I was determinedly optimistic. Jerry had been through enough lately. I wasn't about to put more stress on him now.

"I've done scans of you before, Gloriana, but never noticed anything unusual about your heart. Now you've got me curious." Ian used the GPS to drive into a sketchy part of Stockholm.

I kept glancing behind us but didn't see any cars following us from the hotel. Good. So we'd evaded any of Fredrick's henchmen. I knew he would have had us tailed if he'd realized we were meeting his wife.

"Fredrick wanted to dissect me," I said as Ian pulled up in front of a dark three story warehouse that had seen better days. The double doors were chained shut and an old sign had graffiti obliterating what had probably been the artist's studio logo and posted hours.

Flo shrieked in horror. "He is *il mostro*, a monster."

"You get no argument from me, pal." We climbed out of the car and inhaled almost as one. I recognized Gretchen and Gunnar's scents and nodded. But we were cautious. We walked around the building, deciding to stick together.

Jerry had pulled out a knife while I saw Ian with a gun. Surprisingly Richard also had one. I didn't think of him as the violent type but that was probably underestimating him. Just because he'd been a priest centuries ago didn't mean he hadn't seen his share of wars and battles. Most vampires learned to defend themselves early on or ended up staked.

"Did you hear that?" Flo stopped us with her hand in the air. "Someone with high heels is walking inside. Go around the back. There must be a door open there."

Trust Flo to recognize high heels on concrete. But now that she mentioned it, I heard it too. We crept around the corner and spotted a metal door that was unlocked. It opened without a sound. Someone had been busy oiling the hinges. Inside, our eyes adjusted to the lack of light and I could see there were stacks of canvas, crates and tables against one wall. When a man jumped out from behind an easel, Flo screamed.

"Who are you?" Gunnar wrapped his arm around Flo's throat.

"Let her go, Viking." Richard moved so quickly he was a blur and he pushed his gun against Gunnar's temple. "I would be happy to see your brains splattered on this concrete if you harm even a hair on her head."

"I could snap her neck before your finger could move on the trigger, vampire." Gunnar didn't sound worried. "Is she your woman?"

Richard's growl made the hairs on my arm stand on end. "You'd better believe it."

"Gunnar, she's my friend. It's Glory and Jeremiah. We're here to help you. Please let her go." I didn't dare move for fear someone would do something stupid.

"Gunnar, that's Florence you're holding. Her man Richard is a respected warrior. You know you would threaten to do the same if a man held Gretchen like that. Let her go." Jerry was bold enough to stride up to Gunnar.

"Jeremiah, Glory." Gunnar still held Flo. "Tell him to remove the gun from my head first."

"Like hell." Richard cocked the pistol.

"See reason, Richard." Jerry held out his hand. "Gunnar didn't know you or Florence. He's a hunted man. Can you blame him for reacting like he did?"

"I blame him for touching my wife." Richard looked like he really wanted to shoot Gunnar. A nerve twitched in his forehead.

"Ricardo, I am fine. Put down the gun, *caro*." Flo lifted her foot. "Viking, I will put my heel through your foot if you don't release me at once."

"Fine." Gunnar let go and stepped back just as Richard pulled up the barrel of the gun. "Gretchen, come out now. We have friends, it seems."

"Yes. Are you all going to be nice now?" Gretchen rushed out of the darkness and took Gunnar's arm. "I'm sorry. You can understand, I hope, that Gunnar is a little tense. We have been running for a while and had to spend our death sleep in a very precarious place."

"It was not safe for you." Gunnar glared around the room. "We had to cover ourselves with heavy, dirty rugs in a place Gretchen's family owns."

"A storage facility. It was the best I could do." Gretchen sighed. "Fredrick would never think to look there."

Gunnar had his arm around her waist. "Even so we went to bed at sunrise not knowing if that would be our last sleep and Fredrick's shifters would find us during the day."

"How horrible for you." I ran to Gretchen and gave her a hug. I'd spent some time myself in bad places and scary circumstances. I knew what it was like to have to bury myself in disgusting things and not know if I'd wake again. "We have to finish this tonight."

"I pray so." Gretchen returned my hug then looked over at Jerry. "Jeremiah. I'm glad to see that you recovered from your gunshot. I know about the wooden bullets. You could have been killed."

"I had a rough time but I'm all right now." Jerry

gestured at Ian. "This is Ian MacDonald. He's an excellent doctor. I hate to say it but he saved me."

"A MacDonald helping a Campbell?" Gretchen's eyes were wide. "Thank you. This is a night for surprises."

"MacDonald? The name is known to me." Gunnar stared at Ian, barely acknowledging Flo and Richard as I made the introductions. Richard didn't say a word, obviously still fuming.

"Because you raided the Highlands, no doubt." Ian kept his eyes on Gunnar.

"I was sent by my king. It was not a raid. But a peace mission." Gunnar looked Ian up and down. "What do you care? It was over a thousand years ago. I'm sure you are an old vampire, but not as old as that."

"Perhaps you left something behind. Which king did you serve?" Ian had stepped closer and pulled his gun from behind his back.

"Ian! What are you doing?" I looked from Ian to Gunnar. I couldn't help noticing--

"Hush, Glory. I have my reasons. Tell me, Viking, did you know a lass or two when you made peace in the Highlands?" Ian didn't point the gun at Gunnar but I could see his hand tightening on the grip.

"We don't have time for this, MacDonald." Jerry pushed a shoulder between them. "History can wait. We need to plan, move. Do something about Fredrick and his weapon."

"Wait. I have a burning question." I couldn't hold it in a moment longer and we did need the subject change. "Did Gunnar get his treasure or not?"

"Yes, I did." The Viking gave a glowering Ian one last warning look then walked over to a tarp and moved it to retrieve two bulging hide bags. "Look." He handed one bag to Jerry and the other one to me.

It was heavy. When I opened mine I saw the glitter of gold and silver. Ancient coins. "Wow. These are solid gold and silver?" Ian peered over my shoulder and took a coin out of the bag.

"Plunder from your peace missions no doubt." Ian's sneer made Gunnar move closer.

"Put the coin back." Gunnar held out his hand.

Ian took his time, even going so far as to bite into the coin. "Real gold." He looked it over. "And rare these days." He tossed it back to Gunnar, who snatched it out of the air. "You have any idea how much each one of these might be worth, Viking?"

Gunnar took the pouch when I handed it back to him. "Enough for me to take this woman away from here, I hope. Enough for me to get the kind of weapons that will kill her miserable husband and make her free. That is all I care about."

"Yes. It will get you enough for that and more." Ian looked at Richard then Jerry. "But you'll give away your position if you take any of these to a local coin dealer to cash them out."

"That's true, Gunnar. And I can't use my credit cards, of course. Fredrick will be watching for the activity. That's why I tossed the cards overboard in my purse." Gretchen took the other bag from Jerry. "We will have to wait to deal with this treasure. That is obvious."

"Flo, she tossed a Birkin bag overboard. Bordeaux crocodile. Can you believe it?" I couldn't help myself. I was still in mourning for a bag that could bring up to six figures on the secondary market.

"*Dio mio*! Are you crazy?" Flo stared at Gretchen like she'd lost her mind.

"It wasn't easy but you don't know my husband. He could have put a tracker in it." Gretchen gave Gunnar the bag of coins. "These are desperate times."

"I understand." Flo slipped her arm around Richard's waist. "A purse can be replaced. A special man? Never."

"We can sell the coins for you in Texas. I know some private collectors who will jump on these. No questions asked." Richard nodded toward the pouches. Apparently his interest in history and ancient coins had helped him forget his tangle with Gunnar. "When this is over you might be able to come back with us. Though that's up to Ian, of course. It's his plane at the airport."

"What is Texas?" Gunnar was clearly suspicious of everyone but me and Jerry.

"It's a place, far from here." I was afraid just jumping on a plane for Texas wasn't going to be good enough to get Fredrick off their tails. I smiled at Richard, glad he'd decided to be reasonable, but I could see Ian might be a problem. He'd put his gun away but he kept staring at Gunnar like he was the snake in the Garden of Eden. Hmm.

"Texas is where Jerry and I live. But don't worry about that now. We need to get moving. Gretchen, do you have Fredrick's weapon? Ian and Richard are dying to have a look at it. They are both familiar with modern technology."

"Yes, we are." Richard stepped forward. "Of course we don't have any equipment here. We really need a lab if we're going to figure anything out about it."

"Yes, it's here." Gretchen glanced at the stack of crates against the wall.

"We'd like to take it apart and look at it first." Ian and Richard exchanged glances. "See how it works. Hand it over."

"No. Now that you've seen my treasure this could be a trick. Who's to say you won't paralyze us all and then take off with my fortune?" Gunnar was really very smart to think of that.

Jerry stepped forward. "Gunnar, you can trust these men."

"The man who held a gun to my head? Or the man who is claiming I may have raided his lands and left, what? Bastards there?" Gunnar spit on the floor. "No. You hold it, Jeremiah. And Glory, of course." Gunnar nodded at Gretchen. "We know the Eliminator can't hurt her."

"Really? Glory? How can that be?" Gretchen walked over to a crate and pulled it open.

"It's that long story again, Gretchen. I have a special blood and let's leave it at that. Okay?" I shook my head when I could see Flo wanted to speak up about my demi-goddess thing. Bragging. She'd decided I was like royalty now and being my best friend gave her a certain caché. As if she needed anything to make her more special. I was surprised Gunnar hadn't told Gretchen about my Olympus connection. But then they'd been busy running for their lives. And I wasn't sure Gunnar had really believed me anyway.

"I don't want us to try it on anyone. Certainly I'd hate to see any of you suffer from this. Of course I'll be suffering too, won't I?" Gretchen handed Jerry the weapon. "Notice it has three switches. The one on the right is for mortals. Fredrick says it kills them." She shuddered. "The one in the middle knocks out vampires. I guess that's what he used on you three, Gunnar, Jeremiah and Glory. You don't have to aim it for it to work. It will make any vampire in the room fall down unconscious." Big sigh. "It is horrible."

"What does the one on the left do?" I was afraid I'd already figured that out.

Jerry held the gun so Ian and Richard could see it.

"That one kills vampires instantly." Gretchen clutched the little insert. "It works. I saw him do it. Fredrick killed a vampire in front of me one night. Flipped that switch, aimed it and the man went down, never to see another sunrise."

"*Mio Dio!*" Flo was crossing herself again. "We should destroy it now. Smash it into a million pieces!"

"It wouldn't do any good, Florence. The genius who made this would just make another. We need to figure this out so we can fix this to use ourselves until Fredrick is eliminated." Richard patted Flo's shoulder.

"Yes, Fredrick must die. I see that now. He has a twisted kind of genius and is not fit to live. The vampire he killed." Gretchen's breath was more of a sob. "His body. I saw it. There was a hole where his heart used to be." She bowed her head. "I am so ashamed to carry his name."

"Why, *älskling*? It is not your fault your mate is a monster." Gunnar pulled her into his arms. "We will kill him and you will be free."

"I guess it is the only way." Gretchen leaned against him. "But I loved him once." She looked around at all of us. "Can you understand?"

"Yes, of course. People change." I sent mental messages around the group. Enough Fredrick bashing. She'd come around to our way of thinking. I held out my hand and Gretchen finally handed me the insert.

"Jeremiah, watch what you are doing. Fredrick was always careful to hold the weapon by that padded handle with one hand and to flip the switch with his other hand." She pointed out the parts to me. "I think Glory will have to be the one to try it if you want to see how it works. But I must warn you. Everyone here will fall down unconscious once Glory hits that middle switch. Even if she doesn't aim it at you."

"Are you sure we should test this?" I looked at Jerry and he silently handed the weapon to me. "We have no idea how long you'll be out."

"It's an experiment, Gloriana. Surely if you press the button for only a second, we will only be out for a moment or two." Ian was clearly fascinated. "Are we all game?" No one seemed to want to admit they were afraid to go along with it. Even Gunnar merely grunted and held Gretchen's hand.

"Wait! We fall down if this thing works on us?" Flo frowned down at the dirty concrete floor. "I have on this wonderful coat."

"Maybe you'd all like to sit on the floor. So you won't fall." I studied those switches. Thank God they were color coded so I couldn't accidentally make a mistake. It was the middle one I needed to hit anyway. No chance of an error.

"Seriously, *amica*?" Flo shook her head. "You won't fall too? It will only be for a second?"

"Fredrick was upset that I didn't react to this thing. So

I swear I won't fall. If it does make you faint, you should come to fairly quickly." I hoped that was true. I smiled as I watched my best friend pull a canvas off a stack and turn it over so that she sat on the clean side. She beckoned and Richard sat close to her so he could hold her hand. Everyone else just sat where they stood.

"Here goes." I flipped the switch and watched all my friends, even Jerry standing behind me, fall over. Talk about wielding power. I immediately turned it off again. Then I waited and waited. No one stirred. What had I done?

ELEVEN

It seemed to take forever for them to begin to stir but was actually ten minutes according to the clock on my phone. Jerry was the first to wake up. And he'd been behind me!

"Gloriana. What the hell happened?" He sat up and looked around. "Our friends are still out. My God!"

"I know. Good luck figuring out how this thing works. Is it sound? Some kind of laser? Beats me." I handed him the machine, eager to get rid of it. First, I'd taken the activator out of it. The thing gave me the creeps.

"What could it be then?" Jerry stood but seemed a little wobbly. When I started to go to him, he gave me a warning look. No, he didn't want my help. A breath and a minute to get his bearings and he was good to go.

The others were stirring now too. Gunnar, then Ian. They were the biggest men so I was thinking size might help one recover from whatever the machine did. Richard wasn't far behind. Gretchen moaned and stretched and Gunnar hurried to her side. It took my little buddy Flo the longest. So my size theory wasn't off base. She finally sat up, Richard's arms around her.

"*Mio Dio*, I was knocked completely out. How long did it last?"

I looked at my phone. She'd been out for almost thirty minutes. When I told her she showed her fangs.

"I hate that machine. We need to destroy every one of them. You know how easy it would be to stake me while I am like that?" She stood with Richard's help. "To stake all of us?"

"Or someone could just flip the other switch and kill us all with this thing." Jerry looked like he was seriously thinking about taking Flo's advice and smashing the Eliminator against the concrete floor. "It takes a sick bastard to create something like this."

"We need a place to work and tools. I want to know how this works." Richard was still holding onto a shaky Flo.

"So do I. I have plenty of things we could use in my lab in Austin." Ian nodded. "What the hell. All of you are welcome to come on the plane and go back there. Even you, Viking."

"Fredrick will follow us there." Gretchen was staying on the floor. "He wants the Eliminator back and will want to get even with me for taking off with it. Get even with us all."

"I won't run away like a coward. The bastard must die." Gunnar pulled out his sword. "I will take his head if it's the last thing I do."

"It might be, Viking." Ian frowned. "Your primitive weaponry doesn't stand a chance against something as sophisticated as this." He and Richard had placed the weapon on a table and were trying to open it. Richard produced a Swiss Army Knife with a dozen different blades including screwdrivers. "Glory, you didn't fool with the settings, did you?"

"All I touched was the switch. On and off." I had hated doing that. "With the activator out of it, the thing should be harmless." But was it really? Fredrick could have said that to throw us off. "Be careful!"

"Glory's right. Fredrick could have a booby trap in there." Jerry had joined them.

"We're being careful." Ian smiled, obviously excited at the chance to examine the weapon. "We already took a hell of a chance, lying here unconscious while Fredrick and his men could arrive any minute." He rubbed his chest. "You're onto something though. You said your chest hurt afterwards. So does mine. It's doing a job on our hearts. Richard, we need to think about this."

"Oh, shit. This is a tracker. How long has this weapon been here?" Richard held up a tiny part. "Obviously Fredrick can find it now. Don't know why he didn't sooner."

"I hid it here right after we left the island. But we dropped it here and left. I didn't want us to spend the day where it's so open. Fredrick must not have trusted his men to retrieve it for him and wanted to come personally but the sunrise stopped him." Gretchen buried her face in her hands. "I've led him to us, Gunnar. I'm so sorry."

"No, I want to meet him. To put him down like a rabid dog." Gunnar paced the floor. "It's possible he sent men to take us in our death sleep but, thank Freya, they didn't find us. Now he'll be back for his weapon at least."

"Wait. I see it now. This tracker only comes on when the weapon is used. We activated it when we tested it. He didn't know where the machine was until we turned it on." Richard dropped the tracker to the floor and stomped it with his boot heel. "If we move fast, we might be able to leave before they get here."

But we all knew we were too late when we heard thumps on the roof. Something or things were landing. And then there was the sound of a loud motor outside. A vehicle--and it wasn't a small car either--had just driven up. We were in big trouble. Surrounded.

I held up the activator. "I say we get rid of this thing. Gretchen, you really think the Eliminator is useless without it?"

"Yes, yes! Break it or throw it in the lake outside, Glory. Then at least we can have a fair fight here." Gretchen grabbed a loose board when Gunnar pulled out his sword. "We can't keep running forever."

"*Min modiga kvinna.*" Gunnar gave her a quick kiss. "You heard her, Glory. Get rid of that thing."

Richard and Ian looked pained. They really wanted to know how it worked.

"Hide it instead. It's so little it will take a long time to find. Toss it into that pile of canvases, Gloriana." Richard nodded to Gunnar and pulled out his gun. "Yes, Gretchen is a brave woman, but I'd rather all the women shifted out of here right now."

"*Caro*, I don't run and hide from trouble. And *certamente* I won't leave you alone to fight these *bastardi*." Flo picked up a board too and sat down to strip off her high heeled boots. My little buddy meant business.

"Florence, don't." Richard rushed to her side.

"Try to stop me, *marito*." She got up and gave him a quick kiss. "Glory, toss that thing here." I did and she stuffed it into her cleavage. "Hah! If they get this close to me, there will be hell to pay. Eh?"

Ian burst into laughter and pulled out his gun. "Pity the bastards now. Spread out. They have to come in the back door so they should be sitting ducks. Damn, but I wish we could have used the Eliminator on them. Too bad we'd just incapacitate ourselves as well." He looked at me with narrowed eyes. "Of course Glory could use it and then go around and--"

"Stop right there. Gloriana's not going to stake Fredrick or try to take out all of his shifters by herself. We don't even know if the Eliminator would put his shifters out, do we?" Jerry looked at Gretchen.

"Remember how they took us when we got to the castle, Jerry?" I hadn't forgotten how helpless we'd been. "The shifters didn't go down and neither did Fredrick. I had to be drugged and they all carried us to the dungeon. Fredrick has something that makes him immune to the Eliminator. What, I don't know."

"Glory's right. He used it on me and never would have tried that if it had made him fall down too." Gretchen had kicked off her shoes too and looked ready to rumble.

I was glad we'd figured that out. I had no desire to be the designated killer in this group but I could use some of my Olympus powers. I grabbed a board with a nail in it.

"They will all carry those guns with the wooden bullets. I wish we had bullet proof vests." Gretchen shook her head. "You know Fredrick wears one wherever he goes."

"Wait. The canvases. And that looks like heavy duty steel over there. What if we make our own bullet proof vests?" I ran over to the stacks of material there. "What kind of artist used this place, Gretchen?" I glanced upward. The sounds had stopped. We were lucky they hadn't attacked yet. Probably scouting the area to figure out the best approach. They hadn't realized the back door was the only way in.

"He did metal sculpture. Huge ones that sit outdoors. Paintings too. Why?" Gretchen stood beside me. "What would we need to make such a vest?"

"Brilliant, Gloriana. You're right. That's industrial grade steel. The canvas can be cut to make a vest and the steel should be able to stop a bullet, especially since Gretchen's right and Fredrick's army will be using wooden ones, not metal." Richard started pulling out small pieces of steel, the size of a man's chest. "If they hit us in the head, all bets are off, so watch what you're doing. I wish we could make a helmet of some kind but can't see how with these materials. At least most men trained to fire at vampires automatically go for the heart."

"A breastplate. I like it." Gunnar held a piece of blue metal against his chest.

Ian was by his side, tossing metal into a pile. "Campbell, bring your knife. I'm sure it's sharp enough to cut this canvas. We need arm holes and a hole to put our head through. We'll double it so there's a pouch to hold the metal in front."

"You really think it will work?" I didn't say more. The men must have thought so. They were throwing together makeshift vests at warp speed. Vampire speed actually. The women got theirs first. Chivalry from our ancient men. Then the men slapped together their own. Gunnar hadn't seen Jerry almost die from the wooden bullet but he was used to going into battle well prepared. Soon all of us wore what looked like a canvas bag over our shoulders. They'd found twine to tie the sides together and form pouches for our metal breastplates against our chests and stomachs.

Just in time too. The back door burst open and two men dressed in black rushed inside, guns blazing. The sound was horrendous. I'd hoped to mesmerize the soldiers but realized they all wore goggles with the special lenses that would prevent that. Damn. So I ducked behind the table we'd overturned to use for cover while I thought about how to help. At least our men had guns. Jerry stayed beside me, firing back. Richard and Ian had hidden on either side of the door and jumped the first two shifters, surprising them.

My heart was in my throat as I watched them roll around on the concrete, fighting hand to hand. Flo screamed encouragement in Italian and finally couldn't stand to stay behind her pile of crates. She attacked a shifter who was trying to squeeze the life out of Richard with a metal picture frame. It was just enough distraction for Richard to shoot the man dead.

My pal didn't stop, just picked up the shifter's machine gun and started spraying the doorway with gunfire.

"Get back behind those crates!" Richard, bleeding from a graze on his face, pulled the gun from her hands and shoved her behind him. Flo hit him on his back but did as he said. She shouted what sounded like curses in Italian until he passed her his handgun, keeping the machine gun for himself. More shifters poured into the warehouse.

"That's it, I can't stay here." Jerry jumped over the table and rushed into the melee, firing his weapon and dropping one of the new arrivals. He shouted something in Gaelic and Ian turned just as a man was about to jump on the doctor. Between the two of them, they got his gun and knocked him out. Jerry and Ian actually slapped palms. But there was no time for celebrating when more men came through the doors.

The sound of bullets hitting breastplates was too much for me. I grabbed my board and leaped over the table too. No way was I standing around like a little woman while everyone else was fighting for their lives. Gretchen had taken a position in front of the pile of canvas where we'd stashed the Eliminator, Gunnar by her side. But the Viking moved off, using his sword on one shifter after another. We swung our boards like baseball bats, wild women who were determined to keep everyone away from that weapon. We needed it as part of a plan to get Fredrick where we wanted him.

It occurred to me that the soldiers must have orders concerning Gretchen because they dodged our blows but kept coming. I knew I was right when one jerked her board out of her hand and started dragging her toward the door. I beat him with my stick but he didn't even slow down. Gretchen shrieked Gunnar's name and he turned with a growl.

His sword was covered with blood as he started slicing through men to get to us.

"Let her go!" I screamed, determined to help her. Bullets smacked into my breastplate but I didn't stop, bringing my board down hard on the man who had Gretchen in his arms. It didn't slow him down even though she was kicking and screaming.

Then Gunnar was there. He gestured for me to get out of his way and raised his sword.

"Be careful. You could hurt Gretchen." I didn't like the crazed look in his eyes.

"I know what I am doing." He gave a Viking yell that made my heart stutter then brought the flat of the sword down on the shifter's head. I staggered back, pretty sure I was going to be sick at the sound of that skull cracking.

Gretchen landed on the ground before Gunnar kicked the man's body aside to take her into his arms. The gunfire was sporadic now and bodies blocked most of the door. Were we winning this battle? But where was Fredrick? Surely he hadn't planned to miss this chance to get this weapon back. Ah, one last pair of shifters ran inside and Fredrick appeared in the doorway. He stayed behind them of course. He didn't have an Eliminator, thank God. So he must not have found his spare. Instead he gripped another machine gun.

"Where is it?" He did what we expected and made a bee-line for the Eliminator that we'd left sitting out in plain sight. We let him go to it. He went so fast he left his shifter bodyguard behind, fighting with Jerry and Ian. This was just what we'd planned. Fredrick ran his hands over the weapon, frowning when he realized the activator was missing. "Gretchen, you bitch! Where the hell is the missing part?"

Gunnar roared another of his battle cries which gave me chills. Fredrick raised his gun and bullets smacked into the Viking's makeshift vest, but Gunnar kept going, straight at Gretchen's husband.

"You will not ever harm Gretchen again, you piece of *skit*." He slapped Fredrick's gun away with his sword.

"You're outnumbered. How do you think to win here?" But when Fredrick looked around, he realized his hired guns were deserting him. Their employer was facing an enraged Viking and had lost his own weapon. This battle was as good as over and it hadn't gone their way. The survivors helped the wounded take off to save their own skins.

"I've already won." Gunnar's smile was bone chilling. "I thought I wanted a fair fight with you, but it is not to be. You don't deserve it. Why should I be fair to a man who hurts his woman and turns against his own kind?" And with a mighty swing, he gave another battle cry and took Fredrick's head. It rolled across the floor and landed in a pool of blood. The matted blond hair framed a surprised look, as if even at the end Fredrick had been sure he would win this fight.

"*Herregud!*" Gretchen swayed and I ran to catch her before she fell. "I didn't think he'd go through with it."

"It was the right thing to do." Jerry nodded when the last of the wounded shifters helped each other up and staggered out of the warehouse. "I see no value in finishing the hired help. This way word will spread fast that Fredrick is gone and can no longer provide weapons to our enemies." He looked down at his body armor. "This worked. It's dented all to hell but it worked." He pulled it off over his head and tossed it aside. "Gloriana, look at you. It's a miracle you weren't killed."

"No miracle." I ran to him, dragging off my own armor. "See? My dents are all over my heart." I tossed the makeshift vest to the ground. "Thank God it never occurred to those shifters to go for a head shot." I saw Gretchen was still pale and swaying. I helped her shed her armor then sit down on a crate.

"Fredrick is gone." Gretchen took a shaky breath. She watched Gunnar clean his blade on a piece of canvas then slide it back into its scabbard. "I . . . I must think."

"You are free, *min kärlek,* I hope that makes you happy." Gunnar stopped in front of us and reached for

Gretchen's hands. His own were filthy with the blood of the men he'd killed.

"Happy?" She shook her head. "Would you give me a moment, Gunnar?"

He glanced at me, clearly puzzled.

"You just killed her husband. She'd be a cold woman if she danced for joy. They were married for hundreds of years." I knew Gunnar was only focused on what had just happened and his blood was running hot. Looking around the room and the bodies of men who'd merely done a job, I felt sickened. Okay, so the job they'd hired on for had been to kill us. Couldn't feel too bad about that. They were mercenaries and had known the risks.

And then there was Fredrick. The man had deserved to die, but seeing it happen, and the way it had happened . . . It wasn't the first time I'd seen a head lopped off. But that had been a while back. These days it was rare unless you were caught by a terrorist and I sure didn't watch those videos. Gunnar had done what he'd have done a thousand years ago. He'd meted out justice, Viking style. He was happy with the outcome. And, to be honest, I was happy with it too. I wanted to kick Fredrick's head like a soccer ball for what his men had done to Jerry. I'd almost lost my husband to those damned wooden bullets. And making money by selling to vampire hunters? Good riddance to the asshole.

"Gloriana." Jerry stood beside me. "Let's get out of here. Ian and Richard want to take the Eliminator back to Austin. We've got a couple of weeks left of our honeymoon here. Or have you lost your taste for Sweden?"

"I feel like Gretchen now. Can you give me a minute?" My heart was pounding. My heart which must be different from every other vampire's. Ian wanted to study me. Wanted to study Gunnar too. I glanced at the Viking. He was hovering over Gretchen, trying to figure out what to say or do to make her smile at him. Good luck with that.

"Here is the activator thing. Don't give it to Ricardo or Ian yet, Glory." Flo pressed it into my hand. "I am afraid of that machine and would hate for my man to accidentally put himself into a faint. He might even kill himself with it, you know what I mean?"

"Yes, it is scary." I felt the little piece that looked like an ordinary flash drive and realized it was damp from being in Flo's cleavage. She'd been sweating during the battle. That made me smile. Tough Italian spitfire. "Pal, I will bring it back with me to Texas. After the honeymoon. Tell the guys that. They can wait for a full test then."

"*Grazie.* I thought I wanted an adventure, but maybe this is too much." Flo pulled her coat around her and shivered. She had put her boots back on too. "We plan a little vacation another time, to somewhere cold. When you aren't on your honeymoon. *Bene?*"

"Sounds like a plan, Flo." Jerry pulled me close to his side. "Maybe we can persuade Gretchen and Gunnar to come back with us when we do head to Austin."

"I'm sure the doctor would like that." Flo made a face. "He wants to 'examine' him, as he says. Me? I'd like to ask him about the days of the old Vikings. Is interesting, don't you think?"

"I think we just saw a demonstration of those old days." I shuddered. "He took Fredrick's head like it was nothing."

"It needed to be done, Glory." Flo barely spared

the carnage a glance. "I'm glad he is dead and with no chance to come back to hurt his wife or us. The Viking is a hero." She leaned closer and lowered her voice. "But notice, *amica*, how much he looks like our *medico*. I think Ian suspects the Viking did a little *fare l'amore*--you know what I mean?--when he was in the Highlands."

Jerry just grunted. "I stay out of the MacDonalds' business but it's something to consider. Let's not mention it to Ian or Gunnar now. But later, maybe I'll see what I can find out." He winked at Flo. "If you are right it would certainly be an interesting coincidence."

"Pah, I call it fate." Flo kept studying the two men. "I will put Ricardo on it. The Viking could use some family. *Capiscimi?*"

"I wouldn't wish that family on my worst enemy." Jerry laughed suddenly. "Oh, wait, MacDonald *is* my worst enemy. Poor Gunnar if it's true. You'd better leave it alone, Florence."

But I knew Flo wouldn't. She had an idea and she wasn't going to let it go until she knew the truth.

"You need to put that old feud aside, Jer. Ian saved your life. I'm convinced of it." I pinched his side. "But let's forget it for now and concentrate on our honeymoon. I want to get back to our suite. Flo, you guys should spend one more night, enjoy the hotel. We had a great time in the disco. There's dancing."

"Ah, now you're talking. We can leave tomorrow night then." Flo headed over to Richard.

"Honeymoon and Christmas tomorrow. Did you buy me a present?" Jerry leaned down to kiss me.

"Yes, I actually did. And it isn't the usual, me in nothing but a bow." I laughed and kissed him back.

"Gunnar and I need a place to stay. I wonder if there's room in the Ice Palace for us." Gretchen had obviously calmed down. "Can you call them for me, Jeremiah?"

"Certainly. Will do it now. Why don't we all go outside for this?" He steered us around Fredrick's body. "You need to figure out how to clear the men from your home, Gretchen. Then you can go back there."

"I doubt I'll ever want to live in that castle again. Not with those memories. And I certainly can't trust anyone connected with Fredrick." Gretchen took a deep breath of fresh air once we were outside. "Even the vice president of his company was his lover. You see my problem?"

"Then get in touch with your family. They can advise you. Get a lawyer you trust to untangle the mess. You will need access to your accounts. I know you were wealthy. You can't let all of that go." Jerry was serious then turned his back to make the call.

"We want nothing from that *jäkel*." Gunnar kept his arm around Gretchen.

"I have my own funds, Gunnar. This is not Viking times. I am entitled to my wealth and I intend to have it." Gretchen looked confident and stared Gunnar down.

"Women are different now. Difficult." Gunnar shrugged, like it was a mystery to him.

"Get used to it, Viking." Jerry clapped him on the back. "I have and I like it." He grinned at me. "We're all set. A suite for you two. Unless you want Gunnar to have a separate room, Gretchen. I forgot to ask."

"Really? You want me to stay away from you?" Gunnar managed to look dejected yet hopeful.

"Oh, stop it. You know you are staying with me." Gretchen slapped his arm. "It is fine, Jeremiah. Thank you."

"Did I hear it right? We are all at the Ice Palace tonight?" Flo hurried up to us. "Gretchen, we must take you shopping in the boutique. Since you don't want to go home to pack."

Gretchen still looked a little dazed but decided to go along with it. Before we had time to think twice, Flo had herded us all to the car. I noticed Richard and Ian had tossed the guns they'd taken from the shifters into the trunk along with the Eliminator. They put in extra wooden bullets too that they must have taken out of the dead shifters pockets. I didn't want to think about them searching Fredrick's pockets. But then I saw Ian hand Gretchen a stack of credit cards.

"You should have these. Glory said you tossed yours overboard when you were being chased earlier." At least he'd taken them out of Fredrick's leather wallet.

"Oh, yes. Thank you." Gretchen sighed. "I feel strange. Like this can't be true and yet I am finally free. Am I a bad person to be just a little bit glad he is dead?"

"No, Gretchen. You are perfectly normal. We are all glad he's dead. Sorry, but that's the truth." I looked around and everyone nodded. "The man who died tonight wasn't the same man you married centuries ago, you said that yourself."

"Yes, that is true. That man died a long time ago. This Fredrick was a stranger." Gretchen stood next to Gunnar but moved away this time when he tried to put his arm around her.

"Then it wouldn't be wrong to buy something pretty for yourself." Flo was all for it. "I would like to see you in green. What do you think, Glory?"

"Oh, yes. Definitely green." I glanced at Gunnar. "Hey, Viking, how do you feel about shopping? Want to come along with us?"

We all laughed at his look of horror. Yep, our bad ass Viking had seemed less scared when facing a hoard of armed shape-shifters than at the prospect of shopping with a group of women.

"Oh, one more thing, Gunnar. You have to leave your sword in the car." Jerry gave him an elbow in the ribs.

"What? You would have me go shopping unarmed?" Gunnar reached behind him and gripped the sword handle. "Now you are being unreasonable."

"No, unreasonable is trying to sneak into a hotel with a sword strapped to your back." Flo shook her finger at him.

Gunnar looked at Jerry. "Are you going to do this shopping?"

"No thank you." Jerry shook his head. "You couldn't pay me to do it."

"Then I will not either." He puffed out his chest. "I think it must be women's work."

Gretchen shook her head. "He's missed a thousand years of advances for women. I can see this relationship will be a lot of work if it is to last."

I took pity on him. "That's all right, Gunnar. We were teasing you. Stay with the men. Watch some more soccer on the TV." Jerry and Richard grinned at each other, like they were going to push him to go with us again. "Don't say another word."

"No, we'll keep him. He obviously needs pointers on how to handle women in this century." Jerry laughed. "Don't glare at me, Gloriana. Did I or did I not, just convince you to marry me?"

"Yes, you did. So I'd suggest you remember that you have eternity to look forward to with either a happy wife or a nagging one." I smiled, pretty sure I'd ended that conversation. "I think we need to get in the car now. Gretchen isn't looking so good."

"Thank you, Glory. I am feeling … shaky." She didn't have to say why. It was still hitting her that she had seen her husband murdered right in front of her.

When we all jockeyed for position in the car it became obvious that Gretchen was going to end up on Gunnar's lap. To say it was awkward was an understatement. She got in with all the enthusiasm of a death row inmate on his way to lethal injection

TWELVE

"Gretchen," Jerry looked serious and I realized we had all tried to lighten the mood for his cousin but it wasn't really working. Richard hadn't started the car yet so I figured we had some unfinished business to discuss before we left here.

We'd all crammed into the rental car. The three men from Austin were in the front seat and the rest of us rode in the back. Gretchen *had* ended up on Gunnar's lap but she wouldn't lean against him, her spine stiff. Who could blame her after what she'd just seen him do to her unlamented husband? Well, unlamented by the rest of us anyway. She'd started sniffling quietly.

"What is it, Jeremiah?" She looked up at him, her eyes red.

"We need a clean-up crew at this warehouse." Jerry nodded toward it. "I took a picture of Fredrick's body so it can be safely removed."

"A picture? Why?" I'd seen him do it, wondering about it at the time.

"She will need proof, Gloriana, that the bastard is dead. There will be questions about who should take over the company, all his holdings. And then there's his family…" Jerry looked a question at his cousin.

"I will call Stefan. He will handle everything." She pulled a generic looking phone out of her coat pocket and began to punch in numbers. "Let me out of the car."

We all heard the locks click and Richard jumped out to open the door for her. She stepped into the cold night air and started speaking to someone in rapid Swedish.

"Who's Stefan, Jer?" I wondered if he was from her family or Fredrick's.

"He's her brother." Jerry got out of his side of the car. "I want to hear how this goes."

"Thank God they are both out of here." Ian groaned and stretched. "I couldn't stand being crammed between those two for another minute. I'm shifting back to the hotel. I think I can manage to find my way." He crawled out of the car. "See you later. Text me with any plans." And with that he changed into a black bird and flew off into the night.

"I'm climbing into the front with Jerry now." I opened the back door. "That will give Gretchen some space."

"She needs it. Can you believe she is angry with me? When I try to hold her she acts like I am her enemy." Gunnar had his arms crossed over his chest, clearly sulking. "She should be glad I ended the life of that *jäkel*. If this were in my time, I would have his head in a sack right now, on my way to take it to my king. We would place it on a pike in front of the castle to show everyone what happens to men who betray their own kind." His chin stuck out as if he would still like to do it if he had a clue who ruled Sweden now.

"You did a good thing, Viking. When Gretchen gets over her shock she will be grateful, I'm sure." Flo patted him on one of his beefy biceps. "You were very brave, a hero. *Molto forte.*"

"Thank you." Gunnar smiled at her. "You are a little thing but you were brave too. Where are you from?"

I left them talking to each other and slammed the car door to walk over to Jerry. I slid my arms around his waist and leaned against him while he listened to both sides of

Gretchen's telephone conversation with his vampire hearing. I could hear it too but the Swedish meant nothing to me. Finally, Gretchen broke down sobbing and held out the phone to Jerry. I went to her, patting her back and murmuring words of comfort.

"You must think I'm crazy to have even a bit of sadness about this, Glory. But when I saw him die . . ." Gretchen dug a tissue out of her coat pocket and blew her nose.

"It was shocking. And no matter how bad he was at the end, you must have loved him once." Even I had noticed how handsome he was.

"Yes! You see how I might remember, just for a moment, those days when we were happy." She turned her back on the warehouse. The sea breeze blew the scent of blood toward us and it was impossible to ignore. "But now I need to think about how he was in recent times." Her hand convulsed on that tissue. "I should be glad he's dead because of how he abused me. When I let something slip once to Fredrick's brother about his wooden bullets, he locked me in the dungeon for a week."

"No!" I looked over my shoulder at that warehouse. I had the urge to run inside and make sure that her husband was good and dead. No, there could be no doubt about that. Not even a genius like Fredrick could recover from a severed head. "You should have left him as soon as he released you."

"I couldn't. He threatened to kill my family if I did. Or told anyone about his business or how he treated me." Gretchen sighed. "Now it's hard to remember why I once loved him."

"I guess he changed. People do. But, God, Gretchen." I was at a loss for words.

"Fredrick became a monster. I know it." Gretchen wiped her cheeks with her hands. "I think I'm weeping from relief too. And Stefan is being so kind. My brother will bring men to dispose of the," she took a shuddery breath, "Bodies."

"Good. Then we should be able to leave now. You need a hot bath and a change of clothes." I'd noticed she was still in the ones she'd worn to Birka. She'd spent her death sleep in them and now they were even splashed with blood. Flo had been right about the need for a shopping trip.

"Yes! I would like that." She hugged me. "You've been wonderful about being dragged into my mess. I hope you will be able to enjoy your honeymoon now." She looked up at the sky. "Stefan should arrive soon. He lives not very far from here. But he wanted to get some men together that he could trust to be discreet." Her eyes filled with tears again as she glanced at the car.

"Gunnar. I don't know what to think about him. Did you see how ruthless he was during the fight? He was primitive, barbaric. And the way he killed Fredrick . . ." She shuddered and picked at a stain on her coat, probably blood, before finally looking up at me.

"Wasn't he what you needed? Wanted? A man who could do what was necessary without hesitation?" I wanted to shake her but stepped back instead. This woman needed a reality check. "He was protecting you, Gretchen. You have to know that there was no other way for that fight to end. We had to be sure that Fredrick wouldn't come after you again." I couldn't help myself. I gripped her arm. "He's a Viking warrior, sure. But Jerry, Richard or Ian, given a sword, would have killed Fredrick just like that and been glad to do it. Don't you realize that?"

She closed her eyes and pressed her hands over them. I just waited while she sorted this out in her mind. Finally she nodded, opened her eyes and straightened her shoulders.

"You're right. Of course he had to do it and I'm glad he did." She sniffed. With the tinted windows it was impossible to see if Gunnar was watching us or not. "He is a fine man, Glory. He would have died for me in that place if it had come to that." Fresh tears but this time I knew they were for the right reason.

"Yes, he would have." I nodded. "Show him you

admire him for what he did and he'll follow you wherever you go."

Gretchen managed a strangled laugh. "He's not a puppy, Glory."

"No, he's not. Gunnar is from a time when his sword was his right arm. He did his duty and would like a little praise for that. We know men and their egos, don't we?" I started walking back to the car, Gretchen beside me.

"They want them stroked." She flushed. "Along with a few other things."

I laughed and patted her shoulder. "Now you've got it. He loves you, Gretchen. He's hurt that you aren't acting grateful for his good deed. At least tell him thank you for saving you from a man who hurt you."

"Yes, I can do that." Gretchen lost her smile. "I hope he will understand if I need time to get this straight in my mind. And he needs time too. This is a new century. A new life for him. I don't want to tie him down when he has no idea what's available to him now."

"That's very kind of you. But don't be in such a hurry to give him away, cousin." I nodded toward Jerry who was talking to Richard next to the car. "I've learned that keepers aren't that easy to find." I leaned closer. "How would you feel if you gave him time and another woman swooped in to take your place? Anyone could show Gunnar how the twenty-first century works, including the sexual freedom it allows."

Suddenly her fangs were down. "Another woman in his bed? No, I wouldn't like that." She gripped my hand on her arm. "You see how confused I am, Glory? I hope I don't ruin things with Gunnar. But time will tell." Gretchen walked up to Jerry. "Stefan is on his way?"

"Yes, he said to leave before he gets here. He doesn't want anyone else to see you near the murder scene. It will cut down on gossip. He's going to blame Fredrick's death on a deal with vampire hunters gone wrong." Jerry handed Gretchen her phone and looked in the car. "Where's

MacDonald?"

"He didn't like sitting so close to you so he shifted back." I opened the passenger door. "So now I can sit next to you."

"Good. If we're lucky, he'll get lost on the way to the hotel and we won't have to see him again tonight." Jerry dragged me into his lap once we were in the car.

"This isn't legal, Jer. We need seatbelts." I laughed and gave him a kiss.

"So I'll mesmerize the police if we're stopped." He wrapped his arms around me. "Drive, Richard." He looked back to make sure Gretchen had settled into the back seat. "Cousin, are you all right?"

"Yes, let's get out of here. Glory mentioned a bath and a change of clothes. Now that's all I can think about." Gretchen smiled at Gunnar. "My hero here could use the same."

"Ah, now I'm feeling better. *Tacka*, Gretchen, for calling me that. But I was just doing what needed to be done." Gunnar held out his hand. "Are you sorry I did it?"

"No, now that I'm getting over the shock, I know it was the right thing to do. And that you were very brave tonight." She gripped his hand and placed it over her heart. "I'm safe now, thanks to you, *älskling*."

Gunnar beamed and kissed her cheek. "And I'm still welcome in your bed?"

She flushed and looked around the car. "Of course. Perhaps just to hold me tonight though. This has all has been very upsetting to me."

"Of course. I am not an animal." Gunnar caught my eye and winked. "I can be comforting. I would like to take care of you, Gretchen, and hope one of these men will trade some of their modern money for one of my gold coins. Then I can start paying my own way at the hotel. It would make me feel better about taking you to this Ice Palace and buying clothes."

"Of course." Richard spoke up quickly. "Let me take a

look at a coin or two when we get to the hotel. I'll look them up on the Internet and will give you a fair price for them."

"Richard loves old things. You should see what he has collected. He has a special room in our house filled with religious relics." Flo began to chatter about her husband's obsession with antiques. "Bones of saints. Now that is one collection I don't understand at all. Is *pazzo*."

Gunnar laughed. "There was big business in that even in my time. Be careful, Richard, to check if they are real. I knew a man who dug up old graves and then claimed the bones were from whatever saint the buyer wanted. Made a tidy sum from that business until he was caught one night robbing from his own grandsire's grave."

The conversation went on until Gunnar suddenly shouted. "*Helvete*! Stop the car!"

Richard stomped on the brakes. "What is it?"

"Look! There is the name of my enemy, the one who put me in the ice, on the sign in front of that building. *Fiender*! So bold." Gunnar was desperately trying to get out of the car but the doors were locked and he didn't have a clue how to unlock them.

We all stared at the four story building across the street. Yes, there was a name in giant gold letters over the glass doors. It was a fancy department store and the name was familiar to me. I tried to remember where I'd seen it before.

"Calm down, Gunnar." Gretchen held onto his arm when he tried to break the car window with his hands.

"You don't understand, Gretchen. I have to make them pay. They stole everything from me. More than a thousand years of my life, my family, my position with the king." Gunnar's eyes were wild and, if he'd had room, I had a feeling he would have pulled his sword. "*Helvete*, Richard, unlock the car door! I know you control it." He hit the back of Richard's seat with his fist.

"Wait a damned minute, Gunnar. I'm not going to let you out to make a run at that building. Can't you see the store is closed?" Richard was the voice of reason but that just got Gunnar even more upset.

"I don't care! I have to see, go closer, to know if it's the same name. Gretchen, tell them!" He pressed his face to the glass.

"What's your enemy's name, Gunnar?" Richard asked while Jerry and I exchanged a look. We remembered him mentioning the name when we'd first found him and there it was. The large department store was closed because it was after midnight and it was now Christmas Day, officially at least.

"Brodin. See it there?" Gunnar banged both fists on the door. "Why won't you let me out of this *förbannad* car?"

"Gunnar, that's Brodin's Department Store. There is a chain of them. There won't be a member of the family there, even if it was open which it's not." Gretchen tapped Richard on the shoulder. "Let him out. I'll go with him to show him the truth of it."

"*Tack*, Gretchen. I need to see . . ." The locks clicked and Gunnar wrenched the door open. He was off in a run before Gretchen even got her seatbelt unfastened.

"Let's all go. He could do anything in the state he's in." Jerry opened our door and I scooted out. We all ran across the deserted road, catching up to Gunnar as he stared at a Christmas display in a plate glass window. It featured a beautiful tree that looked like it had been freshly cut from a forest. It was covered with hundreds of colorful lights and had every kind of glittering ornament you could imagine.

Another window had a homey setting that looked like a family just sitting down for a meal. The abundance on the table was breathtaking. Apparently a Swedish Christmas was all about the food and this store must have a famous deli if the array on the table was anything to go by. Mannequins, including lifelike children, sat around the table. The scene looked like it could come alive at any minute with the father at the head of the table saying "Pass the potatoes."

Gunnar leaned against the glass. His voice shook when he started talking. "Look at this. So perfect. So beautiful.

Brodins made this. *Herregud!*" He shuddered and took a moment to gather himself before he faced us.

"Can't you see how they took everything from me? And now they have it all. I lost my family, my favor with the king. These Brodins betrayed me and look how they have prospered." Gunnar grabbed Gretchen's hand. "They are rich. This store clearly serves only people with much money. Who else can afford to buy such wonderful things?"

"You're right. It is a luxury department store. And this is only one of dozens in Scandinavia." Gretchen pushed her other arm under his coat to hug him. "I'm sorry. But surely the family that owns this store is merely descended from the one who was so cruel to you. Should they pay for the sins of an ancestor?"

"Why not?" He looked around at all of us. We'd stayed silent. We couldn't imagine his pain and really had nothing to say that would comfort him. "They are certainly enjoying the effects of his betrayal."

"That is obviously true. If it is the same family." Gretchen suddenly sagged against him. "It's Christmas, Gunnar. The store is closed for the holiday and there will no one to confront, even if we could get inside." She brushed her hand over his cheek. "Can we please talk about this tomorrow night? If you're determined to have revenge, surely you need time to think and plan."

"She's right, Viking. Take a little time to deliberate. This betrayal took place over a thousand years ago. How can you hold these people now accountable for what happened back then?" Richard seemed determined to try to calm Gunnar down. "You did manage to save your treasure. And one more night will not change anything."

"A Brodin put me in the ice, Richard. Would you forget that?" Gunnar was getting worked up again and gestured at the glittering gold sign above our heads. "That name! It makes me crazy. I would like to burn this building down to the ground." He looked around like maybe he'd find a flaming torch handy. His fists worked and he stomped a foot. "Yes! It would make me feel better. A start anyway."

"No! Stop it!" Gretchen dropped his hands and hit him with her fists. "I can't take any more violence tonight. You are never burning down a building if you plan to stay with me, Gunnar. I hope you know that."

Gunnar stiffened, his face harsh in the lights from the Christmas tree. "You would have me forget these wrongs done to me? Woman, you are asking too much."

"And you are asking too much of me if you expect me to lie with you with Fredrick's blood fresh on your hands." Gretchen was shaking as she turned to Flo. "When we get back in the car, trade places with me. I can't stand to sit close to him when he is raving like this."

"Whatever you need." Flo stepped next to Gretchen, obviously determined to ease an awkward moment. "Relax. Gunnar, I know you're not going to burn down anything. Am I right?" She patted his arm. "Tell her."

"No, I won't make promises I may not keep. The Brodins burned my village. I saw it. I had to hide in the hills but I knew they were looking for me. Björn Brodin was jealous of my favor in court. He told lies about me to our king and I know he was the one who put me in the ice while I lie in my death sleep."

Gretchen stiffened and I could tell Gunnar had said something that upset her even more than she already was. "I'm sorry you were put in the ice. I'm sorry your village was burned, Gunnar. But I can't be around you when you keep acting like a crazed Viking. This is a new century. Things have changed!"

"I know. Everywhere I look there is something I don't understand. If I am, as you say, crazed, it is because I am lost here. I killed your husband to keep you safe. I do not apologize for his blood on my hands. So we go from here. Together, I hope." Gunnar tried to get closer to her but she held out a hand to stop him. "Gretchen, *älskling*, you said you would help me in this new time, didn't you?"

"I am tired, Gunnar. I need to go to the hotel and I

need blood. Can you stop pushing me?" She walked on ahead, kicking up snow as she went.

"I'm sorry. You are upset. I just saw the name and, how you say it, Jeremiah?" Gunnar looked at my husband for help.

"Lost your shit, man. That's what happened." Jerry held out his hand and I gripped it as we all started walking toward the car. Thank goodness Gunnar came along quietly.

Jerry walked next to his cousin. "Gretchen, please cut the guy a break. He's just as upset as you are. And he's going to see the name everywhere on buildings now that he's looking for it. Hell, even the boutique in our hotel is run by Brodin's Department Store."

"Oh, gosh, it is." I gave Gunnar a sympathetic look but that didn't mean I wasn't going straight there with Gretchen to help her find a change of clothes as soon as we got to the Ice Palace. The boutique was part of the chain of luxury stores that had just the kind of clothing and accessories my friends and I liked. We got into the car, though Gunnar sent one more hate-filled look back at the store before he slammed the car door. Flo was stuck between the Viking and Gretchen. Jerry's cousin looked as if this ride couldn't end soon enough for her.

"You want me to leave these Brodins alone?" Gunnar reached across Flo, trying to grasp Gretchen's hand. She wasn't having it. "Please, I will wait for this revenge. Perhaps Jeremiah and Richard will help me find out more about the family. How they have prospered since they put me in the ice. Our friends can use their magic box for it."

"The computer, the Internet. Of course, Gunnar. We'll get right on it." Richard broke all kinds of speed limits until finally the Ice Palace loomed ahead of us, brilliantly lit as usual. He slowed the car. "We're here. Now is everyone good? Do we need to get an extra room for someone? Gretchen?"

"It doesn't matter where I spend my death sleep." She sounded tired and discouraged. "I'm sorry if I'm not making sense tonight. But for now if Gunnar will promise to keep his distance…"

"Whatever you need, *sötnos.*" Gunnar looked pathetically eager. "I will even go with you to this shopping if it will make you feel better."

"Oh, I don't think so. But wasn't he nice to offer, Gretchen?" Flo was like Switzerland between two warring countries and she knew better than to drag Gunnar into a boutique with the Brodin name over the door. "We will buy Gretchen something pretty and Gunnar can be cleaning up while we do it. We will get him something to wear too, won't we, Gretchen? Ricardo, you will take care of his money problem, *sí?*"

"Yes. Gunnar can shower in our room while you go shopping and I'll look over his coins and do a little research. What do you think, Gunnar?" Richard pulled into the driveway and popped the locks. A valet ran out to open our doors.

"It's fine with me. Gretchen?" The Viking was trying to catch Gretchen's eye but having no luck.

"We do need clothes. Florence can bring you some. I'll meet you later in the room when I'm ready." Gretchen got out of the car. She still wasn't looking at Gunnar. "Jeremiah, I hope when you called here you arranged for a room with two beds."

"Not sure about that." Jerry gave Gunnar a sympathetic look. "I'll check. You go on and start your shopping. I'll hit the front desk and get your keys." Jerry kissed my lips. "Buy something sexy, Gloriana. Our honeymoon is back on and I'm feeling good. All healed from that wooden bullet."

"Glad to hear it but perhaps I should take a look at that wound, just to be sure." Ian strolled up to our group as we entered the lobby. His hair wasn't even windblown. "Are we celebrating our victory tonight?"

I shook my head. "The mood's not right. I think the men are doing some research on the coins. Check them." I led the girls to the boutique. It was retail therapy and Gretchen made use of her credit cards to pick up everything she'd need for the next few nights. She was serious about not wanting to go back home even to pack a bag. Her phone rang while we were in the dressing room.

"*Hallå.*" She listened for a minute or two then talked in Swedish. Finally she wiped her eyes and ended the call. She turned to Flo and me. "That was my brother. He has taken care of the, um, mess we made in the warehouse. Those were his words." She sighed. "It is done. He is on his way to tell Fredrick's family what happened."

"Sounds like you have a great brother." I hugged her. "How do you think they'll take it?"

"With relief. Lately his family hasn't known what to do about my husband. When they heard he was selling those wooden bullets to vampire hunters, they were horrified, of course." She was talking very quietly and we were all aware of the clerk on the other side of the wall. "The other vampire families got wind of it and wanted Fredrick sanctioned. In Sweden that means put out in the sun."

"Well then maybe we won't have them coming after us for revenge in that case. It seems we solved a problem for the Swedish vampires." I knew that sounded harsh but it was the truth.

"Yes, that's what Stefan is going to say to Fredrick's brother and sister. They are a very powerful family. I'm sure word of the Eliminator got to them too. So I wouldn't be surprised if they are glad he's gone. He hadn't spoken to them since a birthday celebration for his sister turned ugly last summer. She wanted him to stop his work that could hurt vampires. Fredrick mocked her concerns and it turned into a shouting match."

"Family should stick together." Flo has a loving brother. When one was made vampire the other turned so they could be together forever. "But sometimes it's impossible. Did you ever tell them how he was hurting you?"

"No, I didn't dare. Though his sister did have her suspicions. She asked me about it. I had to lie to her or it would have been bad for me once Fredrick got me home. He made that very clear." Gretchen grabbed a red dress that had fit her perfectly. "Enough of this gloom. I am free. I have a handsome man who loves me, though I don't know why. He will be a challenge, that's obvious, but at least he will never hurt me. I almost feel like dancing after what happened tonight."

"No one could fault you for wanting to celebrate your freedom. Gunnar does have a temper, but I can't see him ever laying a hand on you." I picked up my own find, a black number that plunged low in front, just the way Jerry liked it. "We need to figure out a way to satisfy his urge for revenge against these Brodins without going crazy with it." I swear she'd had a funny look when Gunnar had called his enemy's first name. "Gretchen, you know something you want to share with us?"

"I'd rather we wait to see what Richard finds out on the Internet. I know the Brodins of course. Everyone in Stockholm has heard of them. They are very wealthy." Gretchen pulled out one of her credit cards. "And I can understand why Gunnar's so determined, Glory. They did a terrible thing to him."

"*Mio Dio*, not just terrible. The worst thing I've ever heard done to a man." Flo had a big pile of goodies on the counter already and now added a green dancing dress to it. "To freeze a man with no promise that he'd ever be free . . ." She shuddered. "I would want to hurt someone very badly for that. Wouldn't you?"

"Yes. Of course. But surely those responsible are long dead." I signed my tab. Don't you love hotels where you can just charge it to your room?

"We will see what the Google has to say, am I right?" Flo winked at me. "Who knows? Gretchen, are any of the Brodins, um, like us?" We all thanked the clerk and walked out with our packages.

"That's how I know them. Yes, they are one of the leading *vampyr* families and friends of Stefan's. Björn . . ."

Gretchen gasped and dropped her packages. "*Herregud!* What if the man who put Gunnar in the ice is still . . . in Stockholm?"

"No! If this is true, Gunnar will go absolutely apeshit." I put my arm around her, my stomach sinking. Could it be? After over a thousand years? If this was the same man, he'd be powerful as hell. What chance would Gunnar, a lone Viking, have against him? Just the thought of how this news would change things made me tired and Gretchen . . .

"What do you say we hold off on sharing this theory with the guys?" I knew it was a little unfair, but we'd had the night from hell already. Gretchen was already nodding.

"Are you sure, Glory? This is big news. I'm not sure I can keep it from Ricardo." Flo picked up Gretchen's bags and handed them to her. "Gunnar deserves his revenge. I want him to have it and I'm sure you do too, Gretchen. Why wait?"

"I saw Gunnar going, as Glory says, apeshit once tonight, ready to burn down a building. I'm in no hurry to see it again." Gretchen sighed. "It's a good idea. We should wait and see what the research shows. It might be a family name, passed down. Not the same man at all."

"True. Björn Brodin the tenth, maybe. Why get the men all stirred up when it could be nothing." I patted her shoulder. "You've had a rough few days, Gretchen. You deserve a few hours to relax."

"I do." Gretchen clutched her bags to her chest. "I spent many painful years under Fredrick's thumb. Why should I pretend to mourn now?"

We agreed then headed to our rooms. I was so tempted to tell Jerry that Gunnar's ancient history might be alive. No. This was Gretchen's call. Time enough tomorrow night to figure out if there was going to be a Brodin showdown coming. And just when Jerry thought this honeymoon was back on track.

I'd added a sexy nightie to my purchases in the boutique, the Brodin boutique. At least Jer would have one fantastic night for his honeymoon before the drama and possible bloodshed intervened again. I headed to our room and threw open the door. Jerry was dozing on the king-sized bed, freshly showered and naked. Obviously he was ready to prove how he'd healed from his bullet wound which had completely disappeared.

I laughed and did a slow strip tease as I sauntered toward the bed. By the time I got to him, I knew there was no doubt he had survived his gunshot without any ill effects.

"Merry Christmas, husband." I dropped his gift on his bare stomach.

"What's this? You really did go shopping?" He sat up with a grin. "Can I open it now?"

"Of course, it's Christmas." I sat back, excited to see if he liked it. I never gave him presents because he seemed to have everything. But I'd seen this in that hotel boutique and decided to give it a shot. Now I watched as he ripped off the paper.

"Gloriana, it's perfect." He pulled out the silver money clip. It was shaped like a snowflake. "It will remind me of our honeymoon every time I use it."

"That's the idea." I leaned in to kiss him. "Do you really like it?"

"Love it. Stay there. I have a gift for you." He got up and went into the closet, coming out with a small package too. "Open it. Flo helped me with this one."

"Then I know two things—it will be beautiful and expensive." I laughed then opened the box. "Oh!" I lifted out a gorgeous bracelet. It was vintage, the kind of piece I drooled over when I saw estate jewelry. "Victorian! Diamonds and emeralds. Put it on for me, Jerry." I held out my wrist and he fastened it on me. "I love it!"

"Are you sure? Florence was worried because it was old, but we both know you love old things." Jerry kissed my wrist after he fixed the safety chain. "It looks good on you."

"It's perfect." I laughed. He'd said the same thing. "We are on the same wavelength, aren't we?" I pulled him down for a long kiss. "Our first Christmas as a married couple. It's been strange, but somehow we're making it work. I love you, Jeremiah."

"I love you, Gloriana." He pulled me on top of him. "Let's hope all of our Christmases will be happy ones."

We lost ourselves in each other. Were we supposed to meet our friends later? I couldn't remember. If so, we were late. Did I care? Not when I was on honeymoon time.

THIRTEEN

It was still Christmas and dangerously close to sunrise. Gretchen was probably glad of that. It seemed her room had a king-sized bed and she was trying to avoid a confrontation with Gunnar about lovemaking. So she called me. I wasn't thrilled to have our fun and games in bed interrupted but she had a legitimate excuse. They needed some of our synthetic blood. How could we say no?

"I'm sorry." Gretchen said as soon as I answered the door. "Stefan will arrange a delivery for our room tomorrow night. I should have thought of it sooner."

"You had a lot on your mind. We have plenty. Take some with alcohol. It will be good to relax for the few minutes you have before dawn." I glanced at Gunnar who'd gone straight to Jerry and asked to borrow one of his knives for defense. We'd left his sword locked in the car's trunk. This got the men interested in examining my husband's extensive collection which he pulled out of a suitcase. Now they were busy going over about a dozen knives Jerry laid out on the coffee table.

"Relax. Yes, I will try. But all I can see is that bloody sword and Fredrick's head, rolling across the floor." Gretchen shuddered as she followed me to the mini-fridge.

"I know. But look at him, Gretchen. Even now he is thinking about how to keep you safe." I nodded toward where Gunnar had selected a knife and was testing it on his thumb while Jerry nodded approvingly.

"Of course." Gretchen sighed. "I can't stay mad at him when he was just doing what he knows best." She grabbed my arm when I started to open the refrigerator. "But, Glory, he will want to be together tonight. I am not sure." She looked back at him. "It might feel good to be close to him. But--"

"Wait. See how it goes. He's, um, a good lover?" I knew I was pushing it but I wondered if men from a thousand years ago had bothered with foreplay.

"Surprisingly, yes." Gretchen smiled. "I know what you're thinking. At first he was like a wild stallion, starved for sex." She picked up a shopping bag from the boutique and held it open so I could start filling it. "But all I had to do was show him a few things and--Glory!--he has a natural talent." Her face flushed. "Let's just say he likes women and wants to please us."

"Wants to please *you*, you mean." I patted her back. "I'm glad for you. I guess Fredrick didn't."

"Not in the last few years. I was starved for affection too." Gretchen watched the way the trousers hugged Gunnar's butt while I finished loading the bag with blood. "That's why I didn't hesitate to go with the Viking as soon as I met him. I know you thought I was a slut."

I didn't say anything. We were at our door again and it *had* seemed sluttish of her to just offer herself like she had.

"That should hold you until Gretchen's brother brings you more. We have another delivery scheduled for tomorrow night for ourselves." Jerry threw open the door, obviously eager to get rid of them. "You've got less than an hour till dawn. Better get going."

"I know you want to be alone with your new wife." Gunnar grinned at me. "I see the way you look at her, Jeremiah. Even after what your friends tell me is hundreds of years together."

"Yes, we've been together over four hundred years and the passion is still hot between us. So get out of here, you two." Bottles clinked as I thrust the bag into Gunnar's hands and pushed him toward the door.

"We are going." Gunnar laughed and took Gretchen's hand. "I feel some heat myself. You think it is, how they say, contagious?"

Gretchen looked down at their clasped hands. "Glory put some of the special blood with alcohol in that bag. Let me drink one of those and we'll see." She waved at me as I closed the door and locked it.

"Finally, we are alone." Jerry came up behind me and slid down my zipper.

"About time." I'd thrown on my new dress when Gretchen's call had come. Why not? He'd enjoyed seeing me in it.

"Why do we have everyone we know here along on our honeymoon?"

"Because they love us." I turned in his arms as my dress fell to the floor. I hadn't bothered with a bra since the dress had been cut almost to the waist. My tiny panties were the only thing left for him to remove. I unbuttoned his shirt and slid my hands over his chest, so firm, so wonderfully healed.

"They can love us from the other side of the Atlantic." Jerry threw off his shirt, smiling when I opened his pants and dropped to my knees. "What are you doing, Gloriana?"

"Showing you how glad I am that the wooden bullet didn't kill you. But if you'd rather I didn't . . ." I smiled up at him, my hand sliding inside to find him hard and ready for anything as always.

"Whatever pleases you, my love." He rested his hands on my shoulders, groaning when I pushed his pants down to the floor and began to explore him with my lips. "Witch. You are going to make me beg before the dawn comes, aren't you?"

"Beg for what, Jerry?" I used my tongue to trace the vein in his cock, then pulled him deep into my mouth. Before he could do what he usually did, which was to take charge, I held onto his buttocks. The rhythm I set was just what he liked and he *was* begging before I was done with him. He tried to back away, to take this to the bed, even to lift me up so he could do something for me. But I wouldn't let him. I was the one giving the pleasure for a change. My own could wait. He shuddered as I took him higher and higher.

He wanted to resist, I could feel it. I had to dig my fingers into him when he almost broke free. No. He wasn't going anywhere. Not until he lost control. When he finally called my name, his knees almost buckling, I smiled and took what he had to give. It was my pleasure to do it. His hands stayed in my hair and I could feel them shaking. I'd made him fall to pieces, when it was usually me doing the falling. Maybe it had been a little cruel, but when I sat back on my heels, I didn't think he seemed wounded or even upset. No, he had the look of a man who'd been given a fine time. He held out his hand and pulled me to my feet.

"Thank you, lass."

"Was nothing." I was shaking too. It had taken all of my self-control not to let him yank me up sooner so we could come together. Now I was almost hurting with need.

"To bed." He picked me up and carried me to that wide mattress and laid me gently on top of the sheet. He looked at me for a long moment before he stripped off the scrap of lace that the boutique had called panties. "Beautiful."

"Jerry."

"Hush. I want to love every inch of you."

And he did. Until I cried from the sheer exquisite torture of it. Only when the dawn finally pulled us under did he stop pleasuring me. By then we could only curl up in each other's arms. Together. Without even the strength to pull up a sheet to cover our naked bodies.

We met in Flo and Richard's suite soon after sunset. His text said he had something to show us on his computer.

Gretchen looked tense but Gunnar paced the floor. Clearly their last hour before sunrise had not gone well. She'd obviously refused him when he'd made a move. I tried to get her alone but that was impossible. Ian arrived and the seven of us crowded into the small sitting room.

"First, you promised you would take care of my coins. Are they worth anything?" Gunnar came right to the point. He wore the same clothes we'd purchased in the boutique and looked serious, as if it wouldn't take much to make him lose his temper. "I don't like depending on Gretchen's charity. A man should pay his own way."

"I understand. Luckily they are worth a good deal, Viking." Richard held up one of the coins. "This one alone is valued at about twelve hundred American dollars. It's twenty-four karat gold which makes it costly in itself, but to a coin collector, the era and place it is from make it worth even more."

"He has dozens of such coins! Good." Gretchen moved closer to him. "Don't speak of charity again, Gunnar. You did me a service when you killed Fredrick. Taking care of a few expenses for you is the least I can do."

"I am not a mercenary you hired to defend you, Gretchen." Gunnar glared at her. "What I did was out of love. I wish you would believe that."

Gretchen looked away, her eyes full. "It is too soon to speak of love but I am grateful. I'm sorry if I hurt your pride." She faced him again. "At least now you can pay your own way."

"I may have more if these Brodins are the same as the ones who wronged me. Richard says I might be able to claim restitution for the damage done to me." Gunnar looked around the room. "Isn't that what you called it, Richard?"

"If we can prove this family is the same and that their Bjorn Brodin is the one who left you to die all those years ago, I think you might have a case." Richard tapped on his laptop's keyboard. "I've been working on a timeline for the Brodin family tree and their rise in the world."

"They rose from the ashes of my village and gained success by trampling the bodies of my family. What of Bjorn Brodin? Tell me of him and how he went on after I disappeared." Gunnar walked over to stand behind Richard. He studied the laptop screen but clearly the text there meant nothing to him. "What is this you are showing me?"

"Gunnar, be patient." I tried to steer him to a seat. "We all want to hear what Richard has to say." I glanced at Gretchen. She needed to come clean. "Gretchen knows the family. She might be able to add something to this."

"You kept this from me!" So much for Gunnar sitting. He jumped up and approached Gretchen. "You know them? How? Are they *vampyr*? Tell me!"

"Not while you are screaming at me." Gretchen pulled up a chair and sat down herself. "Calm down. I mean it."

"Calm? You're mad! If they are *vampyr* then that means the man who put me in the ice could still be alive. Is he, Gretchen?" Gunnar's sword was still locked in the car trunk but he was obviously wishing for it now. Thank God he didn't pull out Jerry's knife. "*Helvete!* I must know if there is a Bjorn Brodin at the head of this family now and if he is the same man I knew."

Richard looked grim. "According to my research, there is. But it seems unlikely that this is the same Bjorn Brodin, Gunnar. It's probably a family name, passed down from generation to generation."

"Exactly." Gretchen couldn't stay seated either and followed Gunnar as he paced the room. "I've met Bjorn Brodin, Gunnar. He's handsome, in his thirties. He is sophisticated and charming and has many friends. He has a beautiful wife and entertains lavishly in a home that makes Fredrick's castle look like a hovel. Does that describe the monster who put you in the ice? Does it, Gunnar?" Gretchen grabbed his arm and forced him to look at her.

"Please stop and answer me."

"Handsome? How would I know that? He was a man. Big, tall like me, with the kind of wild beard and hair we all had at the time. He had no friends, everyone feared him." Gunnar glanced at me. "Tell her what I looked like when I came out of the cave, Glory. You were scared of me, *ja*?"

"It's true. You wouldn't have known him, Gretchen." I studied the Gunnar we all saw now. He *was* handsome but the wild man who'd rolled in the snow naked had been so unkempt with his tangled hair and beard that I would never have called him good-looking.

"How many Bjorn Brodins are on your list, Mainwaring?" Ian peered over his shoulder.

"I count at least half a dozen. But we know it's possible they are all the same man. With vampires we tend to disappear and reappear years later, pretending to be our own son or grandson." Richard was typing again. "He could have changed of course. You say he has a beautiful wife." Richard smiled at Flo. "We know that can make a man change his ways."

"I want to see this man. Look him in the eye." Gunnar practically growled it. "Can you take us there, Gretchen?"

"I've got an address here, Gretchen, if you're reluctant to take us there." Richard looked sympathetic.

Gunnar stalked to the door. "We go now."

"Wait a minute." Jerry was suddenly beside him. "What if it *is* your old enemy? You can't just show up unprepared. He would kill you on the spot to cover his crime centuries ago."

"He would try anyway. I am not in my death sleep now, am I?" Gunnar puffed out his chest. "He used the coward's way before. This time I face him, man to man."

"He'll have guards if he's smart." Ian frowned at the information Richard was pulling up on his screen. "He's very successful. A man like that won't let just anyone, a stranger, into his house either. Vampires always have to be careful."

"Yes, the family is security minded. We all are. Bjorn

would let *me* in though. I told you I know the family."
Gretchen stayed next to Gunnar.

"You would take us there? You would do that for me?"
Gunnar relaxed his fists enough to reach for Gretchen and
pull her to him.

She touched his cheek. "I pray this Bjorn is not the
same man who hurt you. But you killed Fredrick for me,
Gunnar. The least I can do is help you see if your enemy is
still alive. So you can get the revenge you deserve."

"This could be dangerous. If he is Bjorn, he will attack
as soon as he recognizes me." He scanned the room. "I'll
need more men with me. Can I count on you, Jeremiah?"

"I'm in. Richard? MacDonald?" Jerry frowned. "And
Gloriana won't be left behind I'm afraid."

I'd sent him a mental message and he didn't dare
pretend he hadn't received it or risk ruining his honeymoon.

"Wouldn't miss it." Ian straightened. "Can we use the
Eliminator, Glory?"

"No!" I was keeping the little piece that made it work
safe for now. "You have guns and wooden bullets, I saw you
pick them up. That should be advantage enough."

"True." Richard slammed the laptop closed. "Florence
is making my ears ring with her silent demands so I guess
we're all going. Gretchen, do you need to call to make an
appointment with Bjorn?"

"I'll call Elsa, his wife. We are fairly close. I'll tell her I
have friends and my cousin here from America. I want her
to meet you. That the men would like to meet her husband
as well. It is not unusual for vampires from other countries
to want to network and make alliances when they travel."
Gretchen pulled out her burner phone.

"That's true." Ian smiled at her. "I do it all the time.
Seek out successful vampire businessmen in other countries
and make a connection. You never know when it will come
in handy. Like for a source for synthetic blood." He turned
to Jerry. "Not all of us just pull a mortal into an alley when
we thirst."

"Ian, he's doing better." I could see Jerry's temper rising and I slipped my arm around his waist.

"Don't make excuses for me, Gloriana. I smelled fresh blood on Ian last night. I'm not the only one who likes the taste of a mortal now and then." Jerry was tense where I touched him.

"No one had stocked my room with synthetic." Ian shrugged. "What was I to do?"

"We'll send you some later tonight." I knew he was trying to goad Jerry and I sent Ian a mental warning to back off.

Gretchen pursed her lips. "I hate this cheap phone. I am lost without my own cell. Richard, do you have a phone number in the computer for the Brodins? I hope we can arrange something for later tonight. I'll tell her I'm leaving for America with all of you soon because I need to get away. That Fredrick's death has left me upset and in need of a change." Gretchen punched in numbers as Richard read them to her. "I might as well use sympathy for something good."

We all waited while she made the call. Someone answered and she had an extended conversation in Swedish. Jerry whispered that she was being offered condolences of course. Gretchen pretended to be broken up for a few minutes then you could see on her face that she had changed the subject. It took a little time but soon she was smiling and saying *"Tack."* before hanging up.

"It's all set. Elsa was very gracious. She and Bjorn will be there tonight at midnight and have offered to have us for tea." Gretchen ignored Gunnar's growl. "Vampires in Sweden enjoy entertaining. They import delicacies, things we seem to have no trouble eating. And there will be fine synthetic blood, of course. Elsa is a wonderful hostess."

"I'm sure she is. Look at how beautiful the things were in that store window and in the boutique." Flo was obviously looking forward to it. "Now, Gunnar, you need to calm down and make a plan. How can you prove that it was Bjorn who put you in the ice? Were there any witnesses?"

"Of course there were. His men had to have been with him. There is no way he could have handled it alone. But surely they are all dead. And would not dare have told anyone the truth of that night and risked losing their heads for it." Gunnar collapsed in a chair. "It is to be my word against, how many Brodins, Richard?"

"Looks like the family has grown very large over the years, Gunnar. There are branches in all the major cities where they have stores. I'd say there must be at least one hundred Brodins now. They must do like the Campbells and MacDonalds and have children before they are turned vampire." Richard got up and opened a box he pulled out of a closet. "We should probably arm ourselves in case this comes to a battle. I went back and took these out of the car last night. Valet parking. Never did trust that. Not with weapons anyway." He handed out machine guns, those he must have taken from Fredrick's men, to Jerry and Ian. He also took one for himself. He stared at Gunnar then obviously decided he couldn't give him one without teaching him how to use it. He did pull out the sword which Gunnar took gratefully.

"Now I feel ready to do battle properly." The Viking examined the blade then grabbed a towel and wiped it down.

"Where's mine, Ricardo?" Flo held out her hand. "I think I proved I know how to handle one."

"Darling, you scared the life out of me with your 'handling' of the machine gun." Richard smiled but reluctantly gave her one. "Do you even know where the safety is on this?"

"Why should I need to know that? A machine gun does not need to be safe." She examined it. "Is it loaded?"

"Yes, unfortunately." He handed each of them extra clips. "I don't know how we will explain carrying arms into a tea party."

"We'll put them into bags. Say we're bringing gifts from America." I glanced at Flo. "We saw those canvas duffle bags in the boutique that would work perfectly. The men can carry them in. If this meeting goes south, we can pull them out and go from there."

"I don't like it. We might not have time to pull out anything if this meeting goes--what you say?--South? I guess you mean if the Brodins try to kill me again." Gunnar studied a pistol and decided it would suit him. He stuck it under his shirt at his waist the way he saw Jerry do his. "I guess you expect me to put my sword in there too. No man would allow me past his door if I showed up with that strapped to my back."

"You're right, Gunnar. Storming in there, guns drawn, isn't the smart play. What if these people are innocent? We'd have dead bodies before we gave anyone a chance to explain. That's not going to happen. I don't care what wrong was done to you a thousand years ago." I wanted this clear to everyone in the room. I wasn't carrying a weapon. I didn't need one. I could freeze anyone who tried to hurt my guys and gals and was counting on being able to do that before the first shot was fired. Unless...

"Gretchen, did any of the Brodins buy anti-vampire stuff from Fredrick?" I was thinking about those glasses that kept people from being mesmerized. Hated those things.

"I never heard him mention it. Can't imagine why they would. They haven't made enemies that I know of." Gretchen stalked over to pick out a gun. "I'm a good shot. I'll put one of these in my purse. The bag I bought last night is big enough to hold this." She frowned. "Wooden bullets. I hate these things. Whatever we do, we can't let another vampire get hold of our guns and turn them against us."

"Good point, Gretchen." I glanced at the clock. "I suppose we'd better take the car to the Brodins' place since we've got all this fire power. Flo and I will go buy a couple of those duffle bags then meet you where we did the last time we headed out. Leave the machine guns and sword here and we'll load them in the bags and bring them out with us. Okay?"

"Sounds like a plan." Jerry kissed my cheek then he and the guys took off to get the car. Gretchen stayed behind with us.

"Buying bags for machine guns from the Brodins' own boutique seems wrong somehow." She followed Flo and me down the hallway.

"If all goes well then they'll make the profit on the bags and nobody will get hurt." I pushed open the glass door. "I'd say the likelihood that this is the same Bjorn Brodin is slim and none. The problem is going to be getting Gunnar to accept that he probably won't get a dime from any of them. Why should he?"

"I tell you, Glory." Flo was distracted by a purse display before she finally grabbed the correct bags. "If someone came to me years later and said I owed them for what some ancestor did a thousand years ago, I'd say get lost."

"Exactly." I stepped aside when Gretchen insisted on paying for the bags. She said Gunnar had asked her to do it. That he would pay her back. His problem, his expense. We didn't argue.

"So we're all humoring him. Is that it?" Gretchen let her worry show for once.

"Afraid so." I unzipped the bags when we got to Flo's room. I was sorely tempted to throw something else heavy into them and leave the machine guns there. But I didn't dare. If we got a bad reception and the men needed to protect themselves, I'd never forgive myself if I'd left them defenseless. Besides, Flo was really looking forward to being a bad ass with the machine gun again.

"I pray these will stay in the bags," Gretchen said as she hefted one and started for the car.

"You and me both." I had one and Flo the other. Richard popped the trunk and Gunnar got out to load the bags inside.

"These are heavy. You should have called for help." He patted Gretchen's shoulder. "Thank you all for doing this. I know you did not need to get involved."

"No, we didn't. So promise you won't go crazy when we get there." I took his arm and escorted him to the car. "Stay calm and let's see where this goes."

"I will try, Glory." Gunnar stepped aside so Gretchen could slide in. "Gretchen is doing the talking at first. They are her friends. But talk will stop if I see this Bjorn and recognize him. If he is the one . . ." Gunnar swallowed. "You will need to stand back, that's all I'm saying."

FOURTEEN

The Brodin home was a palace. Not an ice palace this time but one made of stone and surrounded by a forest. The gate had an electronic entry and a guard house. Gretchen gave the man there our names and he checked it against a list. We waited while the beautiful wrought iron creaked open before we sped up a winding road. A butler stood waiting in front of double doors on top of the stone steps. He looked a little surprised when Richard popped the trunk and three of the men each grabbed a duffle bag to carry inside.

Gretchen made light of it. "Hostess gifts. Don't be alarmed, Dalmar, we're not planning to stay the night." She laughed and led us into the massive entryway.

"Welcome, Madame. May I extend my condolences on your loss." Dalmar bowed to her. "The master and mistress are waiting in the blue salon. If you will follow me." He started up the wide staircase, the doors behind us were closed by one of a pair of men in black.

"Bodyguards." Jerry whispered. "I wonder why."

"*I'm* wondering what other colors of salons they have." I held onto him as we walked up the black marble steps. The place was beautiful but a little cold. There were ancient tapestries on the walls but no rugs on the floors. The butler turned left at the landing but we could have taken even more stairs. Clearly there were at least three or four stories to this place.

"Salons? A yellow and a red one." Gretchen turned to Jerry. "If I weren't with you, I'm sure our bags would have been searched." She smiled at the butler. "As you can see, the Brodins are very wealthy and guard their home carefully. It is wise of them to do so, isn't it, Dalmar?"

"Yes, indeed, Madame." The butler stopped at double doors painted with gold leaf trim and carefully opened them. "Mrs. Marken and her guests are here." He bowed and pointed us to a setting worthy of a painting.

Blue salon indeed. Here there was a rug, deep blue with a red pattern in it. The walls were wall papered in a shiny fabric that featured blue birds flying across pale blue skies. The silk sofas were done in the pale blue and the chairs were covered in a various shades of blue from navy velvet to a pale blue brocade. A fireplace kept the room warm with its roaring fire. The marble mantle was white with blue veins running through it. Overwhelming but somehow gorgeous. My antique loving soul shouted "Expensive!"

"Gretchen! *Jag är ledsen om Fredrick!*" A beautiful blond woman dressed in an obviously expensive black dress rushed forward and pulled Gretchen into a hug.

"Please, only a few of my guests speak Swedish. Could we use English please?" Gretchen wiped away a tear. "She said she was sorry about Fredrick." Then she glanced over her shoulder at Gunnar who had stopped near the door.

We all held our breaths waiting for a sign from the Viking. What now? Should we grab our guns? Sit quietly and pretend to drink blood like civilized vampires? Try to figure out how to bring up happenings from a thousand years ago? Gunnar didn't say or do anything as the man walked forward from in front of the fireplace and kissed Gretchen on both cheeks.

"Of course. English. Sorry if Elsa was rude just now. We were shocked to hear of Fredrick's death." He held out his hand. "Bjorn Brodin. Gretchen, would you introduce your guests?"

"Yes, of course." Gretchen pulled Jerry forward. I was attached to him, afraid to let go of his hand. "This is my cousin, Jeremiah Campbell. Though he's going by Jeremy Blade this decade. And his wife Gloriana."

"A pleasure." The men shook hands. "My wife, Elsa. I'd already heard you were here." Bjorn smiled. "Our *vampyr* community loves gossip, I'm afraid. You are on your honeymoon?"

"Yes, we are." Jerry gestured toward Richard and Flo. He introduced them then Ian.

"It seems this honeymoon has turned into a party." Bjorn stared at Gunnar. "And who is this?"

Gunnar signaled to the other men and they suddenly grabbed and unzipped the duffle bags then pulled out their machine guns. He crossed his own arms over his chest as Bjorn tucked Elsa behind a wing-backed chair.

"What is this, a robbery? Gretchen, who have you brought to my home?" He started toward a bell rope hanging next to the fireplace. Ian moved in front of it before Bjorn reached it.

"No, it's not a robbery." Gretchen pulled Elsa, who'd picked up a cell phone, next to her, and grabbed the phone, shoving it into her pocket. She dropped her purse and suddenly had her own gun in her hand. She pointed it at Elsa's heart. "I'm sorry for this but I brought a man who thinks he knows you."

"And that calls for holding me and my wife at gunpoint?" Every other gun *was* aimed at Bjorn.

"Yes, it does. Don't call for help if you want your wife to live. You may die no matter what you do." Gunnar walked forward until he was inches from Bjorn. He had his own gun in his hand. "We have wooden bullets."

"Of course you do." Bjorn's hand dropped to his side.

"Gretchen, I heard Fredrick sold to vampire hunters. I can't say I'm sorry he's dead. But what is this? I had hoped you were his victim, not part of his filthy trade." He wasn't letting his fear show and I admired him for that. He was tall, well-built and had the typical Viking look. In fact, facing Gunnar, he was a match for him in size at least. Gunnar had the advantage in the hatred coming off of him in waves.

"No, I was never a part of Fredrick's dirty business." Gretchen wasn't about to let Elsa go but I could see she hated what she was doing. "Just listen to what this man has to say, Bjorn. Then you will understand why we are here."

"It seems there have been many Bjorn Brodins. When were *you* made vampire?" Gunnar jabbed the gun into Bjorn's stomach.

"Back up, Gunnar. He can take the gun if you do foolish things like that." Jerry knew Gunnar was an amateur when it came to guns. "Of course that would endanger his wife." This was a warning to Brodin.

"Even I know that much." Flo had her own machine gun in hand and waved it around. "I would hate to shoot up this beautiful room. I've never seen so much Fortuni silk in one place." She smiled at Elsa. "You have exquisite taste."

"Enough! Explain yourself." Bjorn didn't grab the gun but I could see he was thinking about making some kind of defensive move.

I stepped up to him. "There is nothing this man would like more than to kill you where you stand. I have the power to freeze you in place so you can't move. Listen to this man and answer his questions or I will paralyze you and you'll be helpless. Must I do that?"

"No, I will listen. Answer any questions. But I don't understand why you are here. Money? I can open my safe. But it's in my office." Bjorn nodded toward the hall door.

"Money is not the first thing on our agenda." I turned to Gunnar. "Tell him your name."

"I am Gunnar. Gunnar Ellstrom." He looked around the beautiful room then straight into Bjorn's eyes. "Does that name mean anything to you?"

Bjorn closed his eyes and his lips moved. In silent prayer?

"Answer him!" I didn't know if it was fear or recognition that made Bjorn stagger over to sink into a chair.

"It cannot be. Gunnar Ellstrom died over a thousand years ago."

"How do you know that?" Gunnar grabbed him by his designer sweater and hauled him to his feet again. "Is it because you led a party of men to find him while he was in his death sleep to bury him in the ice? Is it because you hoped he would melt some bright sunny day and be burned to death? Is that why you think I am dead?"

"I was told it was true." Bjorn didn't fight when he was flung to the floor. "You were vampire. Hated for what you were. It seemed a fitting end for you. Or at least that's what I was told."

"Told. So you are not the Bjorn Brodin who left me for dead over a thousand years ago?" Gunnar stood over him. He tossed the hand gun aside and walked over to the duffle bag that held his sword. "Am I just supposed to take your word for that?" He ignored Elsa's cries. Gretchen held her back when she would have rushed to her husband's side. Gunnar pressed the blade against Bjorn's neck. "The word of a Brodin?"

"I am not a Brodin." The man on the floor didn't bother to defend himself. "Kill me if you think it will right the wrongs done to you, but you might come to regret it." Blood welled as the sword bit into his neck.

"And why would I regret that?" Gunnar stared down at the man. "Not a Brodin. What does that mean? You call yourself Bjorn Brodin to the world. You live in this fancy place, own stores with your name in gold over the door. Are you telling me you are an imposter?"

I held my breath. None of us moved. The machine guns were pointed at the floor. No way could anyone take a shot without hitting Gunnar.

"I was adopted as a young man. Forced by Bjorn to take his name. I didn't want to do it. But it was the only way I could seek revenge for what he did to my father." Tears filled his eyes and ran down his pale cheeks. "You should kill me, *Pappa,* for being so weak that I would betray our name and our heritage."

"What did you call me?" Gunnar's sword shook and I was afraid he would do even more damage to the man, perhaps by accident.

"*Pappa.*" He pushed the sword aside and dipped a finger into the blood at his throat. "The scent of my blood should tell you it is the truth. I am your son, Edvard."

Gunnar inhaled then leaped back. "No! It cannot be. I saw them burn my village, take away my wife and children. I was one man, without a chance to stop them. So I watched and knew I would have to wait to get them back and take my revenge. But I never had a chance. Because I was taken while in my death sleep."

"You don't know me. Of course you wouldn't." The man put his face in his hands. "I *was* a child. Some things I had to do to survive were shameful. Some I regret. The worst was that the *jäkel* stole my name from me." He looked up, his eyes bleak. "Can you ever forgive me?"

"Stop it, Edvard." His wife wrenched away from Gretchen and fell to the floor beside him. "What are you saying? Surely you can't believe this man is who he says he is. What proof does he have?"

"We found him in an ice cave." I'd moved back to Jerry's side. The men still held their weapons but Flo had put hers away. That was a relief. No one in the room wanted my pal's finger on that trigger. "He looked like a wild Viking and had clearly been there for over a thousand years. An ice-quake freed him. It was a lucky thing that we happened to be there that night with blood to offer him."

Edvard raised his head and tears streaked his cheeks. "I believe you. It is a miracle that you survived."

"Your wife called you Edvard." Gunnar had gone very

pale. "She knows?"

"Elsa and my sisters are the only ones who know it is my birth name." He gripped his wife's hand. "It was wrong. I should have died before I accepted the Brodin name."

"No!" Elsa threw her arms around her husband. "He had no choice. Bjorn said you must be dead. Edvard looked for you, Gunnar, so many times. In the ice caves."

"Gunnar, if this man is your son, then what does that mean?" I had a feeling I knew. "What happened to the Bjorn who put you in the ice?"

"Answer her!" Gunnar staggered over to a chair and rested his sword across his knees. He looked confused, like he couldn't figure out what was happening. Ever since he'd fallen out of the ice, he'd had one driving need, to find Bjorn Brodin or his heirs and get his revenge. Now what? Gretchen ran to stand beside him and pressed her hand to his shoulder.

Edvard got up and went to stand in front of Gunnar. "The night he burned our village I saw him take my mother and sisters. I followed him. I was just a small boy and he thought I was unimportant so he let me live." Edvard looked at the rest of us. "Bjorn wanted what my father had. He was jealous. He wanted my mother for his concubine and took her."

Gunnar groaned. "I knew it. Ursula was a beauty."

"He made the rest of us into slaves. But as I grew he came to see that I would be a decent warrior, like you *Pappa*. And no matter how he tried, Bjorn never had a son of his own grow to manhood." He sank down on the blue sofa, his wife beside him. He looked around and noticed that all of us were still standing. "Please, all of you sit. I am not being a good host."

"Don't bother with that. We want to hear this story." Flo found a seat on a needlepointed footstool. "What happened to your mother? And when did you become vampire?"

"Mother?" He glanced at Gretchen who was holding

Gunnar's hand. "She is well. I finally persuaded her to become vampire when she learned it would keep her from having more of Bjorn's brats." Edvard sighed. "She will not believe this news, *Pappa*."

"By Thor's hammer, Ursula still in this world." Gunnar looked up at Gretchen. "It does not change what you mean to me, *älskling*."

That raised Elsa's eyebrows. Oh, yeah, Gretchen had only been a widow for a day and a night. Hmm.

"*Mamma* gave Bjorn many daughters but no sons, much to his disgust. The king liked *Ma* and stepped in to make sure she was taken care of and given her own home when Bjorn tried to set her aside."

"That is good." Gunnar kept staring at Edvard. "It is true? You are my son?"

"Yes, *Pappa*." He sat up straight, shoulders back. "Bjorn finally realized that becoming vampire would give him immortality. He took me with him to the land where we heard you had been turned and we both became *vampyr*. He was older by this time, a tyrant still and head of the family. I bided my time, determined to see him in hell. And now I had forever to plan." Edvard got up and paced in front of the fire.

I could see now how much he resembled Gunnar. His blond hair was close cropped but the broad shoulders, sharp features and blue eyes were the same. There was no reason to doubt his story and I hoped the Viking was ready to accept it. Even his stride looked similar as he stopped in front of the fire and cleared his throat.

"I knew Bjorn was suspicious of me. He caught me going out to the ice fields where I thought he'd buried you. As Elsa said, I searched for your body every chance I got." Edvard stalked over to his father. "I wanted to kill him every day that went by. But he threatened my sisters. He told his warriors that if he died by my hand that they were to slaughter them and all their children at once." His fangs slid down. "You see what a bastard he was."

"Oh, yes. He was without a conscience." Gunnar got up and stared long and hard into Edvard's eyes. "Tell me. Tell me how you avenged the wrongs done to me."

"I gradually made sure that each of my sisters was well protected by men of my choosing. This took years. All of them married well and had children of their own." Edvard smiled at Elsa. "I don't know if you realize it, but you have many fine grandchildren and great-grandchildren. As time went on, some of them chose to become *vampyr* as well. We have prospered."

"Yes, yes!" Gunnar clearly didn't care about that. "Go on, boy."

"I had men in place that I could trust. I made sure we all were ready when I asked for an audience with Bjorn. Before this, he had decided I must take his name. The shame of it." Edvard pressed his fingers to his eyes. "But I had no choice. Now it is too late to turn back. I hope you understand, *Pappa*."

"Yes. We must survive any way we can. Especially if it was part of a plan to get your revenge. You were wise to lull him into a false sense of security. I'm sure once you took his name he thought he could trust you." Gunnar glanced at Gretchen. "And sometimes we do things for love that we might not do otherwise."

"Ah, you do understand. *Tack, Pappa.*" Edvard suddenly grabbed Gunnar and gave him a hug. The men stood there for a moment then pounded each other on the back before stepping apart.

"Are you going to finish this tale or will the sun rise before you are done." Gunnar's voice was hoarse, as if he was close to shedding tears.

Edvard laughed. "It is something Elsa tasks me with constantly. I cannot seem to get my stories out quickly."

"Then come on, boy." Gunnar looked around the room. The men still held their machine guns. "I think you can all put away your weapons. Jeremiah? Will you take my sword for me?" He handed it to Jerry.

"Of course." Jerry smiled. "Sorry that we came in ready to blow you to hell, but we had no idea what we were going to be facing. If it had been the original Bjorn, you know Gunnar would be carrying his head in a sack by now."

"I should hope so." Edvard slapped his father on the back.

Gunnar nodded when the guns were all safely out of sight in the duffle bags.

"We must call for refreshments." Elsa waved an elegant hand when Gunnar protested. "Please, it is important to be civilized and I had ordered some special cakes for us all and premium synthetics. Now I think we have cause for a celebration. Father and son reunited. Do you all agree?"

We murmured the polite thing. Besides, a chance to enjoy cake and blood? No one was going to turn that down. We waited while she pulled the bell rope and ordered Dalmar to serve tea at once. Gunnar paced the floor until the butler and a pretty housemaid had set up the trays then left us to our refreshments.

"At last." Gunnar took a goblet of blood then settled on a sofa. "Tell us the rest, son."

Edvard beamed at hearing the word. "Certainly. Where was I? Oh. So the men were in place to protect my sisters and their families, my own family as well, and I was now called Bjorn Brodin. We were meeting to talk about the stores we had begun building in the capitals in Scandinavia. The old Bjorn had no imagination. He would not change what we offered and the business was suffering. I asked to speak to him alone. He thought it was about new products. He agreed to hear me out because he was convinced he could bully me like he always had." Edvard smiled. "But I was not the timid boy he'd taken as a slave hundreds of years before. The hatred inside me gave me courage. And I'd carefully replaced his guards over time with men loyal to me."

"Wise of you." Gunnar looked around the room. "He is a fine boy, isn't he, Jeremiah? Richard? Ian?"

"Yes, and I can see the resemblance." Ian spoke up. "There's no denying you two are kin. Of course I would be glad to run a DNA test if you would like. Just to be sure."

"What is that?" Gunnar looked to Gretchen as usual.

"It is a special test, to see if your blood matches." She had settled on the sofa beside him, apparently not embarrassed to let the Brodins see their relationship was more than casual.

"Pah, we need no test. I can smell the scent of an Ellstrom on him. He was right about that." Gunnar took a sip from his crystal goblet. "It is a fine drink, Elsa. You have made my son a good wife, I think."

"Thank you, Gunnar. I see the resemblance between the two of you too." Elsa smiled. "Go on, Edvard, you are getting to the best part."

"Yes. I took what Bjorn thought was the new product into the room. It was a spear. Supposedly a toy for children that we would sell at the Christmas season."

"A wooden spear?" Gunnar slapped his knee. "Did the fool not see the danger?"

"He thought himself invincible." Edvard smiled. "I walked right up to him and told him how this would be a fine piece to add to our inventory. He laughed of course and said what use was a spear without a metal tip?"

"And did you show him?" Gunnar was grinning now.

"I certainly did. I held it in front of me and said, 'Sir, it's the perfect weapon for killing a bastard vampire.'" He laughed. "I thought about shoving it into his *jävla* heart right away but then I decided that would be too easy a death."

"Edvard, there are ladies present!" Elsa tried to look stern. "But I am still proud of you. The family has prospered ever since with you at the head of it."

"Wait. You didn't kill him?" Gunnar leaned forward.

"You wanted to torture him of course. It would be no fun for him to die in an instant." Flo had selected a second chocolate cake. "You must tell me where you get these, Elsa. They are delicious."

"My bloodthirsty darling." Richard smiled. "Is she right? Was that what you had in mind, Brodin?"

Gunnar winced at the name. "I hate to hear him called that."

"You must get used to it. We have a prosperous business and large family that use that name. Forget who made us carry it in the first place. We have taken what once stood for a bastard who had no decency and made it into an honorable and distinguished brand that we are proud to claim." Elsa sat next to her husband on one of the sofas and leaned against him. "Now tell them what you did to Bjorn, darling."

"Ah. The fate of that bastard." Edvard got up and walked over to stand in front of the fireplace again. He was restless, as if the telling of the tale had made him relive it. "I had arranged for the guards to come into Bjorn's office and back me up. We surrounded him and chained him so he could not get loose. I had picked out an ice cave high in a mountain where it would be unlikely anyone would find him. My men dug a trench and filled it with water." He paced the room. "It was a very cold winter and the water was already freezing when we dropped him into the trench and piled snow on top of him. He was buried in the ice just as you were, *Pappa*."

"Odin be praised! It is the perfect way to avenge the wrong he did to me." Gunnar jumped to his feet. "You are sure he did not escape?"

"I am sure. I put two trusted shifters on guard during the day. And for weeks after that. I even had men checking once the spring thaw was upon us. But the high mountain never thawed. He was truly buried and is still there to this day." Edvard looked around the room. "You are welcome to check if you don't trust me. I can take you there. I still go at least three times a year. I probe the ice. I can tell if he is there by what the spear hits."

"Hah! I would like to send a spear into him." Gunnar nodded. "We will go see him. I want to end this. Once and for all. If I can escape the ice, so can he. You understand me?"

"Yes. It is a worry now that I see you looking so fit and able to fight." Edvard gestured toward the duffle bags. "You brought machine guns with wooden bullets into my home." He suddenly looked like the formidable warrior he must have once been. "I have guards posted because vampires must be careful. This has reminded me that I should have them search the luggage and bags brought inside from now on." He nodded toward Gretchen. "No matter who accompanies the visitors."

"Yes, you should." Gunnar smiled. "I'm glad we didn't have to kill any of your guards to see you tonight."

"So am I." Edvard's hands were fisted. "Thank God you didn't shoot first and talk later. What a mistake that would have been."

"It's true that we could have." Gunnar looked around the room and picked up an iced cake. "You live very well. And it all started because Bjorn burned down my village and took what was mine."

"Are you thinking this now belongs to you?" Edvard took a step toward his father. "I admit you might have a claim for something. But it was my hard work that made us so successful."

"Oh, yes, I can understand that." Gunnar waved his son back. "Relax. I would not wish to beggar you or start a family quarrel." He took a bite of cake and chewed thoughtfully. "I suppose I should speak to Ursula. I wonder if she considers herself still my wife. It is not an idea I would welcome." He gazed at Gretchen as she got up and walked over to sit in a chair by herself. "Is she living with a man now?"

"Mother swore off men after Bjorn tossed her aside." Edvard studied Gretchen. "I doubt anyone would expect my parents to resume their marriage after a thousand years." He had a solemn look. "But we will see. I can send for her. She lives with us and is upstairs in her suite now. It will take but a few minutes for her to come down here."

"Now?" Gunnar looked as if his son had suggested he face a pack of wolves.

"Why put it off?" Edvard pulled the bell rope.

Flo helped herself to a third cake. "This should be good."

FIFTEEN

The strawberry cake I'd gobbled down sat like a stone in my stomach while Elsa called for the butler and told him to ask Ursula to join us for tea. Gunnar's wife had probably hoped to be asked to meet the strangers from America. Any excitement in an immortal's life was always welcomed. Well, as long as it wasn't a matter of life and death.

"Gunnar, I'm interested in how you met Gretchen. Her cousin finds you in the ice, *ja?*" Elsa sat back, her eyes darting from Gunnar to Gretchen. "But then Fredrick dies so soon afterwards. It is, um, a coincidence perhaps?"

"I killed the bastard." Gunnar wasn't about to let anyone else take credit, even though Gretchen's brother had manufactured a story about vampire hunters and spread it among the Stockholm vampires. He held up a hand when Gretchen made a sound. "Edvard and Elsa are my family. Surely we can tell them the truth." He didn't wait for her permission before he shared the entire story, including Gretchen's abuse at Fredrick's hands.

"By God, I'm shocked and so sorry this happened to you, Gretchen." Edvard, who told his father that he must get used to calling him Bjorn, walked over to take Gretchen's hand. "I wish you had come to us for help. We had our suspicions that he was working with vampire hunters, but could never prove anything." He pulled her to her feet. "I can see how he would use your family as leverage to keep you silent. But he couldn't threaten every vampire in Stockholm, could he?"

"No, you are right. But I never thought . . ." She shook her head. "I felt so alone." She smiled and kissed his cheek. "Thank you. You and Elsa have always been good friends to me, Bjorn. Unfortunately, I was too terrified to think straight. Then I met Gunnar and he wouldn't let me go back home without him. He and Jeremiah, along with Glory, were determined to help me." She turned and held out her hand to Gunnar who jumped up and took it, grinning with relief. "I don't know what would have happened if they hadn't come along."

"What is this?" The woman's voice rang through the room with such command that we all leaped to our feet. "Am I having a waking nightmare or is that Gunnar Ellstrom standing in this salon, holding hands with one of his whores?"

"Madame, mind your tongue!" Gunnar dropped Gretchen's hand and faced the doorway and the woman standing there.

"You were dead, we were told." She looked him over. "I see we were misinformed, more's the pity."

I gaped at her. Ursula Ellstrom was a beauty, even though she must have been past forty when she was turned vampire. She had dark gold hair with a streak of white that ran from her widow's peak like an exclamation point. She had obviously borne many children easily from her ample hips, but they were balanced by generous breasts. She knew how to dress to make the most of her figure and looked voluptuous, not fat, in a navy blue sweater and matching wool pants. Her high heels made her a little taller than me but not by much. When she walked toward Gunnar, her hips swayed with a natural rhythm that had every man in the room watching except for her son. He was busy getting between his mother and father.

"*Mamma*, it is a miracle, isn't it?" Edvard kept his hand on his father's shoulder. "He has been out of the ice for only a few days."

"Out of the ice? Really? Not wandering the world picking up women and finding his bastards?" Ursula turned and stared at Ian. "I see you brought one with you. Really, Gunnar, was that necessary?"

"What the hell?" Ian looked as if someone had poked him with a sharpened stake. "I'm no bastard of this Viking."

Ursula laughed, a peal of bitterness that made me shiver. "Don't bother to deny it. I've seen many of them and you have the look. Scottish by your accent. Gunnar spent many a winter there sowing his seed before he was turned *vampyr*. Didn't you, husband?"

"Let it go, Ursula. I admit I pleased myself when I was on long trips there for the king. A man finds warmth when he has a chance and the women were welcoming." Gunnar eyed Ian. "MacDonald. Do you have a kinswoman named Fiona?"

Ian flinched, his hand going to his waist where I was pretty sure he had a gun tucked under his shirt at his waist. "My grandmother. Say her name again with your last breath." Ian's fangs slid down, his gun came out and he aimed it at Gunnar.

"As I recall the name was fairly common in the Highlands." Gunnar stared at the gun which he knew was loaded with wooden bullets. "Calm down. I'm not claiming you. Though I remember her as a charming widow."

Ian's finger flexed on the trigger and we all stayed frozen in place, afraid to interfere. "I won't listen to this slander another minute. Especially in this company." He stalked over to the door. "I'm shifting back to the hotel."

"Maybe you should take blood samples before you leave, MacDonald. For DNA tests?" Jerry kept a straight face but I could tell he was enjoying this way too much. I pinched him.

"Shut the hell up, Campbell." Ian waved the gun around then slammed out of the room.

"He has your temper, I see." Ursula turned back to Gunnar. "Where were we? Oh, really, Edvard. Step aside. I'll not hurt your father."

"Are you sure you won't try? I've heard you rail against him often enough." Edvard didn't move. "My father isn't the only one known for his temper."

"You heard your mother." Gunnar smiled grimly. "Besides, I think I can handle an angry woman. I've had plenty of practice."

"Should we leave you two alone?" I hated to suggest it. I really didn't want to miss a thing, but it was the polite thing to say.

"No!" Gunnar and Ursula both said it. Apparently they wanted witnesses. I couldn't imagine that they were afraid to be alone together. Not Gunnar anyway.

"Yes, let's get everything in the open. I want Gretchen to hear it too." Gunnar gestured. "Please sit down, all of you. We will try to be civilized. Can you do that, Ursula?"

She laughed again and shook her head. "I can't believe what I'm hearing. Civilized? I had no idea you knew the word. Last time I saw you, you wore the Viking beard and a sword on your back. You were untamed and proud of it." Ursula selected a goblet of blood and settled into a wing chair covered in navy velvet. "You really expect me to believe you've been out of the ice only a matter of days? Surely it takes longer than that for a man of your time to learn this century's manners."

"I'm trying. My new friends are helping me understand this new world. It hasn't been easy." Gunnar grabbed a goblet and drained it in a couple of gulps. He started to wipe his mouth with the back of his hand but obviously realized he'd be showing Ursula how far he *hadn't* come. So he picked up a napkin and blotted his lips.

"Friends. Like Mrs. Marken perhaps?" Ursula narrowed her gaze on Gretchen. "Oh, dear. I forgot to extend my condolences on your recent loss. Was it just last night that your husband, um, lost his head? Gossip has it that someone took it with a sword. If I didn't know better I'd think it was the work of an ancient Viking." She sipped her blood. "Was it, Gunnar?"

"Of course. The man deserved to die. He sold to vampire hunters and hurt his wife." Gunnar didn't blink.

Ursula leaned forward, her face contorting in fury. "If hurting your wife was a killing offense, you would have died many times during our marriage." She shot a malevolent look at Gretchen. "But then I suppose you cared what happened to *this* man's wife."

"I never raised a hand to you in anger, Ursula." Gunnar leaned forward too, his eyes hard. "You will not lay that sin on me."

"There are many ways to hurt besides with your fists, Viking." She sat back.

"Why are you so mad at me?" Gunnar also sat back. "*I* didn't burn our village."

"Didn't you?" She set her empty goblet down so hard the delicate stem snapped. She ignored it and let the pieces of crystal fall onto the table. "You were always off to some foreign land, serving your king, and leaving me to raise our children alone."

"That is what Vikings did, Ursula." Gunnar looked for support then seemed to realize he had no other Vikings around to back him up.

"You more than most. Then you finally ended up in a place where you met the wrong woman." She jumped to her feet when Gunnar opened his mouth to speak. "Don't bother denying it. I knew it was a woman who turned you into a monster. You were always led by your cock. You let a woman get the better of you and came home *vampyr*. I hated you for it. Everyone feared you. I, most of all."

"I know. I am sorry." Gunnar didn't say it hadn't been

a woman. Interesting.

"Too little too late." Ursula was pacing now, her high heels wobbling a little as she stomped her way back and forth in front of Gunnar. "We were in danger because of you. Yes, Bjorn was the one who burned our village and took us as slaves but it could have been any strong warrior. No one wanted a *vampyr* near who might suck one of their children dry and leave them for dead."

"I never did that!" Gunnar was on his feet now too. "I fed from goats and sheep, from willing donors. I never took enough to kill them."

"Willing women you mean." Ursula turned to Gretchen. "You see what he is?"

Gretchen didn't answer her. We were all speechless. The Gunnar we'd met seemed noble, eager to right a wrong and certainly faithful to Gretchen. But then Ursula was right. It had only been a matter of days after all.

"You threw me out of your bed, Ursula. A man has needs."

Gunnar should have kept his mouth shut. Ursula was shaking with anger now.

"You think I don't know that? I was dragged into Bjorn Brodin's bed over and over again for ten long years. Bore him seven daughters in that time. Seven, Gunnar!" Ursula's mouth, painted a rose pink, trembled. "I love my girls, every one of them, but I have to close my mind to the fact that they came from rape. That I was tied to their father's cot and forced so that they could be conceived."

"*Mamma*, enough!" Edvard pushed Ursula into her chair again. "This does no good. Clearly you and *Pappa* have no marriage now. We will ignore the tie and you will both be free to live as you please. Is that your wish?"

"He never acted married anyway. What do I care what he does now?" Ursula accepted a fresh goblet of blood, her hand shaking as she raised it to her lips.

Gunnar sank back into his own chair. "The daughters, they are *vampyr* now too?"

"Of course. I could not let them die while I lived forever." She glared at him. "You will not touch them!"

"No. Of course not. They cannot help who sired them."

"Exactly." Ursula touched Edvard's sleeve. "Our son sacrificed everything to make sure the family thrived. We can both be proud of him. He even took that *gruvlig* name to keep us safe."

"Yes, I can see that. He punished that bastard properly as well. But you see I was able to come out of the ice. So now we must go end Bjorn Brodin's life once and for all." Gunnar stood and looked around the room. "That is the plan, *ja*?"

"What do you mean? Edvard?" Ursula put down her goblet, this time carefully. "I thought you killed him long ago."

"No, *Mamma*. I put him in the ice. Took care of him the same way he did *Pappa*." Edvard scanned the room. "Surely you don't wish for everyone here to go with us."

"It will be a big job. We will need help. The fewer who know what we do, the better." Gunnar glanced at the ornate grandfather clock against one wall. "Is this mountain far away?"

"Far enough that we must wait for another night. We should prepare. We'll have to dig him out and plan how we will end him. How did you get out of the ice?" Edvard was obviously thinking. "Digging into the frozen ground will not be easy."

"Ice-quake. It dislodged the ice and he fell out of the cave wall." Jerry spoke up. "It will be much harder to dig into solid ice. If you need us, I'd be willing to help. You were wild when you were finally free, Gunnar. It is wise to have backup. Richard?"

"Of course." Richard glanced at Flo. "We know this is Brodin family business but the fewer outsiders who are involved the better, I would say."

"Agreed." Edvard faced his mother. "You don't wish

to go, do you, *Mamma*?"

"I wouldn't miss it." Ursula jumped to her feet. "I would like to be the one to take his head but I'm sure Gunnar will do that. It is something I wish you'd had the stones to do a thousand years ago, Viking." Ursula stared at her husband.

"It is true that I was not a good husband. I am sorry, Ursula, that you suffered because of me. It was our way back then. A man took *krigsbyte* when he defeated an enemy." Gunnar surprised her by pulling her into a quick embrace. "I can do this at least. I will kill the bastard."

"What does that *krigsbyte* mean?" I whispered to Jerry.

"The spoils of war." He was nodding. "It's true. Even women and children were considered fair game. As she said, they would have been taken as slaves."

Of course Ursula had overheard him. "Thank God I allowed Edvard to talk me into turning *vampyr*. I have lived to see a time when women are valued." She had already shoved Gunnar away and now looked him over. "I can choose my own lovers now, stay alone or even be with other women if I wish." She wrinkled her elegant nose. "Hairy, smelly Vikings! You think it was a treat to be your woman back then? Hah! The only treat was the gold you would bring back from your travels." Her lips firmed. "What happened to that, Gunnar? All that gold you boasted about getting from the king. I earned a portion of that."

Gunnar flushed and looked around the room, almost daring any of us to mention his treasure. "It's been a thousand years, woman. Would you expect me to have a pouch of gold coins in my pocket today?"

Edvard laughed and hugged his mother. "*Mamma*, of course you should have some, but *Pappa*'s treasure was a myth. Surely you never believed he had one."

Ursula wasn't laughing. "Not a myth, son. And look at your father. Is he laughing? No, he's not. He's hiding something. I knew him well before and I still can tell when he's lying." She slammed her palms onto Gunnar's chest.

"By Thor, as soon as you got out of the ice you went looking for it, didn't you? And you found your treasure."

"Now, Ursula. Surely it is mine." Gunnar plucked her hands off of him, gripping them in his fists. "Look how I suffered for a thousand years in the ice. And you are living well, I see."

"On the charity of my son and his wife!" Ursula struggled to get her hands free. "Let me go, you *jävla* Viking. I will have half of your treasure or you will wish you were back in that ice, freezing your balls off."

"Mother Ellstrom!" Elsa stepped forward and tried to calm down her mother-in-law by patting her back. "Please. It's not charity. We love you."

"Pah! You keep me in a suite so far away from the kitchen I have to use a telephone to call for blood. I could forget to close the drapes when the sun rose and die and you'd never know it. Out of sight, out of mind." Ursula finally worked her hands free and slapped Gunnar's chest again. "We will settle this. As soon as Bjorn is dead. You can be sure I will not forget. Half your gold." With that she twitched her butt all the way to the double doors and flung one open. "I will go with you to the mountain. Don't think to leave without me." The door slammed behind her.

"Wow. The woman knows how to make an exit." Flo picked up her fifth little cake. "And I admire the way she walks in heels. *Ottimo equilibrio.*"

I just nodded. The men soon got into a discussion of logistics, planning the trip to the mountain. Elsa joined Gretchen on her couch and began to quiz her about Gunnar and his fortune. Great. So it seemed Elsa was just as eager to get rid of Ursula as Ursula was to go. I hit the desserts again. At least the food was good. And there was B Negative to drink.

Poor Gunnar. But maybe he deserved to lose half his fortune. He'd been a dog. And if Ian was one of his bastards? The thought made me smile as I selected a dark chocolate candy. Jerry was going to have a field day with that bit of information. I just hoped they wouldn't come to blows about it.

It was a solemn group that rode in four-wheel-drive vehicles to the mountain where Edvard claimed he'd buried Bjorn in the ice. It was a cold, windy night but the Northern Lights were doing their thing and I snuggled up next to Jerry in the back seat of our vehicle. I wasn't eager to see another killing and would have stayed in the hotel if Jerry had let me. No, we were together on our honeymoon, even when it was for something as gruesome as this trip's purpose.

Richard was driving with Flo riding shotgun, almost literally. She had insisted on bringing her favorite toy, one of the machine guns.

"This Bjorn Brodin will be wild when he thaws. You said yourself, Glory, that Gunnar was that way when he finally came back to life. I will be ready to take him down if it's necessary." She had on one of her black leather outfits that she thought made her look combat ready. She'd thrown a brown fox coat over it though to match diamond earrings Richard had given her for Christmas.

"Florence, I wish you would leave that in the car." Richard was still trying to reason with her. "Gunnar will never forgive you if you rob him of the chance to kill Brodin."

"He's right, Flo." I reached forward to touch my friend on the shoulder. "Leave the killing to the three people who have the most at stake." Of course I was a little worried about this too. Ancient vampires could move fast. What if Bjorn got away from us? Jerry had spent the remainder of last night sharpening his knives, excited about a possible battle. I was thinking that my honeymoon was going to hell fast. Sure, we were enjoying a moonlight ride in the mountains but the grim set of the men's faces wasn't exactly the mood for love.

"I'm glad we're not in the car up ahead." Jerry patted my knee. "Did you see how things shook out? Gunnar is sitting in the back seat between Ursula and Gretchen. Elsa grabbed the front seat before Ursula could get it."

"Of course Edvard had to drive. He's the only one who knows where we're going." Richard steered carefully. The road had deteriorated into barely a track that a heavy snowfall had almost obliterated. We kept hitting rocks, too, and I was feeling a little carsick.

"I thought Gretchen was going to stay at the hotel." Flo turned around to look at me.

"So did I. But apparently she changed her mind at the last minute. Gunnar spent the night at the castle so he could catch up with his son. That left Gretchen alone in the hotel yesterday. I guess the idea of sitting there all night alone while we finished what Gunnar had started was just too much for her." I sighed and stared out the car window at what looked like an endless sea of white. "She showed up at our door just in time to go with us."

We all jumped when there was a thump on the back windshield. "What the hell?" Richard stopped the car. "Did I hit something?"

"I'll get out and see." Jerry opened our door and blowing snow and ice made us all gasp. Even worse, a man materialized in front of him.

"Let me in." Ian looked like the abominable snowman. He shivered and gripped the edge of the doorframe.

"What the hell, MacDonald?" Jerry jumped back in the car and scooted close to me so Ian could get in and slam the door shut. "Are you crazy?"

"Probably." Ian held his hands out to the vent that was blowing hot air into the back seat. "I decided to go at the last minute and shifted to follow you. Fucking weather. I realized I was going to have to get in the car."

"Why? I thought you wanted no part of Gunnar and his drama." I'd called Ian when we got back to the hotel the night before, trying to smooth things over. He'd still been in a rotten mood. No one called him a bastard and got away with it.

"I did some research." Ian brushed snow off his head, making Jerry curse him and hit him with an elbow. "Sorry. Anyway, it seems there's some truth to the thing about Fiona. She had an affair with a Viking named Gunnar before she was turned vampire. Bore him a son. That was my father. I called Dad and he admitted the whole thing. Like it or not, Gunnar is probably my Grandda." Ian looked ahead. "You'd better get going, Mainwaring. This weather is worsening and you're about to lose sight of Edvard's car."

"Right." Richard accelerated and we lurched forward. "I'll be damned. So you may be related to Gunnar and Edvard too. That's not a bad connection. Ed's made something great of the Brodin empire."

"I think you should do a DNA test anyway, Ian." I reached across Jerry for his ice cold hand. "You'll feel better if you know for certain. Fiona could have had several lovers. Despite what Ursula said, women did have some freedom back then, I'm sure. Your father wouldn't necessarily be Gunnar's child."

"Thank you, Glory, for calling my grandmother a slut." Ian pulled his hand from mine.

"I didn't mean. . ." I looked at Jerry. He was grinning. "Don't say a word."

"Wasn't about to." Jerry grabbed my hand instead.

Ian turned to us both. "I think the fact that I look like Gunnar and my father, of course, is decent evidence. . ." He shrugged and more snow fell on Jerry. "But I *am* a scientist. So there *will* be a DNA test."

Jerry nodded. "Well, we should be there soon. But this is bad weather for what we'd planned. I hope the cave is big enough to set up the heaters and for all of us to fit inside comfortably." Jerry poked Richard in the back. "What's the odometer say? Are we almost there?" They'd planned the trip down to the exact kilometer. Edvard had programmed a GPS with the coordinates as soon as the technology had become available to him.

"It should be around this next curve." Richard slowed

the car when the one in front of us came to a stop. "Yes, this is it. But I don't see a cave opening. Damn. I wonder if there's been a landslide."

We all piled out of our car in front of what looked like the side of a mountain.

"Thank Odin we are here." Gunnar said after he practically shoved Gretchen out of the back seat of their car. "I would kiss the ground if I wasn't afraid of freezing my lips."

"Go ahead. No one here cares if you have lips or not." Ursula strolled over from the other side of the car. She had on a full length black mink coat and matching hat. Apparently her son's charity was very generous. Her color was high, as if she was in a temper or had been drinking blood nonstop on the way up the mountainside. I had a feeling it was temper.

"I have a generator and a heat gun. Help me get the equipment out of the back and we'll get going on this." Edvard popped the back open on the luxury SUV and the men got busy.

"I'm for getting back in one of the cars." Flo didn't look bad herself in her fur and new boots. Her matching fox hat was pulled down over her ears so that only those dazzling earrings showed. Only Flo would wear diamonds to an ambush. "We can keep the motor running and the heater on."

"I can tell you are from a Mediterranean country. The cold is not for you." Ursula looked her over. "But you have beautiful clothes. Tell me where you got those boots." The two headed back to the second car, heads together.

"I would rather freeze to death than sit another minute in a car with Ursula." Gretchen stood next to me. "She was sniping at Gunnar constantly. Where was his fortune? How had he found it? Did he plan to stay in Stockholm?"

"They were valid questions, Gretchen." Elsa glanced back at the other car. "I understand why Ursula wants her own money. Edvard is very generous with her. Too generous in my opinion." Her mouth tightened. "But she did suffer greatly in the past. As we all did when Bjorn was running the family."

"She landed on her feet. Surely you could have bought her a place of her own. Where she wouldn't be with you all the time." I could understand not wanting your mother-in-law living with you. My own was a nightmare.

"Edvard wouldn't hear of it. You know vampires must be careful. He claimed he couldn't guarantee her safety if she left our home." Elsa shrugged. "I can say no more." She turned to Gretchen. "Are you going to America with your cousin and Gloriana? I know Stockholm must be full of bad memories. You said you haven't even gone to your house to get clothes yet."

"I am thinking about America." Gretchen must have sensed my surprise. "Don't worry, Glory, I wouldn't stay with you. I have money and could afford a nice hotel or apartment. Whatever Jeremiah thinks would be safe for me."

I knew exactly what my husband would say. There weren't any vampire run hotels in Austin. The only safe place for Gretchen would be in our extra bedroom. Hell.

"Keep thinking about it." That hadn't sounded enthusiastic but I was saved from explaining by the sound of the gas generator firing up and the men aiming the heat gun where Edvard insisted the cave opening had to be.

We could see the snow melting while they took turns shooting the blast of hot air at the wall of ice. Soon we saw rocks emerging and the dark space that had to be the cave opening where Edvard had left Bjorn's body hundreds of years before. It took more than an hour but they were finally satisfied that they had cleared enough to make it possible to go inside.

I was pretty sure I'd never feel warm again but I helped the others set up heaters inside the surprisingly roomy cave while the men explored further.

"Here it is, closer to the front than I remembered. I think there have been ice-quakes here as well." Edvard sounded excited. "Look, there are cracks in the ground around him. You can see the body through the snow and ice covering it."

We all hurried to look. It was eerie that you could see the form of a man through that sheet of ice. And I, for one, was scared that the man was close to coming out of his freeze. I couldn't forget how Gunnar had come alive so suddenly.

"Stay back. Get your weapons ready." I knew I wasn't in command but I couldn't help myself. I have intuition about some things--blame it on my Olympus ties. This guy had been thawing while the guys had blasted his cave with the heat gun. Then the heaters near the front were also helping him along.

"Gloriana, we can see that he's still frozen." Ian bent over him, curious as always. That cost him because of course that was when the man in the ice broke through with a roar and reached up to grab Ian by the neck.

SIXTEEN

The rest of the men leaped to help Ian but I thought I had the best solution. I jumped on top of Bjorn and tried to capture his wild eyes, to mesmerize him. He wouldn't look at me, concentrating on the men around him. I grabbed his jaw and forced his face toward me but he still wasn't going to give his attention to a mere woman.

"Let go of the man," I demanded. Damned Viking wouldn't focus on me and it didn't work.

He shook his head, the ice cracking around him. He just kept squeezing Ian's neck until I was afraid my friend was done for. Ian dug at his hand frantically but couldn't break free.

"You have the wrong guy. That's not Gunnar."

The answer was a babble of Swedish that got me nowhere.

"All he heard was my name. Move aside and I'll cut off his arm, Glory." Gunnar loomed over Ian, his sword glinting in the light of the circle of lanterns the men had set up to illuminate the space.

Cutting wasn't necessary. When Bjorn saw Gunnar, he tossed Ian aside and reached for the other Viking instead. I fell back. We'd all agreed this was Gunnar's fight. But, damn, I'd wanted to make this easier.

"Gloriana." Jerry grabbed my waist and dragged me farther away. "You gave it your best shot. Now let's see if Gunnar can handle this."

Bjorn was straining against the rest of the chains Edvard had used to keep him in check when they'd brought him up to this cave. The ice was melting fast and he'd moved enough to do serious damage to the shallow trench where he lay. He strained to sit up, screaming Gunnar's name as he fought to get free. His legs were bound at the knees but his feet were loose and he kicked repeatedly, clearly desperate.

Of course he needed blood. Hundreds of years without it had weakened him. We'd thought about that. Brought some synthetic. Because Gunnar wanted a fair fight.

I looked away. How could any fight be fair with a man barely out of the ice? This whole thing sickened me. I should have gone to the car with Flo and Ursula. Gretchen and I stayed well back when they cautiously passed Bjorn a bottle of blood. He drank deeply and held out a hand for more.

"Finish him, Gunnar!" Ursula came running up behind us, pushing us aside.

Bjorn must have heard her because, with another roar, he broke the chains and was out of the ice. The men were prepared this time and wrapped his arms close to his sides in furs. Then he couldn't grab anyone and wouldn't be able to run either.

There was a lot of Swedish being tossed around. What was he saying? Not pleading for his life that was for sure. He was furious. Surprisingly he didn't look as wild as Gunnar had when he'd escaped the ice. But then Bjorn had been several hundred years older than Gunnar when he'd been stuck in here and had already started his stores. His matted beard and hair weren't very long and his shredded linen underwear was simple. Before he'd been wrapped up, I'd noticed not much of it had survived his struggles.

He was massive, a huge man, but not nearly as good-looking as Gunnar or Edvard. He had the blunt features of a man who'd been hit in the face too many times. I'd say from the scars all over his body that he hadn't been as successful a warrior as Gunnar had been either.

"English. Speak English. We have guests." Edvard shoved Bjorn closer to the heaters.

"*Så?*" Bjorn spit on the cave floor. "Ladies. Are you my English speaking guests? Lift your skirts. I haven't had a fuck in too long. Not you, Ursula. You were never any good at it. I'd sooner fuck a wild hog."

"Shut your filthy mouth." Gunnar back-handed him, knocking him to the ground.

"Defending your wife? You're welcome to plow that field. It bears nothing but worthless girls." Bjorn laughed when Gunnar kicked him. He grabbed at Gunnar's boot and almost succeeded in pulling him down. The other men stepped back, clearly ready to let this confrontation play out . Bjorn's furs fell to the ground. He managed to stand and looked around the cave as if assessing his chances for escape.

"You'll be dead soon. But I can end you now if you're in a hurry to see hell." Gunnar held his sword ready.

Bjorn's eyes blazed then he turned to Edvard. "How long have I been in the ice? You ungrateful *pille*! I gave you everything, even my name. Called you son. And you repay me by ambushing me?" He lunged, going for Edvard this time. Ian and Richard jumped forward, grabbed him and held him back.

"You expected me to be grateful? After I watched you treat my mother like *skit*? And after I heard you brag about what you'd done to my father?" Edvard spit this time, at Bjorn's feet. "I'd kill you myself if I hadn't promised my father that pleasure. Torture you until you cried for the gods to end your suffering."

"That's my son." Ursula whispered as Gunnar slapped Edvard on the back and said the same thing.

"You could call him by whatever name you wished. He has the heart and soul of an Ellstrom and proved it by being a fine warrior and taking the revenge due our family." Gunnar suddenly pressed the point of his sword against Bjorn's heart. "He was never son to a coward like you."

"You think me a coward?" Bjorn struggled against the hold the men had on him until the sword drew blood. "Go ahead and end me. I care not."

"It would be too easy." Gunnar stepped back. "Let him go." Ian and Richard exchanged worried looks but finally released Bjorn. He swayed for a moment.

"How did you get out of the ice, Ellstrom? How? I buried you deep and made sure no one would find you." Bjorn leaned against a rock wall when it seemed like he couldn't stay standing on his own.

"It's a miracle that I survived." Gunnar smiled at Jerry and me.

Bjorn threw back his shoulders. "Hand me a sword and we'll see if you can beat me this time, Ellstrom."

"In a fair fight?" Gunnar looked him up and down. "You didn't give me a chance for one when you took me in my death sleep, did you? Did you give my wife fairness when you raped her? Forced her to bear your brats?" Gunnar threw aside his own sword. "We will see how you fare against me. Man to man."

"*Liggande jävel!* You will die this night. I will tear your head from your body with my bare hands!" Bjorn lunged for Gunnar, surprising everyone with his strength as both men fell to the floor and rolled in the rocks and muck.

"Do something!" Ursula screeched. "You can't let Bjorn win. Not after all this time. Edvard, pick up your father's sword!" She grabbed a rock and threw it at the struggling men.

"I promised *Pappa* I wouldn't interfere. He will win, you will see." Edvard stayed out of the way, as did all the men, but he did grab the sword and hold it ready.

It looked to me like Gunnar was evenly matched, though it didn't seem possible. They were punching and clawing at each other. Bjorn was bigger but Gunnar had better moves, or it looked that way to me. They kept punishing each other and cursing in Swedish. Finally it became obvious that Bjorn was running out of steam. He'd only had that one bottle of blood and hundreds of years in the ice had taken a toll.

Gunnar dragged him to his feet to face him. "Prepare to die, Bjorn Brodin. Do you feel the fires of *Helvete* waiting for you?"

Bjorn said something in Swedish and made a last grab for the sword Edvard was holding. Gunnar roared, the Viking war cry that sent goosebumps racing up and down my arms, and knocked Bjorn aside. Then he wrenched his sword from his son's grasp and faced Bjorn.

"Your greed brought you to this Brodin." Gunnar held his sword aloft.

Bjorn raised his chin, then with all the arrogance in the world, turned to look at Ursula. "Did you tell him, *kär*, that you begged me to raid your village and come for you that night so long ago?" His smile was pure mockery.

"Liar!" Gunnar swung his sword and Bjorn's head flew across the cave, his body falling to the floor.

I couldn't stand it and looked away. Ursula's crow of triumph rang through the cavern. Jerry's arms came around me and I pressed my face to his hard chest. Such a horrible, primitive way to die. And to see it twice in as many days . . .

"It's Viking justice, Gloriana. Do you deny he deserved it?" Jerry whispered in my ear.

I shook my head and kept my arms around him, grateful that, as far as I knew, all of Jerry's ancient enemies were long gone from this earth. I felt a presence near me and realized Gretchen was on Jerry's other side.

"Are you all right, Gretchen?" Jerry held out a hand to her. "You want to go back to the car while we take care of the body?"

"No, I need to speak to Gunnar." She stared at the Viking. He had Ursula by the arm but she was talking fast to him and to Edvard. From the looks of it she was denying

Bjorn's last words. Gunnar finally shrugged and turned his back to her to deal with his sword, cleaning off his blade with a cloth.

"I have told you all how he treated me." Ursula glared at Gunnar's back. "He was a soulless bastard. We should toss his body out in the snow and let the wolves have it."

Ian and Richard nodded and began discussing "disposal".

I shuddered when I heard that word. But no one else seemed bothered by it as Ursula led the men outside to the SUV where she had a tarp they could use for transporting the remains. Jerry went with them, ready to discuss the gruesome details of the final battle with his friends.

Gretchen finally approached Gunnar. "You did well tonight." She wasn't smiling but she did reach out to him.

I knew I should give them privacy but there wasn't a good choice of places to go. There were Bjorn's remains nearby which creeped me out. And a blowing, freezing snowstorm outside. I stayed near the heaters and waited for Jerry to come back with the men. It wasn't hard to hear everything Gunnar and Gretchen had to say.

"Thank you, *älskling*." Gunnar handed the sword to Edvard and motioned him away. "I hope you understand that I must give some of my treasure to Ursula. Bjorn's words disturb me but I am not sure I should believe the claims of such a man."

"He was making trouble to the end." Gretchen moved closer as he clasped her hand. "You must do with your treasure as you see fit. It is not my business."

"But it is. This means I won't be as rich as I hoped when I offer myself to you. So we can be together." Gunnar looked very serious.

She flushed and looked down at their clasped hands. "It is too soon to talk of offering, Gunnar. I must decide how to go on now that I am alone, without a man in my life."

"But you don't need to be alone." Gunnar pulled her

hand to his lips. "That is what I am offering. To take care of you. To be your protector."

"You don't understand this century. Ursula tried to tell you. Women now don't need protecting." She slipped her hand from his. "*I* don't need protecting." But she looked uncertain. "I'm going to see how I feel being by myself and going it alone."

"Will you at least allow me to be your lover?" Gunnar moved closer. "We fit well together I think. Some things are no different than they were a thousand years ago. Our bed sport brings both of us great pleasure. Or am I wrong?"

"You are not wrong." She flushed and looked at the cave entrance where Ursula had come back with the men. "I am thinking of going to America. It is where Ian lives as well. He says he may be your kinsman. Perhaps you would think of coming with me? As my lover?"

"Ah, Gretchen." Gunnar watched the men approach the body and talk to Edvard about what they planned to do. "You wish for me to leave my son after I just found him again?"

"You're right. It is too much. But I hate it here now!" She stepped back. "Everyone will know the truth about Fredrick. Gossip spreads so fast among the vampires here and I am the fool in the center of it."

"If you could wait just a little while." Gunnar reached for her but she scurried back to my side. "Gretchen, please."

"No. My cousin has said I might come stay with him and Glory in Texas. I wish to go as soon as their honeymoon ends. If you feel so strongly for me, you will come too, Gunnar." She turned to us. "I'll be in the car. Florence is out there, in one of them with the motor running. I am tired of this violence." She ran out of the cave.

"I will never understand women." Gunnar exchanged a long-suffering look with Jerry who'd come back to my side. Then he turned back to the disposal crew who were lugging Bjorn's body out of the cave. "Let me help. We must make sure it is in an open spot. It is well if the wolves do feast on him tonight." He looked grimly satisfied. "For once Ursula and I agree."

"God, Jerry. I'm with Gretchen. Let's go to the car. But first we need to talk." I tugged on his coat when he seemed inclined to join the men in their trek outside.

He tore his gaze from the ghoulish procession and seemed to snap to the fact that I wasn't happy. "I meant to tell you that Gretchen talked to me about Austin while you were still getting ready this evening."

"You *meant* to." I knew he'd put it off because he'd been pretty sure I wasn't going to be happy about it. I like Gretchen but three's a crowd when you're newly married, I don't care how many centuries you've known each other. "Just where would she stay, Jer?"

"I haven't had time to work that out. If Gunnar came that would be different. I couldn't possibly expect you to take on another couple in our home." Jerry pulled me close.

I knew what he was up to. He realized we were alone in the cave now. Ursula had gone after the men or back to the car--who cared where she went?--at least she'd quit yelling at everyone. It was quiet and the heaters had made it warm inside. But the men would be back any minute to load the equipment into the car. In the meantime, Jer slid his hands inside my coat and was doing his best to distract me with clever touches. I wasn't falling for it.

"Stop it, Jerry. Let's figure out a place for Gretchen to stay besides our spare bedroom." I grabbed his hands and pushed them away. "I mean it. We can send her back early, on Ian's plane with Flo and Richard. Maybe we can get Flo to call Damian. He's got a big house and lives all alone. Excellent security too."

"You'd throw my cousin to that wolf?" Jerry backed up a step. "Be reasonable."

"Damian is head of the Vampire Council, practically a welcoming committee. And Gretchen can say no to him if she doesn't want to strike up a relationship with him."

"Gloriana, he's not called Casanova for nothing." Jerry

frowned. "Gretchen is vulnerable now. You saw how quickly she latched on to Gunnar."

"So you warn her. I'll give her pointers too." I felt like throwing a full-on hissy fit. "Damn it, Jer. I don't think it's unreasonable for us to want a little privacy when we've been married a little over a week!" I pulled my fur coat together and tramped out of the cave. The icy wind hit me in the face and I shoved my own fur hat down over my ears.

I was sick of sharing what should have been a romantic trip with everyone I knew. I almost ran into the parade of men coming down the hill and the trail of blood they'd left on the way up there. It was a grim reminder that this honeymoon had been full of nothing but trouble since the ice quake that had made Gunnar land in the middle of it.

"Give us a few minutes and we'll be ready to go." Edvard was in high spirits and slapped his father on the back. "My father was a hero tonight. I feel totally free for the first time in a thousand years."

"Thank you, Edvard, but you should take credit too. You kept the bastard on ice for me." Gunnar's voice boomed across the snow. "I look forward to meeting your children. Where did Elsa go? Perhaps when we are in the car she can tell me about them. And the grandchildren."

"If you think to just insert yourself into their family, Gunnar, you are very much mistaken." Ursula came up behind her son. "I have made sure the children know exactly what you were like before you disappeared and left us to suffer."

"Elsa will receive you and help smooth things over. *Mamma*, stop troublemaking." Edvard frowned at her. "Please get in the car. We will be there soon." He nodded when she stomped off through the snow. "You have no idea, *Pappa*, how much I have had to put up with since I got rid of Bjorn. *Mamma* is not an easy woman to live with, always wanting more attention, more money, more of everything! Elsa wanted me to give my mother her own place, but you know vampires are vulnerable. I didn't feel it was safe to leave her alone."

"From vampire hunters you mean?" Gunnar shook his head. "I am still trying to understand how this century works."

"Yes, there is the danger of that. And it is complicated to set up a vampire household. Special servants . . . No matter." Edvard stopped and looked very serious. "I have been thinking about what Bjorn said. Could it be true? That she asked him to burn our village? Yes, he made us slaves, but, when I was a small boy, he treated her well. She had fine clothes and was his favored lady. I don't believe her when she says he forced her. She did not act reluctant to share his bed that I saw. It was only when she gave him nothing but daughters that they became cold to each other."

Gunnar stabbed his sword into the snow and looked toward the cars. "It would be the worst kind of betrayal, son. What she did to me, I can understand. But to sell her own children into slavery? Unforgivable."

"Was it because of your fortune, do you think? Bjorn always talked of it. *Mamma* probably promised it to him, then it was never found." Edvard gripped his father's shoulder. "I pray she did not do it. I have just got my father back. I do not want to lose my mother. But if she did this, she is dead to me."

"We may never know the truth now, son." Gunnar picked up his sword again. "Ursula is a difficult woman and impossible to understand. I married her for her beauty but later regretted it. Why do you think I always asked to serve my king in foreign lands?" Gunnar stared at the cars then jerked as if startled. "What in Thor's name is she doing? Can she drive a car?"

"Of course." Edvard cursed and ran toward the moving SUV. "I'll be damned. She's driving away and leaving us!"

It was true. Ursula had flounced right into the driver's seat and taken off with Flo, Gretchen and Elsa in the car. I realized that left me, Jerry, Ian, Richard, Edvard and Gunnar to cram into the remaining car. That bitch! I just hoped she didn't pull over somewhere and force Gretchen out of the car. Of course she'd have to deal with my buddy Flo if she tried it.

I ran to the other car, the one we'd come up in. No sign of the machine gun in the front passenger seat. I only prayed it was Flo who'd thought to grab it.

"We'll have to leave the equipment here." Edvard looked up at the sky. "The weather is worsening. It will be hard to see the road as it is. Best we start back immediately."

"I'm going after them." I couldn't believe I'd said it but my intuition told me it was the right thing to do. My best friend was trapped in the car with a woman I didn't trust.

"No, you're not." Jerry grabbed my arm. "Stay with me, Gloriana. I insist."

"You aren't trying to order me around, are you?" I gave him a hard look. "I need to do this. I can shift and catch up in minutes. They'll stop for me. If a man tried it, Ursula would run him down."

"She's right about that." Gunnar took my other arm. "You would do that? I'm worried about Ursula with Gretchen. She claims not to care about me, but my wife was always jealous, even when there was no cause." He nodded at Jerry. "Please. Let her go. Glory is a strong woman, with powers. *Ja?*"

"Yes, I am." I looked down to where Jerry held my arm. "Time is ticking away, Jer."

"Go, but be careful." He pulled me close and kissed me. "We'll be right behind you." He released me. "Take no chances."

"Now what would be the fun in that?" I changed into a strong bird with the heft to fight the strengthening winds and raced after the car. It didn't take long to catch up with it. I knew I was taking a chance, but I changed so that I ended up in the road in front of it, allowing for braking on an icy patch. Ursula almost hit me anyway.

"What the hell are you doing out there?" She barely

cracked her window and didn't unlock the doors.

"Can I have a ride? I am sick of those men, ordering me around like I have no sense. Would you believe they wanted me to fetch the blood out of the car after you left? Walk into this blizzard while they stayed near the heaters?" I gestured at the almost whiteout conditions. I figured appealing to Ursula's feminist agenda would get me into the car and I wasn't wrong.

"Fine. Get in the back seat." She unlocked the doors. "We will be stopping shortly. I have something I need to do."

I was afraid I knew what that something was. I'd seen Flo's machine gun tucked neatly next to Ursula's hip beside the driver's door.

"We should hurry down the mountain. It's not safe to linger. This weather is getting really bad. I don't know how you can see the road as it is." I jumped in next to Flo who gave me a wide-eyed look. I had a feeling she'd been forced to give up that gun. In fact there was a rip in the sleeve of her fabulous fox coat. She stroked it and muttered Italian curses then nodded toward Ursula.

"Four against one," she whispered. "We watch for our chance, *si?*"

I shook my head. Crazy moves could get everyone hurt. I sent her the mental message that Ursula had her beloved machine gun very close. That made Flo swallow and cross herself.

"Listen to her, Ursula. We shouldn't stop." Elsa was in the front seat and she wasn't happy either.

"I've been driving in these mountains since the automobile was invented, Elsa. Quit telling me what to do. Soon I will have Gunnar's fortune, all of it." Ursula glanced in the rearview mirror. "What? Did you really think to have him and his money too, Gretchen? Tell me where he has his gold and I might let you live. Might." She fought the steering wheel as the car slid on the ice. "*Helvete!* These roads."

"Gunnar will never let you have his gold. He's counting

on it to give him a new start in this century." Gretchen gripped the armrest on the other side of Flo. "I'm not telling you a damned thing."

"Gunnar has lived too long." Ursula laughed. "I'd like to see him survive a heart full of wooden bullets. *Tack*, Florence, for telling me about those." She reached down with her left hand and lifted the machine gun so we could all see it. Gretchen gasped. Elsa didn't seem surprised but I guess she would have seen it as soon as she got in the car.

"I was playing. They aren't really wooden. Ricardo wouldn't trust me with a real weapon. You know how men are." Flo kicked the front seat with her boot.

"Quit trying to fool me. You think I didn't check for myself?" Ursula glanced into the back seat. "Make me lose concentration on my driving and we could all end up stuck in this blizzard. Is that what you want?"

"No. Keep your eyes on the road!" I patted Flo's knee, trying to calm her down. "Give Gunnar a break. He just spent all those years in the ice."

"What do I care what he went through? I went through worse. He slept for a thousand years. I suffered. This little bitch made sure I never had a free moment, even after Bjorn was gone. I was her unpaid servant until the stores finally made enough money to hire others." Ursula reached over and yanked a handful of hair from Elsa's head.

"Ow! Stop it!" Elsa scratched Ursula's hand and the car lurched off the track and bounced wildly until it ground to a halt with a loud screech.

"Now look what you made me do." Ursula slapped Elsa across the face. "Shut up and sit still or I swear I'll put you out in the ice right now."

"No!" Elsa put her hand to her red cheek. "I'll be still."

Ursula nodded then fiddled with controls, probably putting the car into four-wheel drive and reverse. The car rocked, the motor raced but there was no movement.

"The rest of you, get out and push." She turned in her seat, pointing the gun at us. "Now! Stand in front of the car.

I'll have the thing in reverse and you must push when I honk the horn."

"It's a blizzard out there. We'll freeze." Gretchen was trembling.

"As if I care. All of you. Out!" Ursula spit the words.

"Come on. The sooner we get out, the sooner we get back in." I heard the doors unlock again and opened mine. Oh, the misery of that icy wind in my face. I pulled my gloves on before I climbed out and immediately sank thigh deep into a snowdrift. "This doesn't look good, Ursula."

"I don't care how it looks. Get out and put some shoulders to it. All of you!" She motioned with the machine gun and Flo scrambled out after me. Gretchen had climbed out the other side of the car.

"It's cold and wet. I can barely see my hand in front of my face!" She yelled across the top of the car. "I wonder how far we are from town?"

"Too far to make a run for it." Ursula screamed. "Shut the *jävla* doors and get ready to push."

"My coat and hat are getting ruined." Flo bumped the car door closed with her hip. "I will get that woman for this. Gunnar is not giving her one single piece of gold. That's a promise."

"Right. Now let's push this thing out of the snow." I scrambled over the pile of rocks that had obviously stopped the car. A closer look made my breath catch. We were on a mountainside and there was a steep cliff behind that rock pile. "Careful. Watch your step or we could end up taking a bad fall."

Gretchen grabbed me as she slipped on a rock. "I wish I had one of Jeremiah's knives. Somehow I would stick it in that bitch's back. Ordering us around like we're her slaves!"

"Come on, let's work together. Use your anger as fuel." I put my hands on the car's hood. "When she honks the horn, we push." We stood shoulder to shoulder and did just that when Ursula leaned on the horn. We did have vampire strength and shouted when the car slid backward on the first try.

"We did it, *amica*!" Flo and I hand slapped. Gretchen did the same with both of us. Then we got the bad news.

"She's leaving us!" Gretchen stumbled toward the deep ruts the car had left in the snow. "No, she can't do that!"

"It seems she can and did." I exchanged a look with Flo. Why was I not surprised? A figure staggered out of the blizzard toward us. Of course. She'd dumped Elsa too.

"Family means nothing to that *jävla tik*." Elsa shivered then shook her fist at the car that had already disappeared from sight. "I just hope to God she has to face her son about this. He will make her suffer for it."

"Okay, now that we're stuck in a blizzard, let's figure out our next move." I knew better than to be cheerful as three sets of eyes swiveled toward me.

"The men should be driving down this way any minute. *Ja?*" Elsa had lost her hat somewhere. Oh, yeah, when her mother-in-law had torn out her hair.

I studied the scenery. "I wish I could say yes, but I'm afraid Ursula got off the path or road or whatever it was." I spit snow out of my mouth and unwound the scarf I had around my neck. "Elsa, put this over your head."

"Thanks, Glory. When they find our frozen bodies next spring, at least I will have my ruined hair covered." She laughed until she cried then sat on a rock and put the scarf over her head. "I wonder how long before sunrise."

"Don't even think about it." Flo shook her finger at her. "*Pregare*. Do you believe in God? He will send someone to find us."

"While you wait for divine intervention, I'm shifting and looking for the car with the men in it." I hugged Flo. "And praying too. Thanks, pal." I did my shift into that sturdy bird and winged away in the direction I hoped would take me back toward the road and the cave. I read the wind, remembering that it had been blowing into my face when I'd followed the road before. So I put it at my back and struggled aloft. I sent God all sorts of arrow prayers as I flew.

My wings grew heavy with ice and I was about to give up when I heard the noise of an engine below me. The car was covered in white so it was nearly invisible. But it had to be our guys. Now it was going to be a matter of using my instincts to lead them back to my friends. And Elsa.

I swooped down and did the change thing, taking no chances on being hit. This time I did what Ian had done and hit the driver's side window. The car was moving slowly enough that I had no trouble making that happen. It stopped immediately and the window came down a few inches.

"Glory?" Edvard stared at me. "What are you doing out here?"

I told him a short version, trying not to make his mother sound like a total psycho. It wasn't easy.

"You mean my wife is out there in this weather? Unprotected? *Mamma* just left her there?" Edvard was dumbfounded.

"For God's sake, man, open the fucking doors and let her inside." Jerry was coming unglued, banging on his window in the back seat and rocking the car in his effort to get to me.

"Yes, of course." He unlocked the doors and Jerry was out in an instant, wrapping me in his arms and dragging me into the backseat with him. He held me in his lap, trying to stop my shivering by holding me close and folding his coat around me.

"Gretchen?" Gunnar sat in the front, riding shotgun. "What of her?"

"She's waiting out there in the cold as well. I think Ursula really wanted to kill her but didn't take the time to do it. Your wife wants all your gold now, Gunnar, but Gretchen wouldn't tell her where it is." I was finally starting to warm up. "Go slowly, Edvard. I think Ursula got off the road because we were really near a cliff and got stuck. Do you know where that could be?" I stuck my hands inside Jerry's coat, under his arms.

"God, Gloriana, your face is coated with ice." Jerry kissed my cheeks over and over again. "Ursula's gone mad."

"Can you blame her? I'm sure looking at Bjorn again drove her over the edge. Brought back memories she'd shoved into the back of her mind." I shuddered. "Edvard, do you see anything?" The blizzard was getting worse. I was worried sick about Flo and touched Richard who was rigid beside me. "Richard, what do you think we should do? Would it be stupid to get out and shift? Search from the sky?"

"Damn it, Gloriana, let me out of the car and quit reading my mind." Richard reached forward to grip Edvard's shoulder. "Stop the fucking car. I've got to get out of here."

"My wife is out there too, Mainwaring! It would be madness. Then we'd have one more lost in this mess. Give me a few moments more. This is my mother we're talking about. I think I know where she might have gone off the track." The car lurched. "There! Do you see something moving?" He stopped the car and wrenched open his own door. He was out on a run. We all piled out of the car, though I still clung to Jerry.

"Stay in the car, Gloriana." He tried to put me back inside. The motor was still running and the vehicle was a haven of warm air.

"No! I have to help." I peered into the driving snow and ice. "I can't see a damned thing." I closed my eyes and tried my other senses but they were overwhelmed by the cold and wind and the shouts of the men. Even Ian had taken off toward what Edvard had insisted were dark spots against the snow. "Be careful!" I screamed. "You could fall off the edge of a cliff." I rushed forward, Jerry beside me, refusing to let me go.

"Gretchen!" Gunnar sounded frantic as he stumbled through the snow. "Answer me! I will come with you wherever you go! I swear it!"

"I've found them! They're huddled together for warmth." Richard shouted repeatedly so we could follow his voice. "This way. They're all right, just suffering from the cold."

We all rushed to where he held Flo against him. He was murmuring to her and rubbing his hands over her face which was a sickly shade of blue. Gunnar grabbed Gretchen, lifting her into his arms and hurrying back toward the car. Edvard did the same for Elsa.

"We need to get them warm as quickly as possible. I should check them over. At least they were dressed for the weather. But hypothermia is still dangerous." Ian looked at me as we raced back to the car. "Gloriana, how do you feel? Any numbness or tingling in your feet or hands?"

"All of the above." I wondered how we were going to fit into that car. By the time we got there, Gunnar was in the front passenger seat with Gretchen in his lap. Somehow Edvard had put Elsa in sideways in front of him in the driver's seat. So Ian, Richard with Flo in his arms, Jerry and I crammed ourselves into the back seat and forced the doors closed. We all breathed a sigh of relief as the warmth of the car heater blew over us.

"How are you going to drive this machine like that, Edvard?" Gunnar stopped rubbing Gretchen's hands long enough to ask.

"We're figuring it out. But that is not the question on my mind now." Edvard helped Elsa sit up between the front seats, on the console. I was sure she was very uncomfortable but it couldn't be helped. "I am wondering what in hell I will do about my mother. She just tried to kill my wife. I can't forgive her for that."

Elsa clasped his hand on the steering wheel. "Will you kill her for me?" She looked around the car. "Oh, stop staring at me. I won't actually make him to do it. Though it would give me great pleasure." She sighed and leaned against his shoulder. "Just take me home, *min kärlek*. It will be enough to toss that bitch out into the snow. See how she likes it."

Edvard kissed the top of her head. "It will be done."

He put the car in gear and started down the mountain.

I held onto Jerry and stared at Gunnar in the front seat. Had I heard him promise Gretchen he'd come to Austin with her? Great, just great. Let the honeymoon go on down the drain. I could hear the gurgle.

SEVENTEEN

"Where do you think Ursula was going?" I knew we were all wondering the same thing. I was just the one to ask it out loud.

"The hotel." Flo sounded miserable as she said it. "I wasn't thinking when I told her where we were all staying. She asked me about my boots and I told her about the boutique. Of course it is a Brodin Boutique, Edvard."

"Yes, then you must be staying at the Ice Palace. Is that where you're keeping your gold, *Pappa*?" Edvard had been concentrating on getting us down the mountain successfully and we'd been silent while he'd done it. Now we were on a paved highway.

"Yes. I'm sure all she will need to do is ask for our room number." Gunnar grunted. "But half of my gold is in your room, Richard. You were researching the values of the coins."

"The people at the front desk won't just give out your room number, Gunnar." I felt compelled to tell him. "There are privacy issues. Especially if Ursula goes in claiming she's your wife and looking mad. You checked in with another woman. Hotels are not going to get involved in extramarital affairs."

Gretchen shifted on Gunnar's lap, clearly uncomfortable both with the subject and the fact that she was sitting on a big man's lap in a fairly small space. "The room is in my name anyway. I am the one with the credit card. She will probably use mind reading on the mortal workers to get the information she needs." Gretchen leaned against Gunnar's shoulder. "I am so sorry."

"Why? This mess is of my making." He kissed her cheek. "No, it is of Ursula's. I can't imagine her thinking, leaving all of you in the cold to die. I will make her suffer for that."

Jerry's arms tightened around me. "I'm beginning to think this honeymoon destination was one of my worst ideas ever."

"Well, I won't confirm or deny that." I smiled and kissed him. But I was really beginning to wish for a warm place like my cozy apartment in Austin.

"Sweden is a beautiful country. And peaceful." Elsa looked at me from the front seat. "You have fallen into a family quarrel that is unusual. And that is putting it mildly."

"No, I fell into their honeymoon." Gunnar looked back at me too. "You saved me and I won't forget it. But it was not the romantic wedding trip Jeremiah planned, *ja*?"

"I was thinking about the advantage of your long nights, not about the cold. I'll admit it." Jerry nuzzled my cheek. "We have had those. But they've been full of the kind of bloodthirsty battles and killing my new wife hates. There should be no more of it, no matter how mad at Ursula you are, Gunnar."

"This just means you'll owe me a second honeymoon someday, Jerry. In a warm place." I smiled and slid my fingers inside the neck of his sweater.

"I'm sure you want to see an end to this as much as we do, Glory. And to get warm again," Edvard said.

"Son, thank you for all you've done." Gunnar reached behind Elsa to clap him on the shoulder. "You have made me proud. Please do not feel bad when I make your mother pay for what she did to Gretchen."

"Hah! Stand in line, old man. She tried to kill my wife and has been a pain in my backside for hundreds, no, a thousand years. If she did conspire with Bjorn, we should end her." Edvard's hands tightened on the steering wheel. "Glory will just have to leave the room."

"Enough killing. You cannot do that to your own mother, Edvard. As much as that would gladden my heart." Elsa covered his hand with her own. "But we will make sure she leaves Sweden." She looked back at me and winked. "And not go to Texas either. That would be too cruel, eh, Glory?"

"You are so right." I leaned back against Jerry. "So we're going to the hotel to try to stop her? Do we have a plan for when we get there?"

"Let's see what we find." Gunnar was sounding reasonable. Who knew it was possible in a Viking? "Just make this machine go fast, Ed, uh, Bjorn. I know Elsa is uncomfortable and, even though I am enjoying holding her close, Gretchen's legs are pushed against this piece of metal in front of us. There are too many people in here."

"You're right, *Pappa.* I'm putting the pedal to the metal." Edvard grinned. "And call me Edvard. I'm forsaking that bastard's name from now on. I'll explain to the world that my long lost father has come home and I'm taking back my birth name. No one in the *vampyr* community will question it and I don't care what others think anyway." He laughed.

"I am Edvard Ellstrom again. Damn, that feels good to say." He reached for Elsa's hand. "I'll even rename the department stores. It is time for the Brodin name to disappear forever."

Gunnar laughed with him. "Even if I have no gold at all, I feel rich this night."

It was a good thing he felt rich, because Ursula was

doing her best to make him poor. She'd obviously read mortal minds and had latched on to our favorite bellman, Viktor. We saw him, shaking and white faced, as soon as we entered the lobby.

"I'm so sorry, Mr. Ellstrom. The woman wouldn't take no for an answer. I don't know how she did it, but I ended up opening your door for her." Viktor turned to Gretchen. "Well, it was your door too of course, Ms. Marken. She dragged me down the hall and insisted. I couldn't help myself."

"It's all right, Viktor. We understand." I stood next to him while the rest of the crew surged down the hall toward Gunnar and Gretchen's room. I'd spotted the telltale marks on Viktor's neck. "Come with me. I want to tip you, to compensate you for your trouble. The money's in my room." Not true. I had money on me, but I needed to erase those marks. Ursula obviously had enjoyed a fortifying drink and hadn't bothered to remove the evidence.

"Not necessary, Mrs. Blade. Really. You are always very generous with me." Viktor swayed. "I'm going off duty now. My shift is over and I'm not feeling too well. I need to lie down."

Damn it. How much blood had that woman taken? "Come with me, Viktor. I want you to promise to go to the restaurant and buy a steak. Rare. You are very pale and I think such a meal will help with that faint feeling. Will you do that? I'm paying." I pushed him toward the restaurant.

"Oh, thank you, Madame, but they won't like that. I'm in uniform. It's not allowed." Viktor tried to resist but a good stare into his eyes and he was putty in my hands. After I pulled him into a closet and erased those marks, we arrived in the doorway of the main restaurant which was open twenty-four hours a day.

"This man has done me a special service," I told the maître d. "I know you will allow him this once to sit at a table in his uniform and enjoy a meal on me. Won't you?" I pressed a large bill into the man's hand and we were soon at a table in a dark corner. A waiter appeared at my elbow. "You will serve Viktor a rare steak and..." I turned to the bellman. "Would you like some fried potatoes with that?" I smiled.

"Sure." Viktor collapsed into a chair. "You are being very kind after I did something . . ." He shifted the silverware in front of him. "I'm sorry."

"No, don't be." I told the waiter to give me the check and I signed it, adding a generous tip. "Let him stay as long as he likes. He's been very helpful to me and my friends." I started to walk away.

"Mrs. Blade." Viktor set down his glass of water. "I need to tell you something. I'm afraid it's important. That woman asked me to tell her ..."

"What, Viktor?" I leaned closer.

"She wanted the room numbers for others—yours and the Mainwarings'. Doctor MacDonald's too." Victor sighed. "I know it's against policy but it was as if I didn't have a choice. If you tell management what I did, I will lose my job." He hid his eyes behind his napkin. "The worst is that she took my passkey. I may be fired anyway if I don't get it back."

"Oh, Viktor!" I gripped his shoulder. He was shaking again. "That woman took advantage of you. It's our fault. We let her know where we were staying and that we have something... Never mind. I'll get your passkey back for you. I promise." I patted him on the back. "You won't lose your job. Now please, enjoy your dinner." I left him babbling thanks as I sprinted for Flo and Richard's room. I'd be damned if I'd let that woman have all of Gunnar's gold.

When I got to the door I heard noise from inside. Luckily she hadn't shut the door completely and I eased it open, hoping I could take her by surprise. She was tearing through the drawers, dumping them out in her search. Flo was going to have a fit when she saw all of her lingerie on the floor. Ursula spotted me as soon as I stepped inside but didn't stop searching.

"Looking for something?" I could see Richard's computer had bitten the dust but no sign of a bag of gold. If he had locked it in the safe, she was out of luck.

"You know what I'm looking for. Where is it?" Ursula lifted the mattress and flung it aside.

"Gunnar's gold? Haven't you heard? It's a myth." I wondered if she had Flo's machine gun somewhere. I was going to grab it as soon as I saw it.

"Do you think I'm stupid? Or without vampire skills?" She laughed. "I read Gretchen's mind. She was so afraid I'd get her lover's fortune that it was all she could think about-- finding it on that island." Ursula came closer. "Gunnar was actually clever, hiding it in that gravesite. I had no idea he had the brains to think of that."

She whirled and walked over to the closet. "There's a safe in here. Do you think it could be looked inside there?"

"If I had a bag of gold, it's where I'd put it." I looked around for that gun. I knew my buddy Flo had her jewelry jammed inside the safe. I doubted if Richard had added the gold to her stash. He was a brilliant man and liked clever hiding places. I had a feeling it was around here and almost in plain sight. Luckily I was one of the few vampires who could block my thoughts. Ursula could try reading my mind and she'd hit a wall.

"I want the combination." Ursula was almost frantic as she paced around the room.

"Well, don't look at me. Flo is with her husband, your son and Gunnar. What do you think your chances of surviving an encounter with that crowd would be?" I was enjoying this. Watching Ursula unravel. Had she really set up Gunnar to be frozen? I tried to probe her mind but her thoughts were all about money. She was obsessed with it. Well, she clearly was guilty of something and I'd like to see her get her due. But then Jerry was right, I'd had enough killing the past few days to last me forever.

"Call her. You're her best friend. She told me that in the car. Tell her you need her. For something silly like to match a sweater to a skirt. That's her kind of expertise." Ursula snarled and looked me over. "Empty headed bitches, both of you, more interested in your wardrobes than in what's important. I'd like to see you do the kind of things I had to do in order to survive all these years."

Now that offended me. This woman had no idea what I'd done to stay alive for over four hundred years. No idea who I really was. She'd made a snap decision based on my appearance. Which I admit was pretty smoking hot tonight in my brown leather coat which matched my boots perfectly.

"Make me." I looked her over. "You talk tough but I have special skills. Want to go one on one and see?"

She'd tossed her mink coat and hat on a chair and reached under the coat. Damn. There was that machine gun. She aimed it right at my heart.

"Yes, your friend Florence was bragging about your skills. So I won't look you in the eyes, will I?" She kept the gun steady. "But I won't need to when I pull the trigger and kill you. Now sit down and call the little bitch. Get her to come here." She threw the phone at me.

I picked it up off the floor and sat on the couch. "Seriously? You think I'll get Flo here so she can unlock her safe? Not without a promise that you won't touch her. Or her jewelry. We both won't be hurt or it's no deal."

"Do I need to put a bullet in your leg first?" She moved the barrel down to aim at my foot.

"That would be stupid, Ursula. The noise would get the rest of the gang here on the run. Not to mention the police." I was happy to point that out. I sure didn't want a wooden bullet in my leg either.

"Okay, so I promise not to hurt your little friend or take her jewelry. All I'm after is the gold. It's what Gunnar owes me." Ursula's eyes gleamed though as she must have realized Flo's jewelry was probably worth a fortune. Which it was. She really must think me an airhead if I would believe any promise she made. I didn't have to bother to read her mind this time when she was so obviously out to get whatever she could.

"So you didn't find Gunnar's stash in his room?" I wasn't about to start dialing, but Ursula grabbed the phone anyway and put it on speaker before she handed it back.

"Well, yes, I did. But I think I should have it all." Ursula nodded toward her mink.

"What makes you think that wasn't all of it? He had a bag of gold. What are you doing here looking for more?"

"Gretchen's mind, stupid. She was worrying about the half Gunnar had given to your pal's husband. Thinking about the value and if it would be enough to make him rich." Ursula laughed. "Ancient coins. They're worth a fortune now. I know people who will pay a good price for them. But it won't be Gunnar who will enjoy those riches."

"He earned them, didn't he?" I couldn't take my eyes off that gun. I hoped she knew what she was doing. It could go off and I'd have those damned wooden bullets inside me. After seeing Jerry hurt so...

"No, I earned them." Ursula gestured with that machine gun. "You have no idea how I suffered at Bjorn's hands. The man had sex like he was trying to break a speed record. I wasn't kidding about smelly Vikings either. He didn't bathe or clean his teeth." She shuddered then poked my leg with the gun barrel. "Dial or I'll knock *your* teeth out. One hard hit with this gun and you won't ever bite into your husband's jugular during sex again. How would you like that? Your friends won't hear that hit either." Her gestures became more alarming, the gun butt so close to my face, I knew she was serious. I made a grab for the gun but she was too quick for me.

"What are you waiting for?" She kicked my shin. "Hurry!"

"I can't do it." I gasped when she jammed that gun butt down on my foot. It hurt so bad that my eyes watered. "Shit!"

"That's just the start. Trust me, your teeth are next. Get with it. When I have what I want, I'll be out of here. I don't want to kill you or your friend and, you're right, the noise of the machine gun will attract attention I don't want. I just need to get the gold. Now do what I said." That white stripe in her hair was quivering. The look in Ursula's eyes and my throbbing toes convinced me she would be happy to torture me until I obeyed her.

One of my skills is that I can dematerialize--disappear from one place and reappear in another. I'd been waiting for my chance to do that so I could overpower Ursula with the element of surprise and take that gun. I decided now was the time. But I'd left it too late. The pain in my foot made it impossible to concentrate and I couldn't vanish. Damn it.

Plan B: I was pretty sure reinforcements would help me figure a way out of this. I dialed.

"Flo? I'm at your room." I could hear the sounds of the rest of the gang in the background. "Can you hear me?"

"Yes, of course. What is it? We are busy here. Gunnar's gold is gone and he is ready to tear someone's head off. Ursula's if he can find her."

I glanced at the woman. She smiled and gestured with the gun.

"You remember the cute T-shirts we saw in the boutique? I just couldn't resist them. I went by there and bought us each one. So we can match. You are always helping me. I had to get you something as a thank you." I had emphasized the "helping". "Don't bring Richard and Jerry along with you. Let's make it a surprise." I hoped she understood what I was trying to tell her. I'd emphasized the key words—"bring", "Richard," "Jerry," and "along"— saying them louder than the rest of the sentence. I couldn't do more than that to send her the right message.

"Matching T-shirts, *amica*?" Flo clearly knew something was up. My fashionable friend would die before she put a T-shirt on her body and she knew I was aware of that. "What color? You know I'm not going to wear yellow, don't you? That is for cowards."

"You are always brave. No need to prove it to me." I

got a sick feeling in the pit of my stomach. Ursula was frowning, like she was getting suspicious of this conversation. "Really, Flo. If this isn't a good time ..."

"I'm coming." She hung up.

"Satisfied?" I handed the phone back to Ursula. She really was being cagey and I'd tried but hadn't been able to capture her gaze to mesmerize her or turn her to stone. Now I'd have to wait for Flo to get here. Oh, God. Wooden bullets. I didn't like that machine gun aimed at me. I didn't want it aimed at Flo either but two against one meant we might have a chance to distract Ursula. If only Flo had taken my hint and would show up with the men.

"You did very well. I'm surprised. I thought you'd fight me harder on calling your little friend." She sat on the bed but kept that machine gun steady. "Of course I would have happily broken every bone in your body to make that happen."

"You already broke a couple of my toes. I'm not into pain." I wondered if I found the bag of gold first if I could get Ursula to just leave. Probably not. Now that she knew about the jewels, she wanted them too. But it was worth a shot. I scanned the room. Surely if I concentrated, I'd find Richard's hiding place. Then I saw it. There was a bag of dirty laundry hanging on the back of the door with an interesting lump at the bottom. Knowing Richard, he'd dropped the coins there on his way out the door. I got up and limped over to it. Damn, but my toes hurt.

"Where are you going?" Ursula waved the gun at me.

"I'm going to let her in. You don't want Flo running away when she sees you, do you?" I leaned against the door. Sure enough, I felt the hard bulge at the bottom. It was the right size and shape to be Gunnar's gold coins. I could pull it out and throw it at Ursula. Perfect distraction.

"Is that door shut this time?" Ursula got up to check, still wary around me. "She must use her key. I expect you to pull her inside and close the door after her. Get it?"

"You're crazy. I hope she runs like hell when she

realizes you're here." I really didn't want to do this. I was trying to get to the gold without Ursula noticing while I heard Flo's key in the lock.

"Glory! How did you get in my room?" Flo gasped when she saw Ursula. "*Mio Dio!* It's a trap!"

I looked behind Flo, scared and disappointed that the men weren't with her. Of course this could have turned into a blood bath if they'd come in with their guns blazing.

"Yes, *my* trap. And it worked perfectly, *kvinna.*" Ursula smiled and stood, her gun on Flo now. "Shut the door then come over and open your safe."

"What? You are stealing my jewels?" Flo grabbed my arm. "Glory! How could you call me for this?"

"Seems your best friend gave you up because she didn't want her teeth knocked out. So much for loyalty." Ursula stepped closer and jabbed the gun into Flo's stomach. "Get over here. Open the safe and give me Gunnar's gold."

Flo pushed the gun barrel away from her stomach. "You are hurting me. For nothing. Gunnar's coins are not in there. I have filled the safe with my pretties. I told Ricardo he would have to find his own hiding place. I don't know where he hid the gold." She glanced at me. "Tell her, Glory. I don't travel without my jewels. I have many of them. Enough to fill the hotel's little safe to the brim."

"It's true. Look at her new earrings, a Christmas present from her husband. Chocolate diamonds set in gold to match her coat today. The rest are kept locked up close to her at all times. Read her mind if you don't believe us." I was watching for my chance to grab that gun. I'd almost had it when she'd moved toward Flo but I was afraid, with Ursula's finger on the trigger, that a sudden move would get Flo shot. "I'm sorry, Flo. I didn't want to call you down here."

"It's okay. I don't want you to die or lose your smile. Jeremiah would never forgive me." Flo reached out for me. "But if we are buried, we *should* be in matching T-shirts, *capiscimi?* Not yellow, of course. I won't even wear a yellow diamond. It is not my color. But a pretty pink perhaps. I look good in pink and so do you, *amica*. We will have to decide someday. Coral is nice. What do you think?" She winked, obviously working on a distraction so I could make a move.

"Stop all this silly talk." Ursula was quivering she was so mad. "Open the safe, *slyna*! Or I will hurt you and you will know it!" Ursula waved the gun around, her finger finally off the trigger as she got ready to hit Flo with the stock as she'd hit me.

This was my chance. I grabbed the barrel, jerking the gun out of Ursula's hands. She screeched in outrage, lunging at me, determined to wrestle it back.

"No, *cagna*! You cannot have it! Get her, Glory! Make her a statue!" Flo jumped on Ursula's back, raking her hair with her fingernails until she had a handful. She twisted and pulled while Ursula screamed.

I tossed the gun aside and held onto one of Ursula's ears while Flo kept her hair in a firm grip. Ursula couldn't move her head. She squeezed her eyes shut but I poked at them with my fingers until she was forced to open them. In seconds the woman was turned into stone.

"There. Relax, Flo, she's out of commission now." I almost fell over when Flo launched herself at me for a tremendous hug. Then she let go, both of us out of breath.

"*Grazie a Dio*! We did it!" Flo grinned. "I couldn't believe it when you called and started talking about matching T-shirts." She laughed and hugged me again. "I knew then that you had either hit your head and gone crazy or were in trouble. I had to come."

"Right into danger." I wanted to smack Ursula for what she'd done to me and to Flo, but it's no fun hitting a statue. "Thank God she didn't hurt you."

"You are limping. She hurt *you*." Flo stared down at my foot. "And she ruined your boot. *Cagna inutile*." She smacked Ursula on her arm then ran to pick up the machine gun and quickly took out all the bullets. "This thing. I hate it. If it had killed either one of us . . ." Just then the door flew open and

Richard stood on the other side.

"What is this? Florence? I wondered where you ran off to. Ursula is here?" He rushed inside and gathered Flo in his arms.

Jerry was right behind him. "What the hell, Gloriana?" He saw Ursula's strange position next to me. "You caught her? What happened?"

"She was trying to force Flo to give her Gunnar's gold. She wanted Flo's jewels too." I grabbed Jerry and held onto him. "Thank God that's over."

"Is it?" Gunnar strode inside. "Where is my gold?"

I smiled at Richard. "Behind the door there. Show him, Richard."

"Maybe I'm not as crafty as I thought I was." Richard walked over to the door and pulled down the laundry bag. "Did you really find it, Glory?"

"Yes. But Ursula didn't have a clue. She assumed it was in the safe. She had me call Flo for the combination." I leaned against Jerry. "I'm sorry I did that but I don't think--"

"Sorry?" Richard tossed Gunnar his sack of coins then turned on me. "You endangered my wife and just say 'Sorry'?"

"Ricardo, it's all right." Flo threw her arms around him and looked up at him, her eyes blazing. "Don't get all macho on me. Glory and I handled it. She gave me enough hints on the phone that I figured out she was in trouble. I could have brought you with me, but I decided the two of us could take care of one evil bitch." She turned to grin at me. "We knew what we were doing, didn't we, Glory?"

"I'm not so sure." I took a breath and stepped away from Jerry. "I never should have involved you, Flo." I blinked back tears. "She could have killed you. When I saw her press that machine gun against you . . . Well, it made my heart stop."

"By God!" Richard's hands were fisted.

"Don't say a word, Mainwaring." Jerry wrapped his arms around me again. "Gloriana was alone with a deranged woman. She did what she had to and obviously Florence made the decision to come on her own. They both acted on impulse. Thank God this did end well."

"But is it at an end?" Edvard pushed into the room, Ian and Elsa behind him. "What am I to do now? Is my mother permanently like this?" He motioned toward Ursula who hadn't moved or blinked since I'd put her into that state.

"I can unfreeze her at any time. But you need to decide, Edvard, you and Gunnar, what you want to happen next. She has half your gold in her coat pocket, Gunnar. The half that was in your room. If you let her go, she's going to need a place to live." I sighed, sick to death of the lot of them.

"I'd let her starve. Put her on an ice flow like the Eskimos used to do." Ian was being typically hard ass.

"Not a bad plan." Elsa nodded. "But I can't see it working. My husband is too forgiving." She'd been standing with her hand on Edvard's arm, not letting him out of her sight. "She will not stay with us though, Edvard. Not a minute longer." She let go of her husband and looked resolute.

Edvard reached for her and pulled her close again. "I agree, my love. She will never set foot in our home again." He looked at his father. "We'll have to make a deal with her. She must leave Sweden and go somewhere else. Far away. If you agree to give it to her, she could take enough of your coin to get settled, *Pappa*."

"I would really like to kill her, but there's been enough of that. Glory, if you can release her from this spell, we will take her away from here and figure this out. Fredrick had a nice dungeon. I would like to see Ursula inside it." Gunnar turned to Gretchen. "What do you think, *älskling*?"

"Of course. Use the dungeon as long as you wish. I must go back home some time. To pack if for nothing else." Gretchen held his hand.

"Yes. Pack. For your trip to the Texas." Gunnar smiled at Gretchen then turned to Edvard. "I will go away too. I'm sure Elsa does not need more family coming to live with her."

"But *Pappa*..." Edvard looked conflicted.

"Not now, anyway. We will give you time to recover from this latest disaster. And you will have much to do if you truly wish to erase the Brodin name." Gunnar smiled at Elsa. "Does that please you, Daughter?"

"Thank you, *Pappa*, for understanding. Later, you will be welcome to come back. To get to know all of the family." Elsa walked up to him and hugged him. Then she picked up Ursula's mink and found the other bag of gold. "Here's your coin. Are you sure Ursula should have any of it? It would be right if she had to leave Sweden penniless and fend for herself."

I thought about Ursula's taunts. What she'd done to survive. Surely her survival hadn't been at stake if she'd asked Bjorn to burn their village and take her own children as slaves. She'd denied that but I wondered... I couldn't imagine being so coldly calculating, but I knew what it was like to be a woman, poor and alone. Gunnar looked around the room, as if seeking advice.

"It would be cruel to just toss her out with nothing. Been there, done that. Why not give her enough money for a decent start? I don't think you want her out there somewhere, so filled with despair and bitterness that all she can think about is how to get revenge. Do you?" I reached for Jerry's hand. He kissed my cheek, probably remembering how alone I'd been when he'd first met me. I'd been lucky enough to find him. My love. I doubted Ursula in her present mood would welcome love again. And I certainly wasn't in the frame of mind to hope for it for her.

"No, I never wish to lay eyes on her again. We can make that a condition of her leaving with funds." Gunnar nodded. "I hope that she will not ever have to be a worry to any of us."

Ursula would certainly not be a worry to me. But what about Gunnar? He'd announced that he wasn't staying in Sweden. Gretchen was looking up at him like a love sick puppy and a clear "Full speed ahead". Which meant the Viking was on his way to "the Texas" too. I sagged against Jerry as I finally got that message. Damn it all. Here we go again.

"Is there a key card in that coat pocket, Elsa? I need to give that to our bellman before he gets fired. It's how Ursula got into the rooms here." I was relieved when she waved it around. Jerry grabbed it and we'd deliver it to Viktor later.

"Can Ursula hear us when she is under this spell, Glory?" Gunnar clearly wanted this settled before everyone left the room.

"Yes, she can. I've been turned to stone before by someone with the same power. I heard and remembered everything that happened while I was like that." And it was the most frustrating feeling imaginable. Not that I felt sorry for Ursula.

Gunnar walked up to his wife and put his large hand on her neck. "Hear me, woman. We will give you enough money for a fresh start somewhere far away. But you are never to bother me or our family again. I could take your head right now and no one would blame me for it." We could all see his fingers tighten on her throat. "It would be easy and more merciful than a thousand years in the ice, *ja*? So think hard. Will you agree to go away and not return?" He glanced at me.

"She can't answer until I release her. Are you ready for me to do that?" I admit I was nervous about it.

"Go ahead." Gunnar stepped back. We could all see his fingerprints on Ursula's neck.

I looked the woman in the eyes. "Don't be foolish, Ursula. They can still kill you if you come out fighting." I touched her shoulder and she instantly relaxed.

"*Min Gud!*" She looked around the room as if trying to find an ally. Edvard looked as implacable as his father. "I heard."

"You accept our terms?" Gunnar held his sacks of gold.

"I seem to have no choice." Ursula was eyeing his fortune.

"No money until travel arrangements have been made." Edvard stalked toward her. "You also heard that we are putting you into Gretchen's dungeon until you leave town. You will be guarded so there is no chance for escape. Of course that would be foolish. Leave there before we put you on a plane and you would miss the chance for money to take with you. Do you understand, *Mamma?*"

"A dungeon! But surely that isn't necessary. I will cooperate!" Ursula looked indignant.

"Don't waste your breath." Elsa stood on her other side. She held her mother-in-law's mink coat and hat and showed no signs of handing them over. "Servants will pack your things and your luggage will be sent to the airport when the arrangements are final."

"Let us go then." Gunnar, with Gretchen beside him, stopped to say goodbye but I knew we'd see them again soon. "Thank you for helping me. This is a good ending, I think. Or good enough."

Edvard and Elsa hustled Ursula out between them. We all breathed a sigh of relief to see the last of her.

Ian stared after them. "Well, I still think she's getting off lightly."

I tugged Jerry to the door but sent a mental message to Flo first that I was going to give Richard and her some space for a while. He was furious with me and I didn't blame him. But no one tells my best buddy what to do. She ran across the room and hugged me.

"We will be leaving here tomorrow night, Glory. I love you, *amica*. Don't let Ricardo's upset hurt you. I will see you in Austin when you are home from your honeymoon."

"I love you too, *amica*." I smiled through my tears. Guilt will do that to you. I'd almost gotten her killed. She'd had a part in that decision, but I could have done something to stall Ursula, maybe even chanced taking a bullet before making that stupid phone call. I didn't like what I'd done tonight. Maybe I deserved to have my apartment overrun by cousins and their lovers.

EIGHTEEN

The next night we got a call from the front desk reminding us that it was our turn for the hot tub gondola ride. We'd almost forgotten about it. Jerry was jazzed.

"Remember, we reserved it when we first checked in. We sit in a hot tub, just the two of us, while we ride over the mountains in a cable car and watch the Northern Lights together." He was packing champagne blood for our trip.

"Maybe we should cancel. Stay in and just relax here in our own bathtub." I was trying to figure out how this could go wrong. We'd thought a sleigh ride with Rudolph had sounded like a romantic idea too. Look how that had ended.

"Now, Gloriana, we can't let one mishap turn us into hermits."

I was about to start an argument when there was a knock on the door. "I can make our tub in our own bathroom here very interesting, Jer." I threw open the door.

"I'm sure you could, Glory." Ian grinned at me. Of course his vampire hearing hadn't let a closed door keep him from joining the conversation. "I've come to say goodbye or I'd offer myself as a third party. Now *that* would be interesting, I can promise you that."

"A MacDonald and a Campbell in the same bathtub? At the same time, with the same woman?" I laughed. "Would there be swords?"

"Of course, darling." Jerry laughed. "I know you're kidding or there already would be. Goodbye, MacDonald." Jerry was ready to slam the door in Ian's face.

"Wait. I have news. Something that Glory will be happy to hear." He pushed his way inside. "Florence told me she's already been by to say her farewells and she and Richard are waiting in the car. My news is that Gretchen and the Viking are leaving with us."

"Really?" I held onto Jerry, afraid to believe it. "They're leaving with you? On your plane?"

"Yes. Since I'm fairly sure we're kin, I've invited Gunnar and Gretchen to stay at my house while they're in Austin." Ian laughed at my expression which I was sure was pure relief. "I know your place is just an apartment. I have plenty of room and, frankly, I want to run a few experiments on the man."

"He won't like that." Jerry had his arm around me. He was actually holding me up. I felt a little weak in the knees from happiness. I wasn't going to have house guests.

"Probably not, but I told him I needed to confirm our relationship and Gretchen explained the DNA test to him. It will be on me to persuade him to do the rest of it." Ian seemed sincerely happy too for a change. For the usually dour Scot it was quite a difference. "I don't mind telling you I'm a little excited to have discovered this relationship. If it proves true, I may eventually take Gunnar home to Scotland. To meet the clan."

"I can imagine how that will go. You say Fiona is still around?" Jerry squeezed my shoulders. "Gretchen won't be eager for that visit."

"No, she won't." I pulled myself together and moved to give Ian a farewell hug. "Thank you for taking them on. I mean it." I stepped back. "As to the Scotland trip, I wouldn't rush it, Ian. That could sabotage Gunnar and Gretchen's relationship. You need to give those two a chance to get to know each other better. Who knows if Gretchen will even stick with Gunnar after the dust settles? She really is on the rebound from Fredrick. Gunnar's fresh out of the ice too. He may want to play the field as well, once he gets used to this century."

"I don't interfere with relationships, Glory. Those two can do as they please." Ian exchanged a guy to guy look with Jerry. "Toes all right? Ursula did a number on you last night." Ian looked down at my bare foot. "Do I need to examine you?"

"They're fine. Thanks for asking. A couple of bottles of synthetic and I healed." I knew Jerry did not want Ian touching my foot and I was telling the truth. Have to love the vampire powers. Jerry had moved close and wrapped his arm around me again.

"All right then. We're pushing off. See you in Austin." In typical Ian fashion, he was out the door.

"I can't believe they're all gone. And no visitors in the apartment when we get home." Jerry picked up the insulated bag he'd packed. "You going to keep grinning, Gloriana?"

"Of course." I kissed his smile.

"Then let's go." We were picking up our coats when there was another knock on the door.

"I knew it was too good to be true. What now?" But I smelled a familiar scent and threw open the door. "Flo! We already said goodbye."

"I know, *amica*, but Gunnar was fussing in the car about a reward." Flo was glowing in another beautiful cold weather outfit. This one was red leather with matching boots.

"I told him we didn't expect one." Jerry glanced at me. "He mentioned it when he thought he'd lost his gold. I'm sorry, Gloriana. I know you hoped…"

"Yes, it should go to Glory. She found him in the ice." Flo waved a piece of paper. "Gunnar had a handful of coins to give you. I told him that was silly. What would Glory do with old coins? Though some of them were quite pretty. So I persuaded Ricardo to write you a check for their value, Glory. It is not much, but it made the Viking feel better." She handed me the check. "And to him it is a fortune. Money isn't worth what it once was, you know."

I looked at the check. Fifty thousand dollars. That was a good chunk of change to me too. I knew Gunnar had ended up giving Ursula plenty just to get rid of her. I really shouldn't take this. Though it would pay some important bills for my shop. I tried to hand it back.

"I can't take this. Finding Gunnar was a fluke. And Jerry helped."

"No, you must take it. It is a matter of pride." Flo smiled at Jerry. "You understand, right, Jeremiah? The man must pay or he will think you give him charity."

"Take it, Gloriana. Use it as you see fit. You were the one who insisted we dig out the man." Jerry nodded. "And started the mess that made this one memorable honeymoon."

"There, you see." Flo hugged me. "We go now. Ricardo has calmed down. We will be fine once you come home to Austin. I make him buy me a new ring because he yelled at you. Hah! So it worked out for both of us. See you after the honeymoon!" She waved and headed down the hallway, her high heeled boots not making a sound on the Oriental runner.

"Well. I never expected this." I folded the check and put it in my purse. I was locking both in the hotel safe while we were enjoying our cable car ride. "Seems like we're salvaging this honeymoon after all."

"Careful, darling. You know statements like that can bring on disasters." Jerry waited by the door. "Let's get out of here before someone else knocks."

Thirty minutes later we were settled in a cable car, equipped with a hot tub, as it lurched into motion. An attendant had shown us to a dressing room where we could undress and we'd taken advantage of it. So we were naked and sitting in steaming water, the wide windows around us giving us fabulous views of the mountains and the snow below. In the distance we could see the lights of Stockholm. Above, through the glass roof, we could see the cables carrying us up to the mountains. It was a quiet ride except for the bubbling water in the tub as we kept gliding ever higher. The Northern Lights were giving us a brilliant show.

"What do you think?" Jerry poured champagne blood into a flute and handed me one. He'd explained to the attendant who'd wanted to set up our "refreshments" that he had brought us a special vintage. She'd just provided the glassware. We'd declined the offered snacks with a wink. She'd laughed and given us a knowing look. Obviously honeymooners never ate much on these rides anyway.

"I think, husband, that you have definitely managed to turn this honeymoon around." Just then the cable car lurched. I grabbed him with one hand and steadied my glass with the other. "I hope I didn't jinx us by saying that."

Jerry laughed and pulled me into his lap. "That bump was because we just went over a section connecting the cables. It was nothing to worry about." He took my glass and set it and his in the special holders that would keep the liquid from spilling. "Come here, wife." He rearranged my legs so that I straddled him. "That feels better."

I sighed. Better? It felt heavenly to be pressed against him so intimately. I loved the feel of his strong body and guided him inside me. "Mmm. Have I told you lately that I love you?" I kissed his cheeks, his forehead, then his mouth before I began to move.

"Only when we woke up together at sunset." Jerry held onto my hips. "You are the love of my life, Gloriana. I will never let you go." He surged into me, causing a mini tidal wave. Fortunately the water level allowed for some vigorous action and we were in no danger of swamping the car.

We moved together, our eyes on each other. There was no need to read minds. We knew what we would find there. It had taken me a long time to give my heart fully. This man could be demanding and commanding. But I'd learned to accept him as he was. And to make him understand that he'd get more from me with a less autocratic attitude.

He'd learned things along the way too. That I would do anything for the man I loved willingly. But I would not be ordered or coerced into following his lead. We were partners in this marriage. In some things, he was stronger. There was no doubt he was the better businessman. I didn't resent him for that and looked forward to his help with my shop when we got home. And he acknowledged that I'd always have some special powers that he would never be able to achieve. If it came to a battle—God forbid—I could do things with them that would make his sword useless.

We were reaching the mountaintop in more ways than one. Tension rose inside me, the spiraling need for release that was more than physical. In some ways it could only be satisfied by this man. My lover quickened his moves and I gripped his waist with my thighs. He kissed me hard, taking my mouth with the same thorough hunger that he showed as he drove into me, harder and deeper until I threw back my head and panted his name over and over again.

"Take my vein! Jerry! Please!" I leaned forward, offering my jugular to him.

He struck hard and true, taking my life force fiercely, the pull resonating through me until I trembled with an orgasm that made my toes curl and my nails rake his shoulders. He drank for endless moments before he released me then licked the punctures closed, kissing the spot before just holding me. He soothed me with soft touches until I finally came back to myself, my heart pounding as I let my head fall to his shoulder. I saw the damage I'd done and kissed away the marks.

"How do you do that? Make me lose my mind every time?" I sat back and ran a finger over his lips. "I know it's coming and yet you continue to surprise me." I could feel the aftershocks where he still pulsed inside me. "You are a stallion."

"And you are the one woman who can make me lose *my* mind." He smiled and sucked my finger into his mouth. "Remember when Gunnar wondered how we could still be so hot for each other after four centuries? It made me think."

"I don't have to think about it." I pulled my hand back before he bit that finger. "We are what they call soul mates. It was written in the stars as they say." My gestures toward the sky made him grin. "Oh, mock me, I don't care. I'm a romantic. You obviously are not. So what were you thinking?"

"That Gunnar hasn't met his soul mate yet or he couldn't ask that question. You know I've pursued you for all of those centuries, Gloriana. I'm not mocking your soul mate statement. It is just the truth." He ran his hands up and down my back. "We are one now. In God's eyes because of our marriage, yes. But we were two halves of a whole looking for one another when we met. I knew it then. It just took you longer to realize it."

"Jerry." My eyes filled with tears. "That is the most beautiful thing you've ever said to me." I kissed him then, pouring all my love into it. By the time I pulled back, I'd made a decision. Our honeymoon had been exciting, horrifying and wonderful. But it was time for our marriage to start. We needed to do it where we would spend our lives together.

"Husband, it's time for us to go home."

DICTIONARY

I hope you enjoyed REAL VAMPIRES AND THE VIKING. I sprinkled in some foreign words, mostly Swedish, used by my Viking and his family. I've included a short dictionary. The words are in the order they appear in the book. Native speakers may disagree with some of my translations. If so, blame the Internet. I write fiction, so I do take a few liberties. Many of words are a bit obscene but that's the way the story goes...

After the Swedish section, there's a little bit of Florence da Vinci's Italian vocabulary. Have to love our Italian spitfire. Thanks for reading!---Gerry Bartlett

Gunnar's Swedish Dictionary

1 Skitprat=bullshit
Stopp! Vi är stang da!=Stop! We are closed.
Gullig=sweet or darlingtjuv=thief
Min kärlek=my love
Vad hander?=What's happening?
Fostra av Gud!=Mother of God!
min sota=my sweet
Flotta=fleet
Jaklar!=Damn!
10 Fiende=enemy
Herregud!=My goodness or My God!
Batars=boats
Min modiga kvinna=My brave woman
En timmes=one
hourjakel=devil or bastard
älskling=darling, sweetheart
förbannad=cursed, damned
liten pojke=little boy
sötnos=honey
20 pultron=cowardjävla=fucking
jävla tik=fucking bitch
min fina= my precious
gruvlig=horrible
köttiga=fleshy
krigsbyte=booty
slyna=slut, bitch, whore
pille=prick
min vackra lady=my beautiful lady
Skit=shit
30 Det gör mig galen= It makes me crazy.
Liggande jävel=Lying son of a bitch
Tack=Thanks
Kär=beloved

Florence da Vinci's Italian Dictionary:

Amica=friend
Teppisti=thugs
Capiscimi?=Understand me?
Molto irritante=very irritating
Caro=dear
Dio mio!=My God!
Bene=good, OK
Fare l'amore=lovemaking
Molto forte=very strong
Pazzo=crazy
Ottimo equlibrio=good balance
Pregare=pray
Grazie a Dio!=Thank God!
Cagna inutile=worthless bitch
Cagna=bitch

If this is your first experience with the **Real Vampires** series, welcome! Here's a complete list of the series. You might want to read from the beginning and see how Glory and Jerry got to the honeymoon stage. Here goes and thanks for reading! You can always come to my website at **http://gerrybartlett.com** for more information about the series or to sign up for my newsletter. My email address is also there. Hope to hear from you!

Gerry Bartlett

Real Vampires have Curves
Real Vampires Live Large
Real Vampires Get Lucky
Real Vampires Don't Diet
Real Vampires Hate Their Thighs
Real Vampires Have More to Love
Real Vampires Don't Wear Size Six
Real Vampires Hate Skinny Jeans
Real Vampires Know Hips Happen
Real Vampires Know Size Matters
Real Vampires Take a Bite Out of Christmas (Novella)
Real Vampires Say Read My Hips
Real Vampires and the Viking
Rafe and the Redhead—Spinoff about Rafael Valdez

ABOUT THE AUTHOR

Gerry Bartlett is the nationally bestselling author of the Real Vampires series, featuring Glory St.Clair, a curvy vampire who was bloating when she was turned in 1604. Gerry is a native Texan and lives halfway between Houston and Galveston where she has an antiques business that lets her indulge her shopping addiction. You can see her purse collection on Pinterest.

Would she like to be a vampire? No way. She's too crazy about Mexican food and sunlight. You can reach her on http://gerrybartlett.com or follow her and her dog Jet on Facebook, twitter or Instagram. Her latest release is Real Vampires and the Viking (Real Vampires #12) available now.

CPSIA information can be obtained at www.ICGtesting.com
Printed in the USA
LVOW08s0014140616

492399LV00031B/1011/P